LUMBER-JACKULA

LUMBER-JACKULA

MAT HEAGERTY   SAM OWEN

Simon & Schuster Books for Young Readers
New York   London   Toronto   Sydney   New Delhi

SIMON & SCHUSTER BOOKS FOR YOUNG READERS

An imprint of Simon & Schuster Children's Publishing Division

1230 Avenue of the Americas, New York, New York 10020

SIMON & SCHUSTER BOOKS FOR YOUNG READERS

and related marks are trademarks of Simon & Schuster, Inc.

For information about special discounts for bulk purchases, please contact

Simon & Schuster Special Sales at 1-866-506-1949 or business@simonandschuster.com.

The Simon & Schuster Speakers Bureau can bring authors to your live event.

For more information or to book an event, contact the Simon & Schuster

Speakers Bureau at 1-866-248-3049 or visit our website at www.simonspeakers.com.

Interior design by Tom Daly

The text for this book was set in S Owen Comics.

The illustrations for this book were rendered digitally.

Manufactured in China

0422 SCP

First Edition

10 9 8 7 6 5 4 3 2 1

Library of Congress Cataloging-in-Publication Data

Names: Heagerty, Mat, author. | Owen, Sam, 1989- illustrator.

Title: Lumberjackula | Mat Heagerty ; illustrated by Sam Owen.

Description: First Simon & Schuster Books for Young Readers hardcover edition. |

New York : Simon & Schuster Books for Young Readers, 2022. | Audience: Ages 8-12. | Audience: Grades 4-6. |

Summary: Jack, who is half-vampire and half-lumberjack, struggles to choose between a vampire academy and a lumberjack school when all he really wants is to dance.

Identifiers: LCCN 2021009660 (print) | LCCN 2021009661 (ebook) | ISBN 9781534482586 (hardcover) |

ISBN 9781534482579 (paperback) | ISBN 9781534482593 (ebook)

Subjects: LCSH: Graphic novels. | CYAC: Graphic novels. | Identity—Fiction. | Dance—Fiction. | Vampires—Fiction. |

Loggers—Fiction. | Family life—Fiction. | Schools—Fiction.

Classification: LCC PZ7.7.H396 Lu 2022 (print) | LCC PZ7.7.H396 (ebook) | DDC 741.5/973—dc23

LC record available at https://lccn.loc.gov/2021009660

LC ebook record available at https://lccn.loc.gov/2021009661

To Ollie and Wilder—
keep on dancing to your
own beats
—M. H.

For Andy and Huck—
do what you love
—S. O.

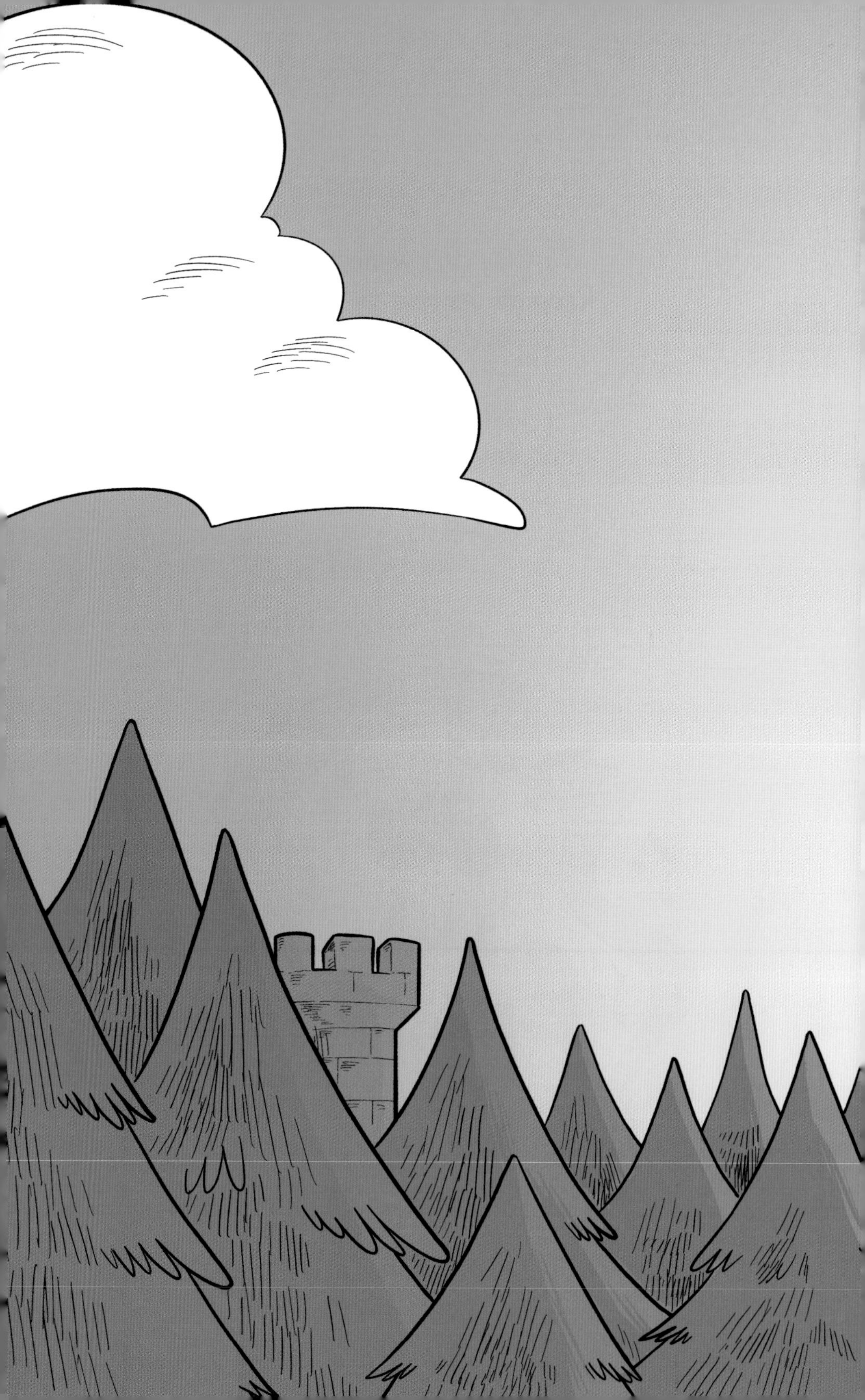

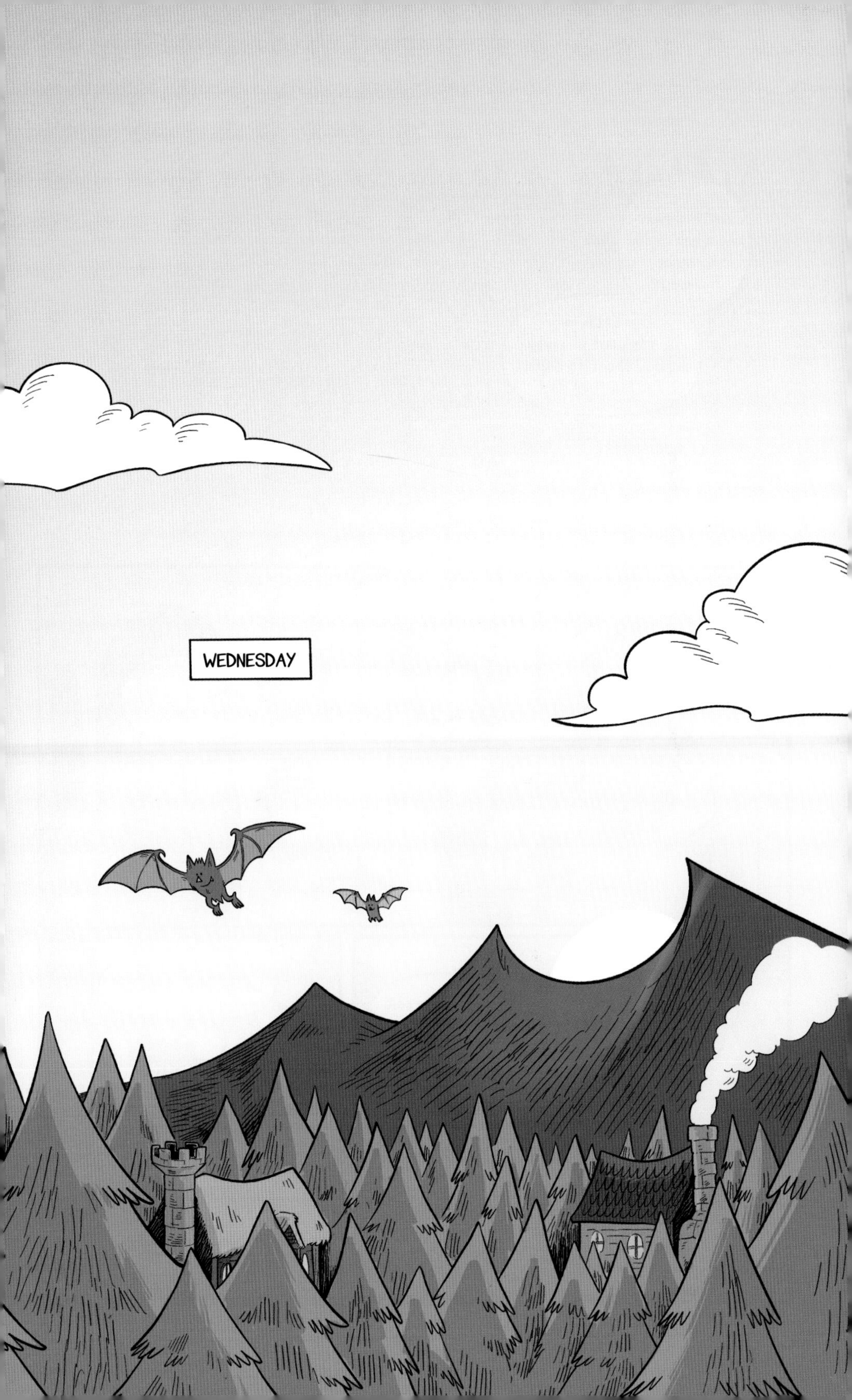
WEDNESDAY

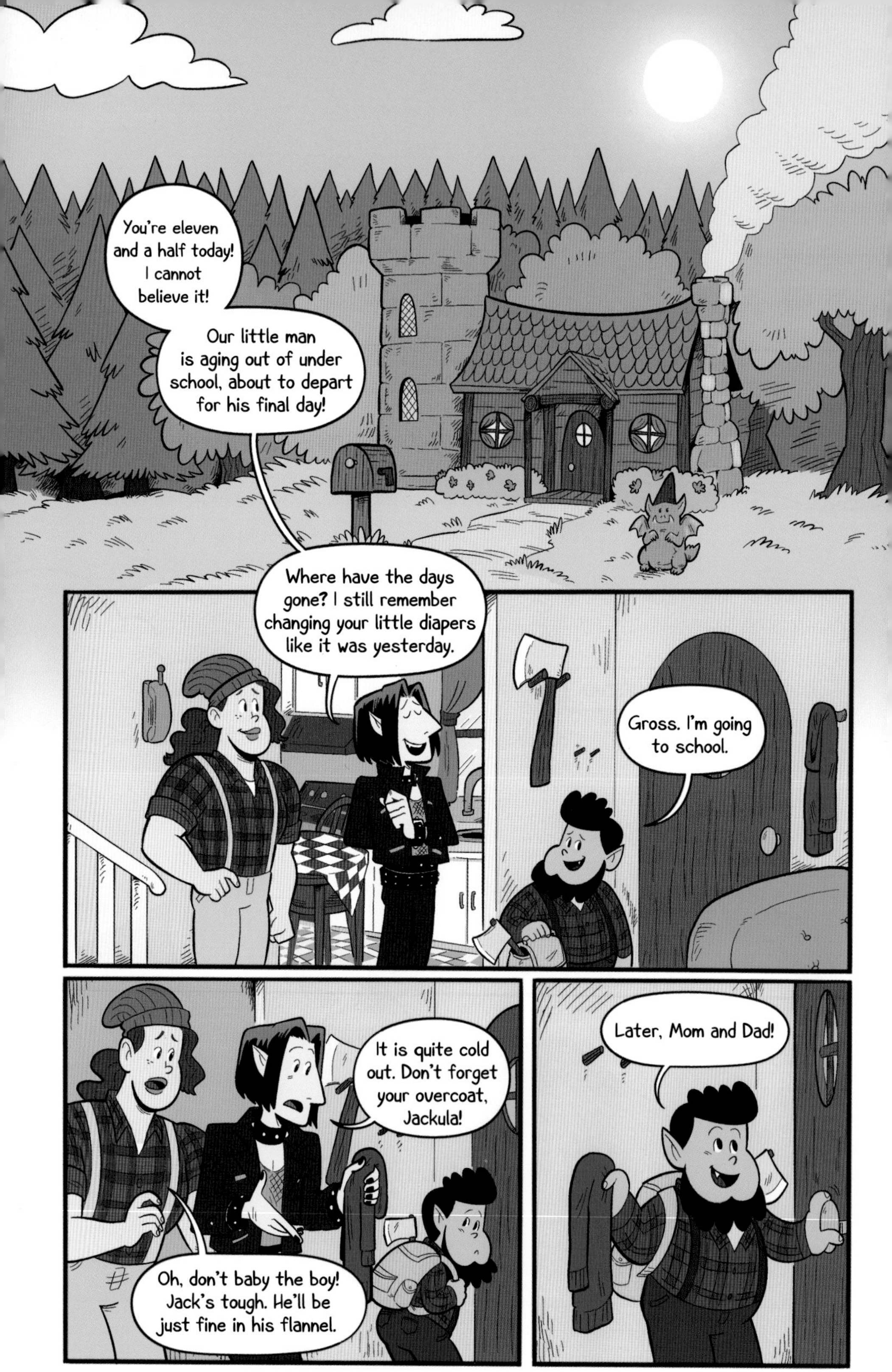
You're eleven and a half today! I cannot believe it!
Our little man is aging out of under school, about to depart for his final day!
Where have the days gone? I still remember changing your little diapers like it was yesterday.
Gross. I'm going to school.
It is quite cold out. Don't forget your overcoat, Jackula!
Oh, don't baby the boy! Jack's tough. He'll be just fine in his flannel.
Later, Mom and Dad!

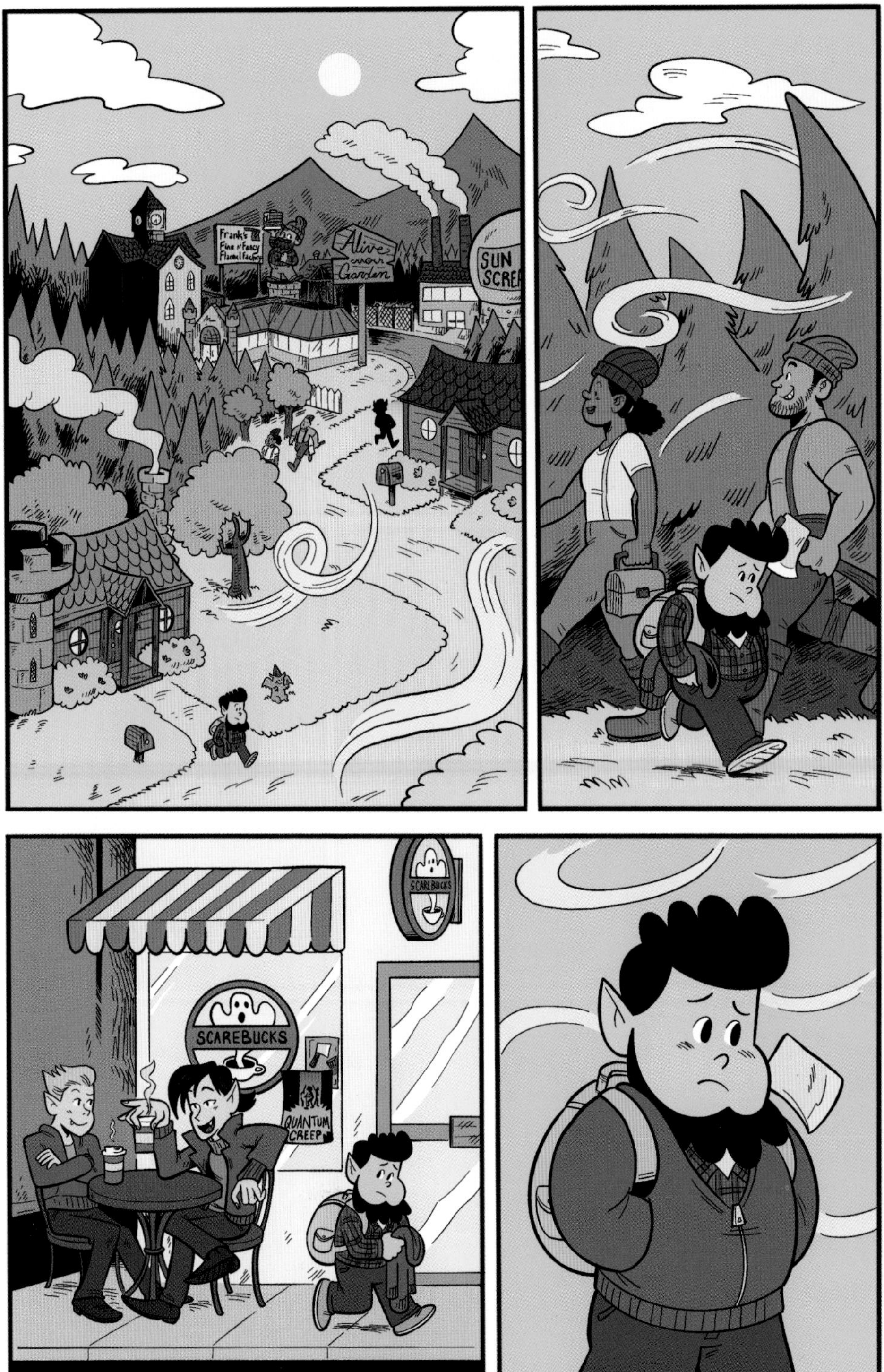
Frank's Fine n' Fancy Flannel Factory
Alive Garden
SUN
SCAREBUCKS
SCAREBUCKS
QUANTUM CREEP

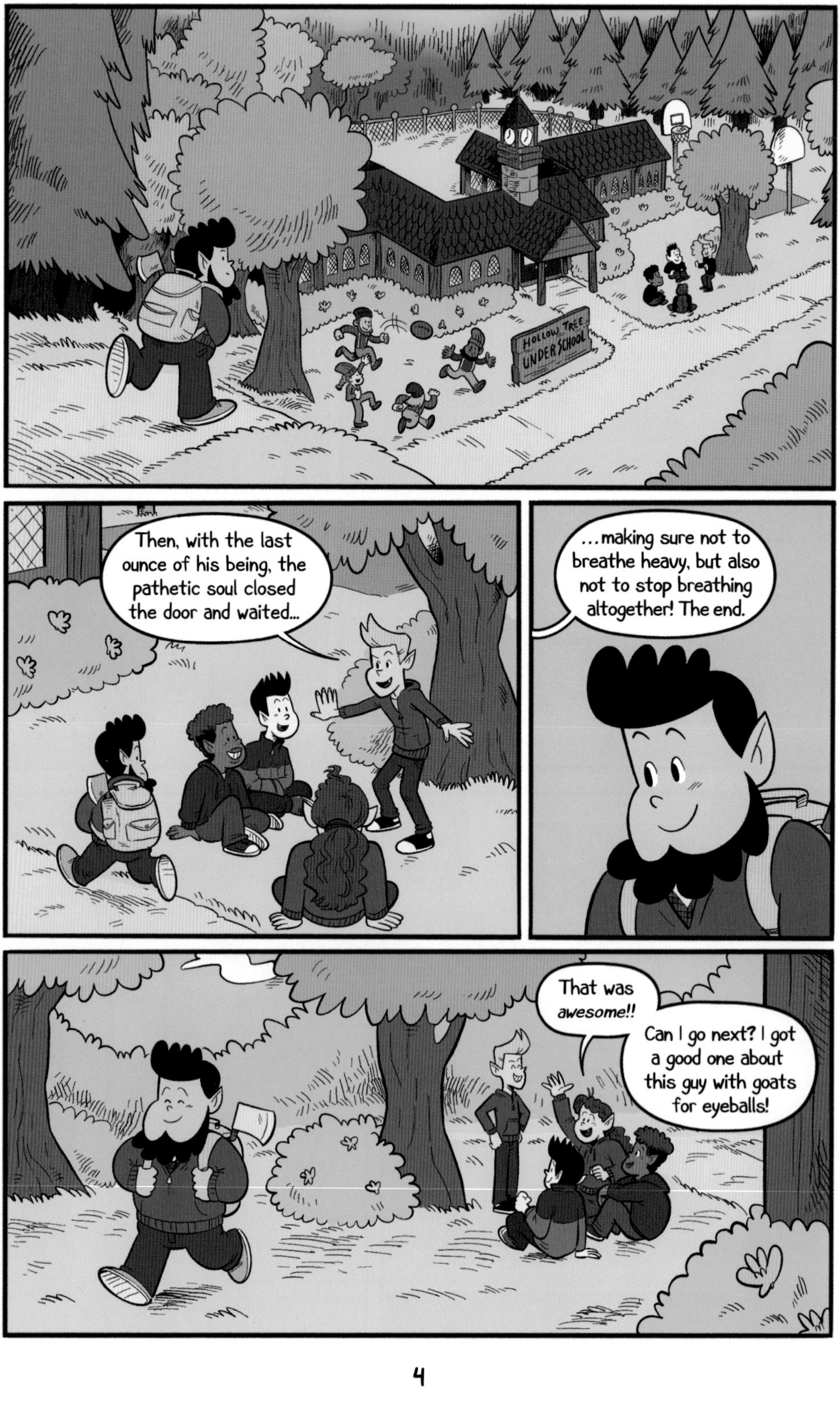
HOLLOW TREE UNDER SCHOOL
Then, with the last ounce of his being, the pathetic soul closed the door and waited...
...making sure not to breathe heavy, but also not to stop breathing altogether! The end.
That was *awesome!!*
Can I go next? I got a good one about this guy with goats for eyeballs!

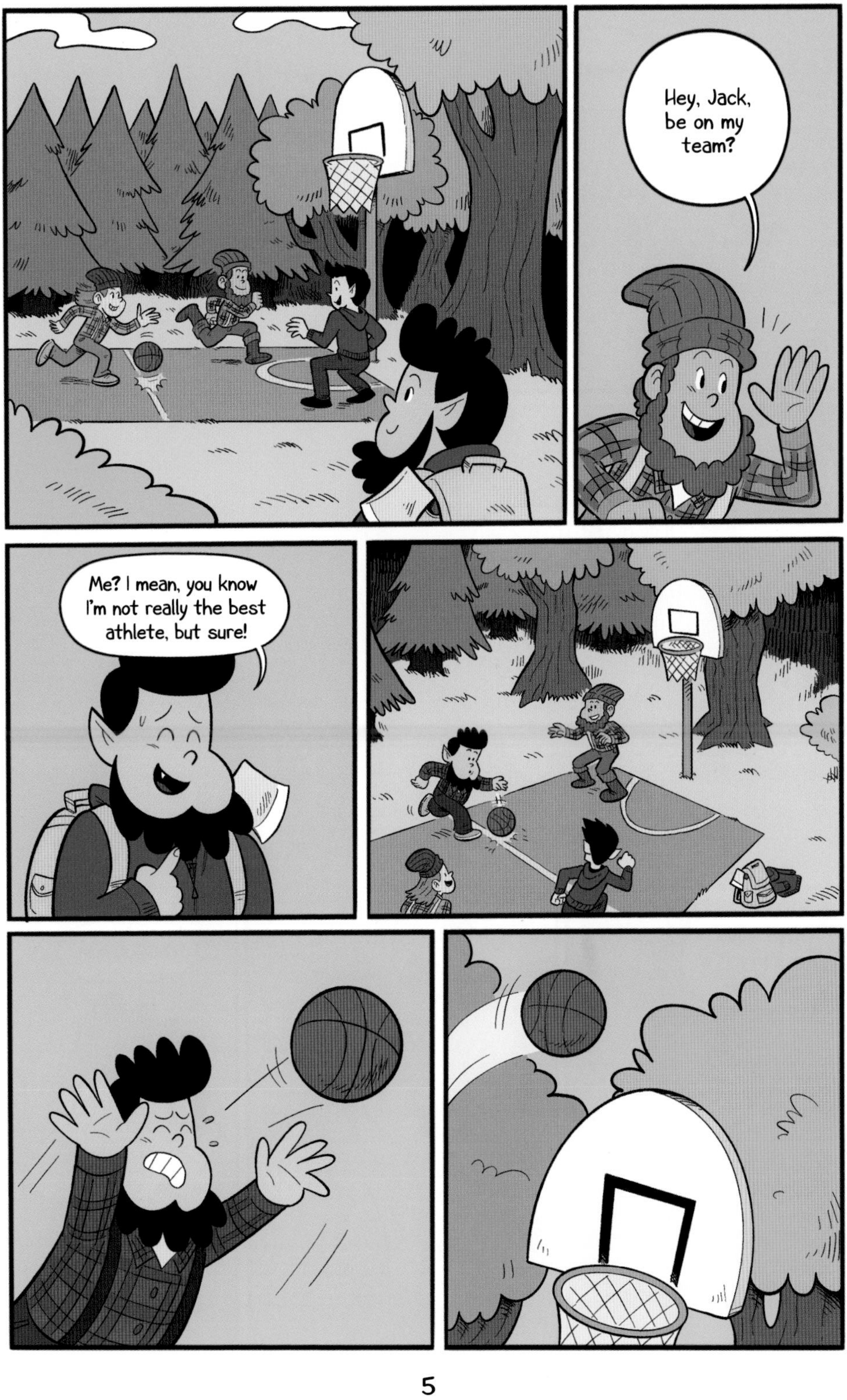
Hey, Jack, be on my team?
Me? I mean, you know I'm not really the best athlete, but sure!

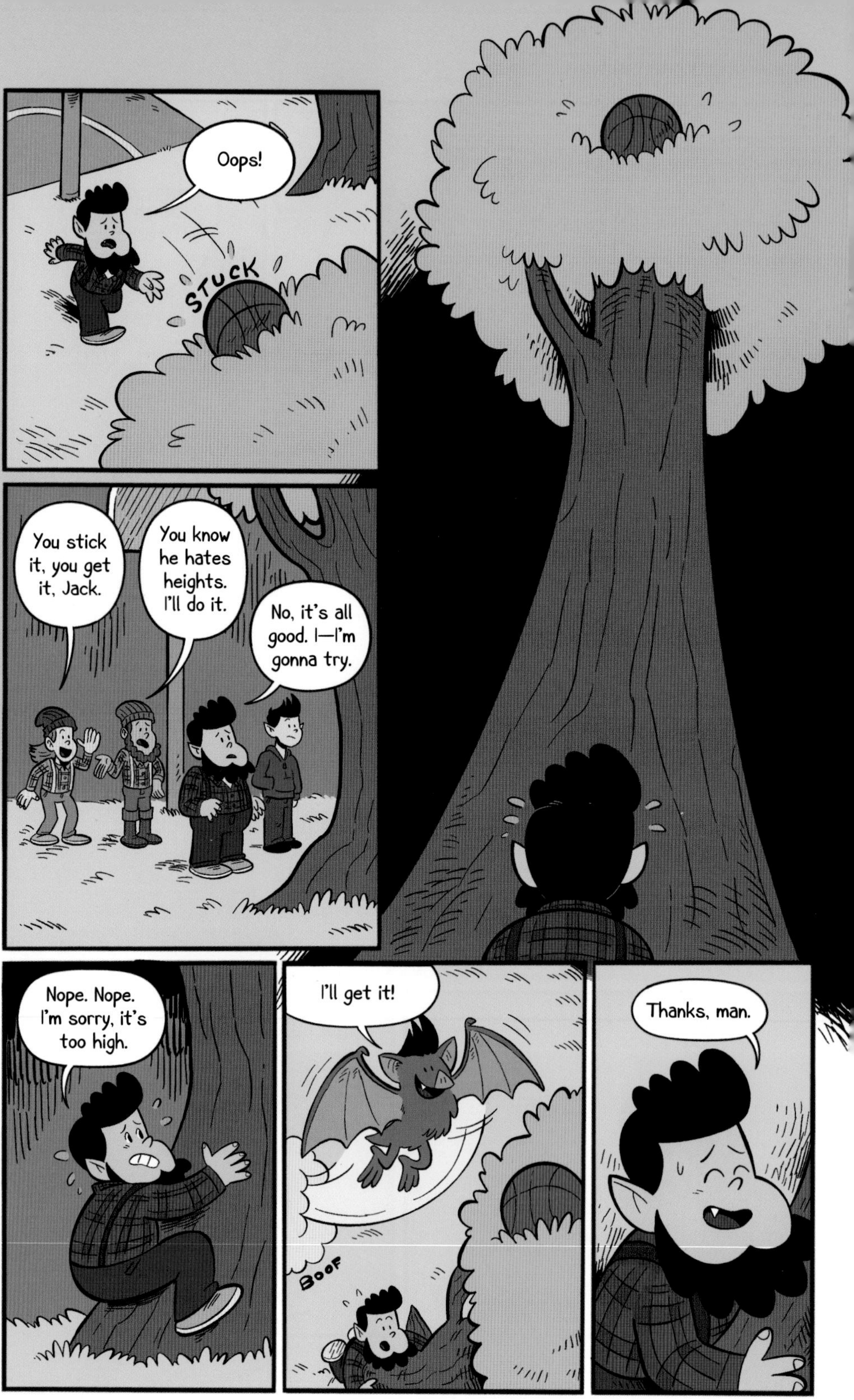
Oops!
STUCK
You stick it, you get it, Jack.
You know he hates heights. I'll do it.
No, it's all good. I—I'm gonna try.
Nope. Nope. I'm sorry, it's too high.
I'll get it!
BOOF
Thanks, man.

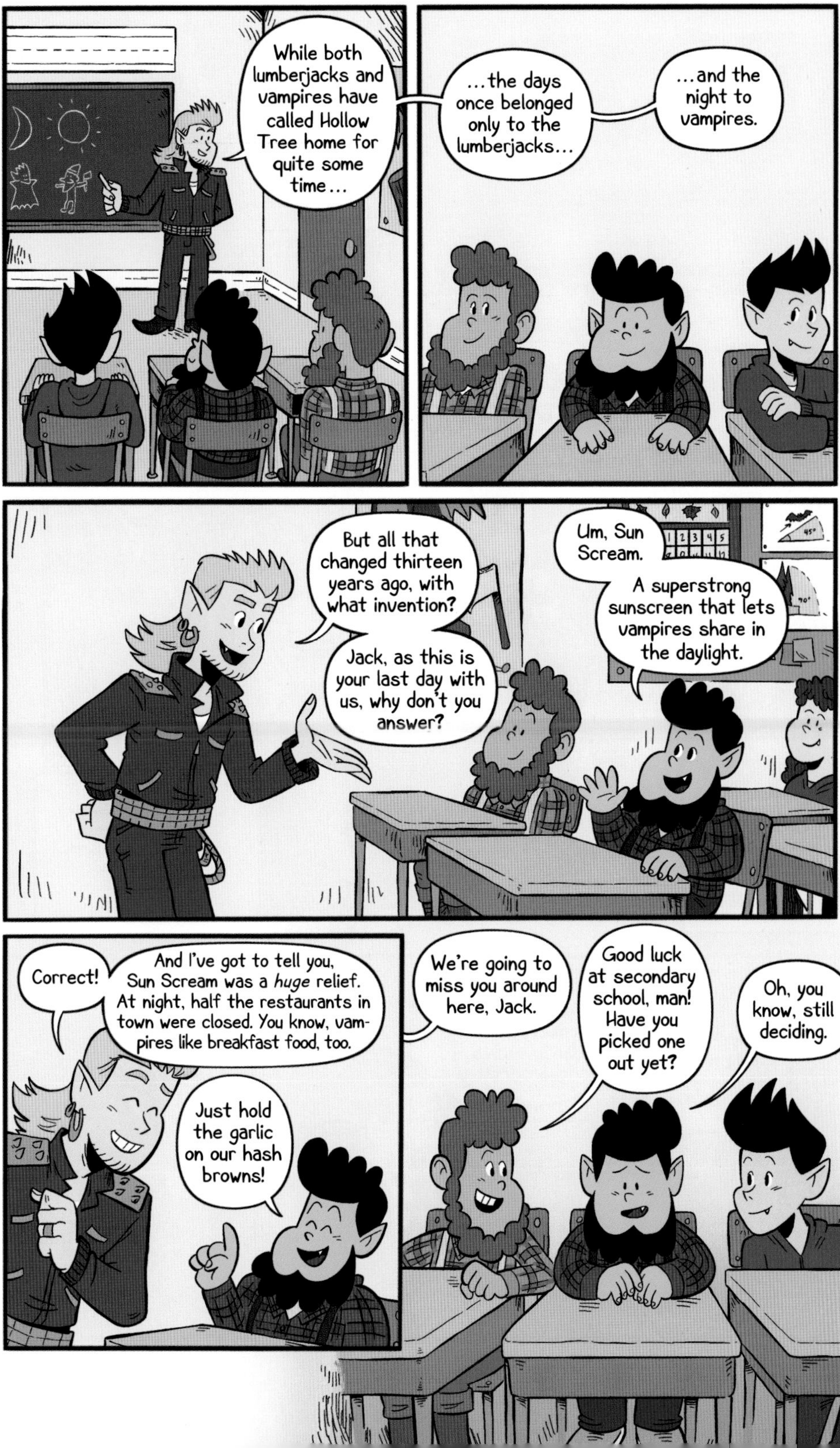

While both lumberjacks and vampires have called Hollow Tree home for quite some time…
…the days once belonged only to the lumberjacks…
…and the night to vampires.
But all that changed thirteen years ago, with what invention?
Jack, as this is your last day with us, why don't you answer?
Um, Sun Scream.
A superstrong sunscreen that lets vampires share in the daylight.
Correct!
And I've got to tell you, Sun Scream was a *huge* relief. At night, half the restaurants in town were closed. You know, vampires like breakfast food, too.
Just hold the garlic on our hash browns!
We're going to miss you around here, Jack.
Good luck at secondary school, man! Have you picked one out yet?
Oh, you know, still deciding.

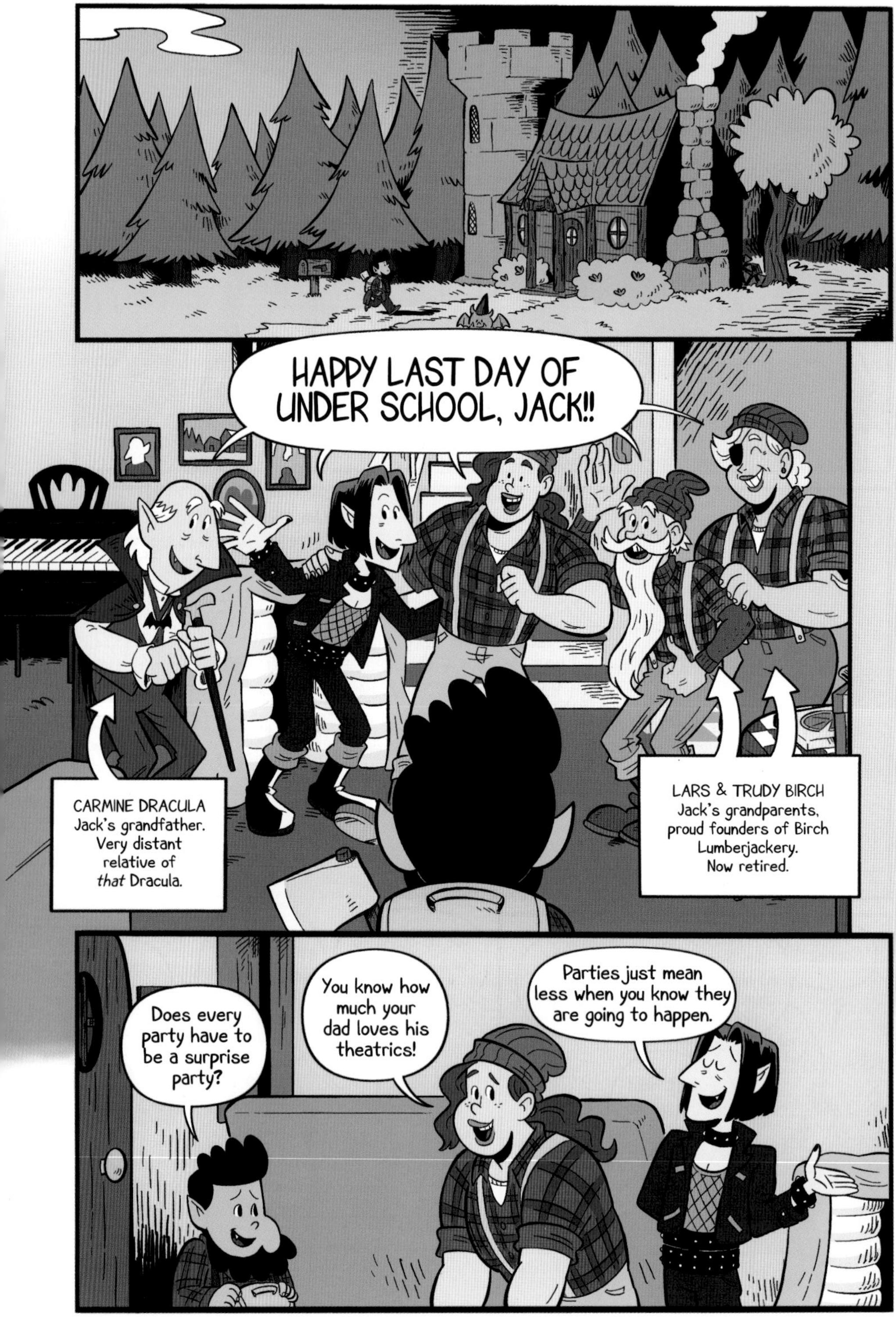

HAPPY LAST DAY OF UNDER SCHOOL, JACK!!
CARMINE DRACULA Jack's grandfather. Very distant relative of *that* Dracula.
LARS & TRUDY BIRCH Jack's grandparents, proud founders of Birch Lumberjackery. Now retired.
Does every party have to be a surprise party?
You know how much your dad loves his theatrics!
Parties just mean less when you know they are going to happen.

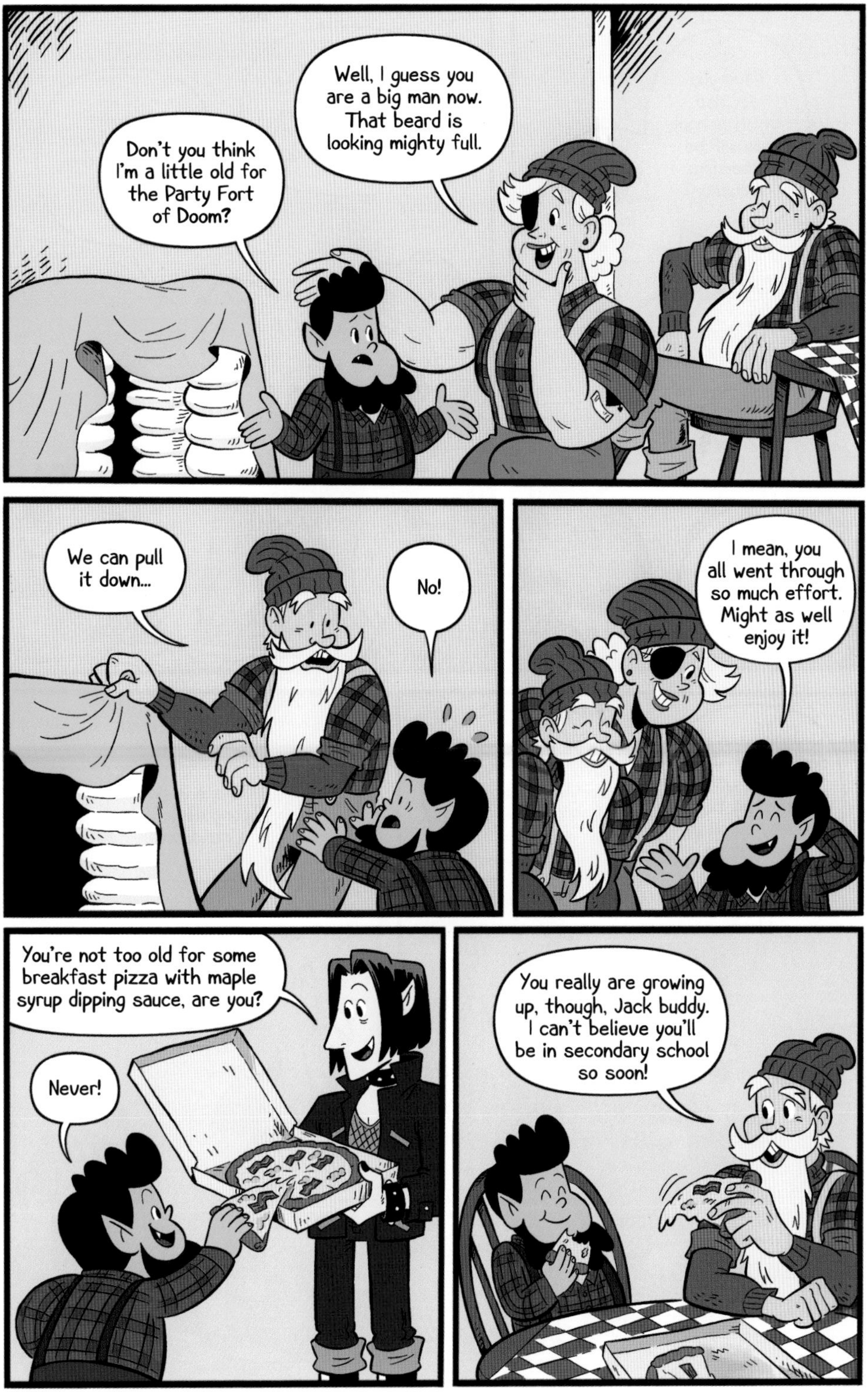
Don't you think I'm a little old for the Party Fort of Doom?
Well, I guess you are a big man now. That beard is looking mighty full.
We can pull it down...
No!
I mean, you all went through so much effort. Might as well enjoy it!
You're not too old for some breakfast pizza with maple syrup dipping sauce, are you?
Never!
You really are growing up, though, Jack buddy. I can't believe you'll be in secondary school so soon!

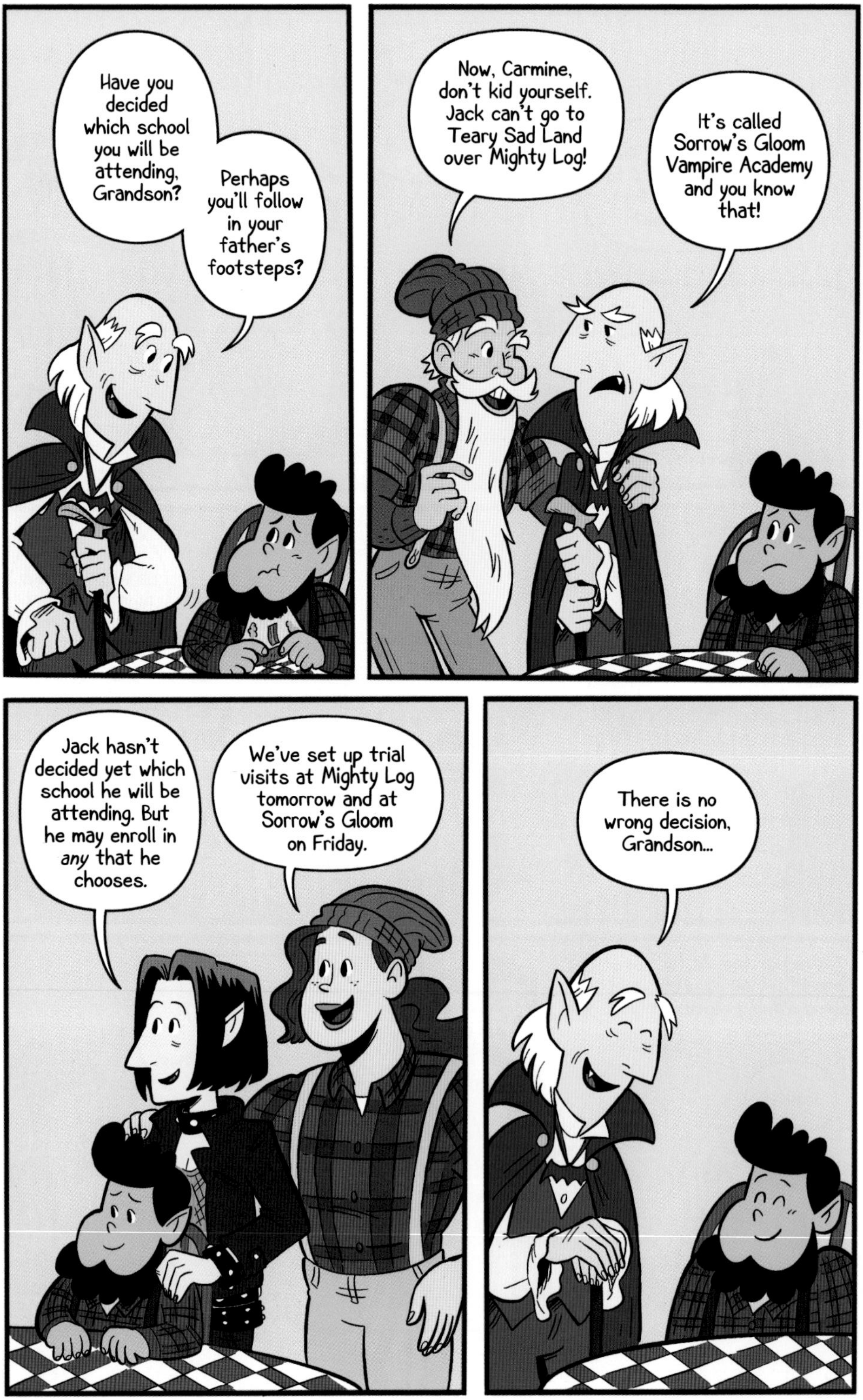
Have you decided which school you will be attending, Grandson?
Perhaps you'll follow in your father's footsteps?
Now, Carmine, don't kid yourself. Jack can't go to Teary Sad Land over Mighty Log!
It's called Sorrow's Gloom Vampire Academy and you know that!
Jack hasn't decided yet which school he will be attending. But he may enroll in *any* that he chooses.
We've set up trial visits at Mighty Log tomorrow and at Sorrow's Gloom on Friday.
There is no wrong decision, Grandson...

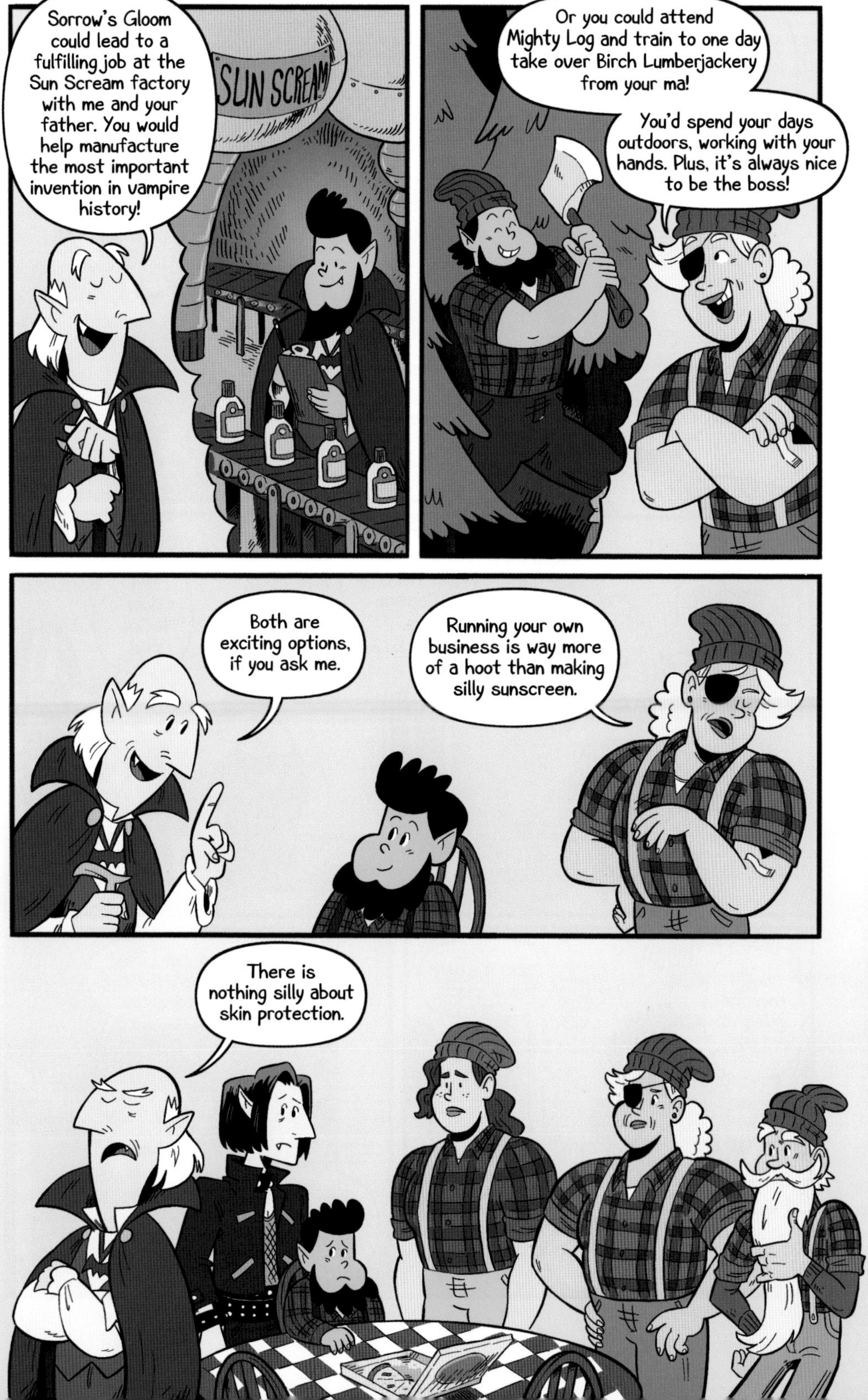

Sorrow's Gloom could lead to a fulfilling job at the Sun Scream factory with me and your father. You would help manufacture the most important invention in vampire history!
SUN SCREAM
Or you could attend Mighty Log and train to one day take over Birch Lumberjackery from your ma!
You'd spend your days outdoors, working with your hands. Plus, it's always nice to be the boss!
Both are exciting options, if you ask me.
Running your own business is way more of a hoot than making silly sunscreen.
There is nothing silly about skin protection.

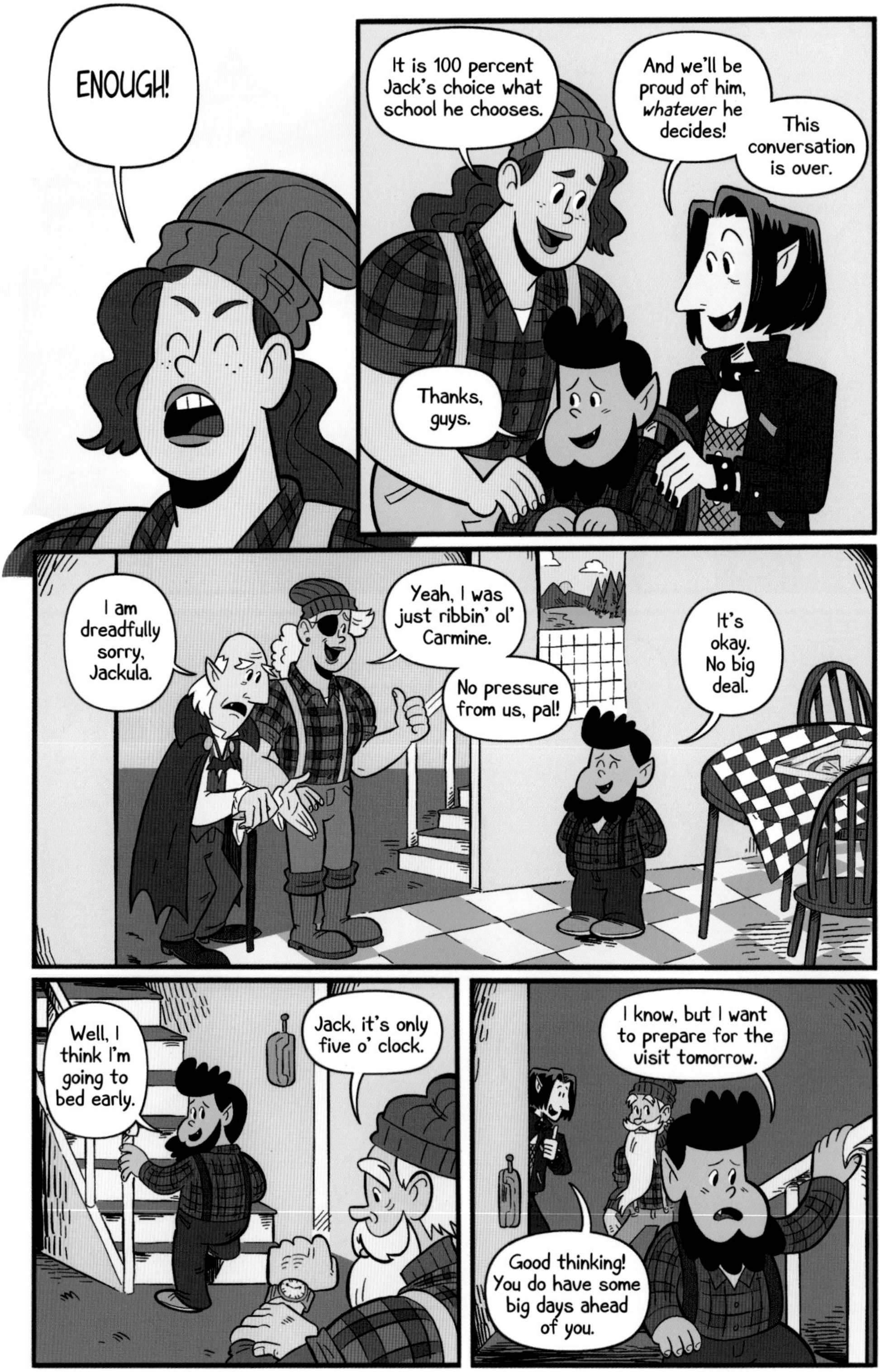
ENOUGH!
It is 100 percent Jack's choice what school he chooses.
And we'll be proud of him, *whatever* he decides!
This conversation is over.
Thanks, guys.
I am dreadfully sorry, Jackula.
Yeah, I was just ribbin' ol' Carmine.
No pressure from us, pal!
It's okay. No big deal.
Well, I think I'm going to bed early.
Jack, it's only five o' clock.
I know, but I want to prepare for the visit tomorrow.
Good thinking! You do have some big days ahead of you.

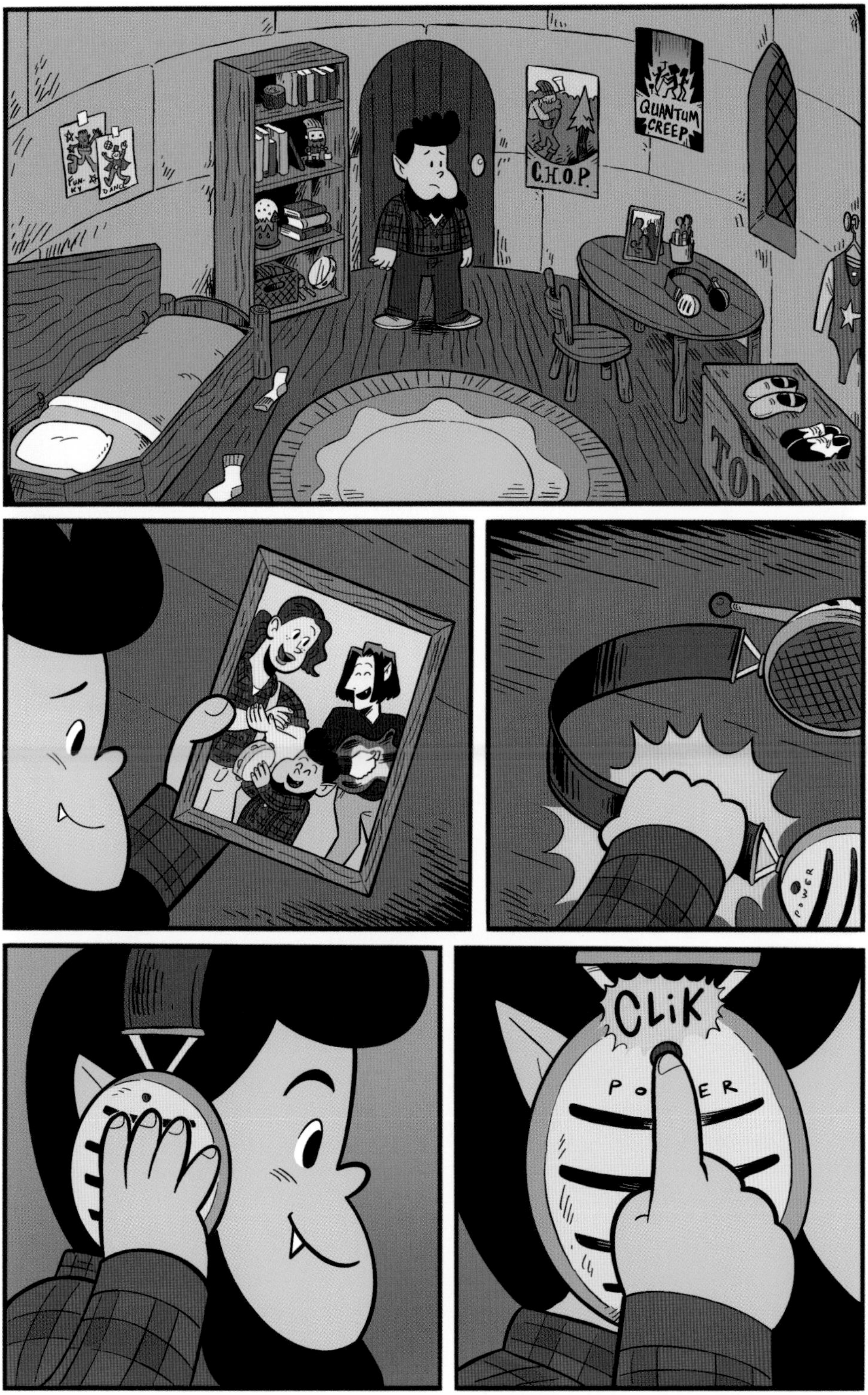
FUN-KY
DANCE
C.H.O.P.
QUANTUM CREEP
POWER
CLIK

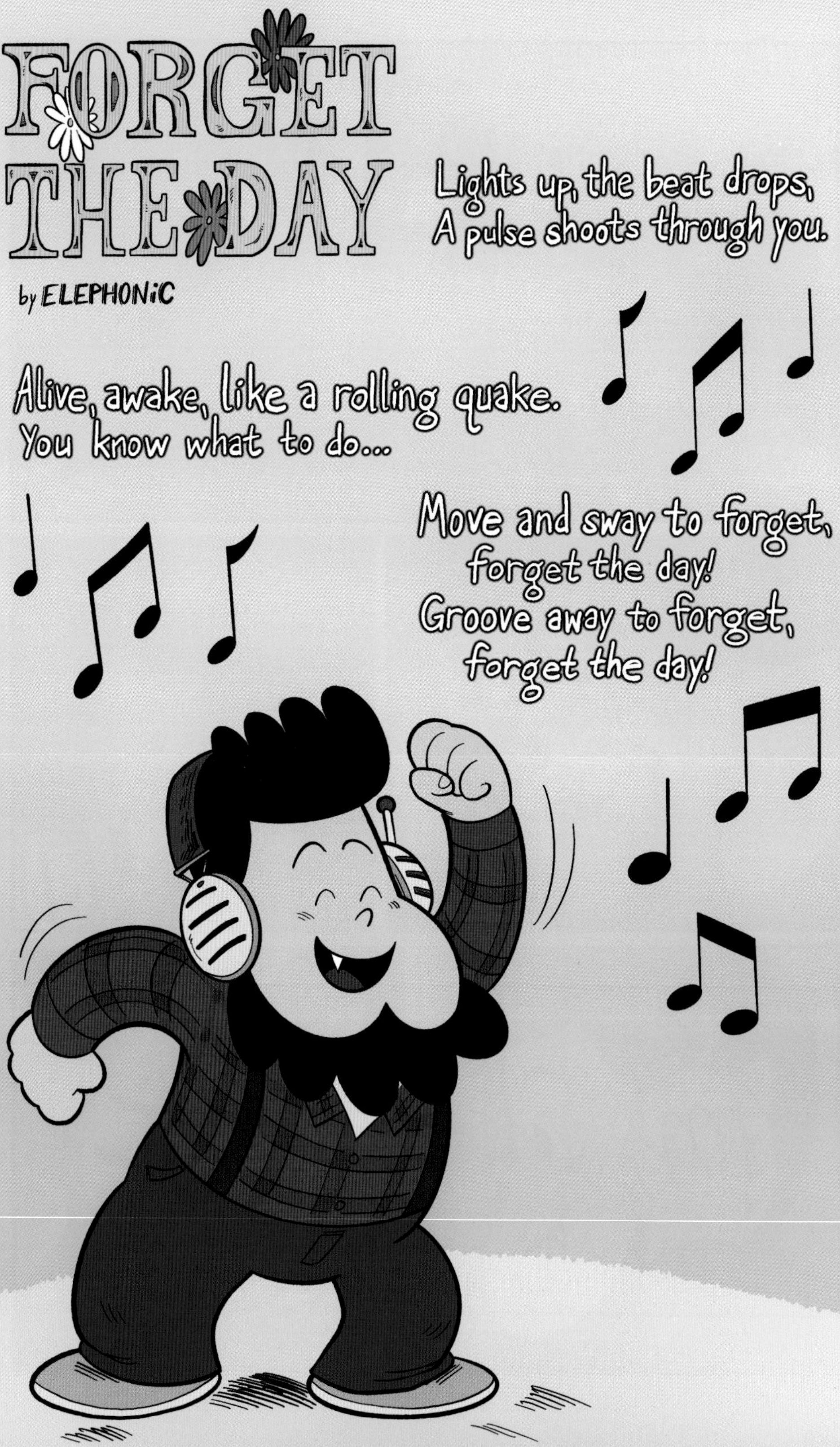
FORGET THE DAY
by ELEPHONiC
Lights up, the beat drops,
A pulse shoots through you.
Alive, awake, like a rolling quake.
You know what to do...
Move and sway to forget,
forget the day!
Groove away to forget,
forget the day!

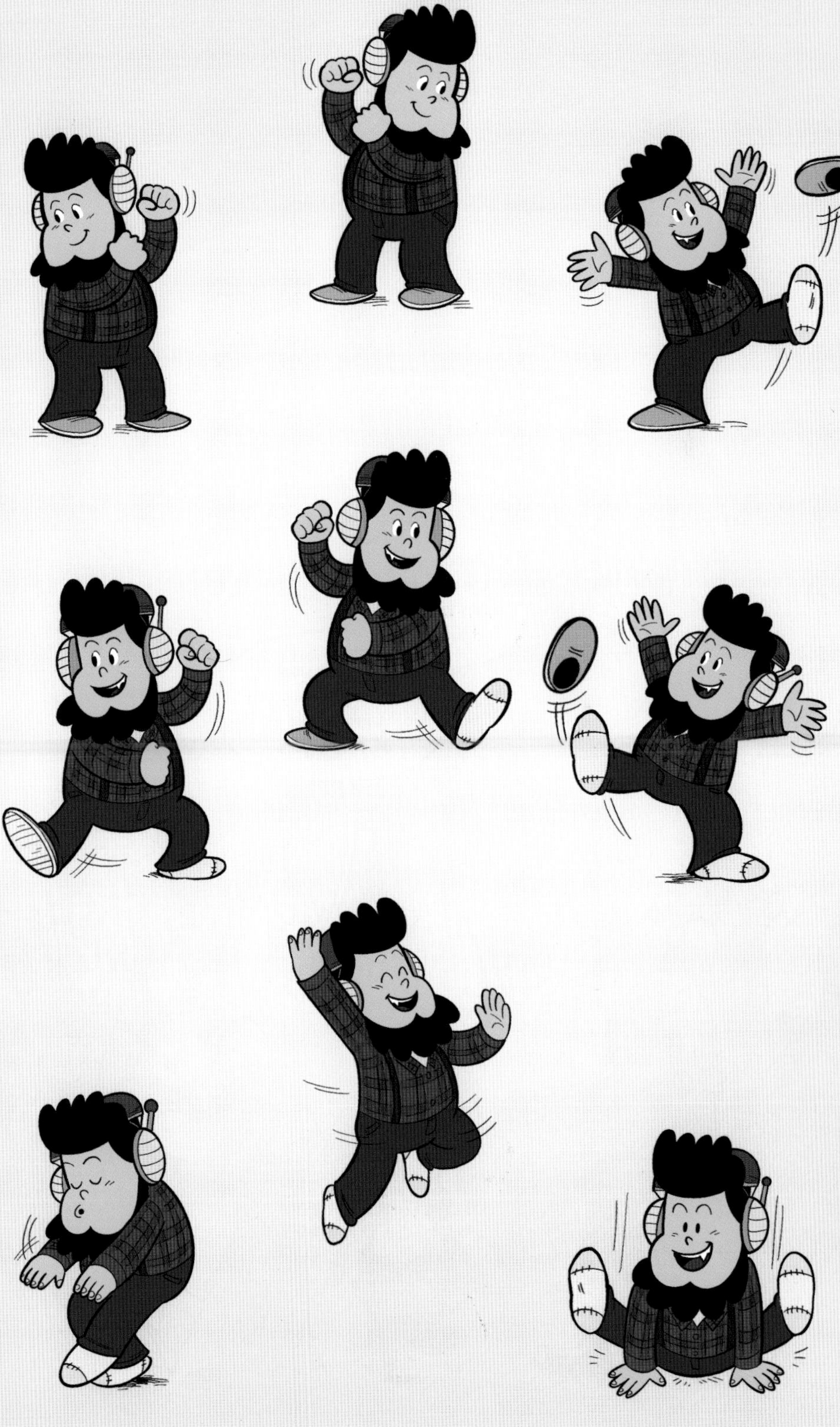

THURSDAY

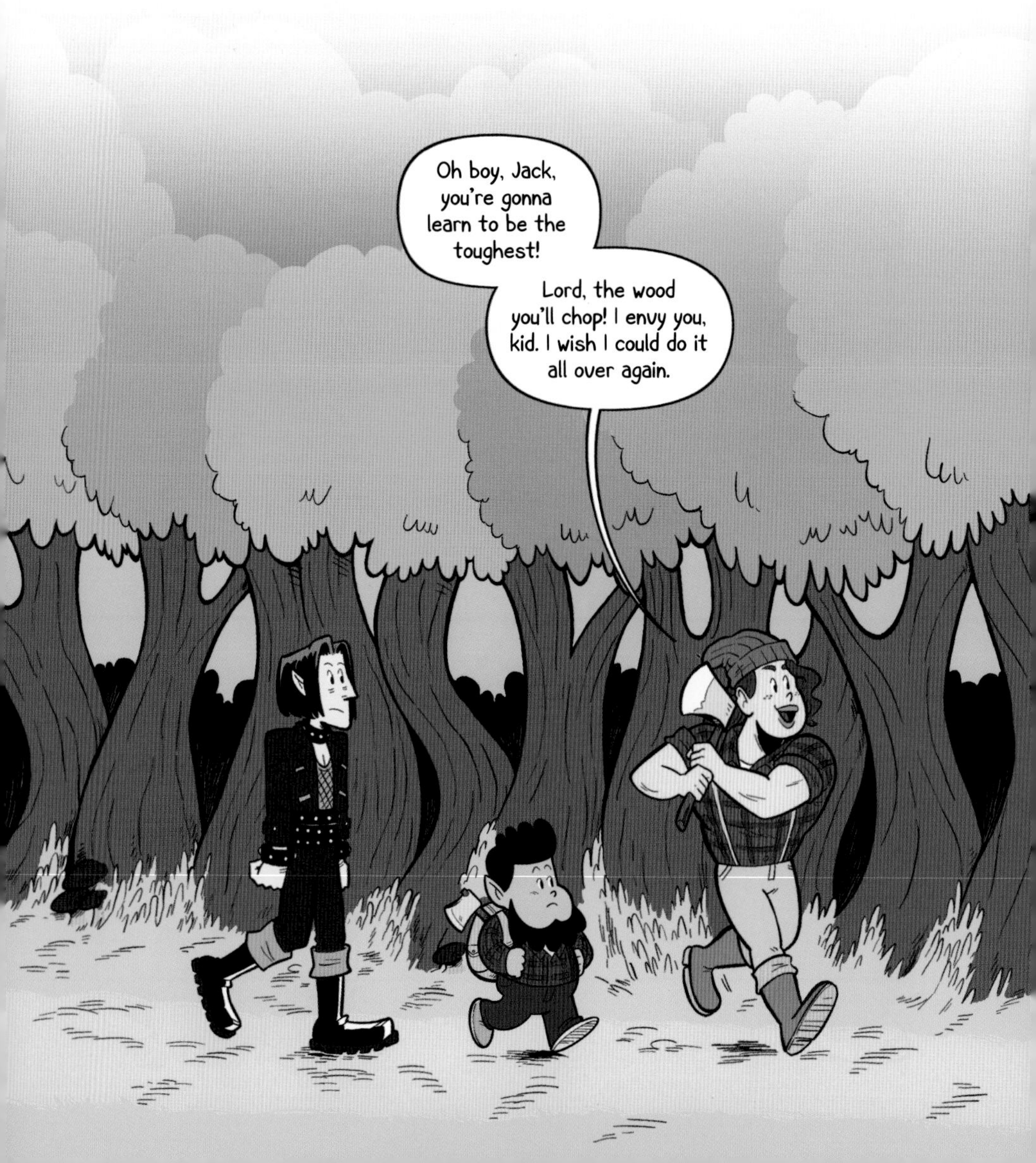
Oh boy, Jack, you're gonna learn to be the toughest!
Lord, the wood you'll chop! I envy you, kid. I wish I could do it all over again.

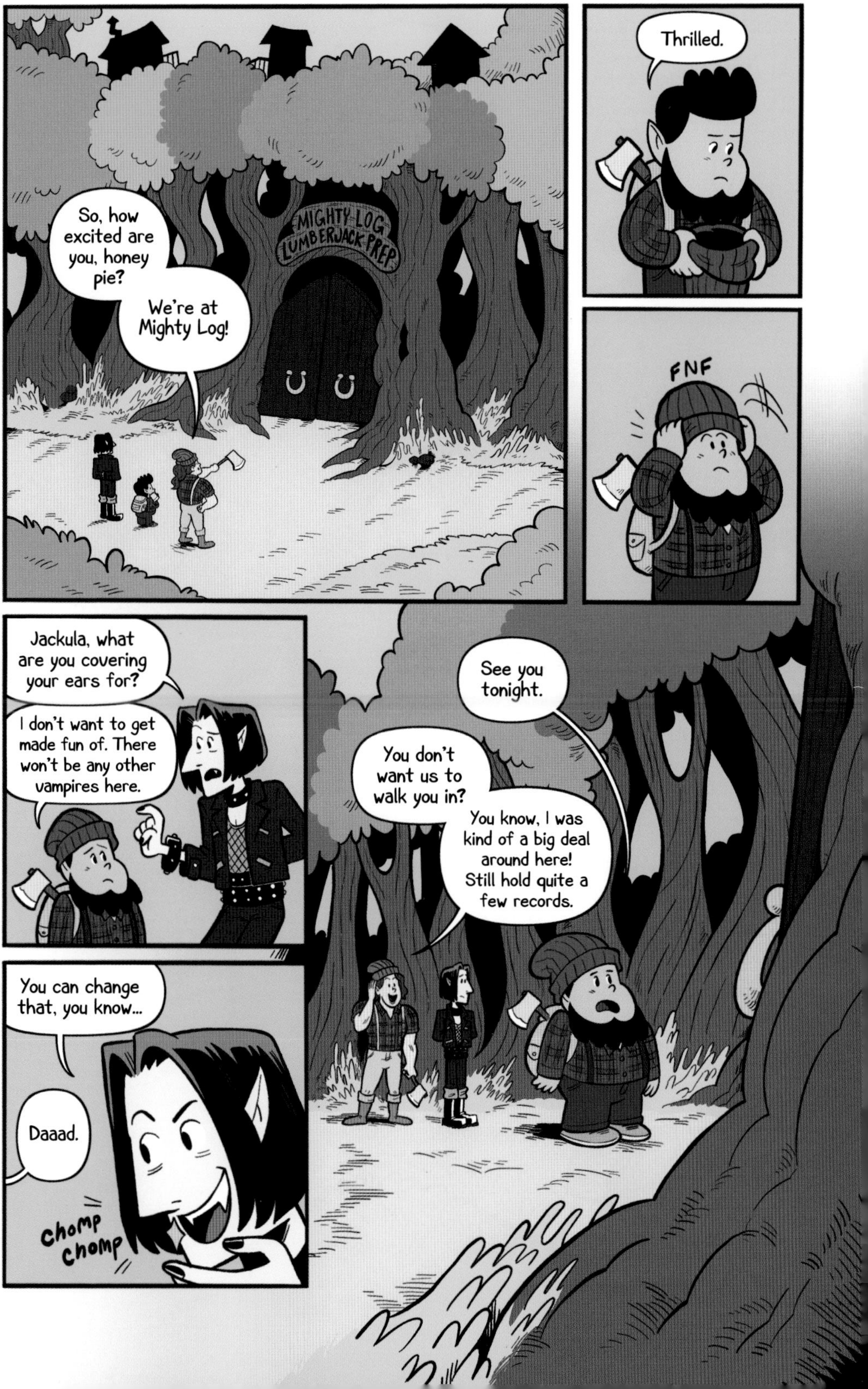

MIGHTY LOG LUMBERJACK PREP
So, how excited are you, honey pie?
We're at Mighty Log!
Thrilled.
FNF
Jackula, what are you covering your ears for?
I don't want to get made fun of. There won't be any other vampires here.
You can change that, you know...
Daaad.
CHOMP CHOMP
You don't want us to walk you in?
You know, I was kind of a big deal around here! Still hold quite a few records.
See you tonight.

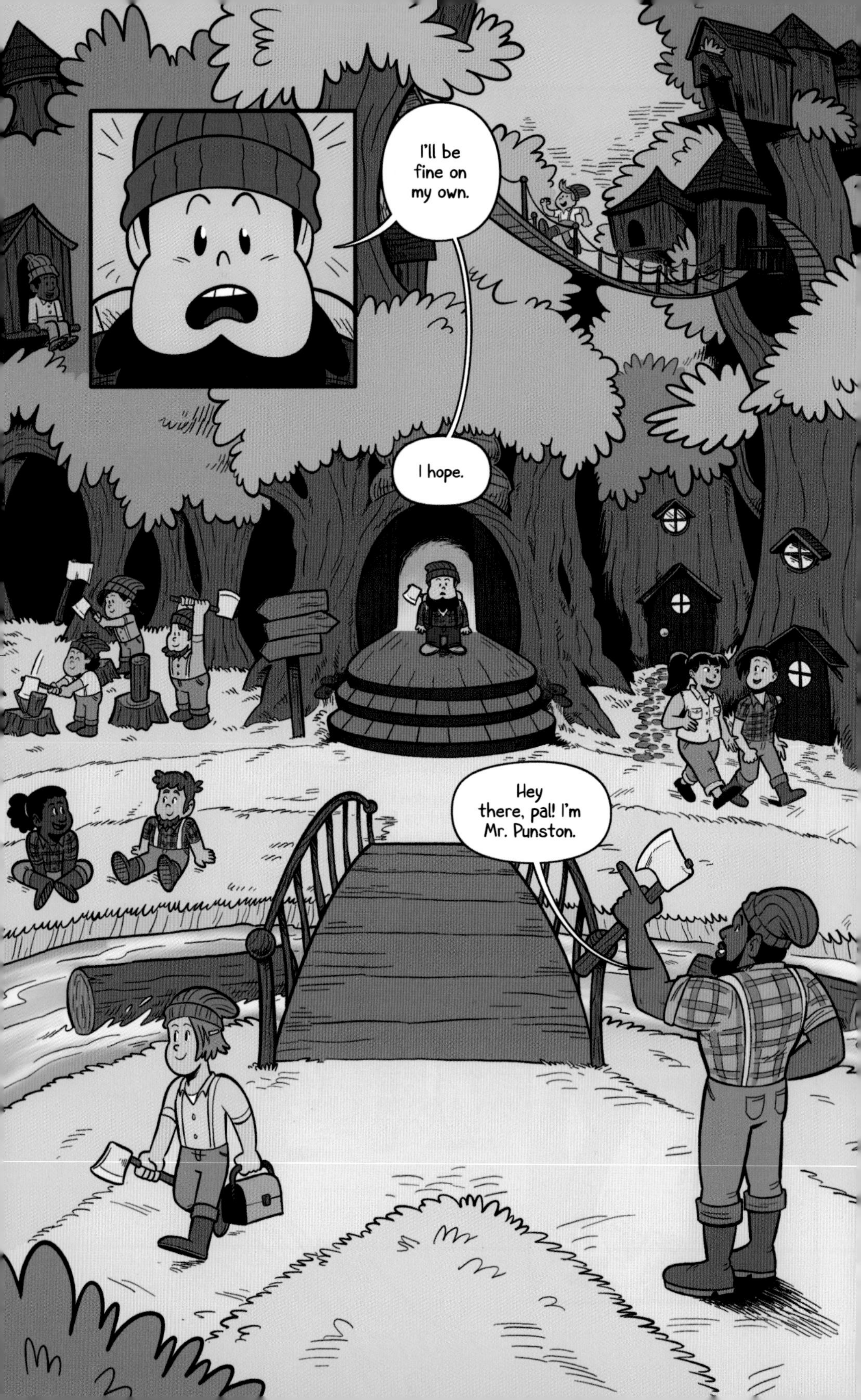
I'll be fine on my own.
I hope.
Hey there, pal! I'm Mr. Punston.

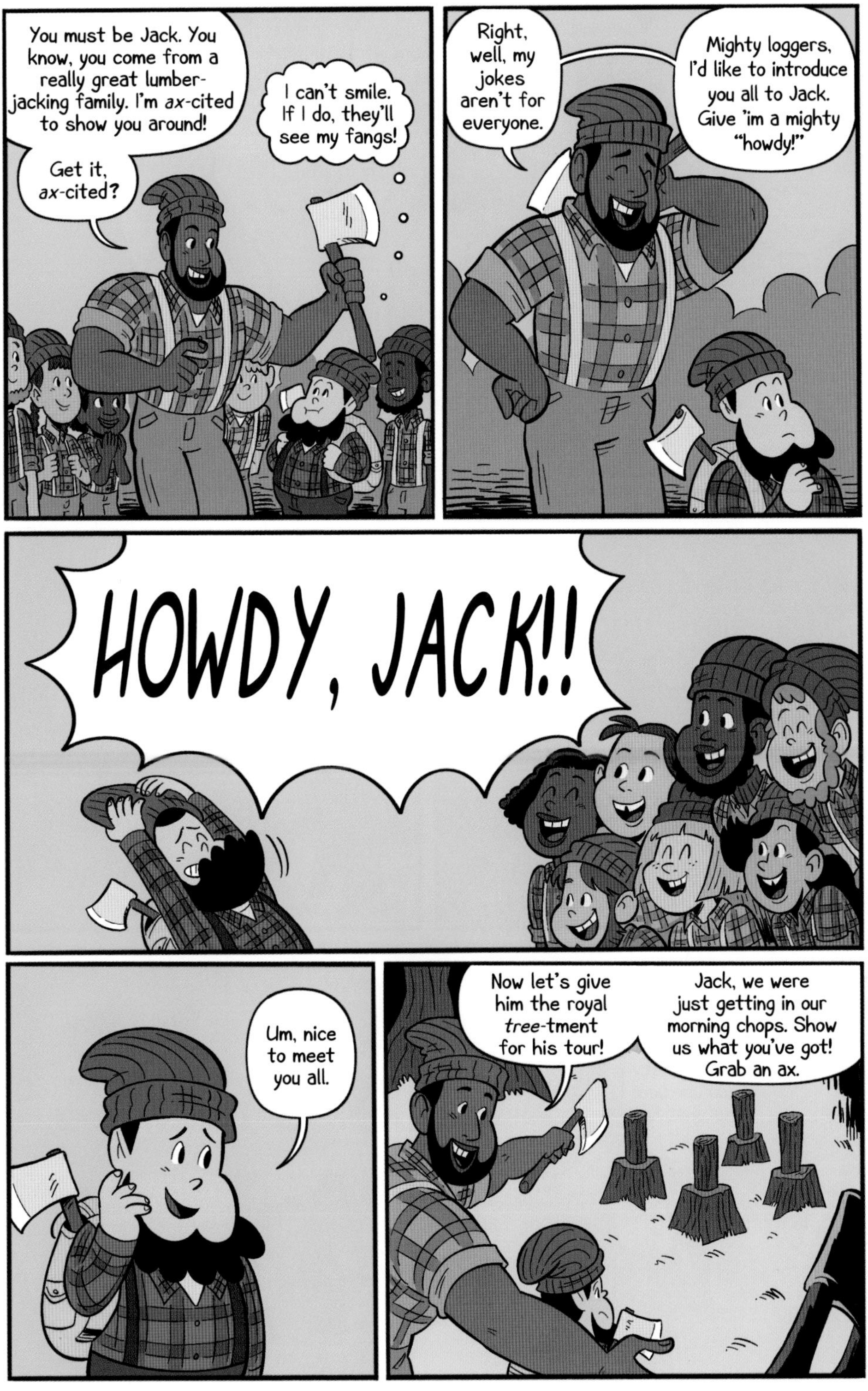
You must be Jack. You know, you come from a really great lumber-jacking family. I'm *ax*-cited to show you around!
Get it, *ax*-cited?
I can't smile. If I do, they'll see my fangs!
Right, well, my jokes aren't for everyone.
Mighty loggers, I'd like to introduce you all to Jack. Give 'im a mighty "howdy!"
HOWDY, JACK!!
Um, nice to meet you all.
Now let's give him the royal *tree*-tment for his tour!
Jack, we were just getting in our morning chops. Show us what you've got! Grab an ax.

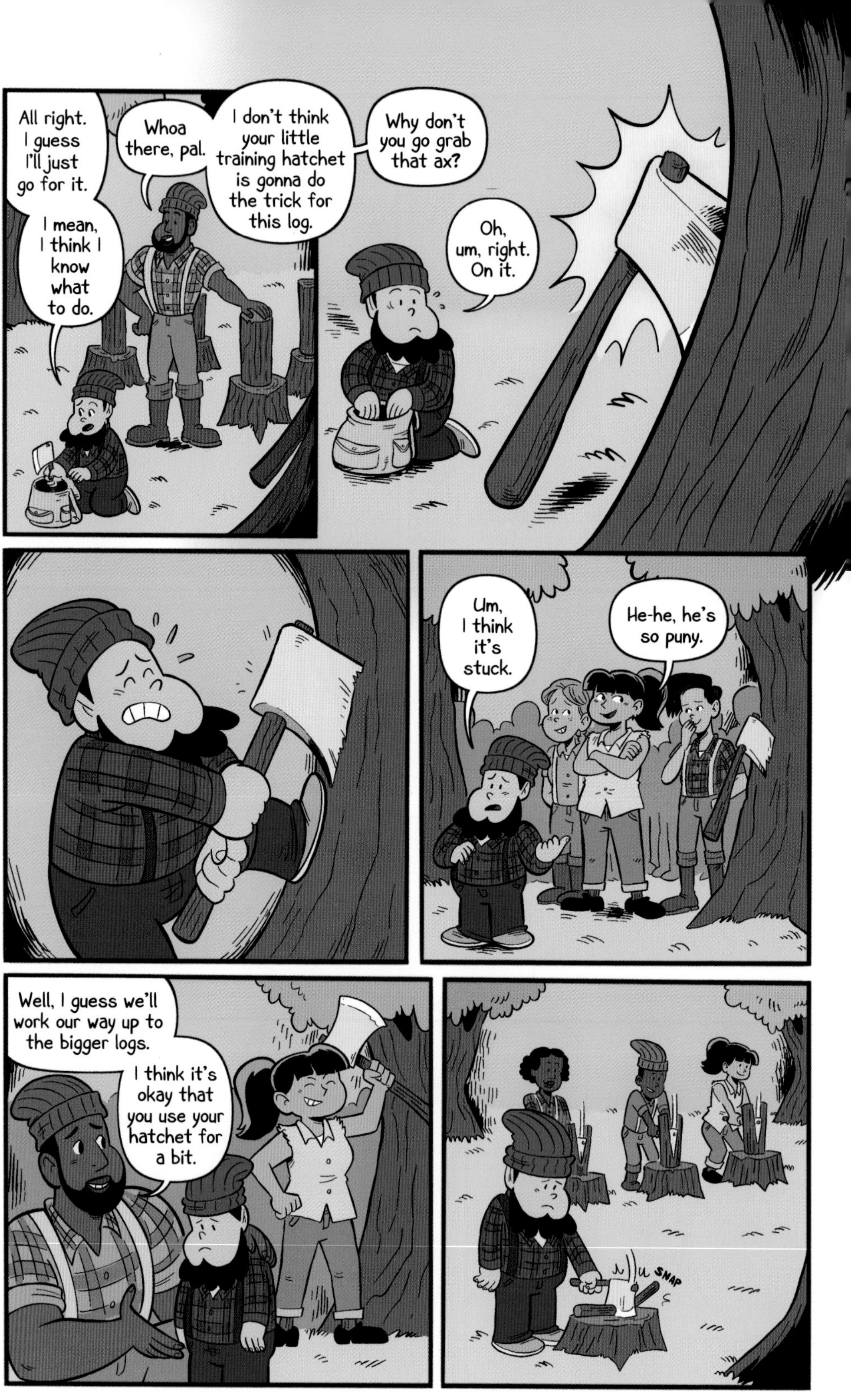
All right. I guess I'll just go for it.
I mean, I think I know what to do.
Whoa there, pal.
I don't think your little training hatchet is gonna do the trick for this log.
Why don't you go grab that ax?
Oh, um, right. On it.
Um, I think it's stuck.
He-he, he's so puny.
Well, I guess we'll work our way up to the bigger logs.
I think it's okay that you use your hatchet for a bit.
SNAP

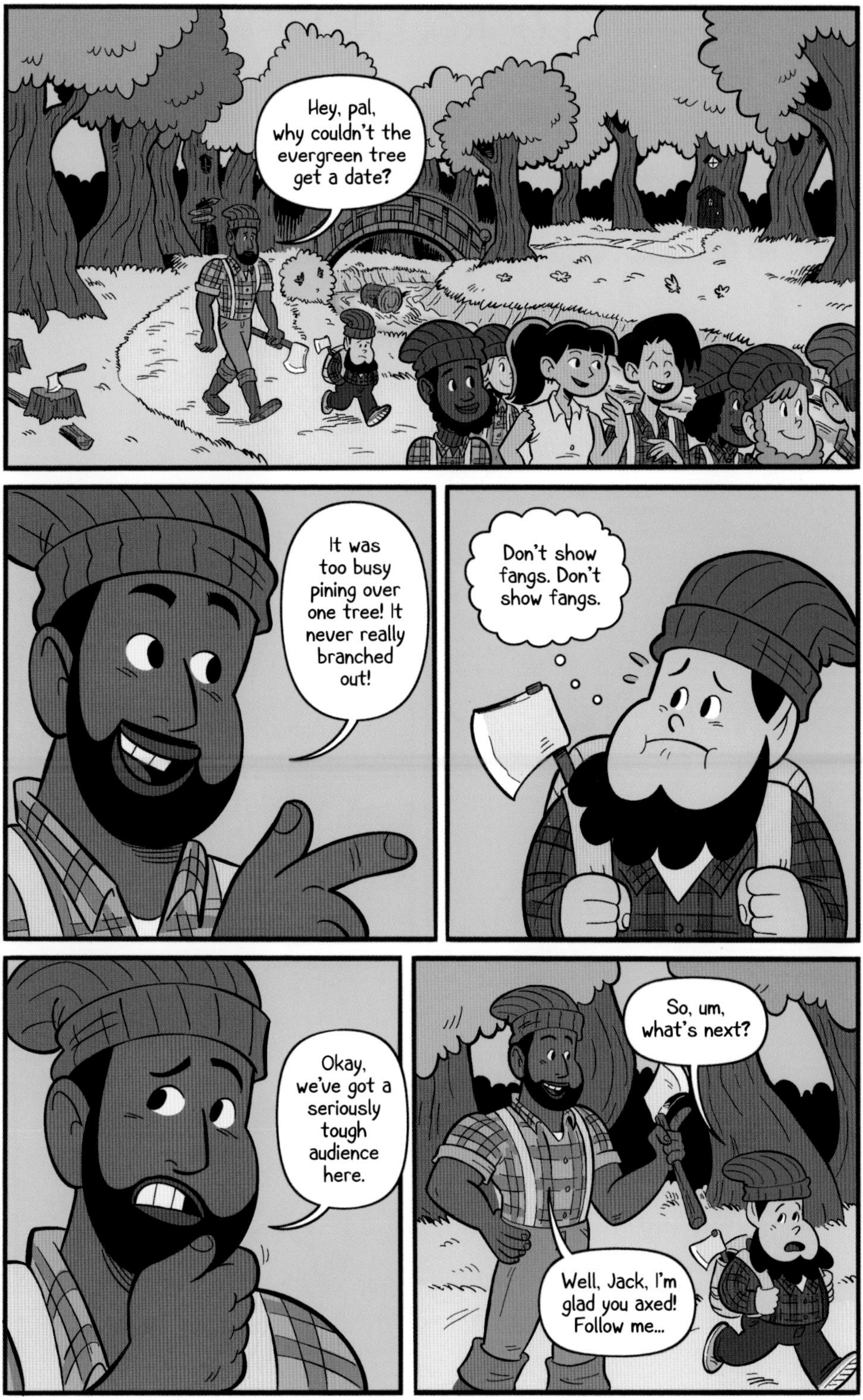
Hey, pal, why couldn't the evergreen tree get a date?
It was too busy pining over one tree! It never really branched out!
Don't show fangs. Don't show fangs.
Okay, we've got a seriously tough audience here.
So, um, what's next?
Well, Jack, I'm glad you axed! Follow me...

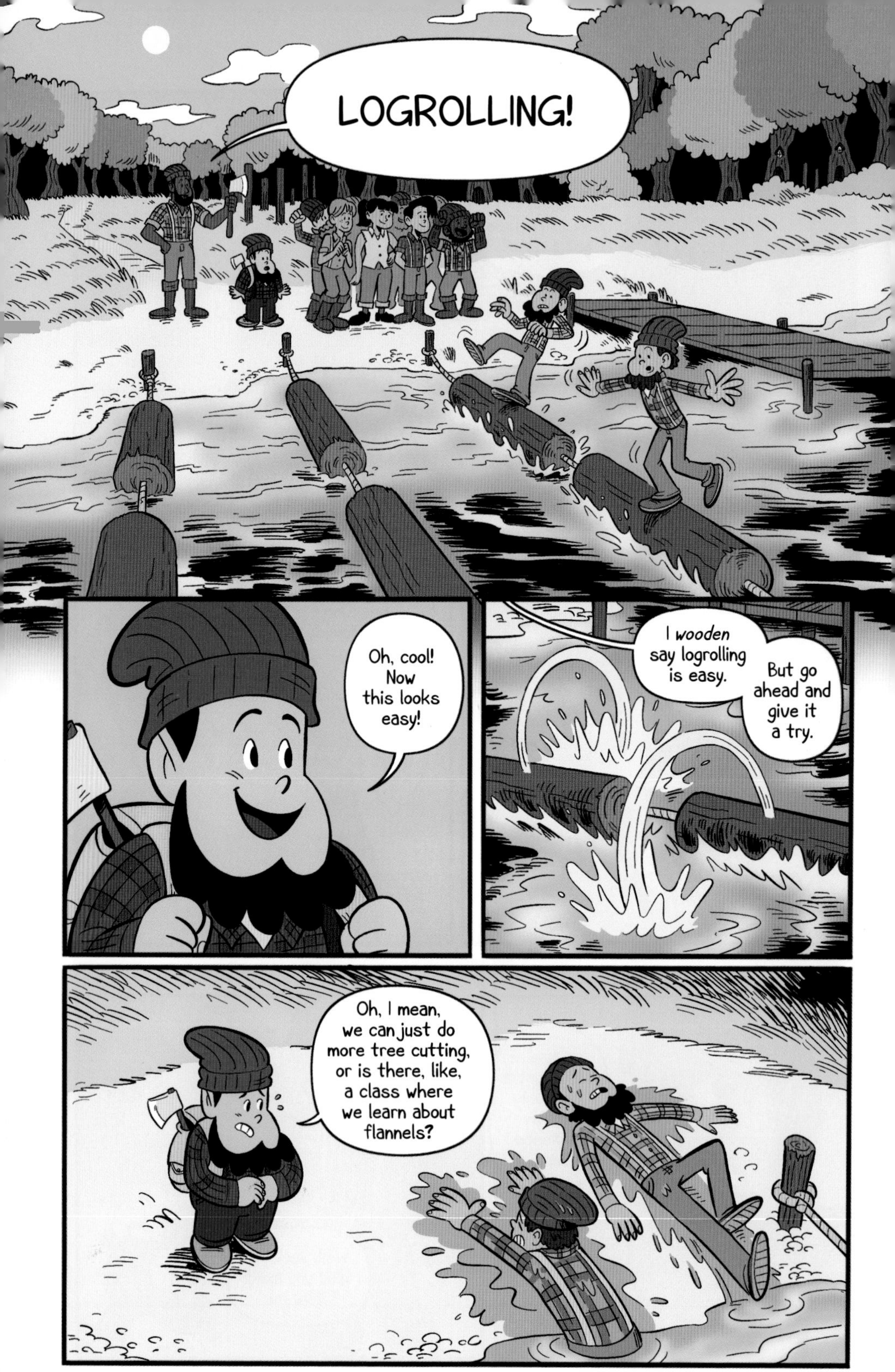

LOGROLLING!
Oh, cool! Now this looks easy!
I *wooden* say logrolling is easy.
But go ahead and give it a try.
Oh, I mean, we can just do more tree cutting, or is there, like, a class where we learn about flannels?

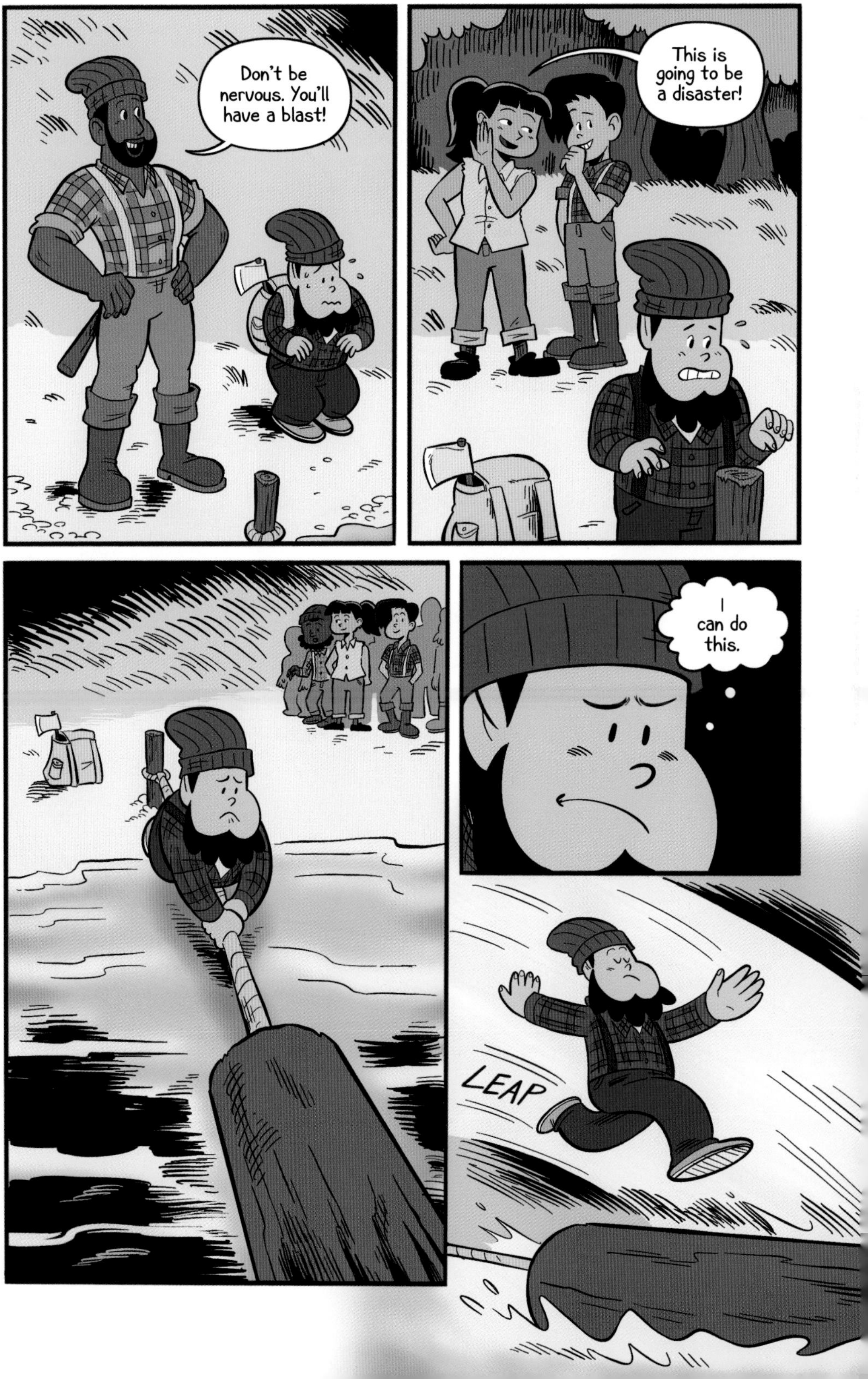
Don't be nervous. You'll have a blast!
This is going to be a disaster!
I can do this.
LEAP

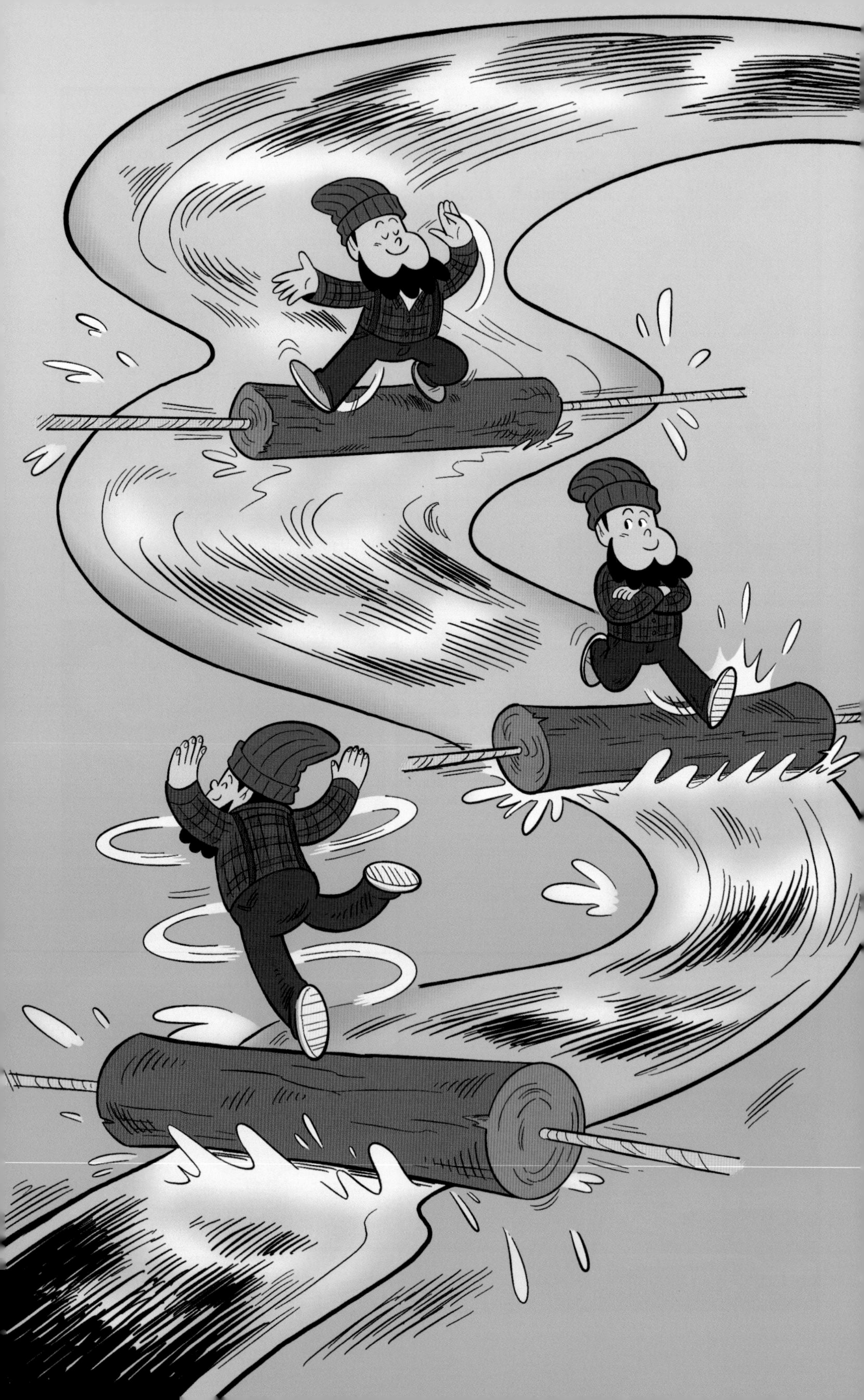

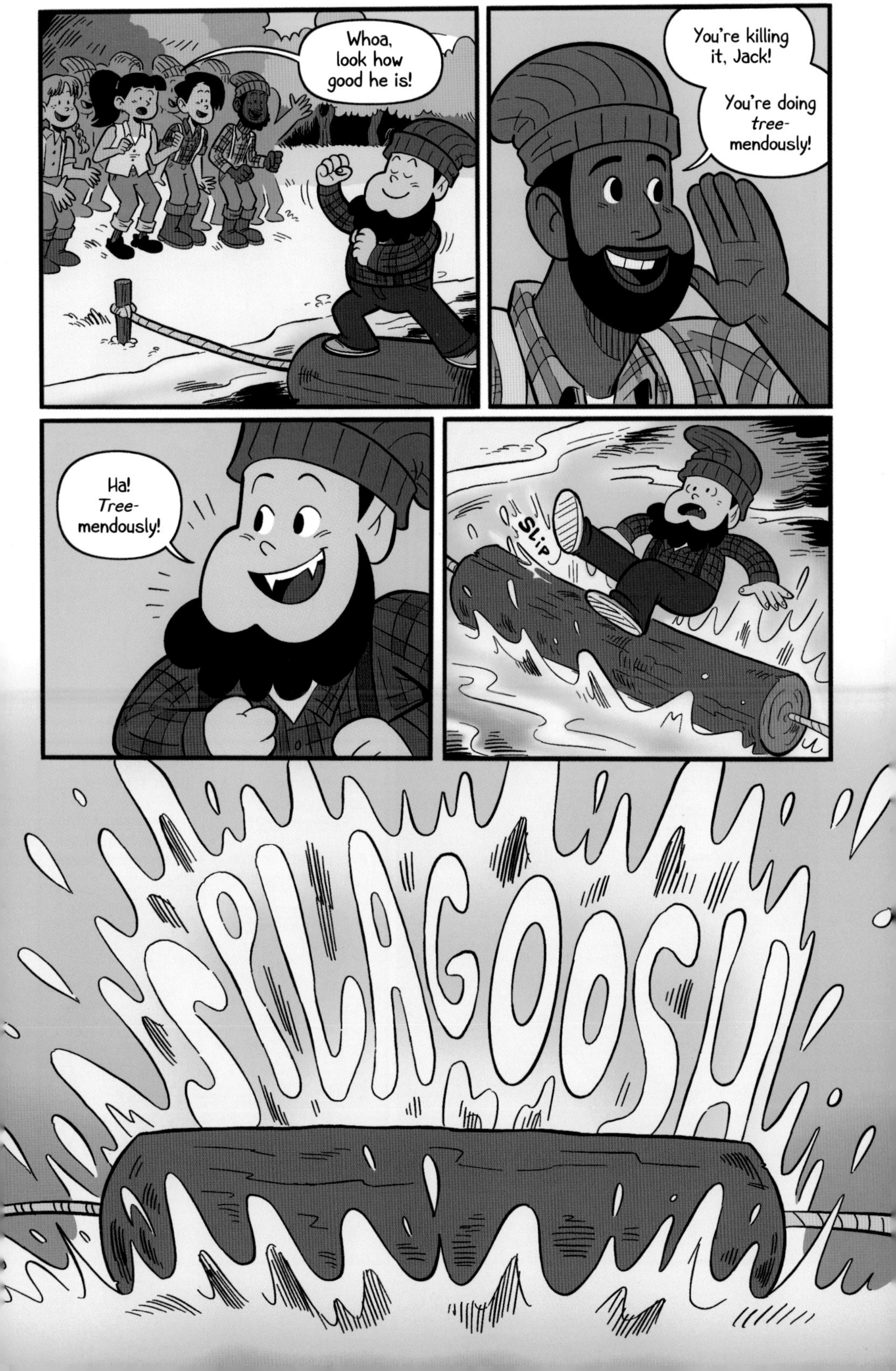

Whoa, look how good he is!
You're killing it, Jack!
You're doing *tree*-mendously!
Ha! *Tree*-mendously!
SLIP
SPLAGOOSH!

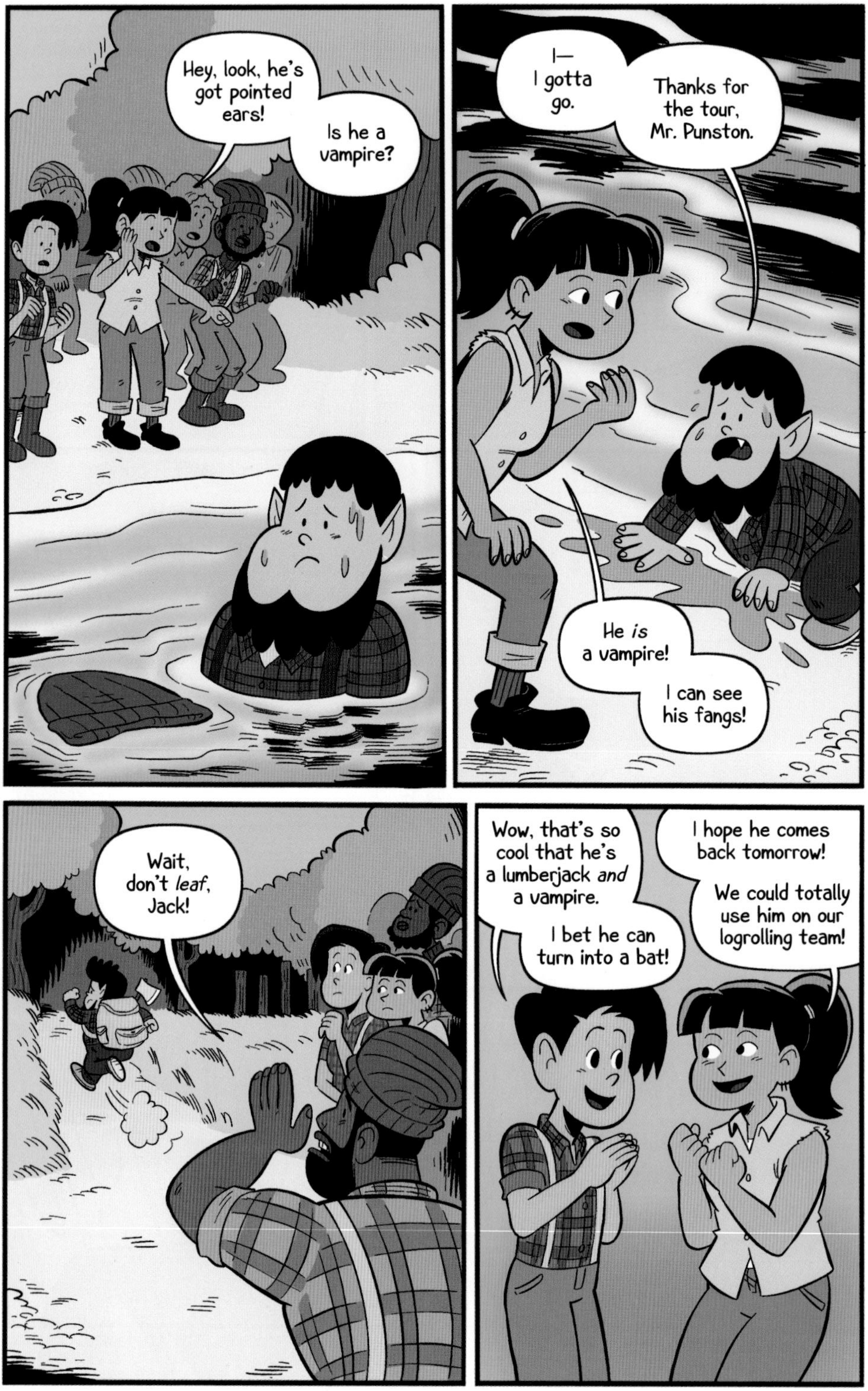
Hey, look, he's got pointed ears!
Is he a vampire?
I—
I gotta go.
Thanks for the tour, Mr. Punston.
He *is* a vampire!
I can see his fangs!
Wait, don't *leaf*, Jack!
Wow, that's so cool that he's a lumberjack *and* a vampire.
I bet he can turn into a bat!
I hope he comes back tomorrow!
We could totally use him on our logrolling team!

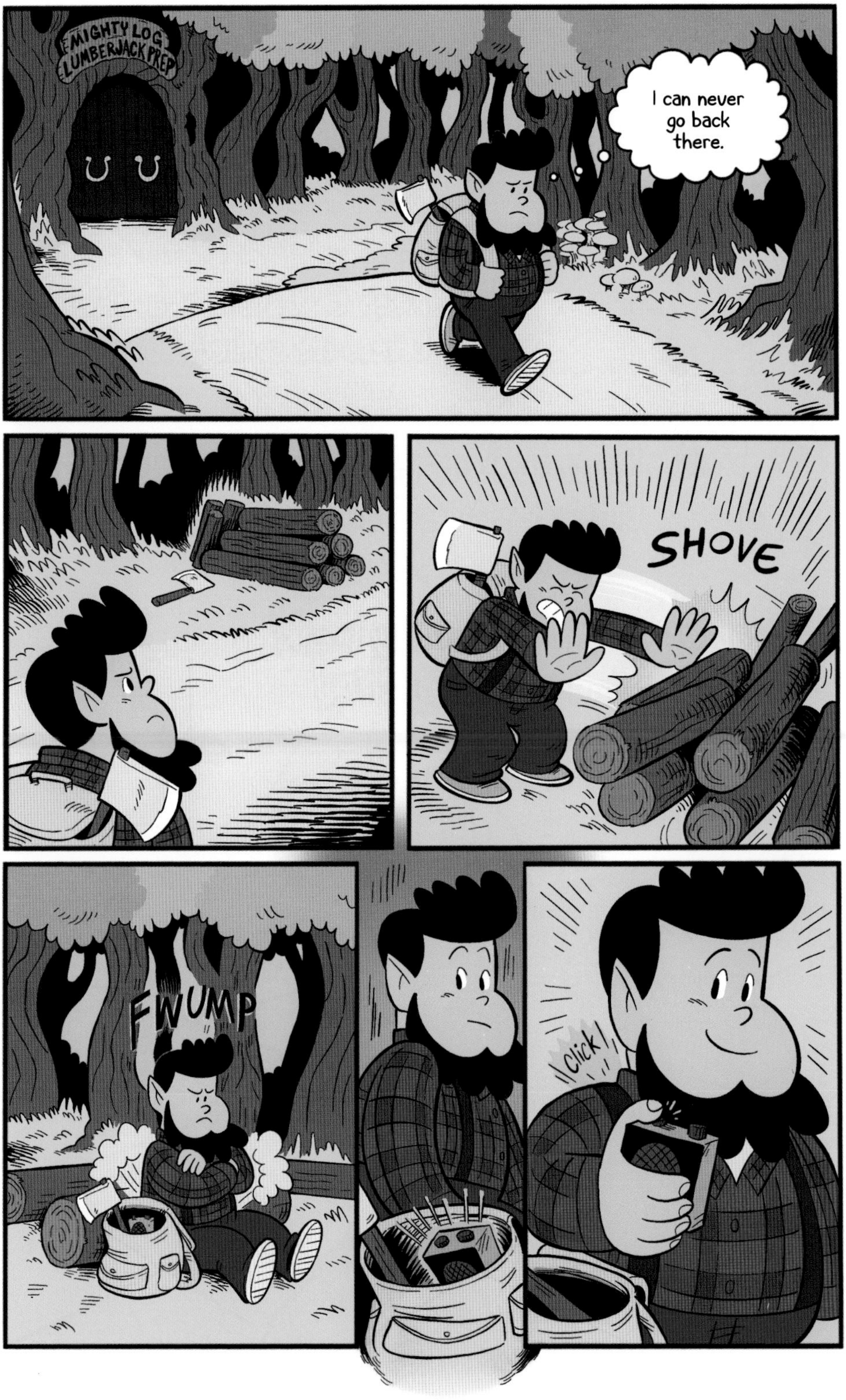
MIGHTY LOG
LUMBERJACK PREP
I can never go back there.
SHOVE
FWUMP
click

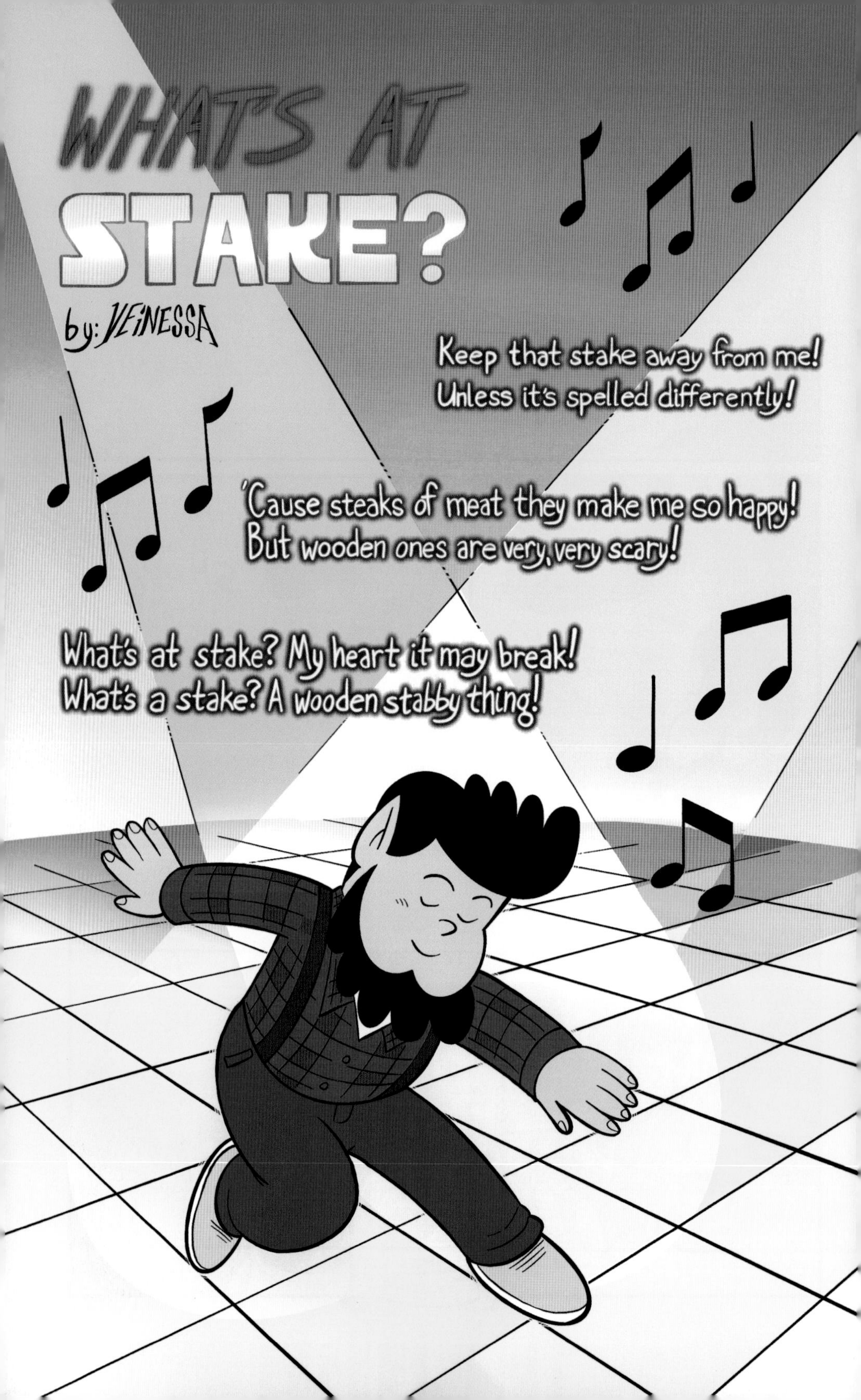
WHAT'S AT STAKE?
by: VEINESSA
Keep that stake away from me!
Unless it's spelled differently!
'Cause steaks of meat they make me so happy!
But wooden ones are very, very scary!
What's at stake? My heart it may break!
What's a stake? A wooden stabby thing!

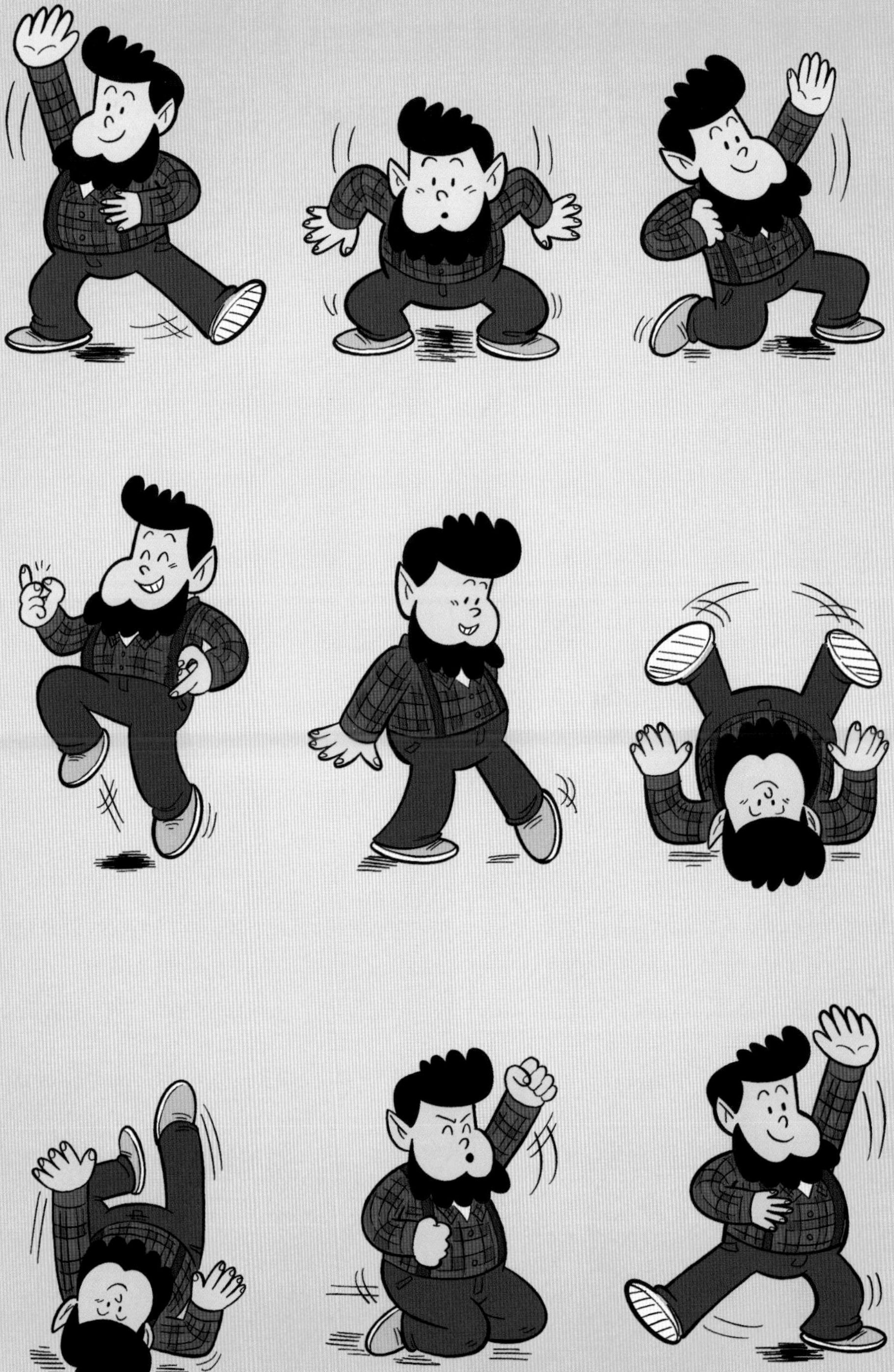

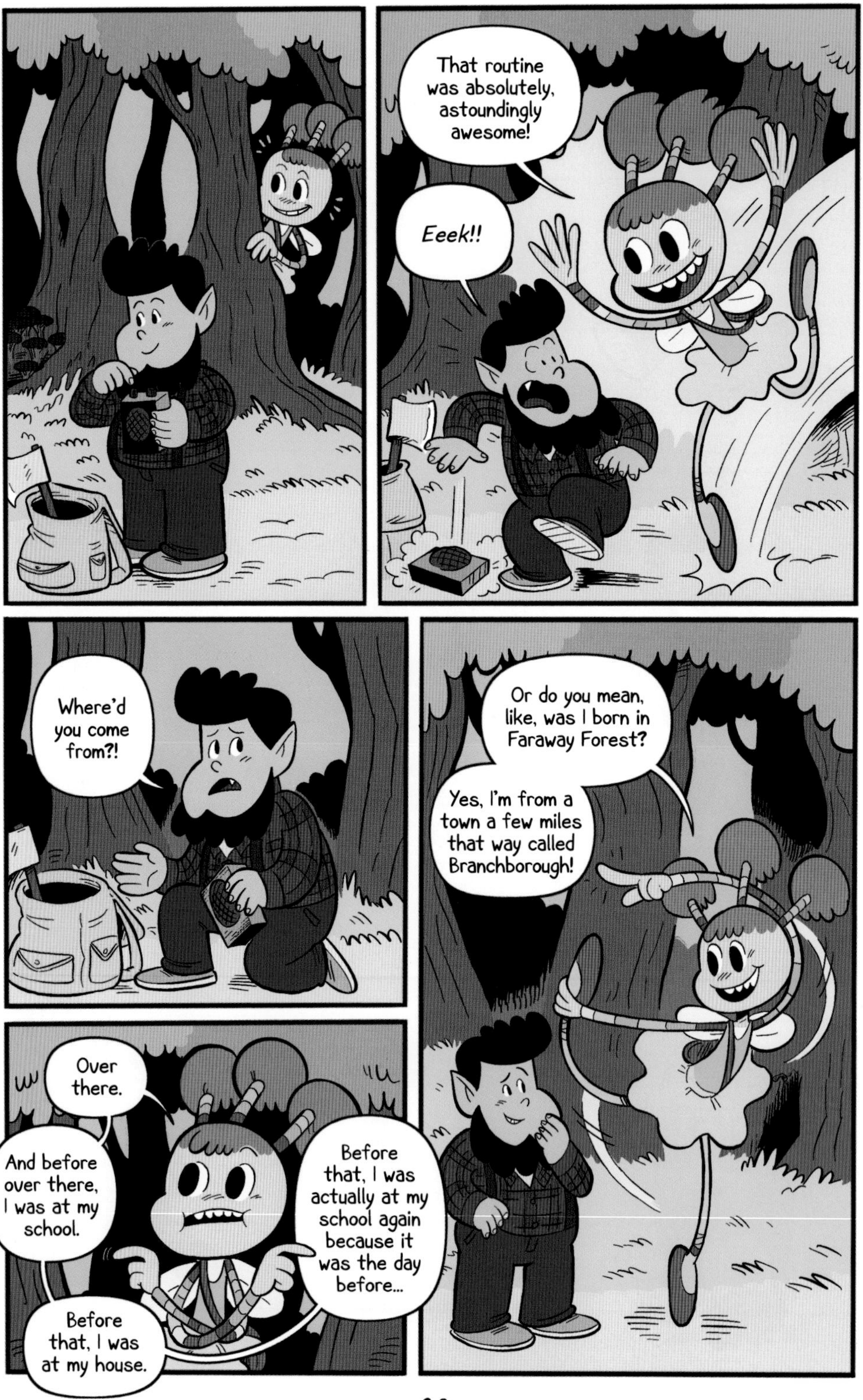
That routine was absolutely, astoundingly awesome!
Eeek!!
Where'd you come from?!
Or do you mean, like, was I born in Faraway Forest?
Yes, I'm from a town a few miles that way called Branchborough!
Over there.
And before over there, I was at my school.
Before that, I was at my house.
Before that, I was actually at my school again because it was the day before...

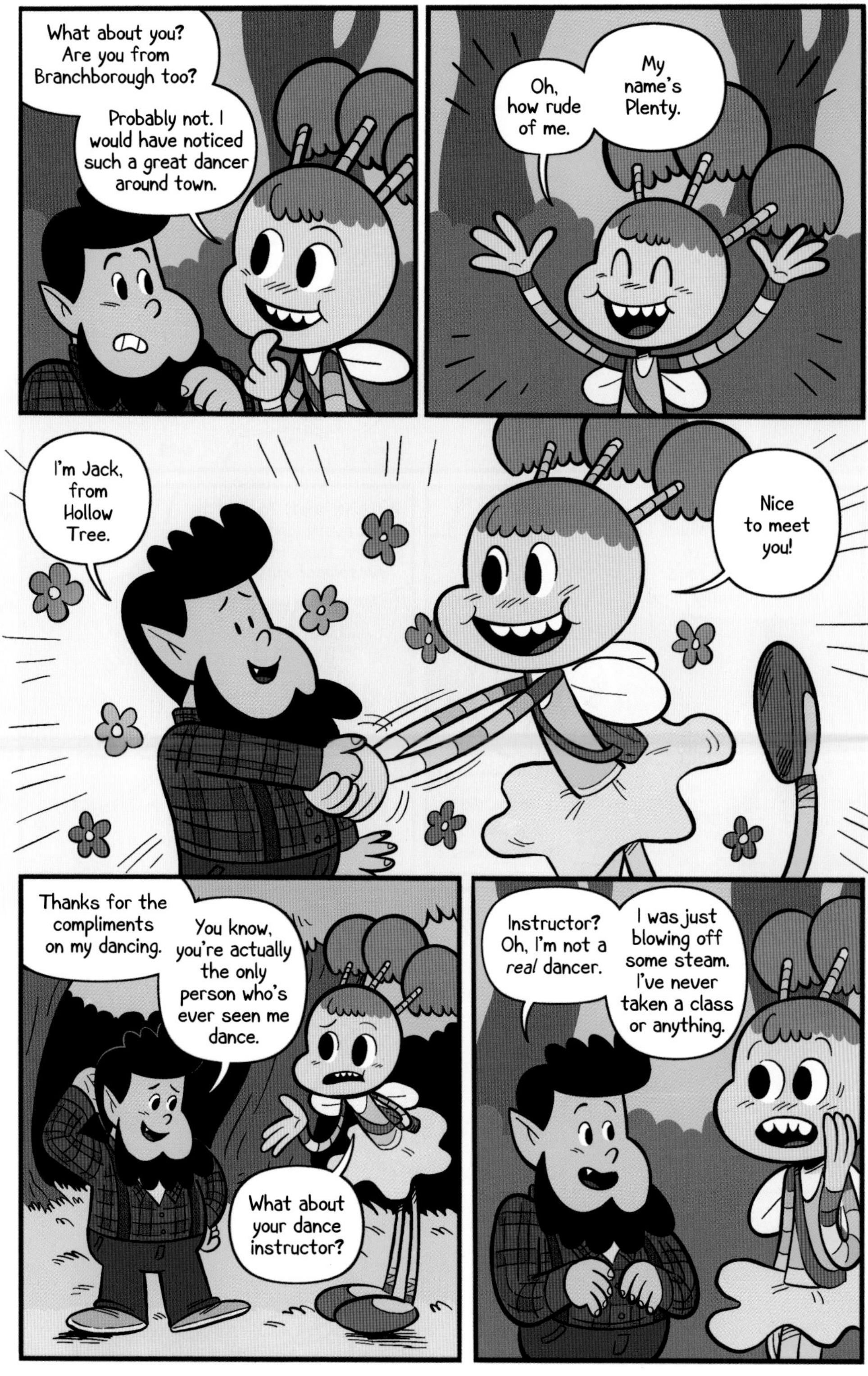
What about you? Are you from Branchborough too?
Probably not. I would have noticed such a great dancer around town.
Oh, how rude of me.
My name's Plenty.
I'm Jack, from Hollow Tree.
Nice to meet you!
Thanks for the compliments on my dancing.
You know, you're actually the only person who's ever seen me dance.
What about your dance instructor?
Instructor? Oh, I'm not a *real* dancer.
I was just blowing off some steam. I've never taken a class or anything.

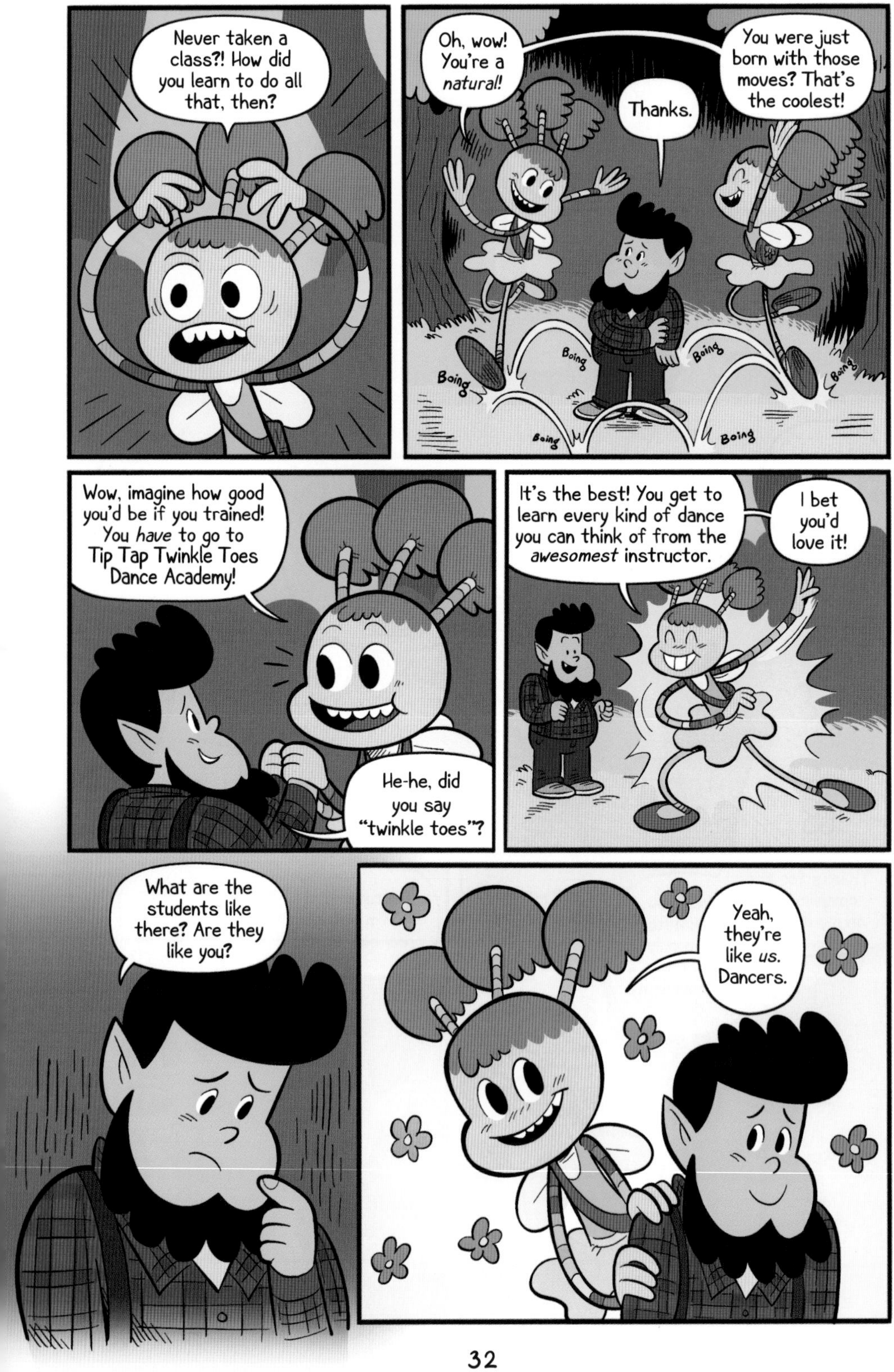
Never taken a class?! How did you learn to do all that, then?
Oh, wow! You're a *natural*!
You were just born with those moves? That's the coolest!
Thanks.
Boing
Boing
Boing
Boing
Boing
Boing
Wow, imagine how good you'd be if you trained! You *have* to go to Tip Tap Twinkle Toes Dance Academy!
He-he, did you say "twinkle toes"?
It's the best! You get to learn every kind of dance you can think of from the *awesomest* instructor.
I bet you'd love it!
What are the students like there? Are they like you?
Yeah, they're like *us*. Dancers.

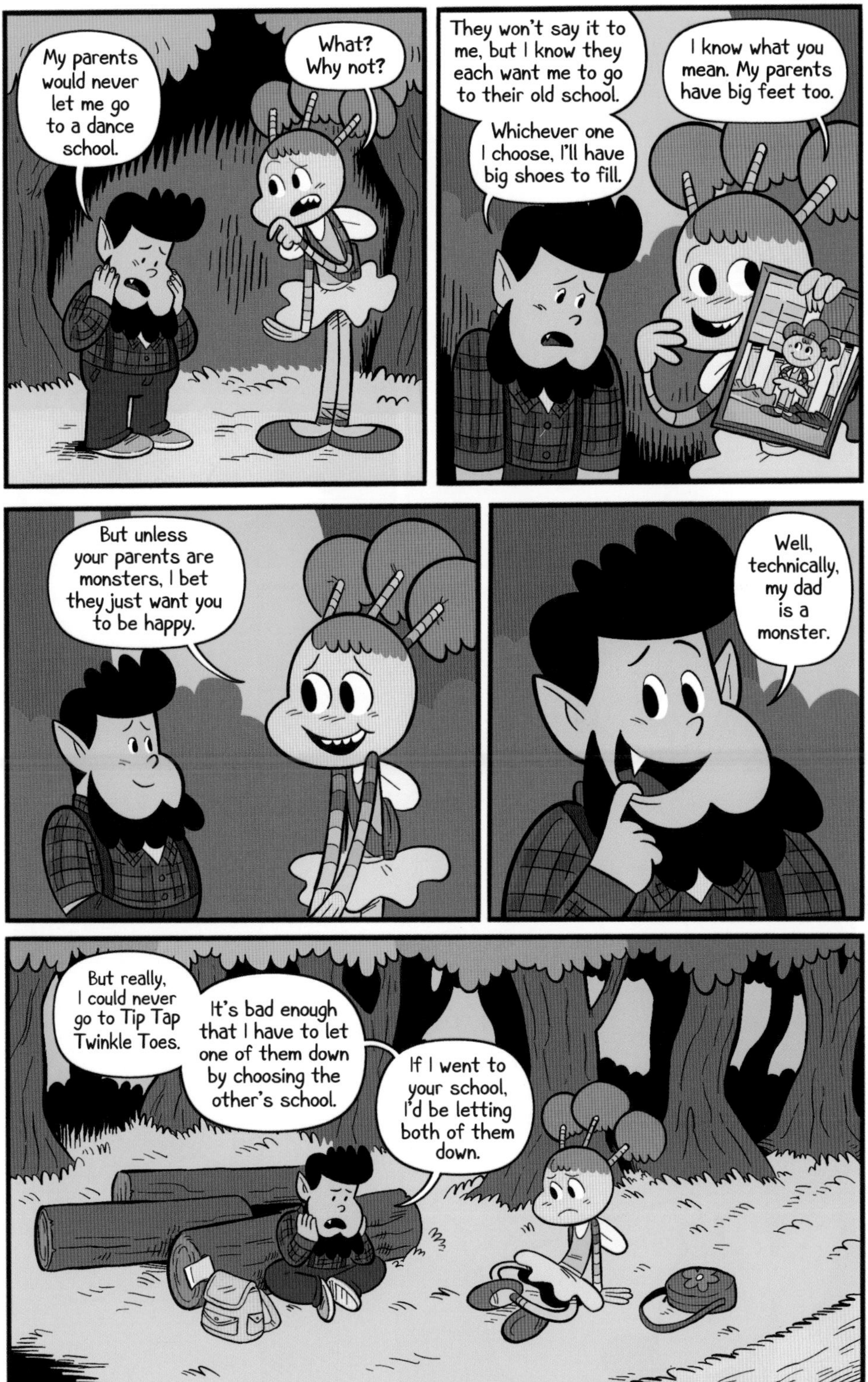

My parents would never let me go to a dance school.
What? Why not?
They won't say it to me, but I know they each want me to go to their old school.
Whichever one I choose, I'll have big shoes to fill.
I know what you mean. My parents have big feet too.
But unless your parents are monsters, I bet they just want you to be happy.
Well, technically, my dad is a monster.
But really, I could never go to Tip Tap Twinkle Toes.
It's bad enough that I have to let one of them down by choosing the other's school.
If I went to your school, I'd be letting both of them down.

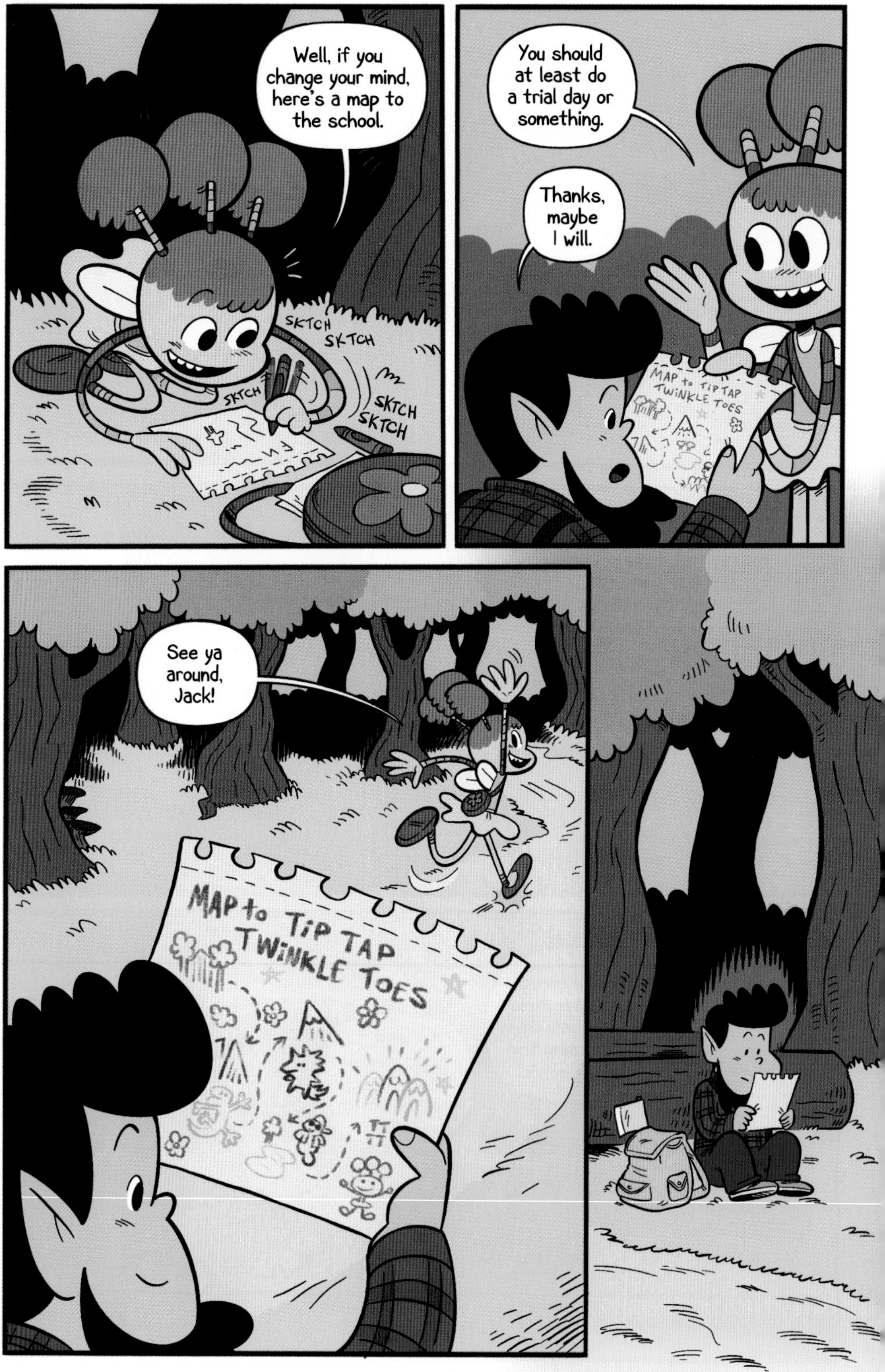
Well, if you change your mind, here's a map to the school.
SKTCH
SKTCH
SKTCH
SKTCH
SKTCH
You should at least do a trial day or something.
Thanks, maybe I will.
MAP to TIP TAP TWINKLE TOES
See ya around, Jack!
MAP to TIP TAP TWINKLE TOES

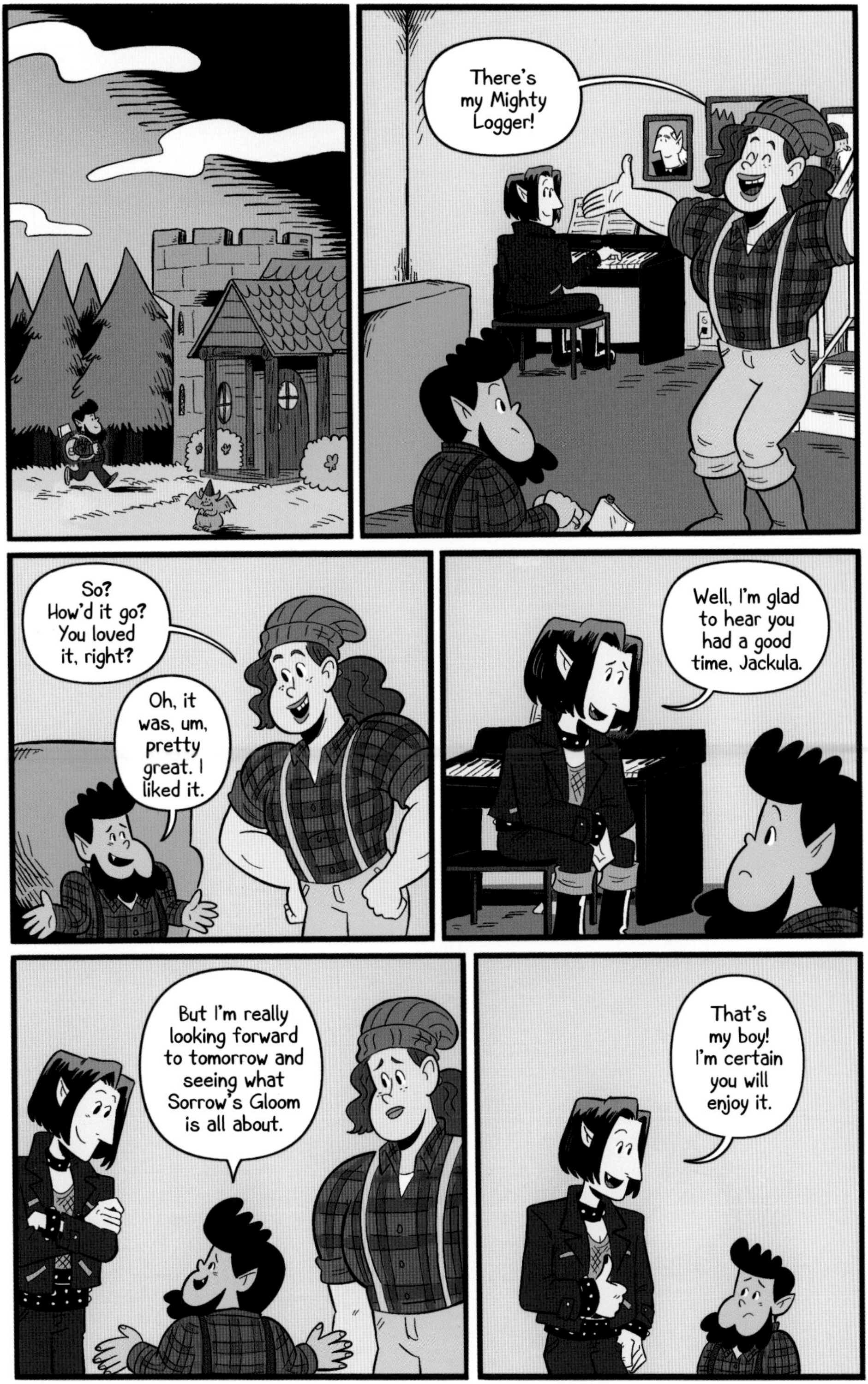
There's my Mighty Logger!
So? How'd it go? You loved it, right?
Oh, it was, um, pretty great. I liked it.
Well, I'm glad to hear you had a good time, Jackula.
But I'm really looking forward to tomorrow and seeing what Sorrow's Gloom is all about.
That's my boy! I'm certain you will enjoy it.

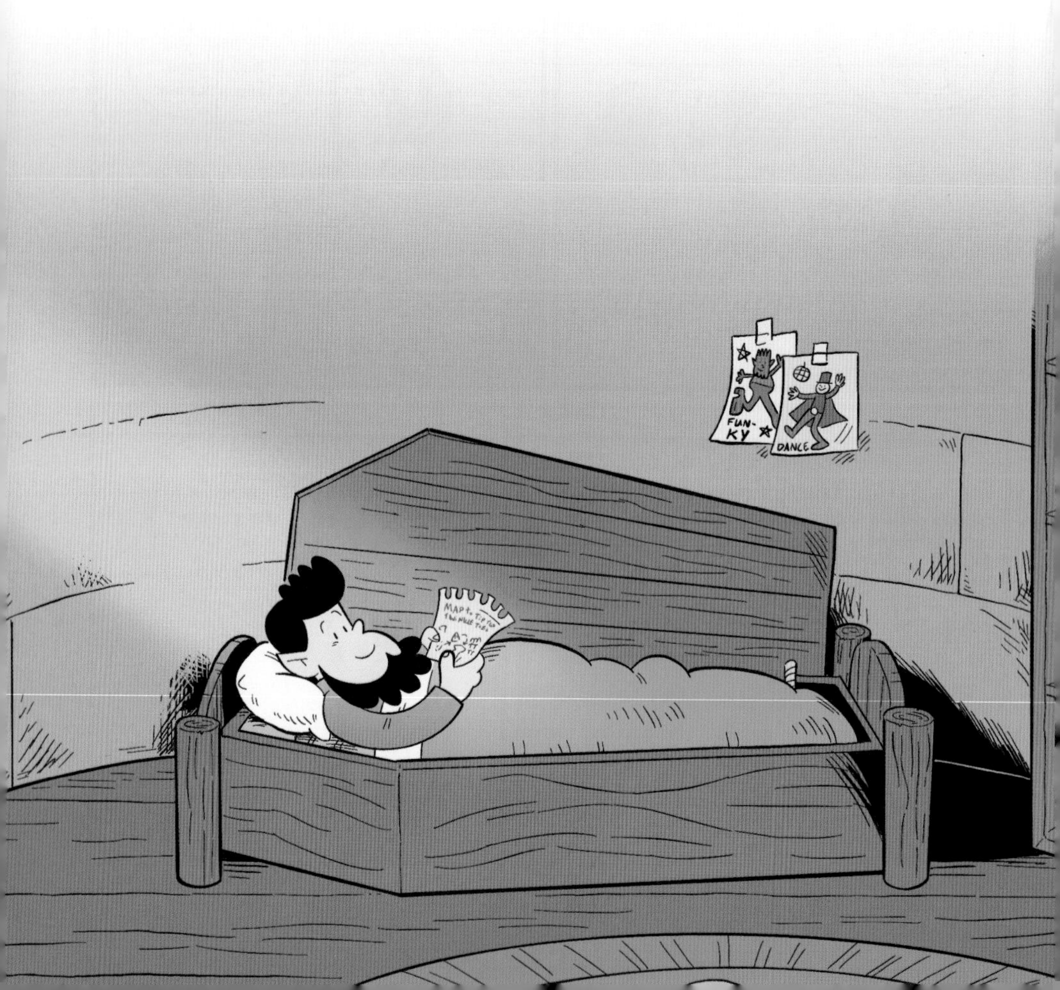
FUN-
KY
DANCE

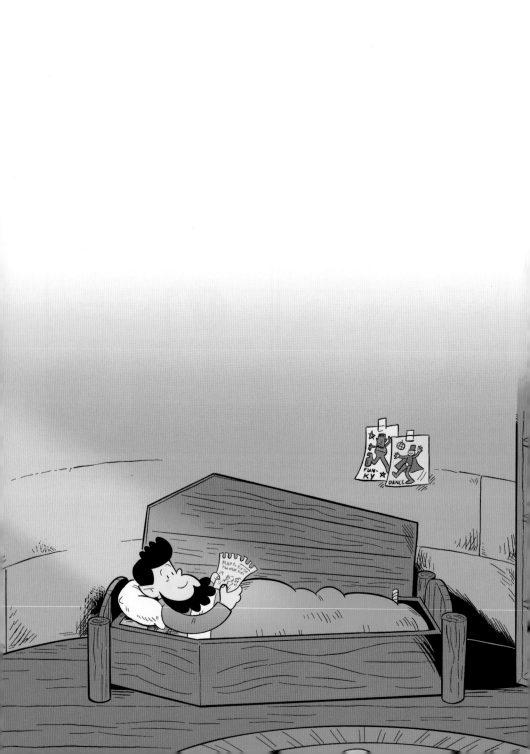

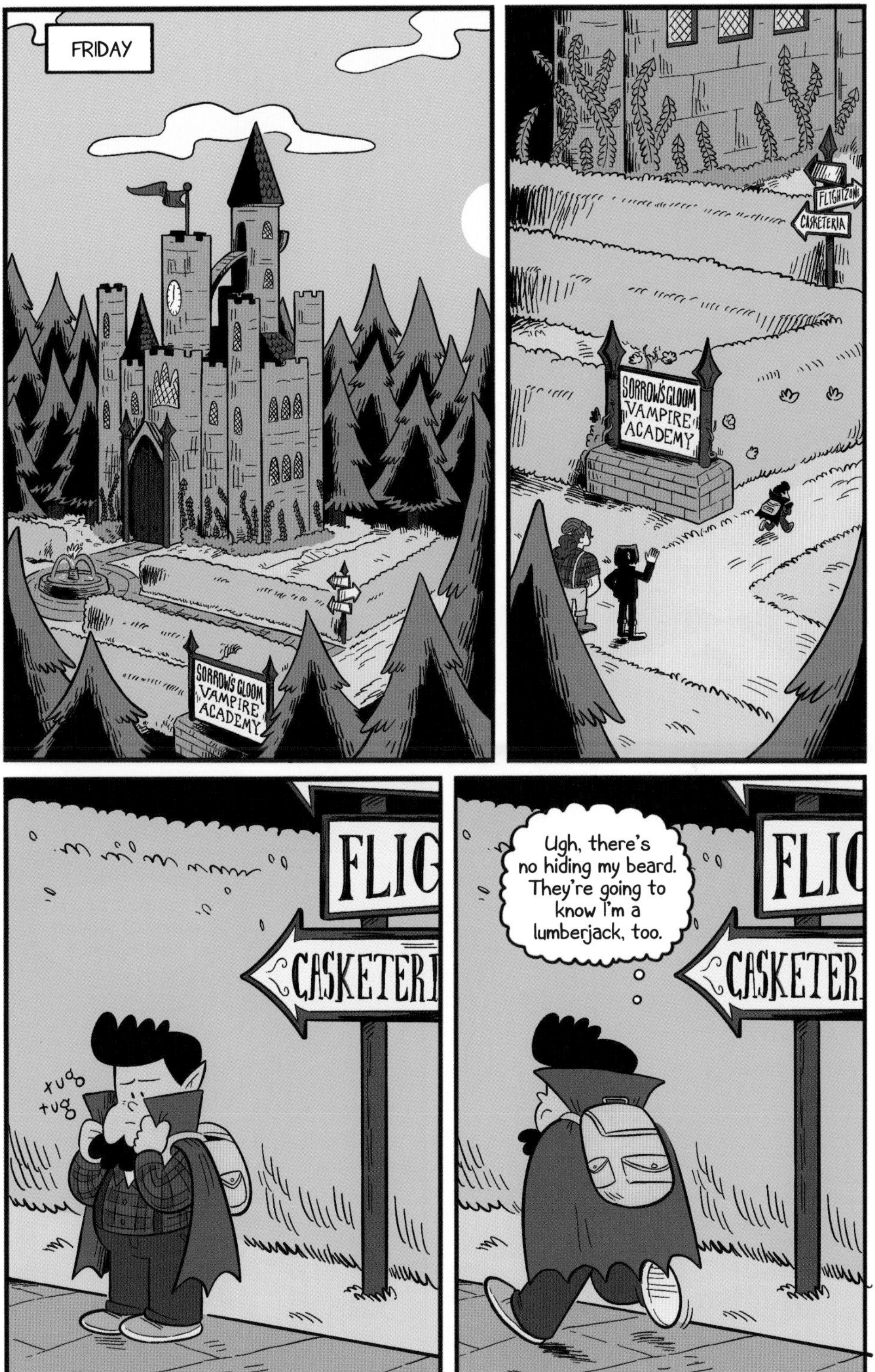
FRIDAY
SORROW'S GLOOM VAMPIRE ACADEMY
FLIGHTZONE
CASKETERIA
SORROW'S GLOOM VAMPIRE ACADEMY
FLIG
CASKETERI
tug tug
Ugh, there's no hiding my beard. They're going to know I'm a lumberjack, too.

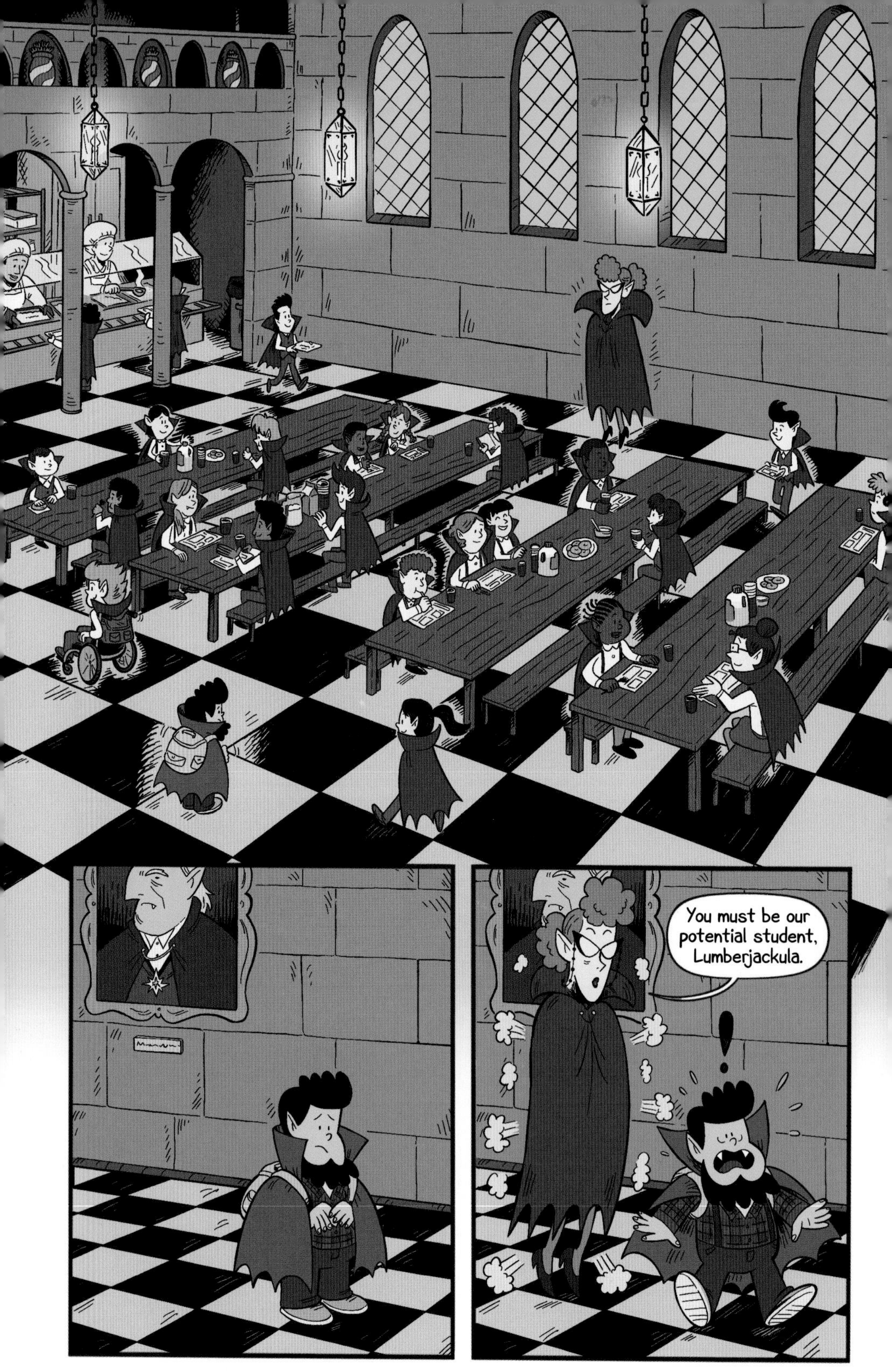
You must be our potential student, Lumberjackula.
!

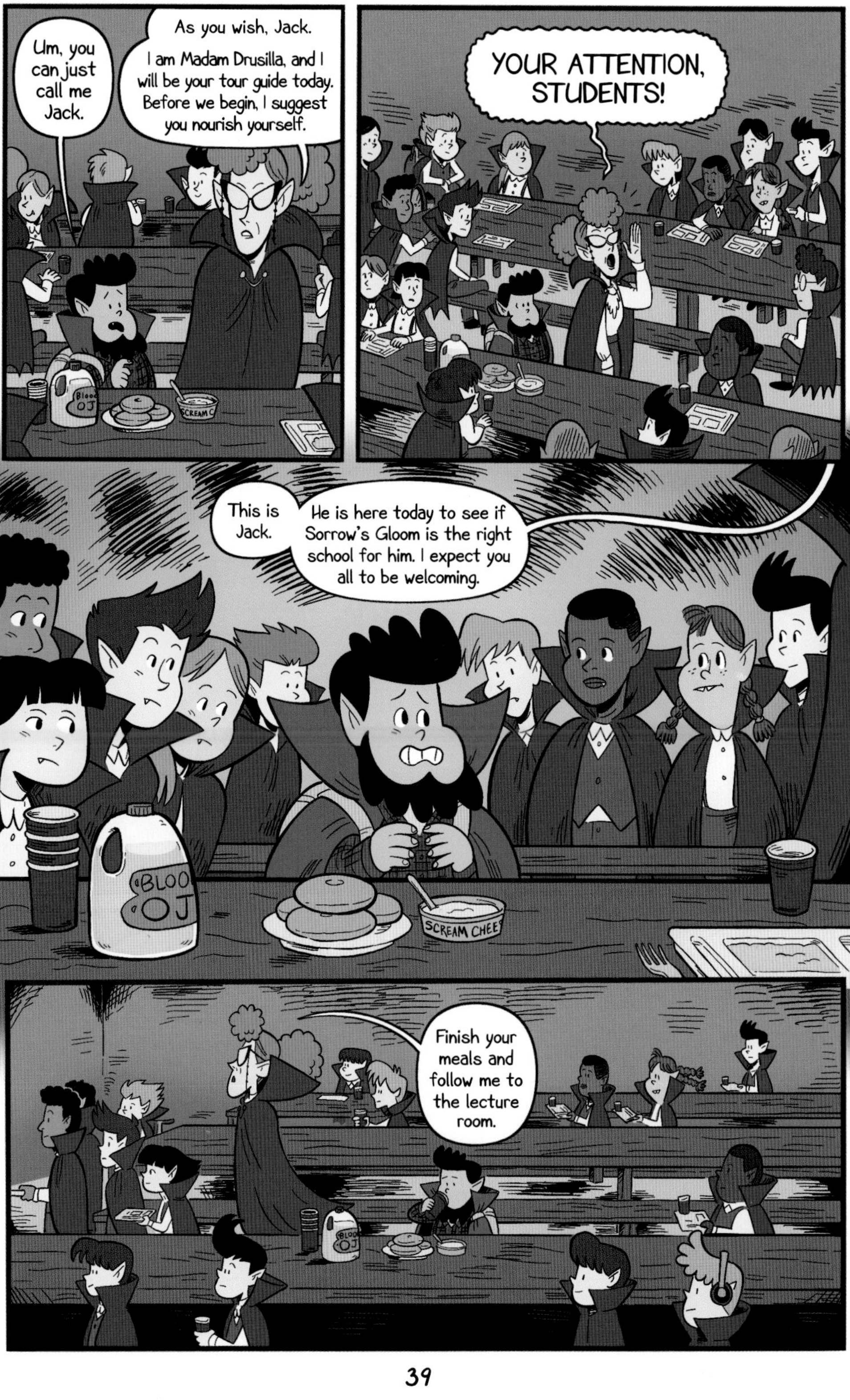
Um, you can just call me Jack.
As you wish, Jack.
I am Madam Drusilla, and I will be your tour guide today. Before we begin, I suggest you nourish yourself.
BLOOD OJ
SCREAM C
YOUR ATTENTION, STUDENTS!
This is Jack.
He is here today to see if Sorrow's Gloom is the right school for him. I expect you all to be welcoming.
BLOO OJ
SCREAM CHEE
Finish your meals and follow me to the lecture room.

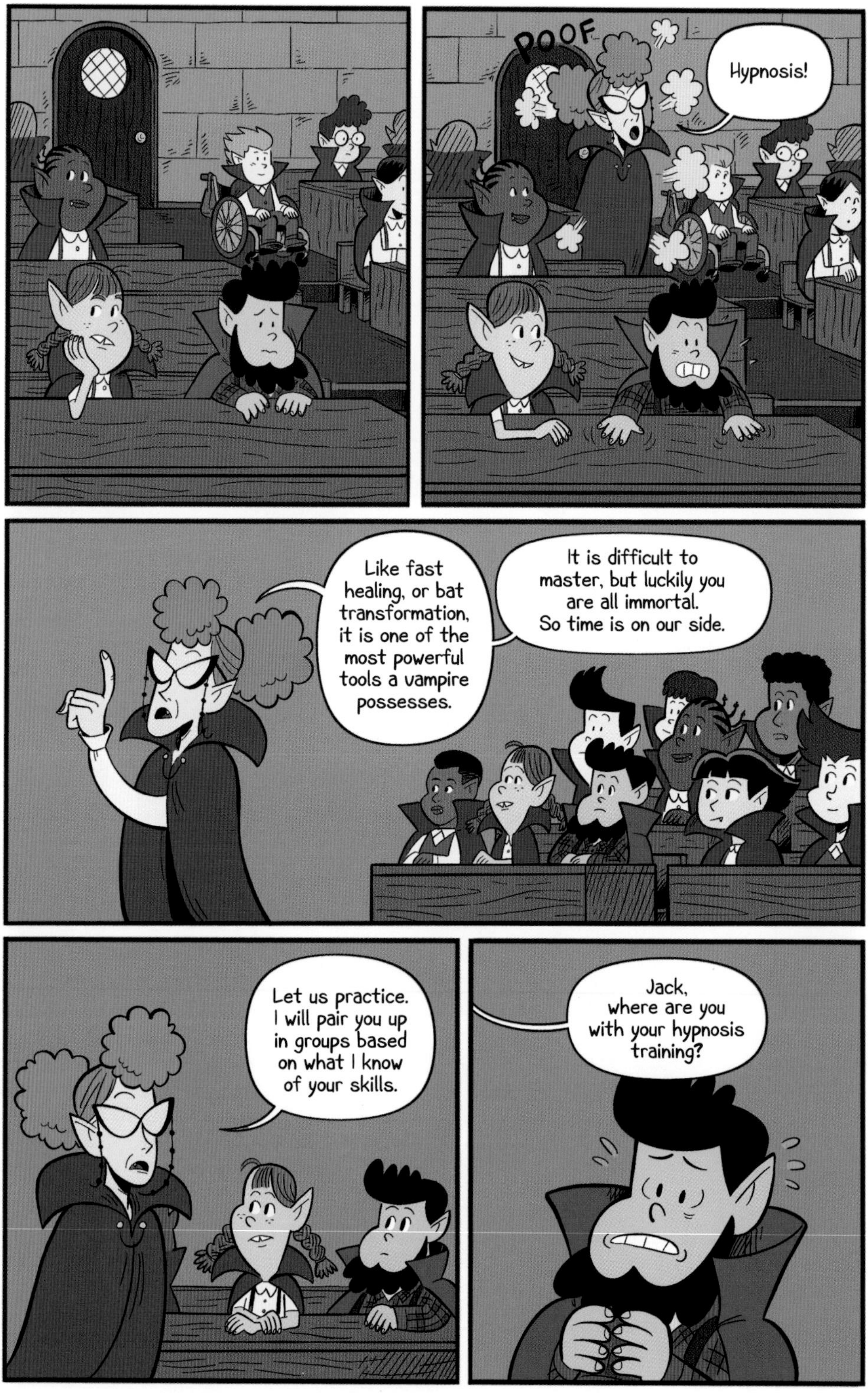
POOF
Hypnosis!
Like fast healing, or bat transformation, it is one of the most powerful tools a vampire possesses.
It is difficult to master, but luckily you are all immortal. So time is on our side.
Let us practice. I will pair you up in groups based on what I know of your skills.
Jack, where are you with your hypnosis training?

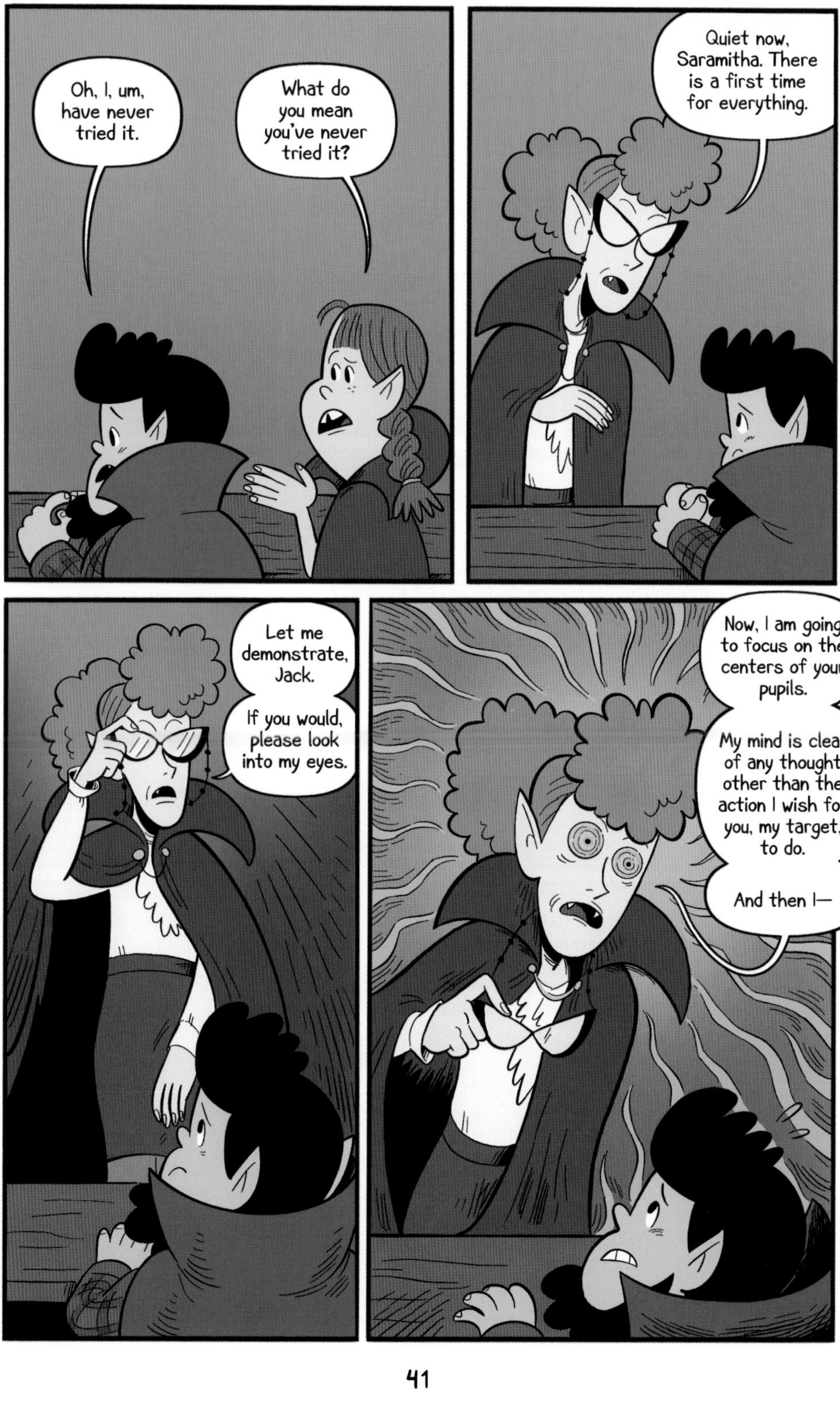
Oh, I, um, have never tried it.
What do you mean you've never tried it?
Quiet now, Saramitha. There is a first time for everything.
Let me demonstrate, Jack.
If you would, please look into my eyes.
Now, I am going to focus on the centers of your pupils.
My mind is clear of any thought other than the action I wish for you, my target, to do.
And then I—

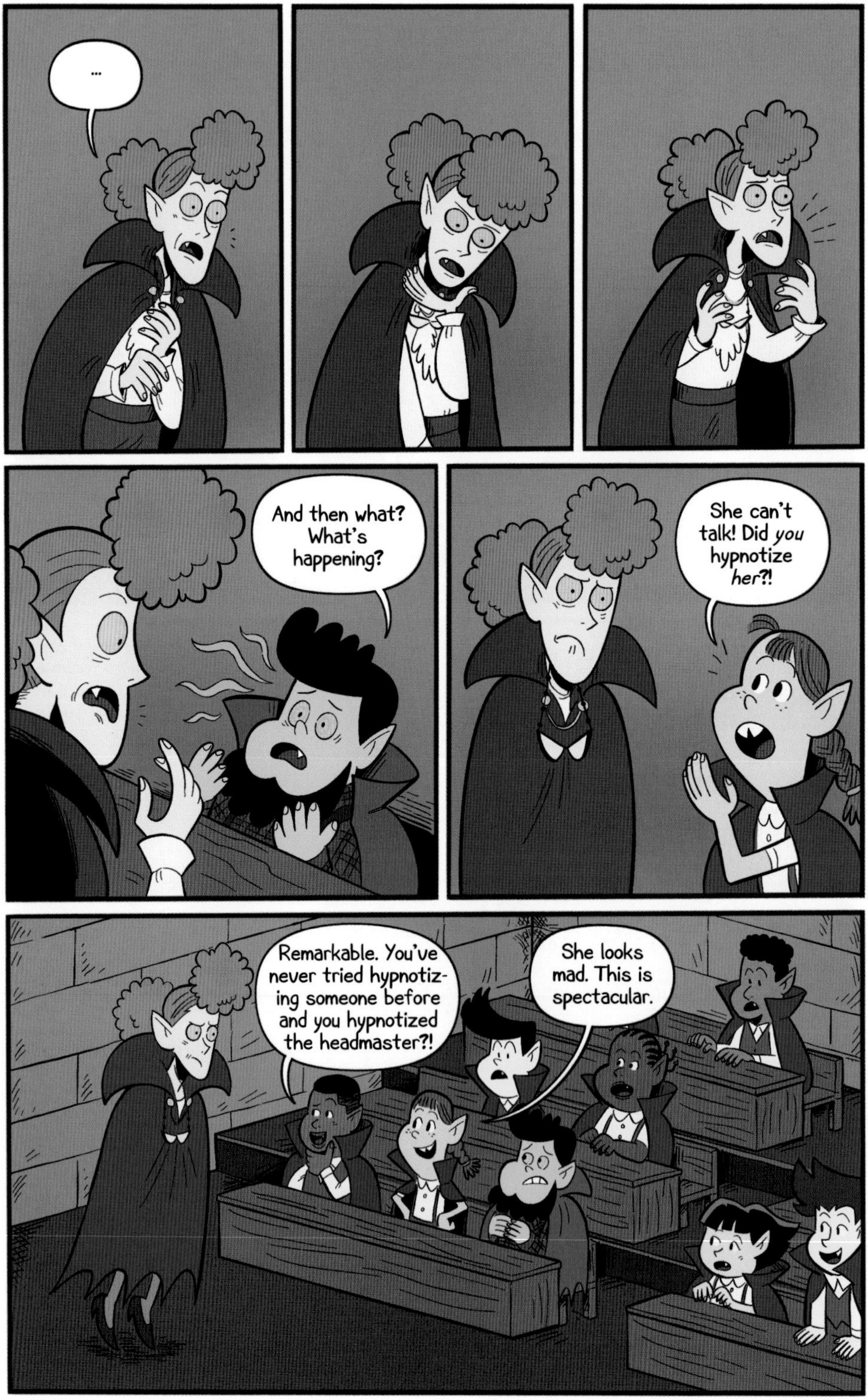
...
And then what? What's happening?
She can't talk! Did *you* hypnotize *her*?!
Remarkable. You've never tried hypnotizing someone before and you hypnotized the headmaster?!
She looks mad. This is spectacular.

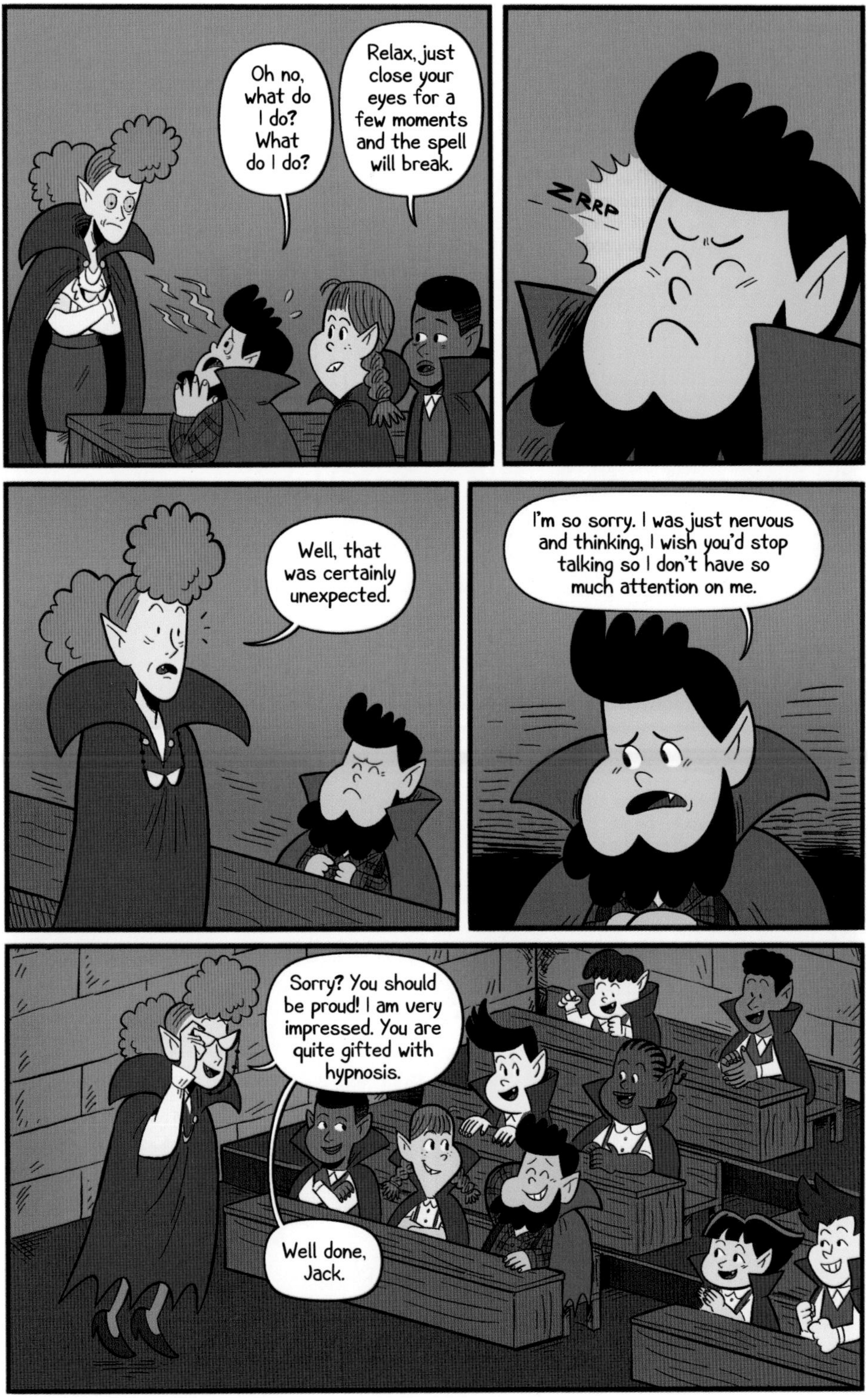
Oh no, what do I do? What do I do?
Relax, just close your eyes for a few moments and the spell will break.
ZRRP
Well, that was certainly unexpected.
I'm so sorry. I was just nervous and thinking, I wish you'd stop talking so I don't have so much attention on me.
Sorry? You should be proud! I am very impressed. You are quite gifted with hypnosis.
Well done, Jack.

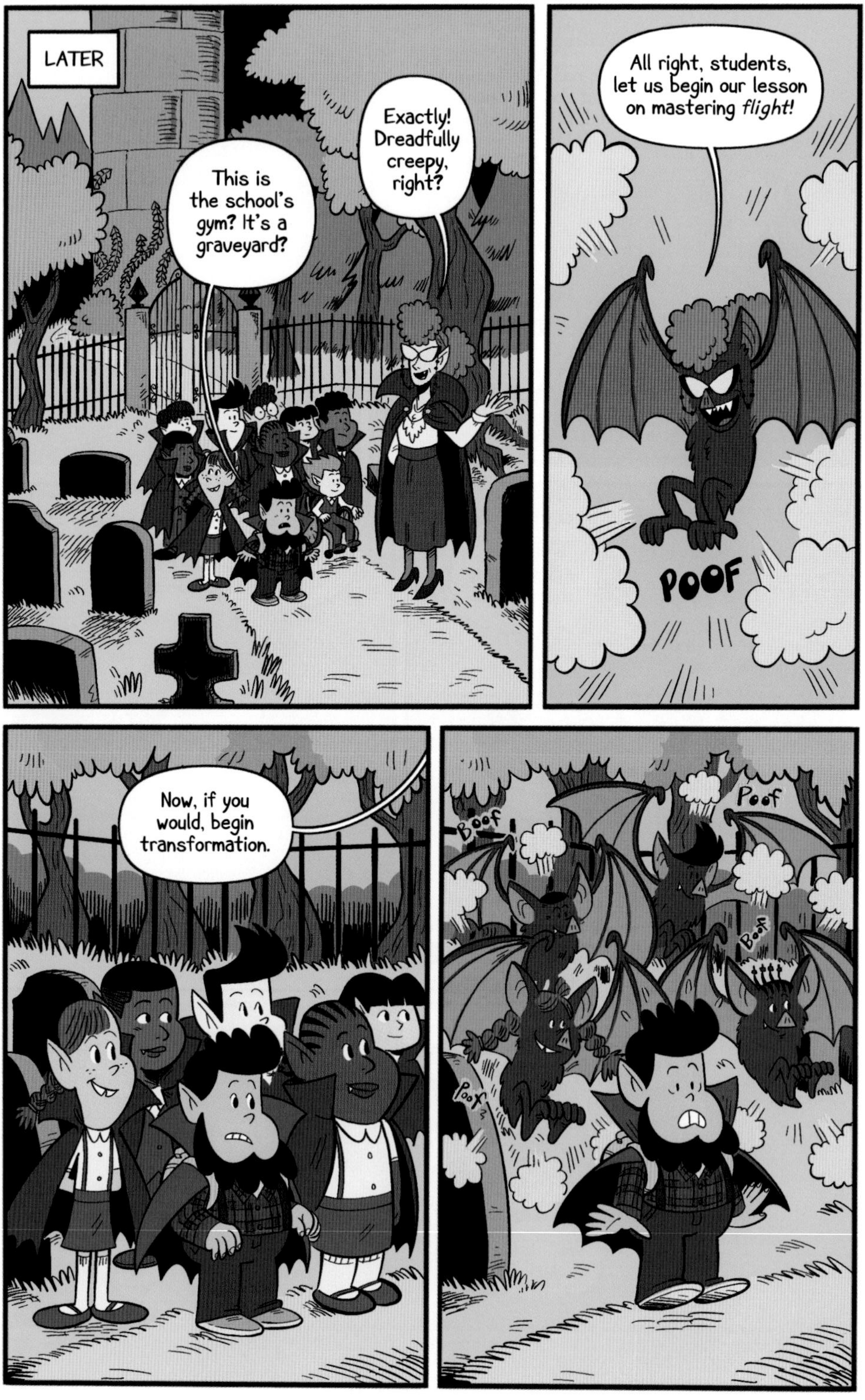
LATER
This is the school's gym? It's a graveyard?
Exactly! Dreadfully creepy, right?
All right, students, let us begin our lesson on mastering *flight*!
POOF
Now, if you would, begin transformation.
Boof
Poof
Boof
Poof

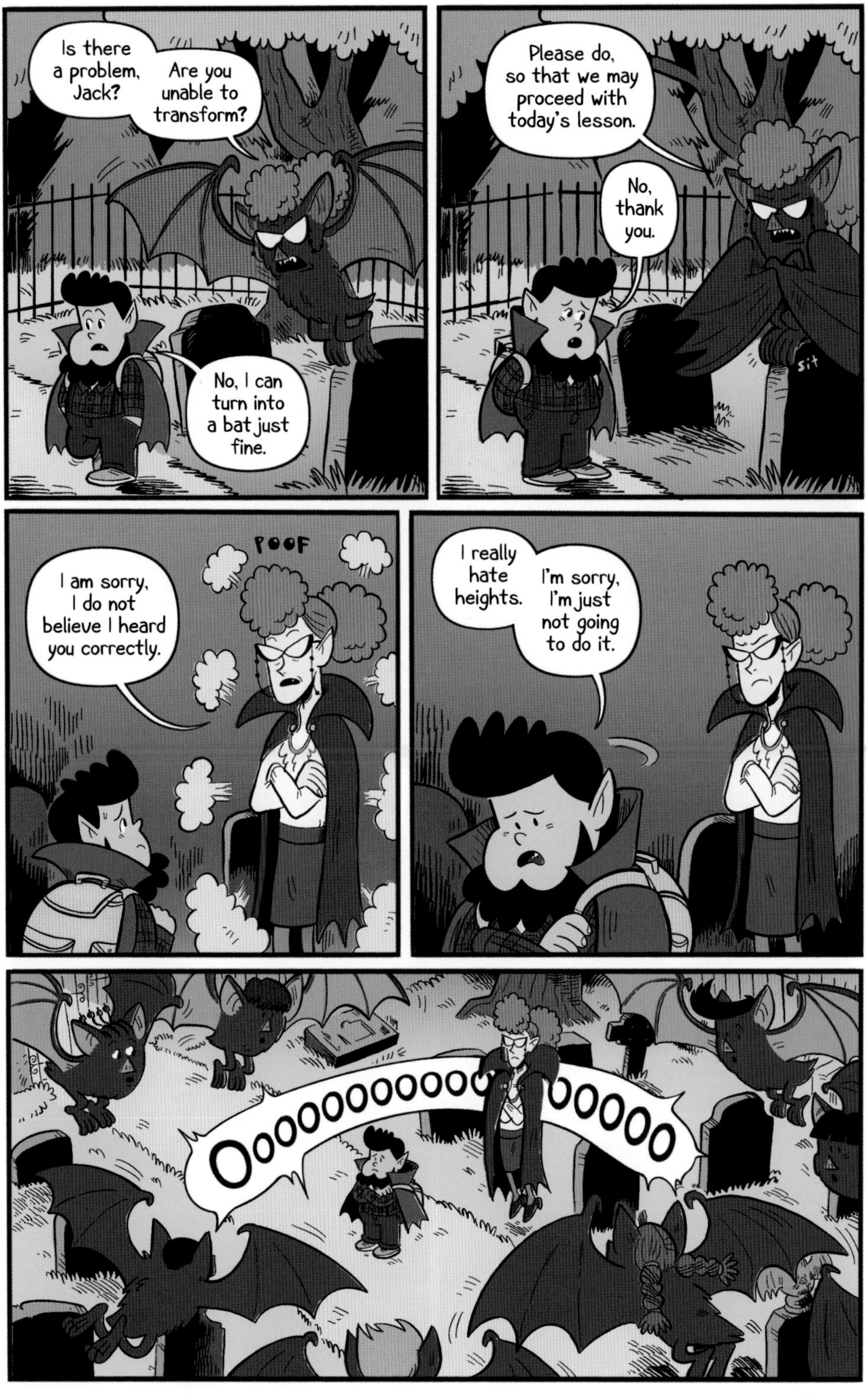
Is there a problem, Jack?
Are you unable to transform?
No, I can turn into a bat just fine.
Please do, so that we may proceed with today's lesson.
No, thank you.
sit
POOF
I am sorry, I do not believe I heard you correctly.
I really hate heights.
I'm sorry, I'm just not going to do it.
Oooooooooooo ooooo

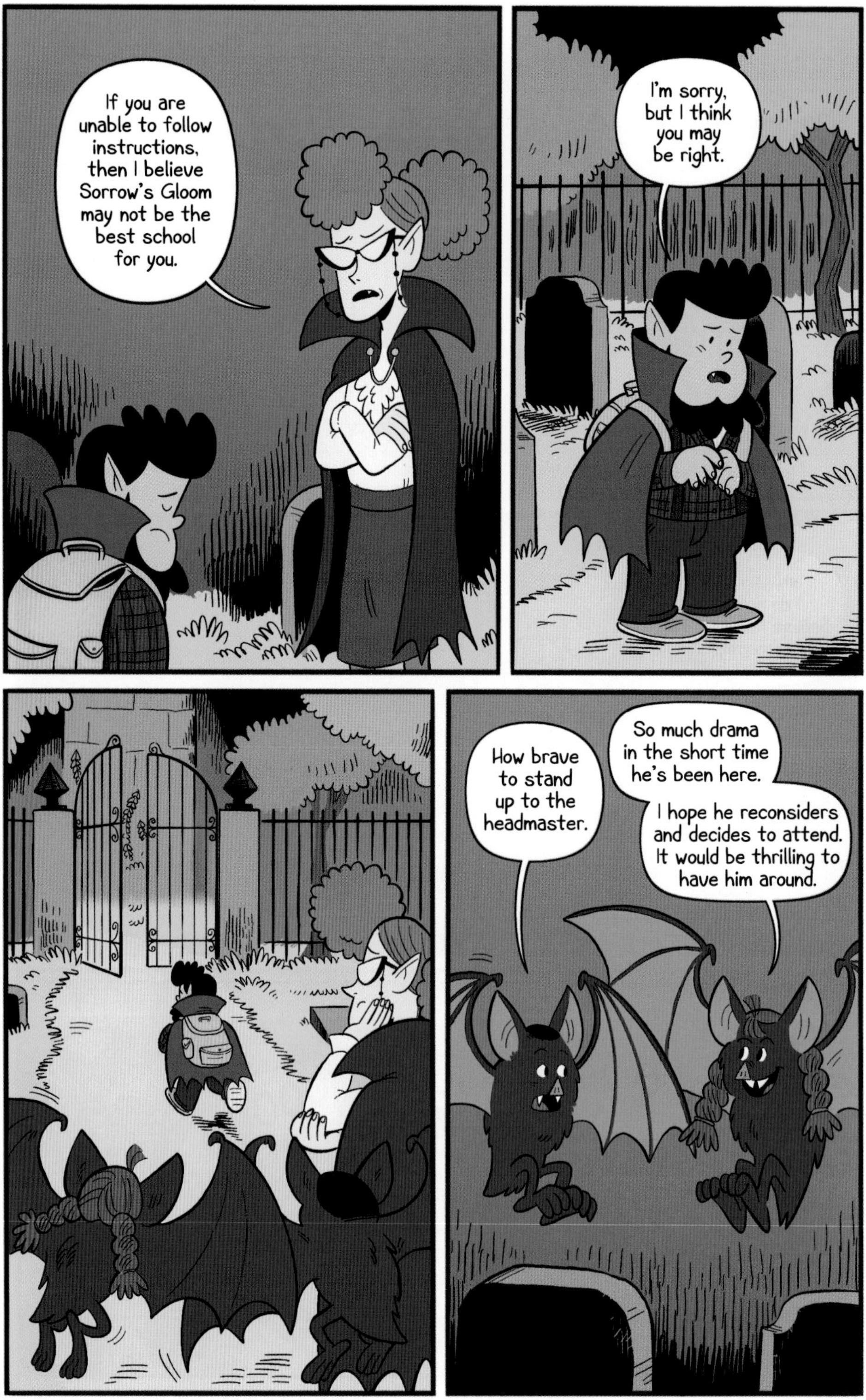

If you are unable to follow instructions, then I believe Sorrow's Gloom may not be the best school for you.
I'm sorry, but I think you may be right.
How brave to stand up to the headmaster.
So much drama in the short time he's been here.
I hope he reconsiders and decides to attend. It would be thrilling to have him around.

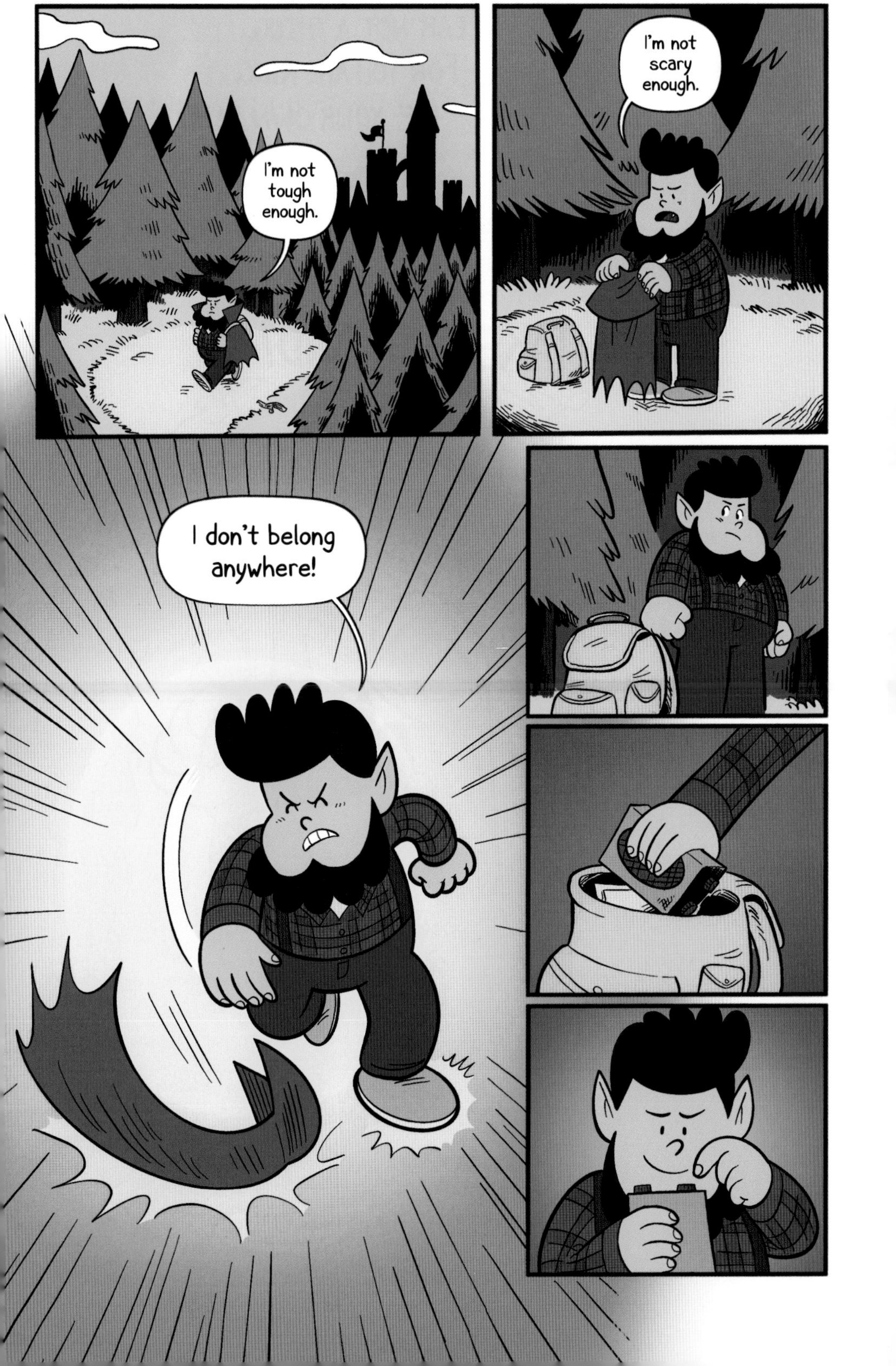
I'm not tough enough.
I'm not scary enough.
I don't belong anywhere!

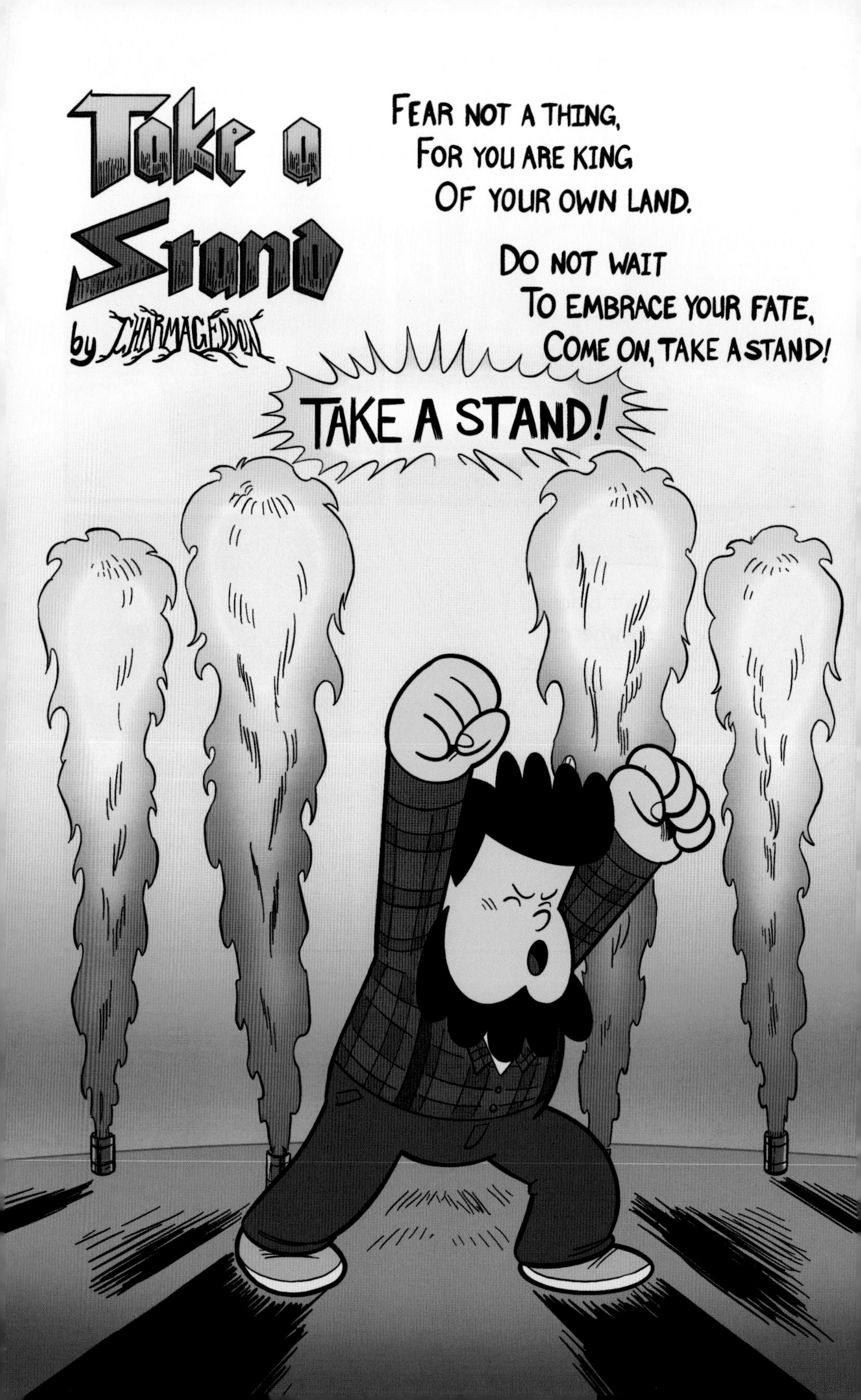
Take a Stand
by CHARMAGEDDON
FEAR NOT A THING,
FOR YOU ARE KING
OF YOUR OWN LAND.
DO NOT WAIT
TO EMBRACE YOUR FATE,
COME ON, TAKE A STAND!
TAKE A STAND!

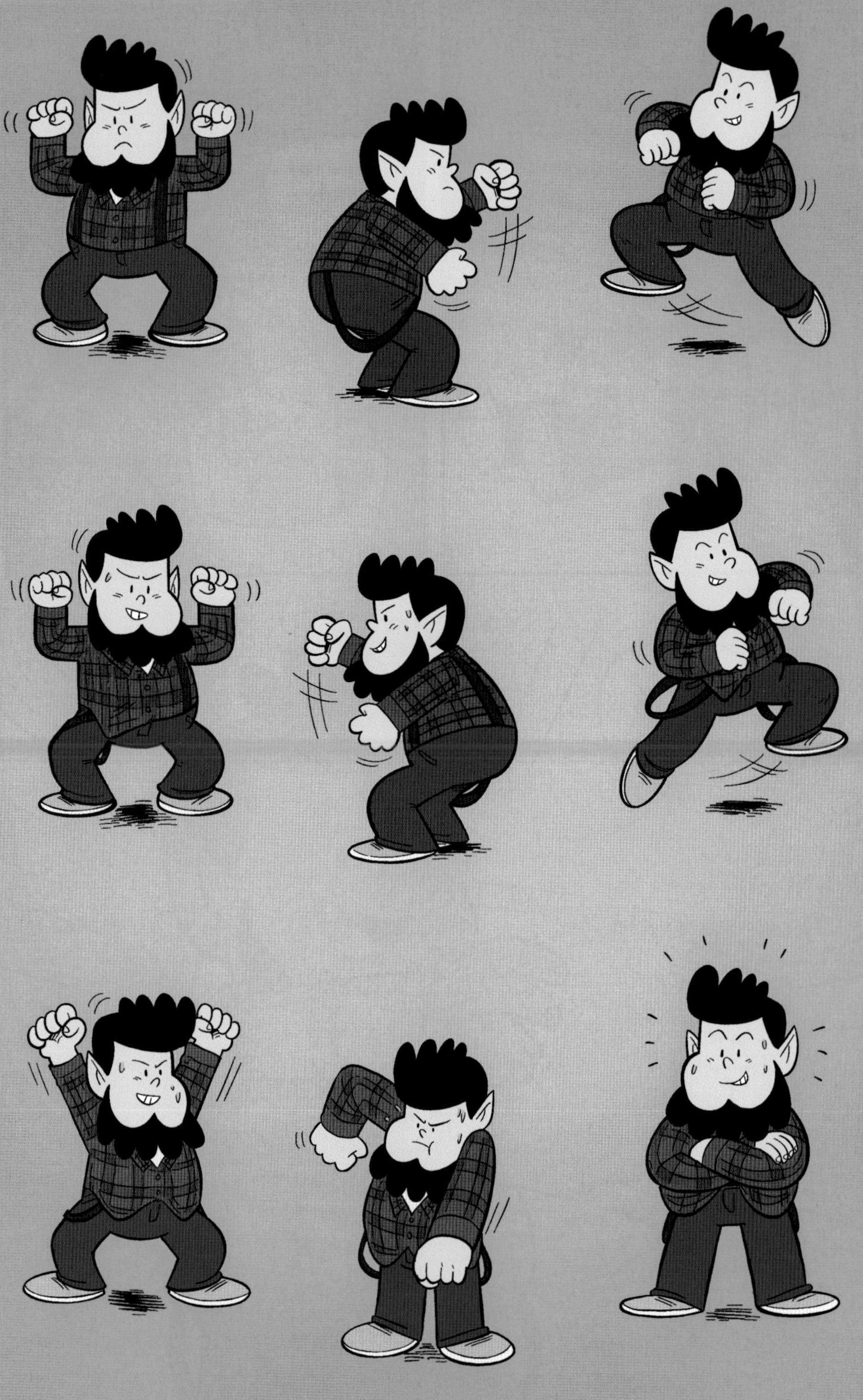

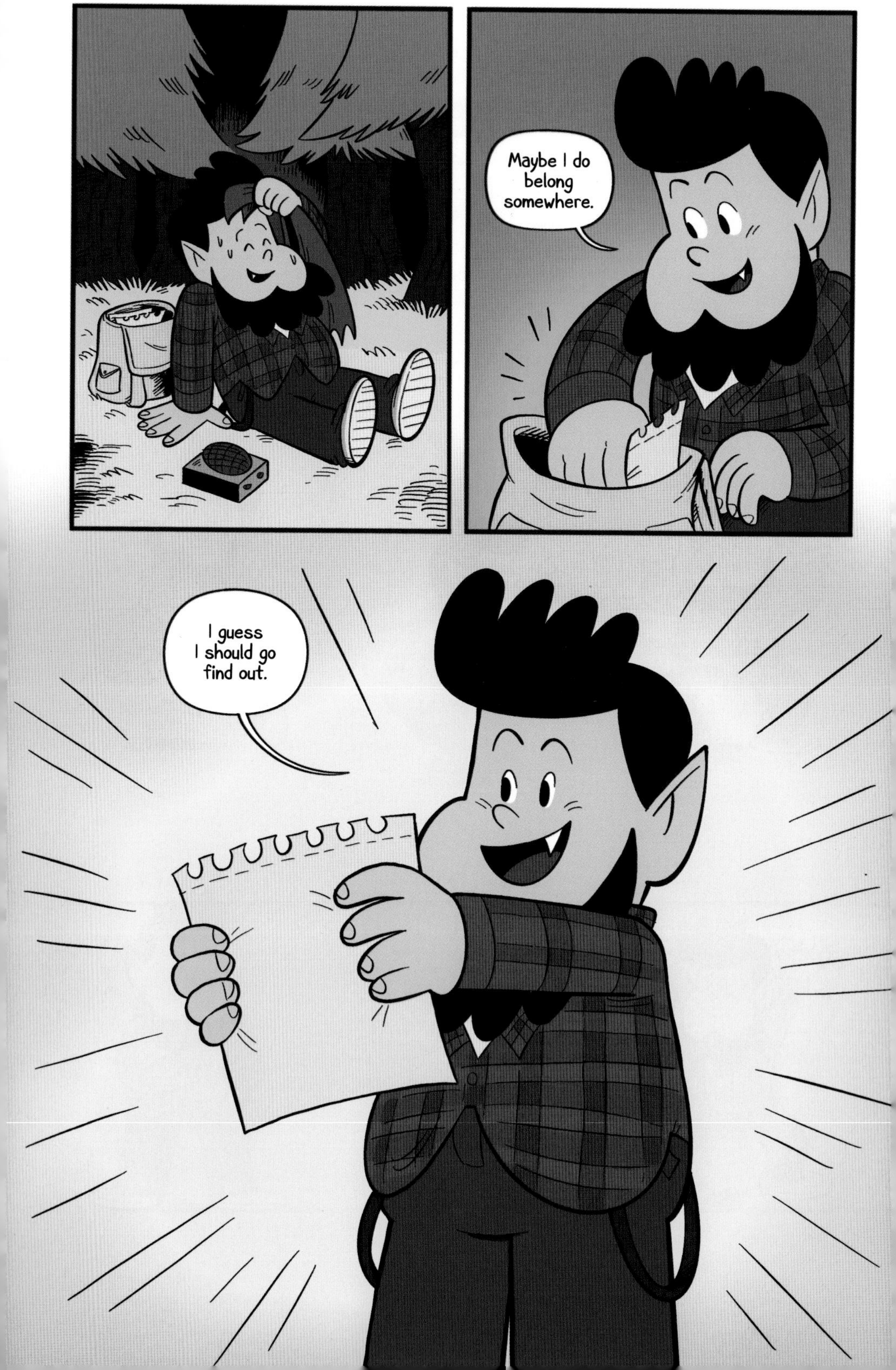
Maybe I do belong somewhere.
I guess I should go find out.

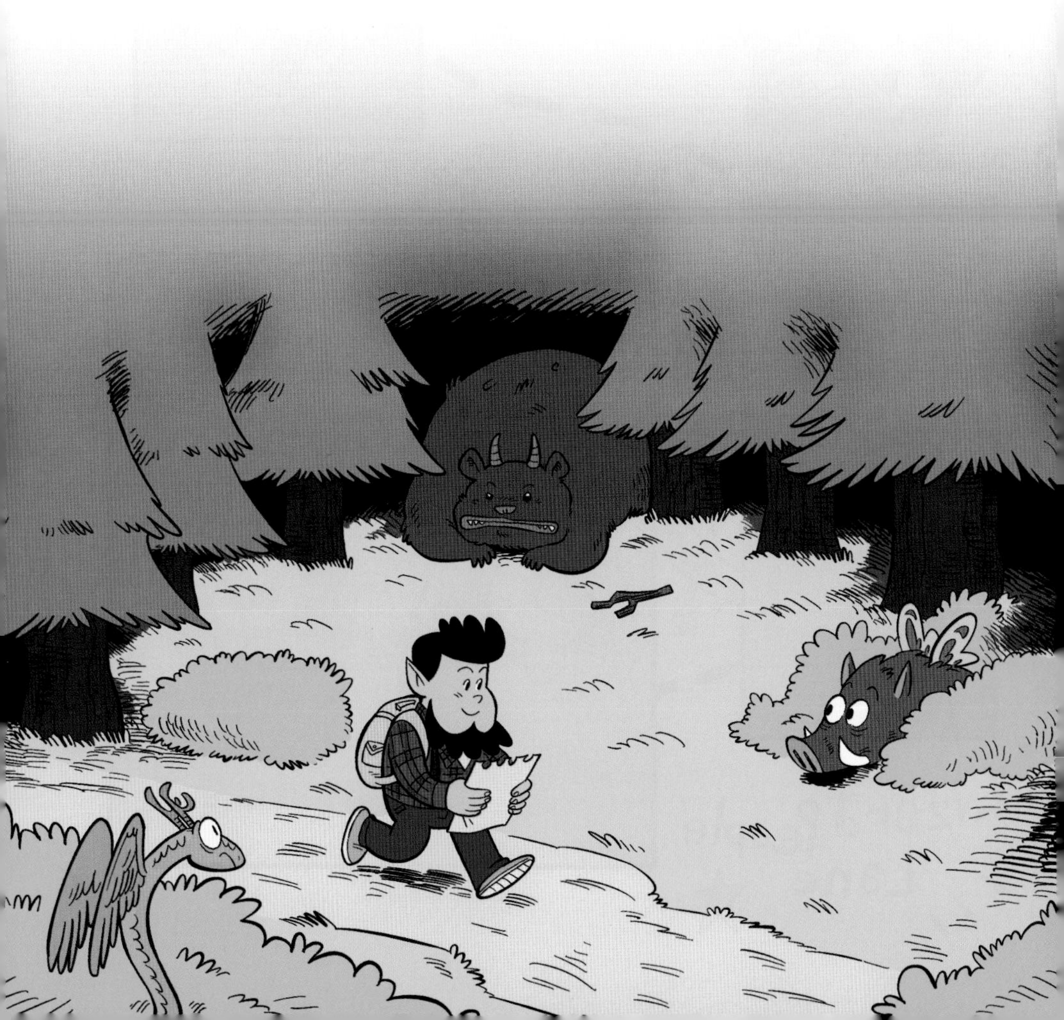

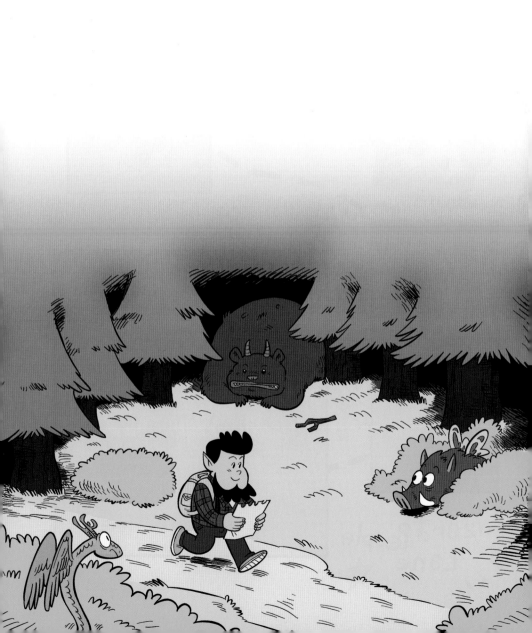

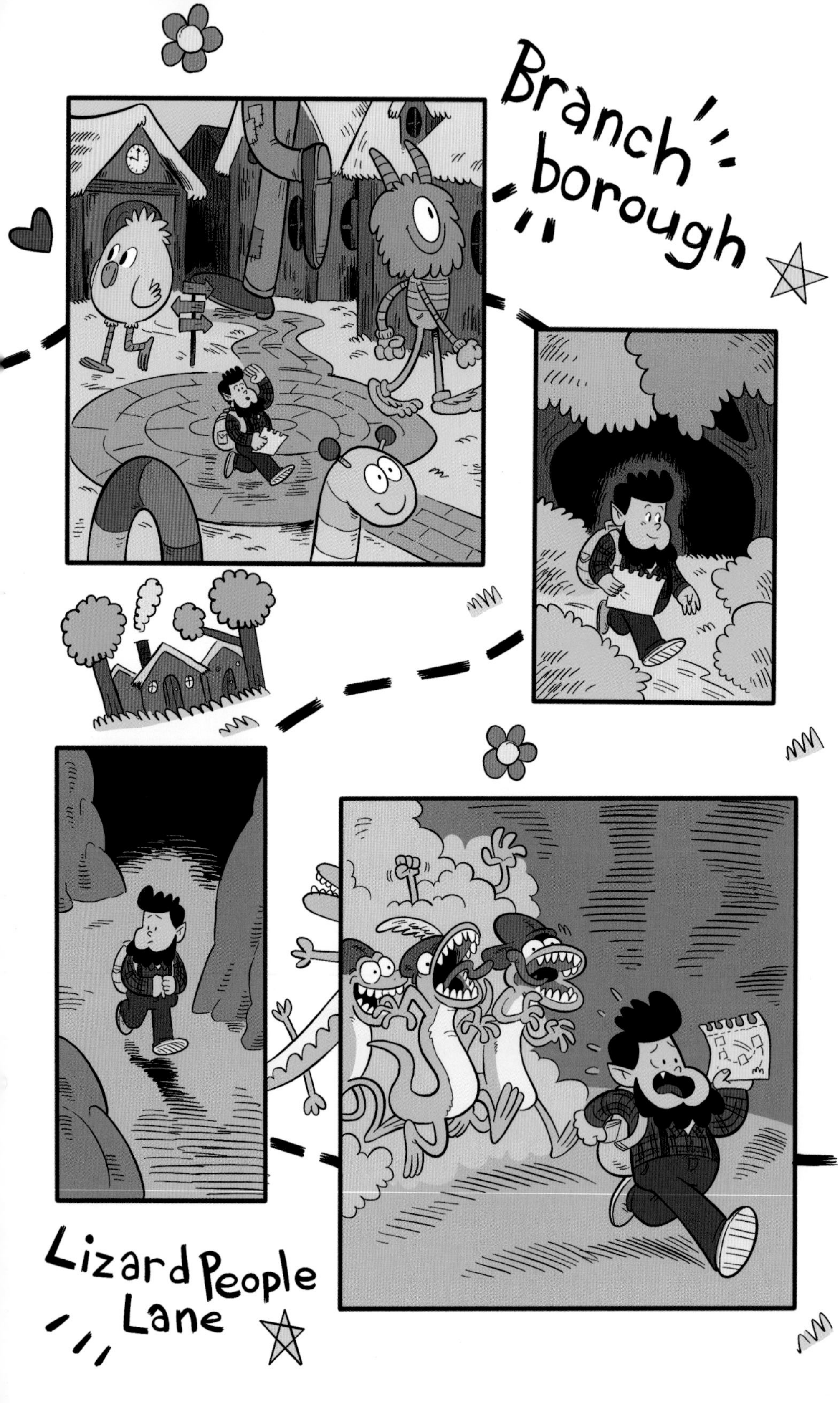
Branch borough
Lizard People Lane

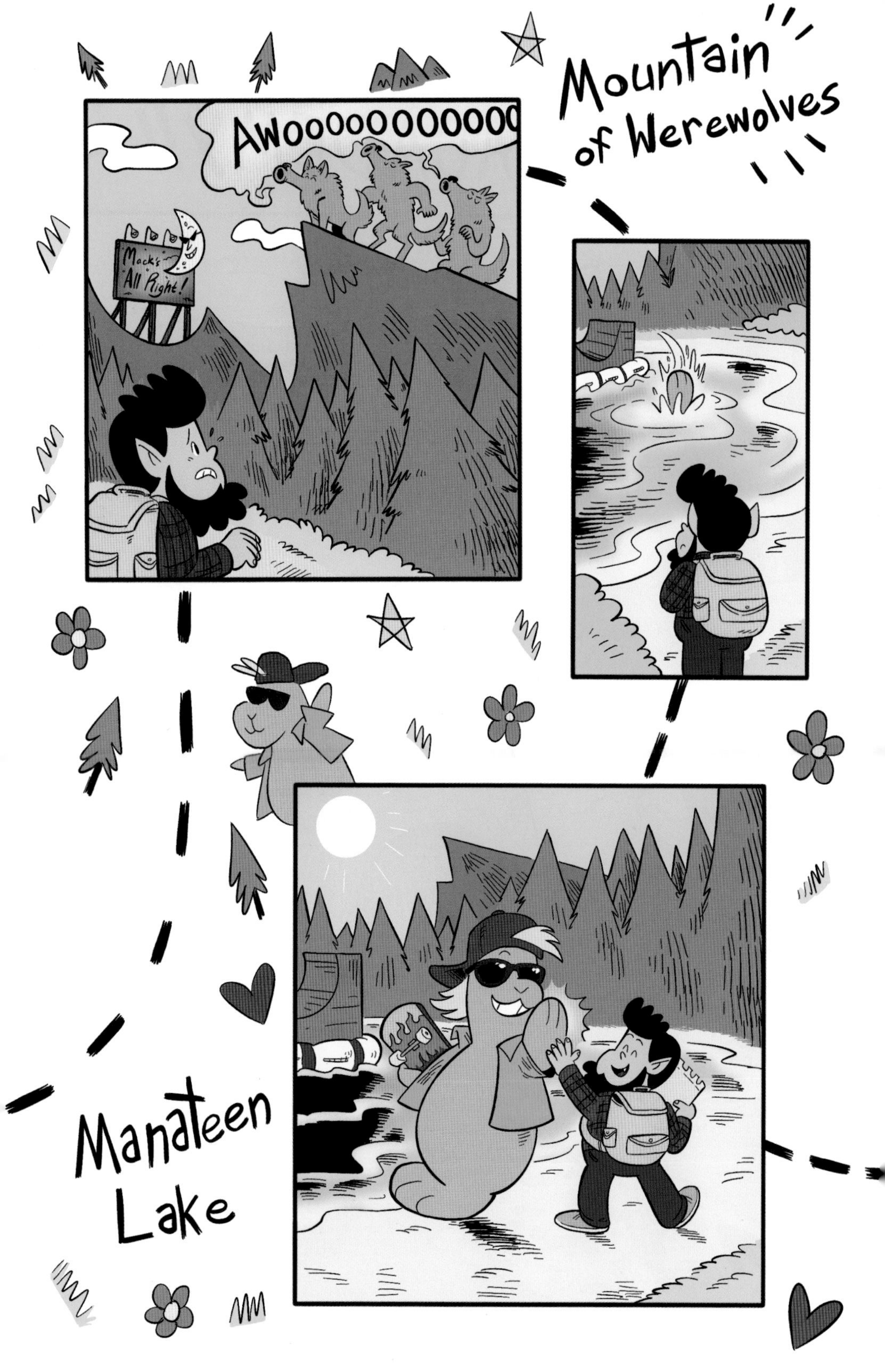
Mountain of Werewolves
Awoooooooooo
Mack's All Right!
Manateen Lake

TIP TAP TWINKLE TOES ACADEMY!!

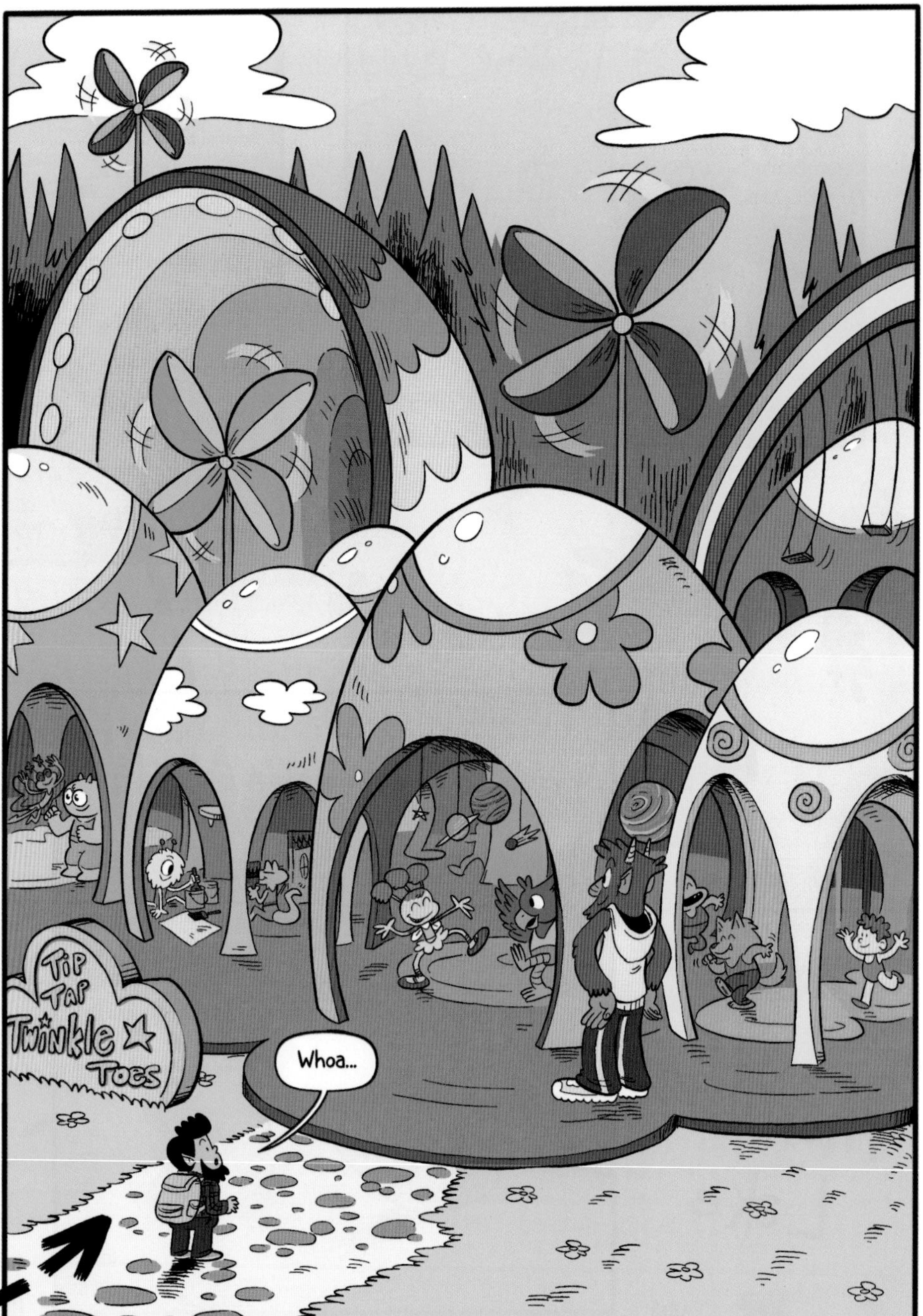

Tip Tap Twinkle Toes
Whoa...

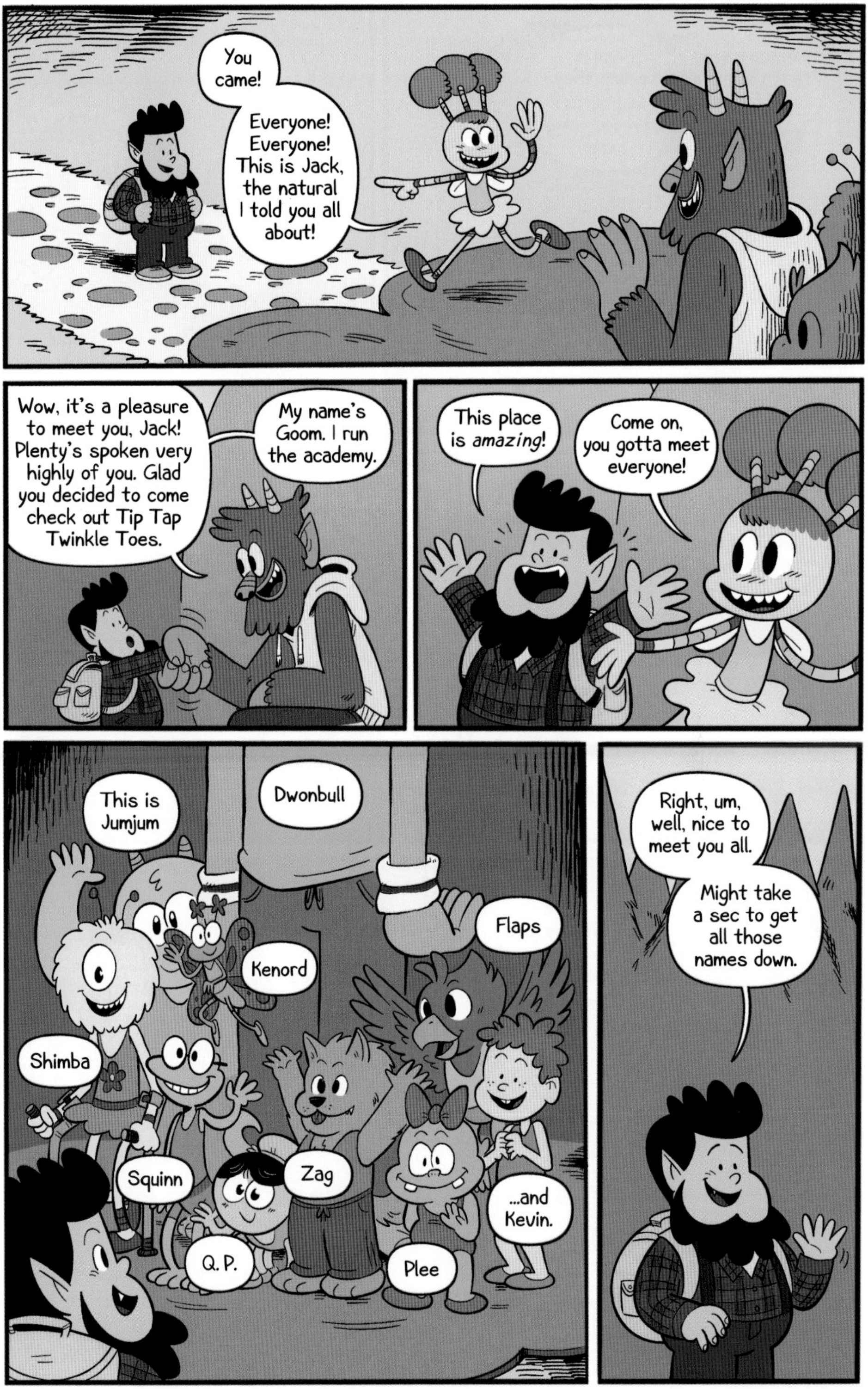
You came!
Everyone! Everyone! This is Jack, the natural I told you all about!
Wow, it's a pleasure to meet you, Jack! Plenty's spoken very highly of you. Glad you decided to come check out Tip Tap Twinkle Toes.
My name's Goom. I run the academy.
This place is *amazing*!
Come on, you gotta meet everyone!
This is Jumjum
Dwonbull
Flaps
Kenord
Shimba
Squinn
Zag
...and Kevin.
Q. P.
Plee
Right, um, well, nice to meet you all.
Might take a sec to get all those names down.

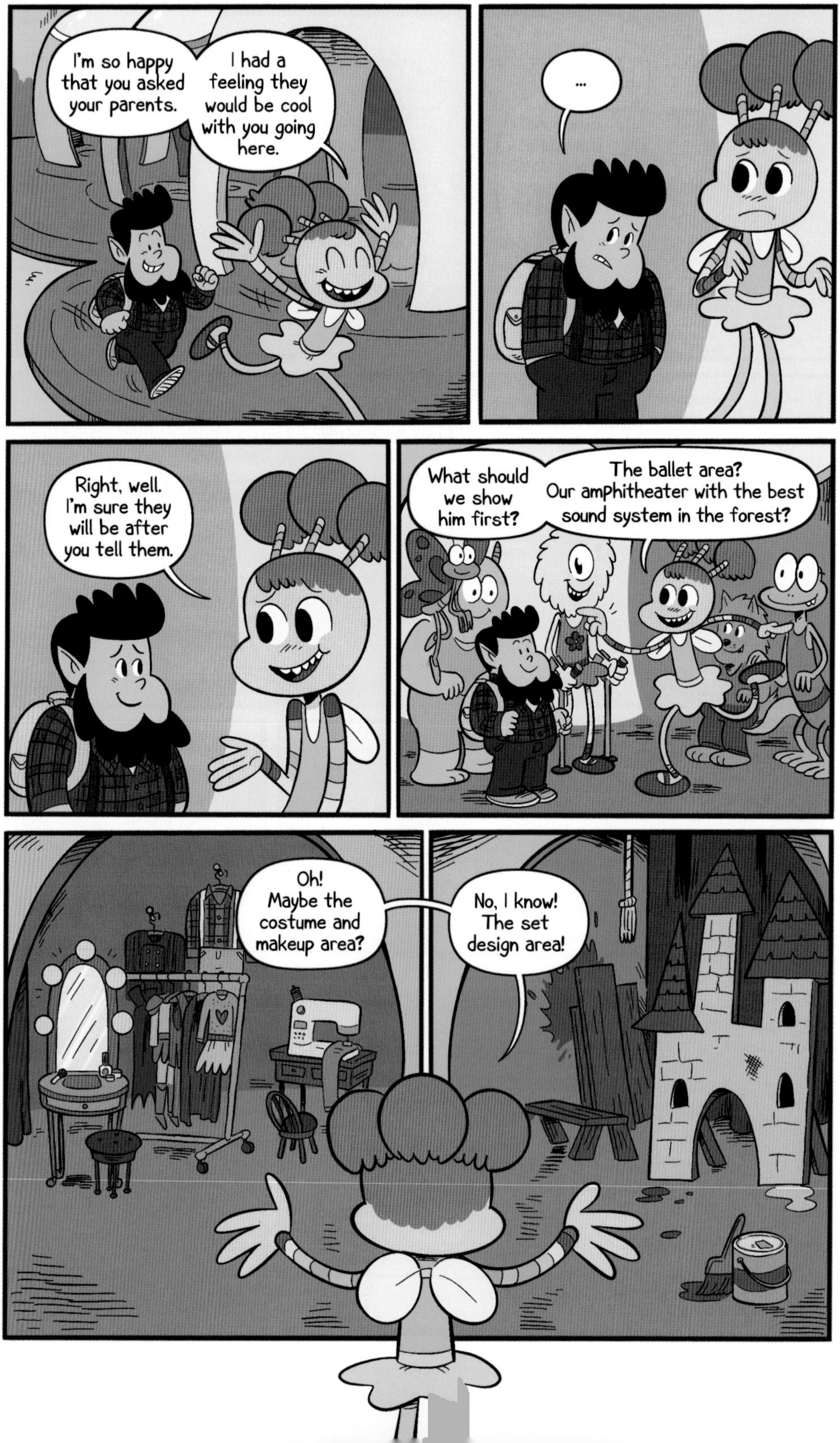
I'm so happy that you asked your parents.
I had a feeling they would be cool with you going here.
...
Right, well. I'm sure they will be after you tell them.
What should we show him first?
The ballet area? Our amphitheater with the best sound system in the forest?
Oh! Maybe the costume and makeup area?
No, I know! The set design area!

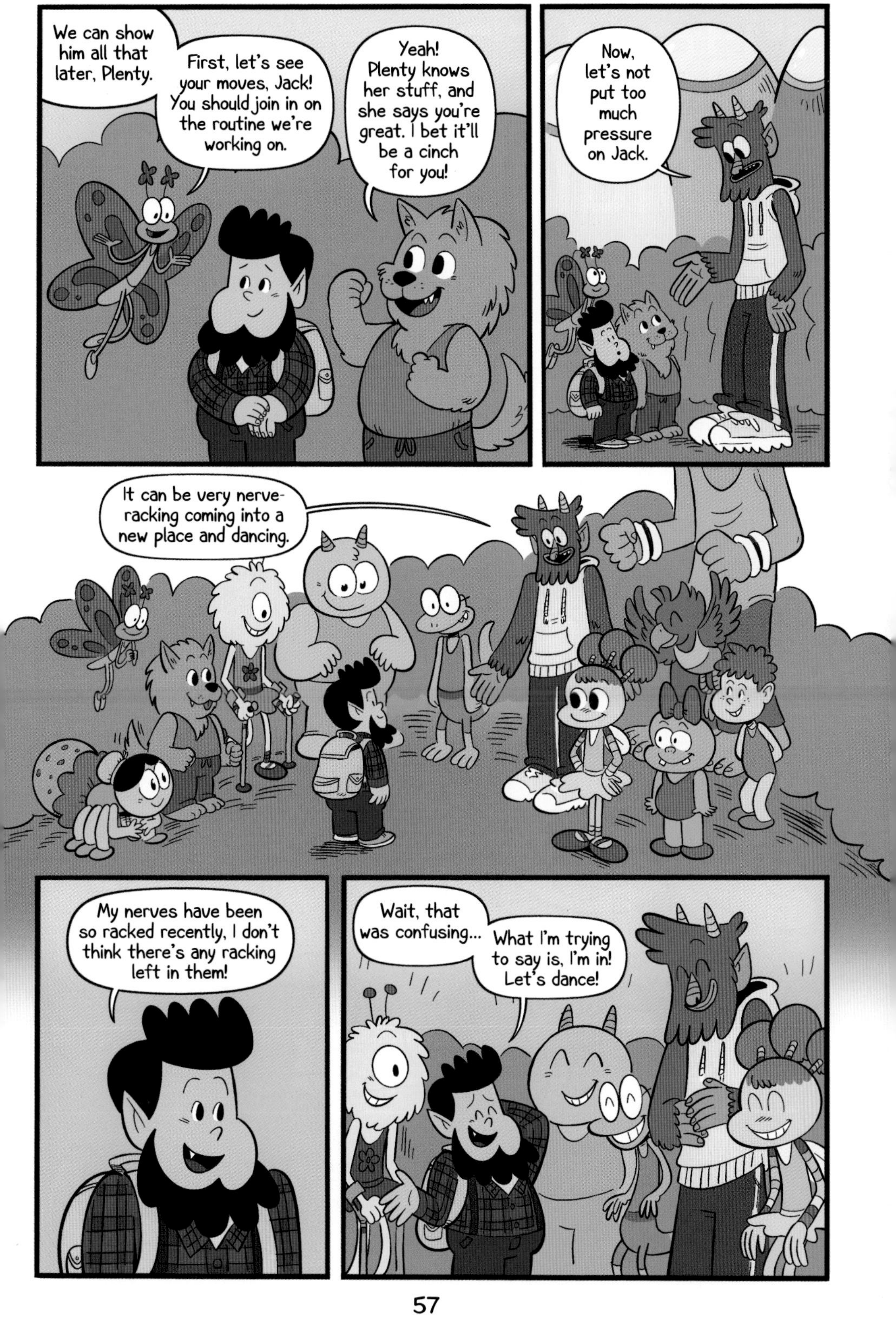
We can show him all that later, Plenty.
First, let's see your moves, Jack! You should join in on the routine we're working on.
Yeah! Plenty knows her stuff, and she says you're great. I bet it'll be a cinch for you!
Now, let's not put too much pressure on Jack.
It can be very nerve-racking coming into a new place and dancing.
My nerves have been so racked recently, I don't think there's any racking left in them!
Wait, that was confusing...
What I'm trying to say is, I'm in! Let's dance!

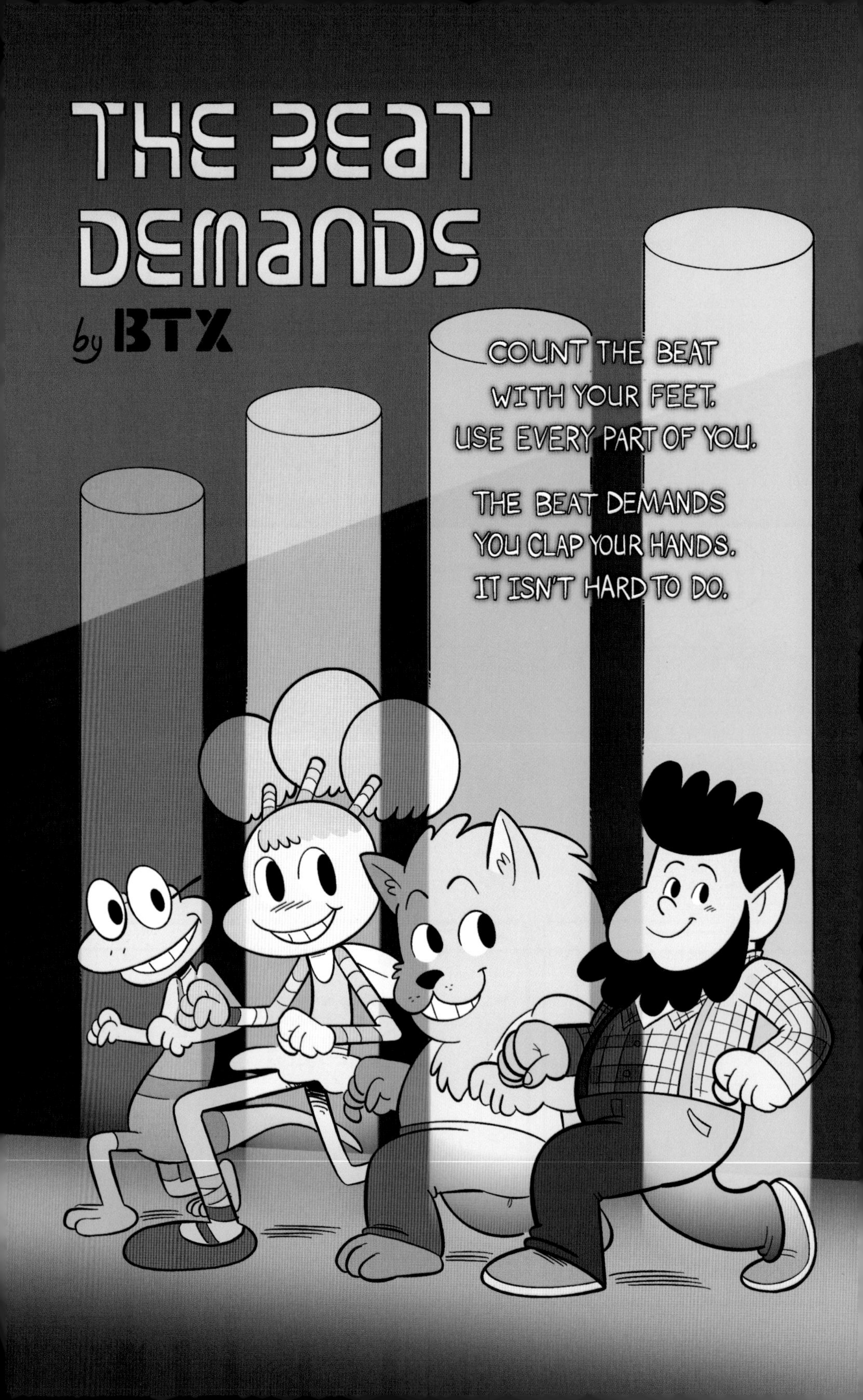
THE BEAT DEMANDS
by BTX
COUNT THE BEAT
WITH YOUR FEET.
USE EVERY PART OF YOU.
THE BEAT DEMANDS
YOU CLAP YOUR HANDS.
IT ISN'T HARD TO DO.

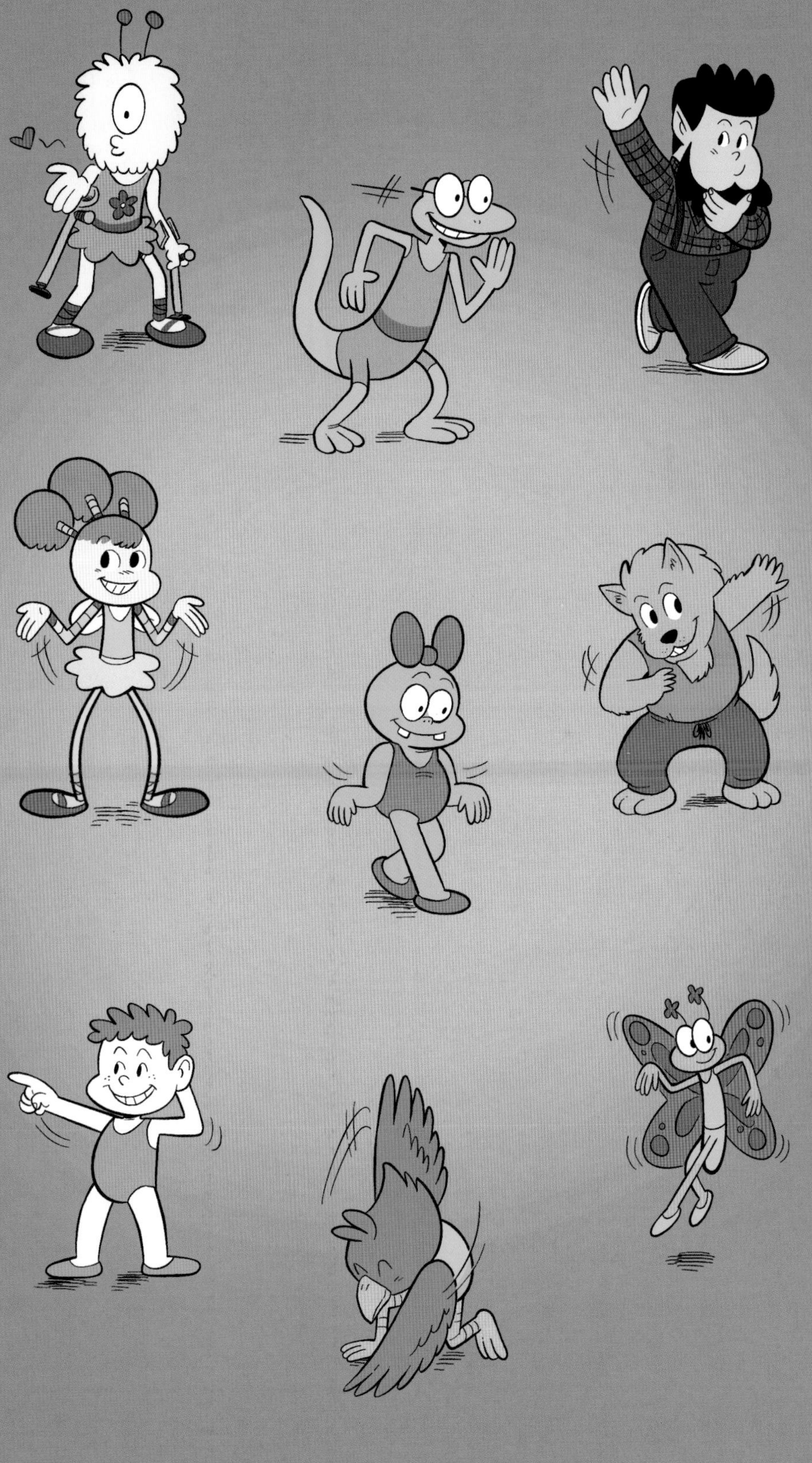

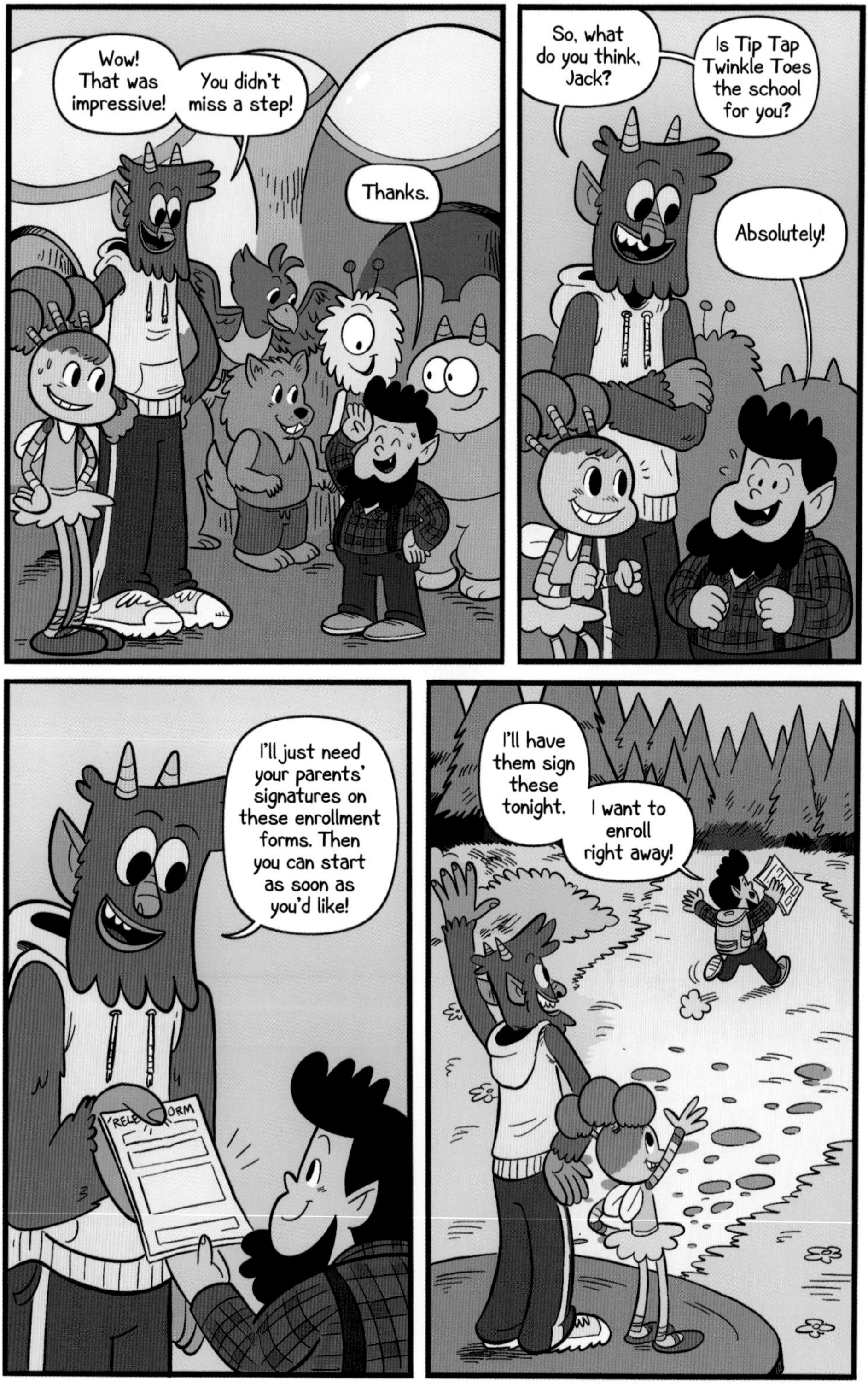
Wow! That was impressive!
You didn't miss a step!
Thanks.
So, what do you think, Jack?
Is Tip Tap Twinkle Toes the school for you?
Absolutely!
I'll just need your parents' signatures on these enrollment forms. Then you can start as soon as you'd like!
I'll have them sign these tonight.
I want to enroll right away!

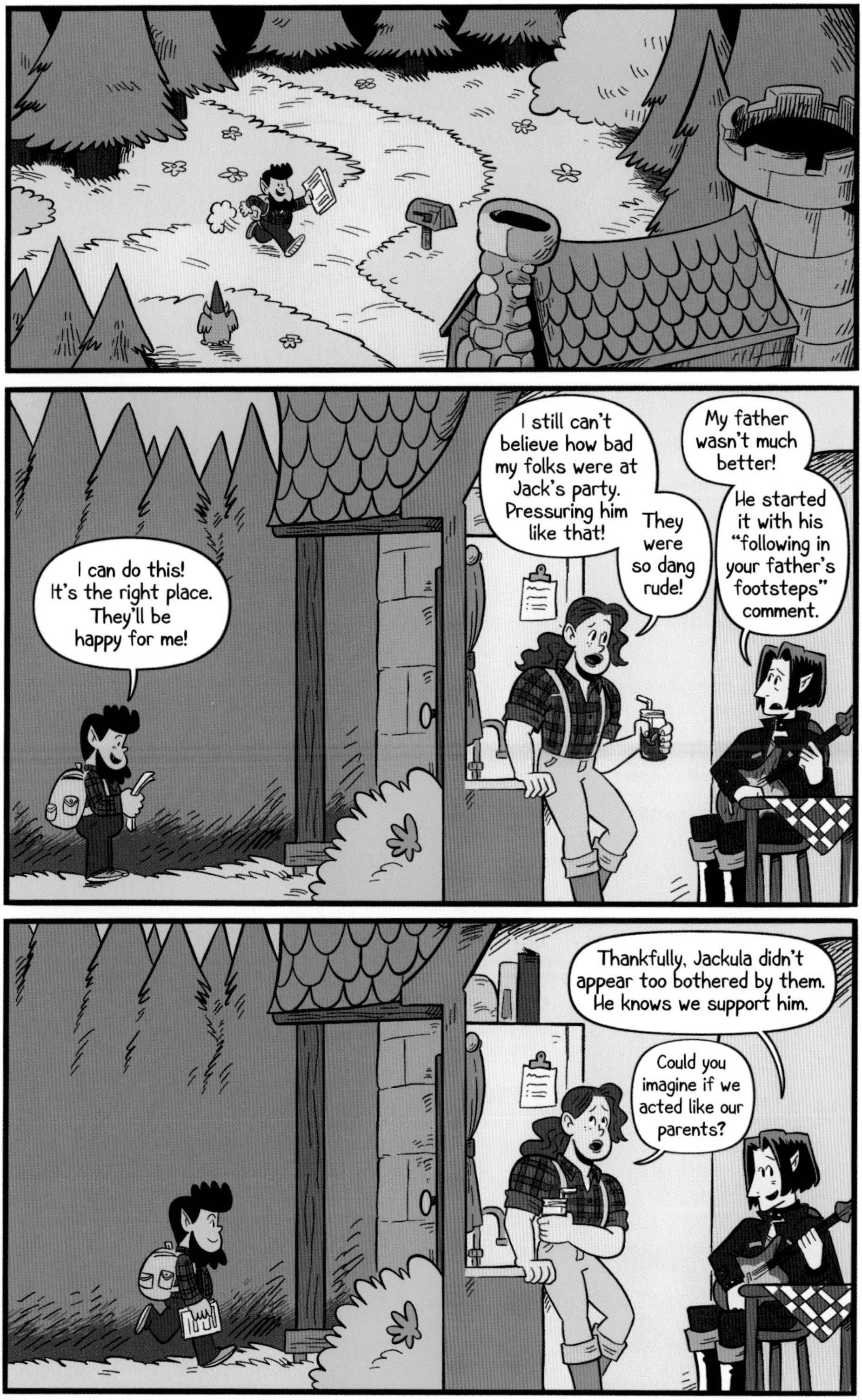
I can do this! It's the right place. They'll be happy for me!
I still can't believe how bad my folks were at Jack's party. Pressuring him like that!
They were so dang rude!
My father wasn't much better!
He started it with his "following in your father's footsteps" comment.
Thankfully, Jackula didn't appear too bothered by them. He knows we support him.
Could you imagine if we acted like our parents?

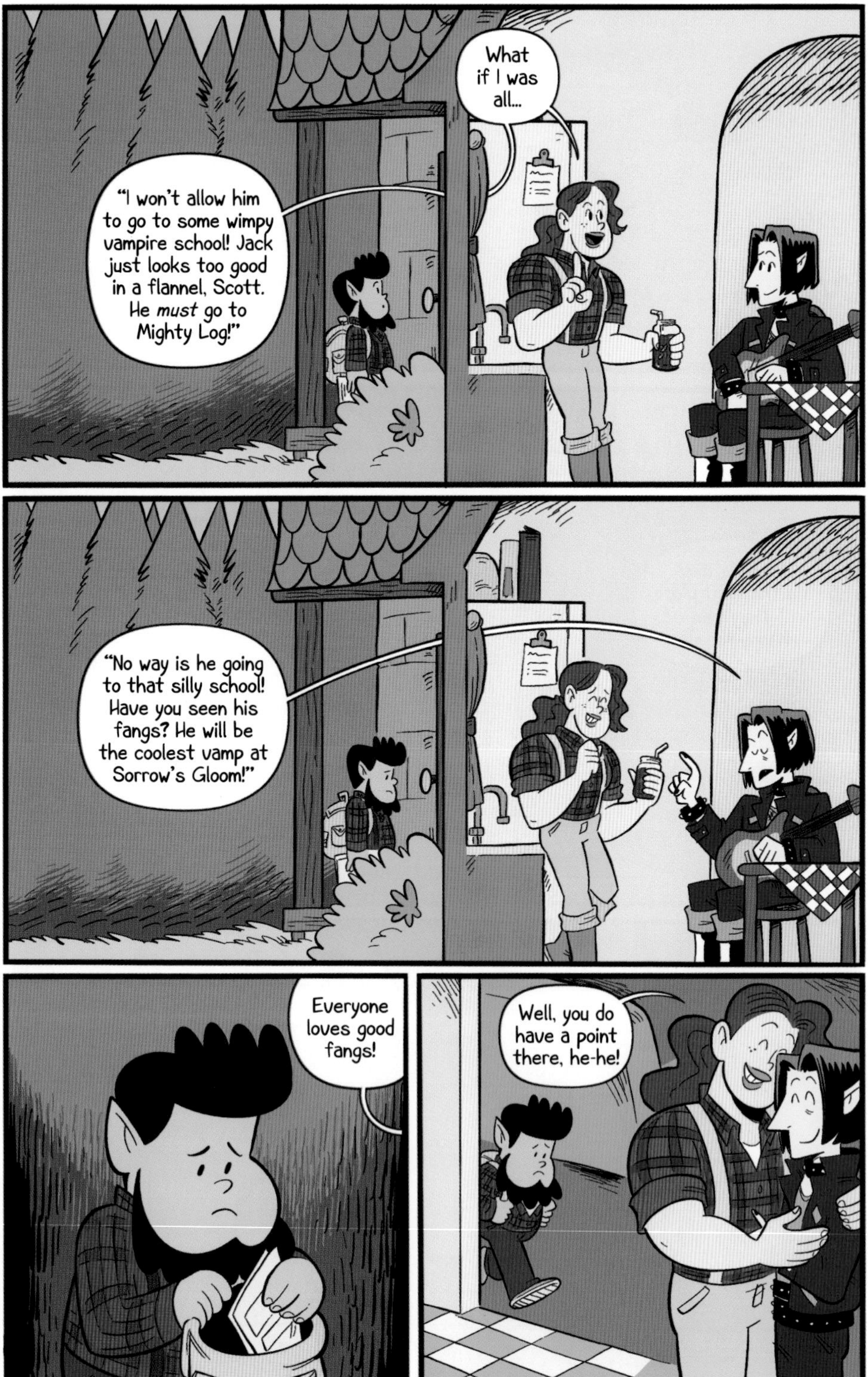
What if I was all...
"I won't allow him to go to some wimpy vampire school! Jack just looks too good in a flannel, Scott. He *must* go to Mighty Log!"
"No way is he going to that silly school! Have you seen his fangs? He will be the coolest vamp at Sorrow's Gloom!"
Everyone loves good fangs!
Well, you do have a point there, he-he!

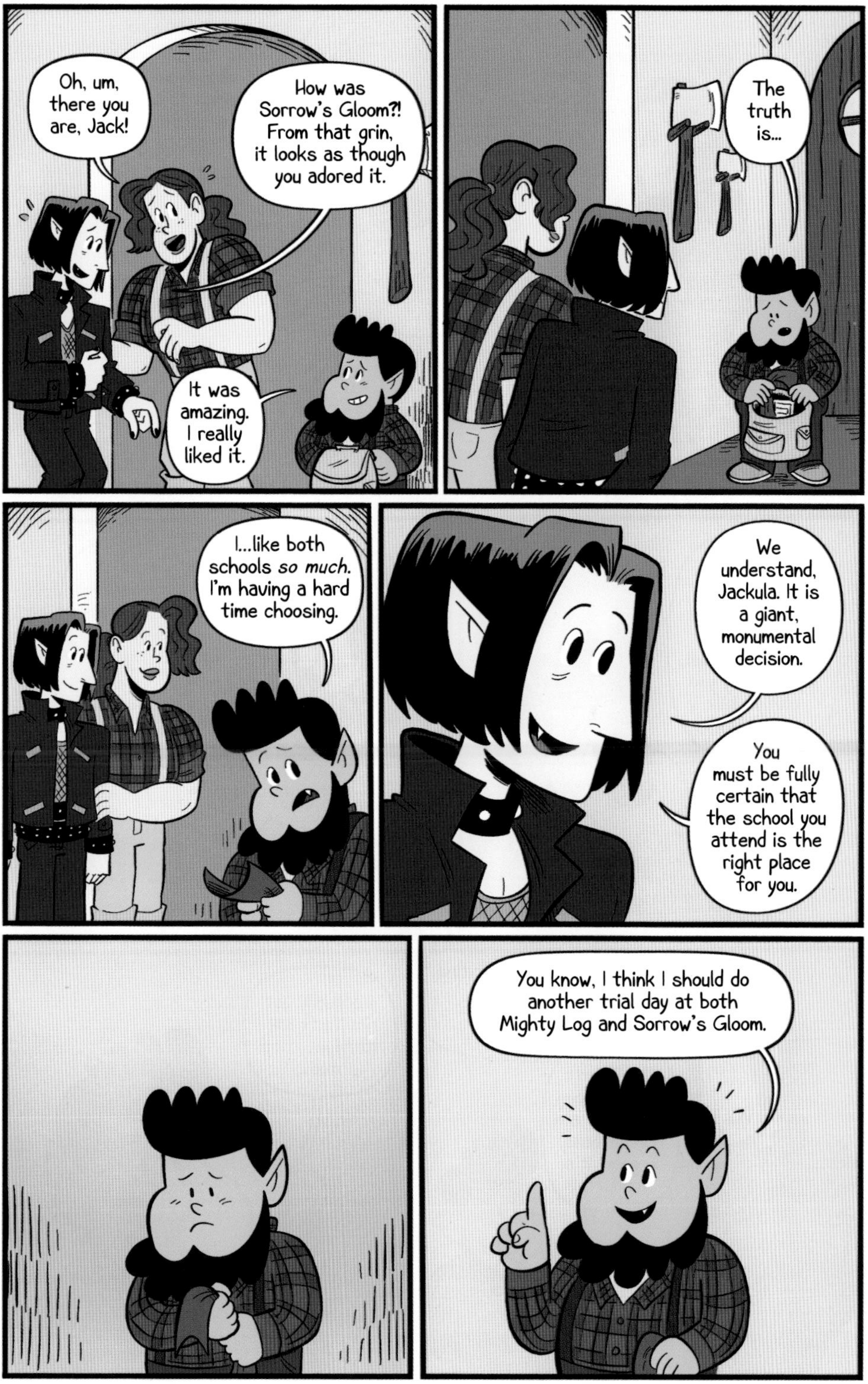

Oh, um, there you are, Jack!
How was Sorrow's Gloom?! From that grin, it looks as though you adored it.
It was amazing. I really liked it.
The truth is...
I...like both schools *so much.* I'm having a hard time choosing.
We understand, Jackula. It is a giant, monumental decision.
You must be fully certain that the school you attend is the right place for you.
You know, I think I should do another trial day at both Mighty Log and Sorrow's Gloom.

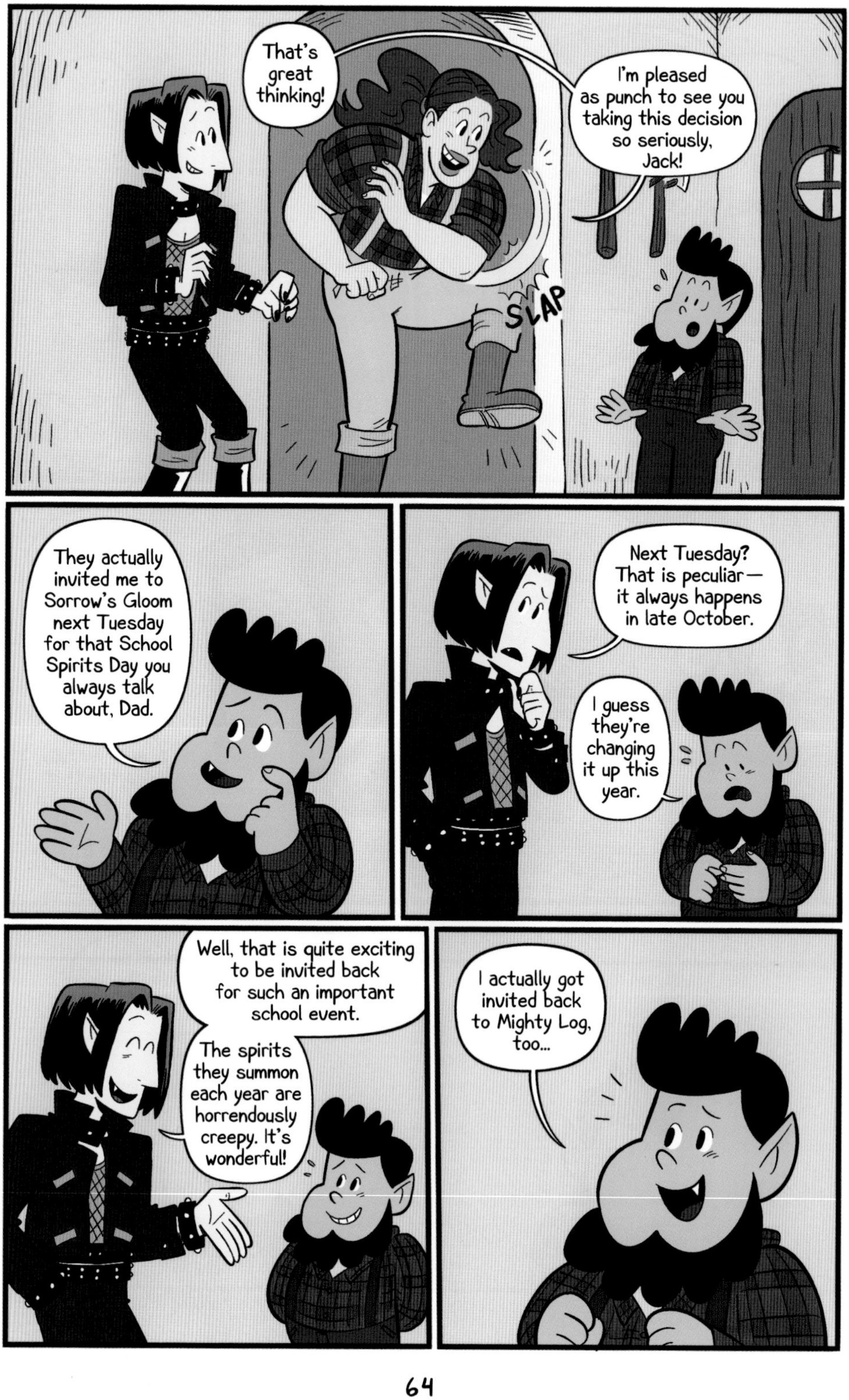

That's great thinking!
I'm pleased as punch to see you taking this decision so seriously, Jack!
SLAP
They actually invited me to Sorrow's Gloom next Tuesday for that School Spirits Day you always talk about, Dad.
Next Tuesday? That is peculiar— it always happens in late October.
I guess they're changing it up this year.
Well, that is quite exciting to be invited back for such an important school event.
The spirits they summon each year are horrendously creepy. It's wonderful!
I actually got invited back to Mighty Log, too...

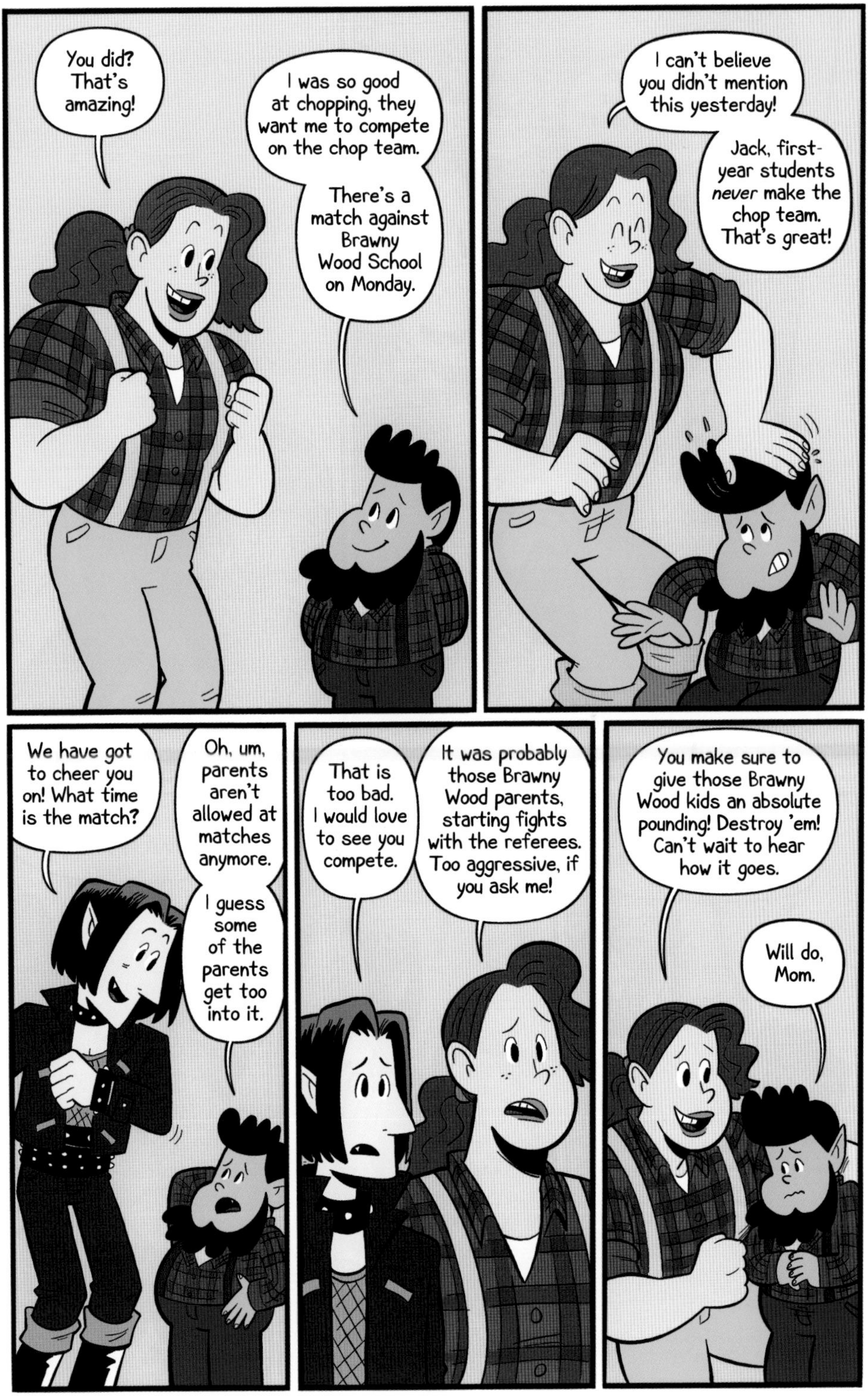

You did? That's amazing!
I was so good at chopping, they want me to compete on the chop team.
There's a match against Brawny Wood School on Monday.
I can't believe you didn't mention this yesterday!
Jack, first-year students *never* make the chop team. That's great!
We have got to cheer you on! What time is the match?
Oh, um, parents aren't allowed at matches anymore.
I guess some of the parents get too into it.
That is too bad. I would love to see you compete.
It was probably those Brawny Wood parents, starting fights with the referees. Too aggressive, if you ask me!
You make sure to give those Brawny Wood kids an absolute pounding! Destroy 'em! Can't wait to hear how it goes.
Will do, Mom.

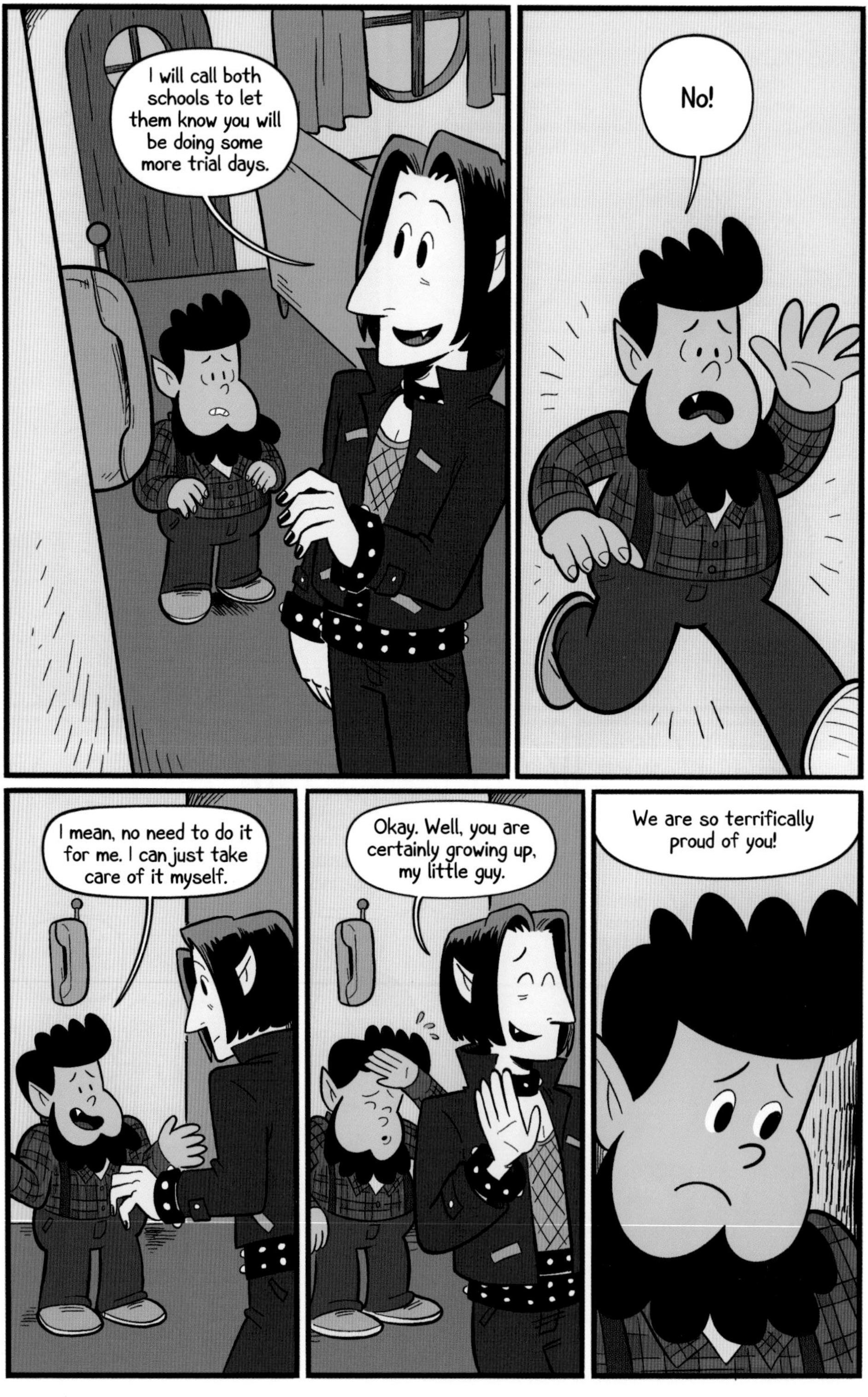

I will call both schools to let them know you will be doing some more trial days.
No!
I mean, no need to do it for me. I can just take care of it myself.
Okay. Well, you are certainly growing up, my little guy.
We are so terrifically proud of you!

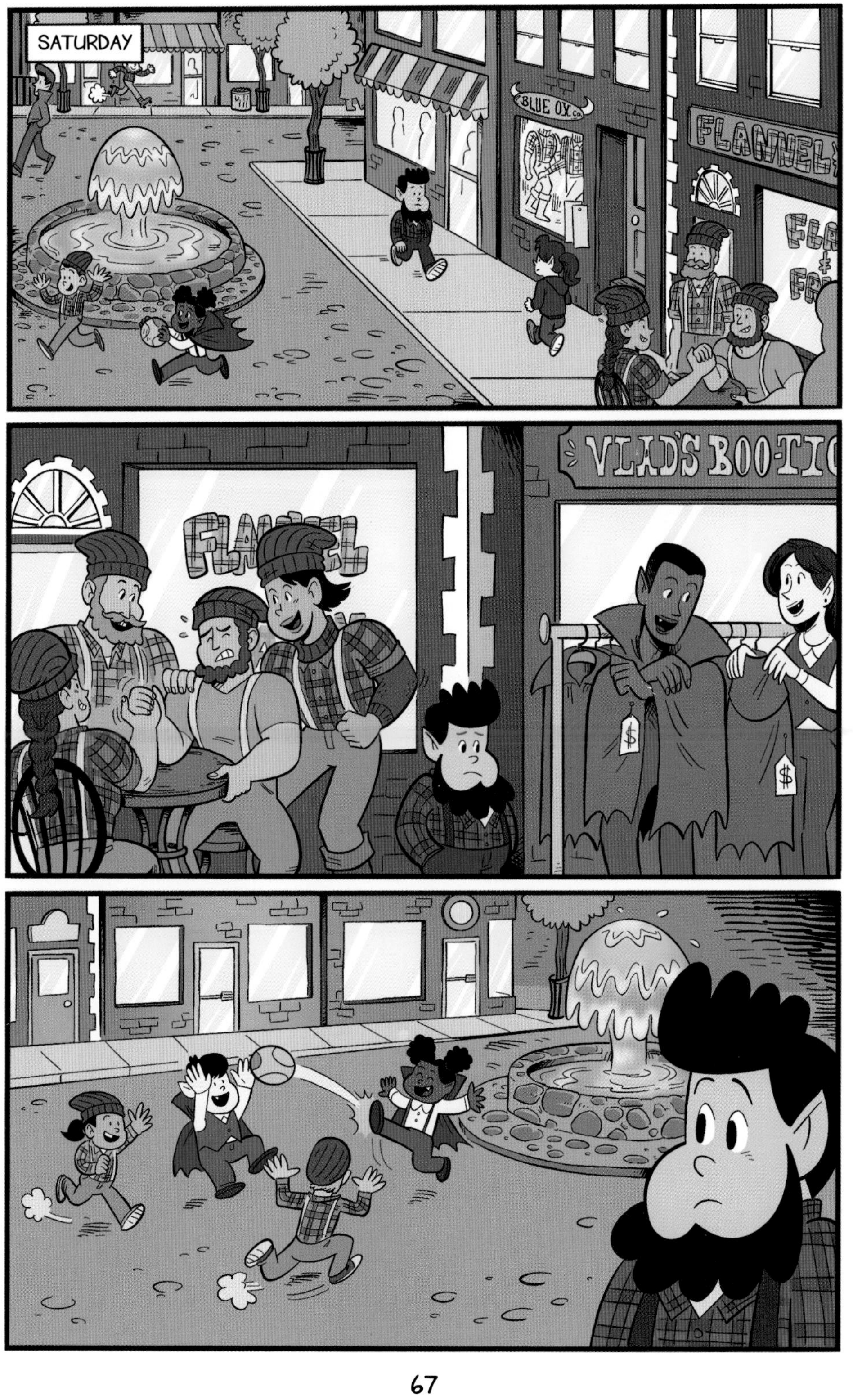
SATURDAY
BLUE OX Co.
FLANNEL
VLAD'S BOO-TI

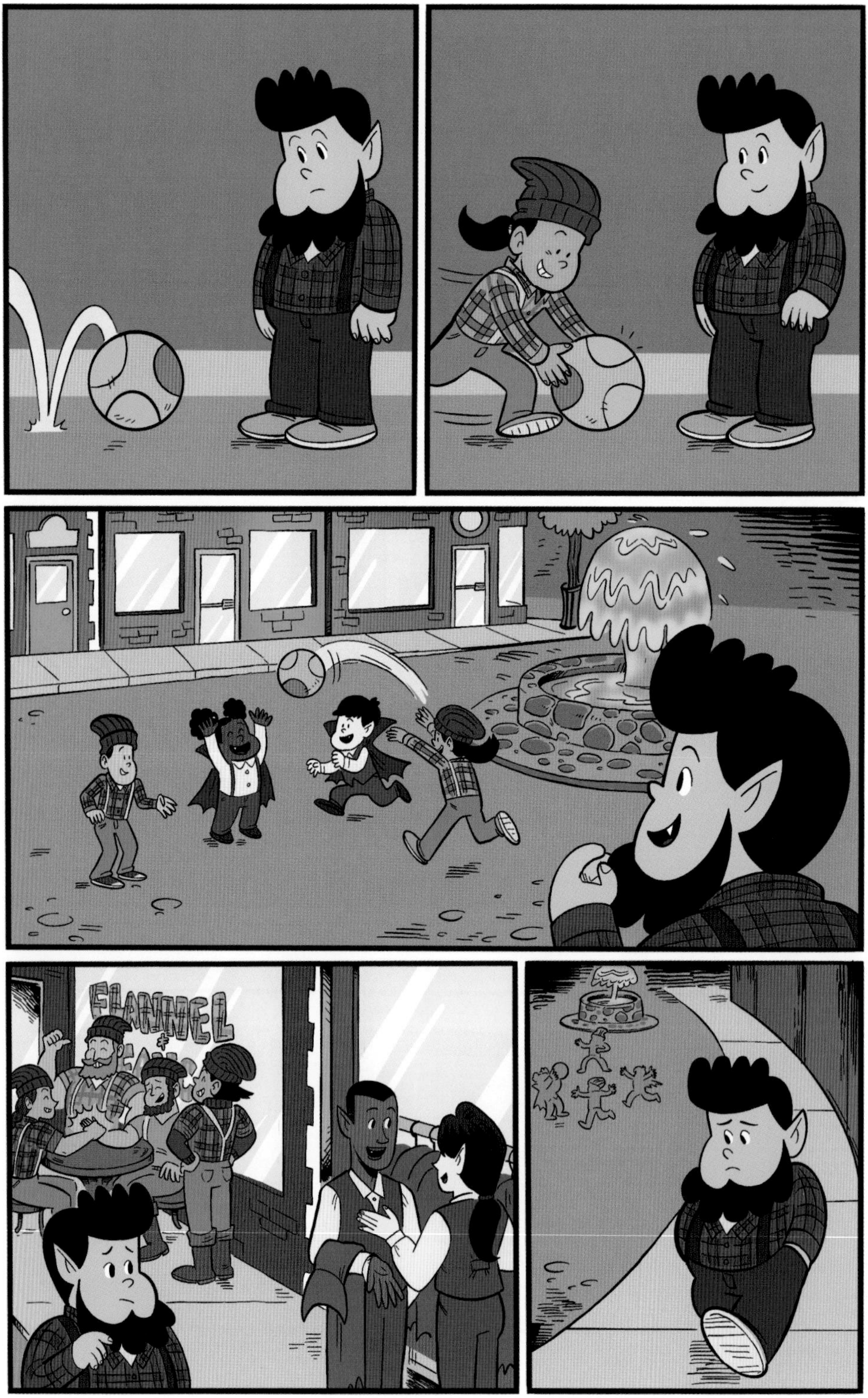
FLANNEL

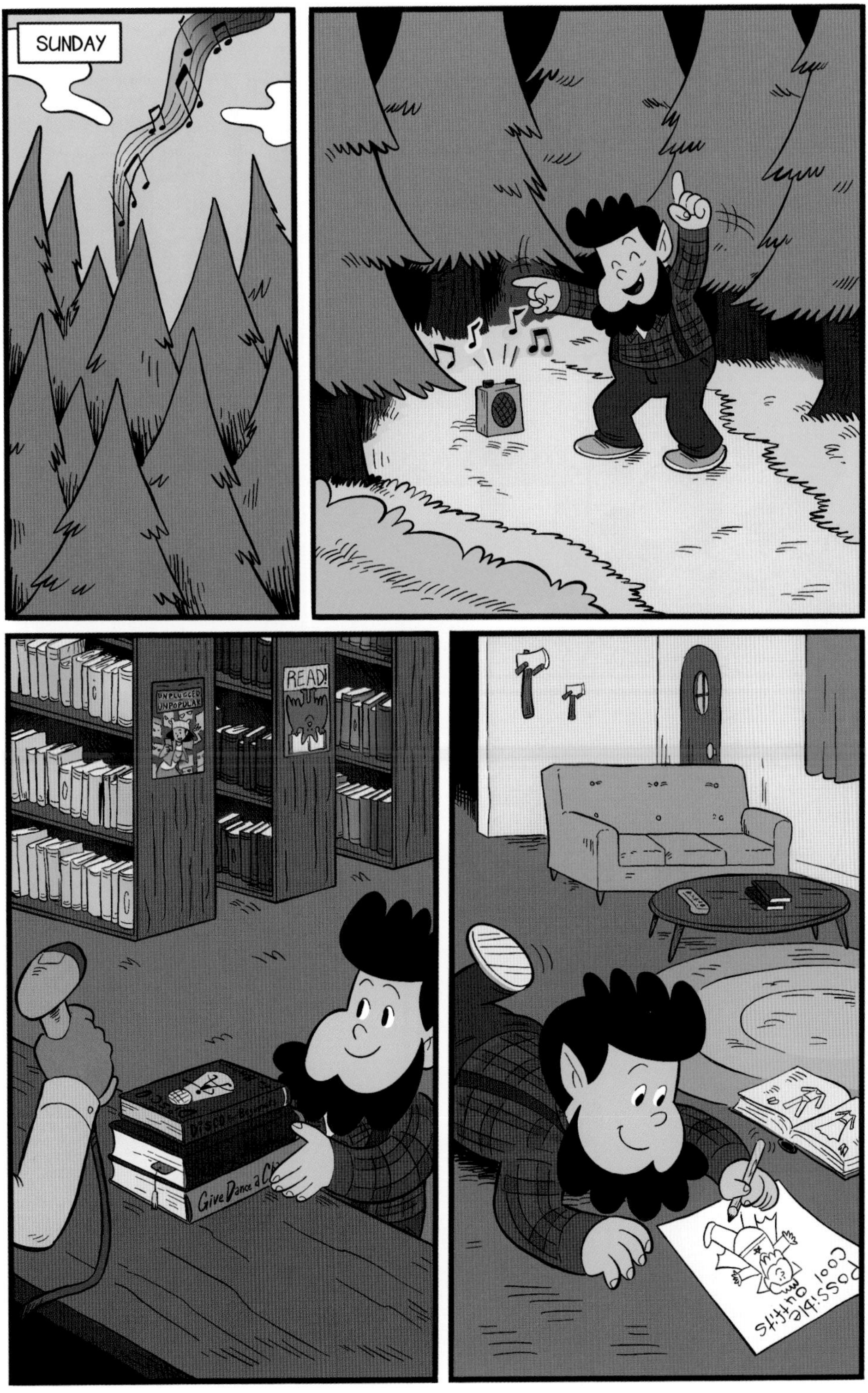
SUNDAY
UNPLUGGED
UNPOPULAR
READ!
DISCO
Possible
Cool Outfits

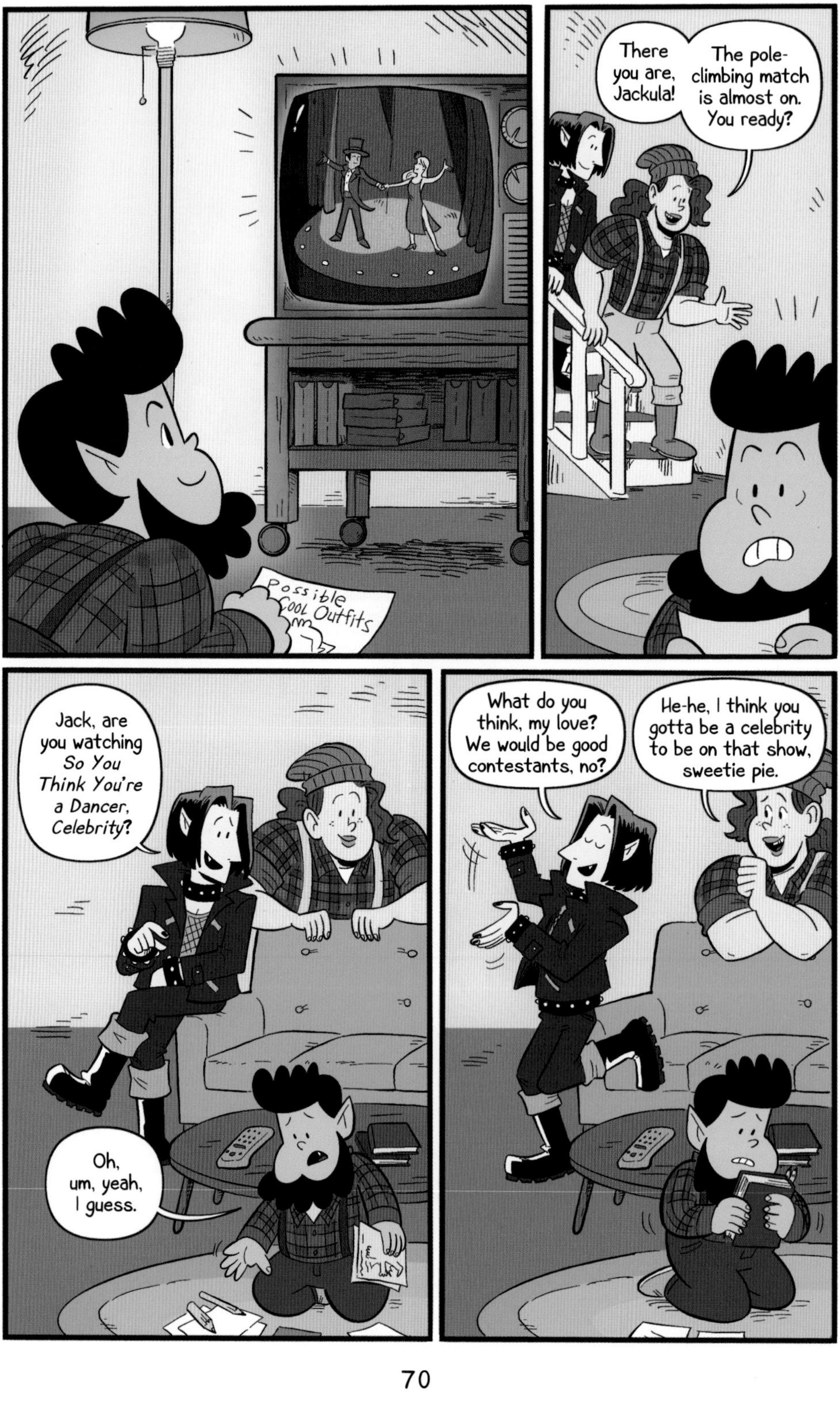
Possible Cool Outfits
There you are, Jackula!
The pole-climbing match is almost on. You ready?
Jack, are you watching So You Think You're a Dancer, Celebrity?
Oh, um, yeah, I guess.
What do you think, my love? We would be good contestants, no?
He-he, I think you gotta be a celebrity to be on that show, sweetie pie.

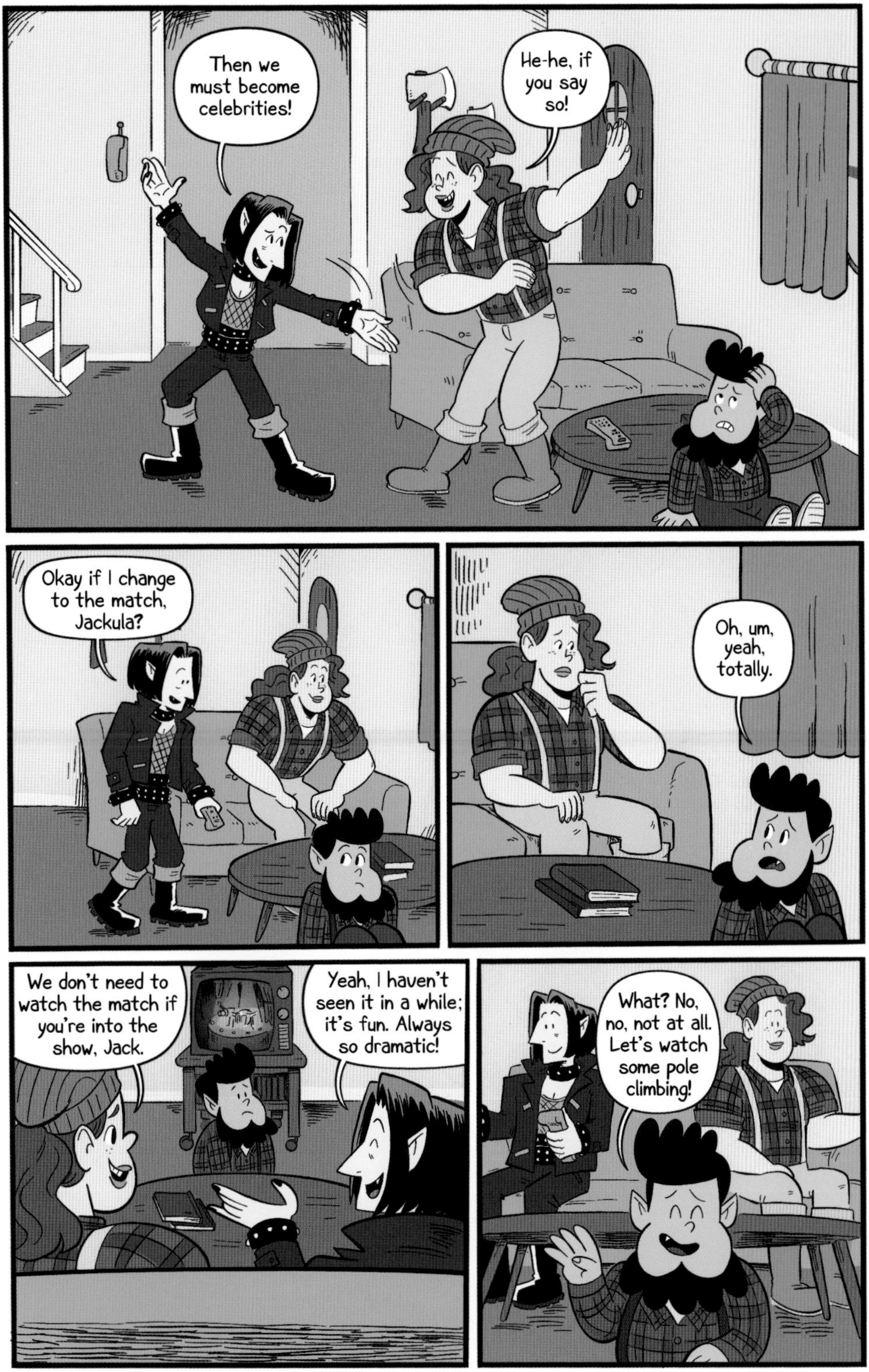
Then we must become celebrities!
He-he, if you say so!
Okay if I change to the match, Jackula?
Oh, um, yeah, totally.
We don't need to watch the match if you're into the show, Jack.
Yeah, I haven't seen it in a while; it's fun. Always so dramatic!
What? No, no, not at all. Let's watch some pole climbing!

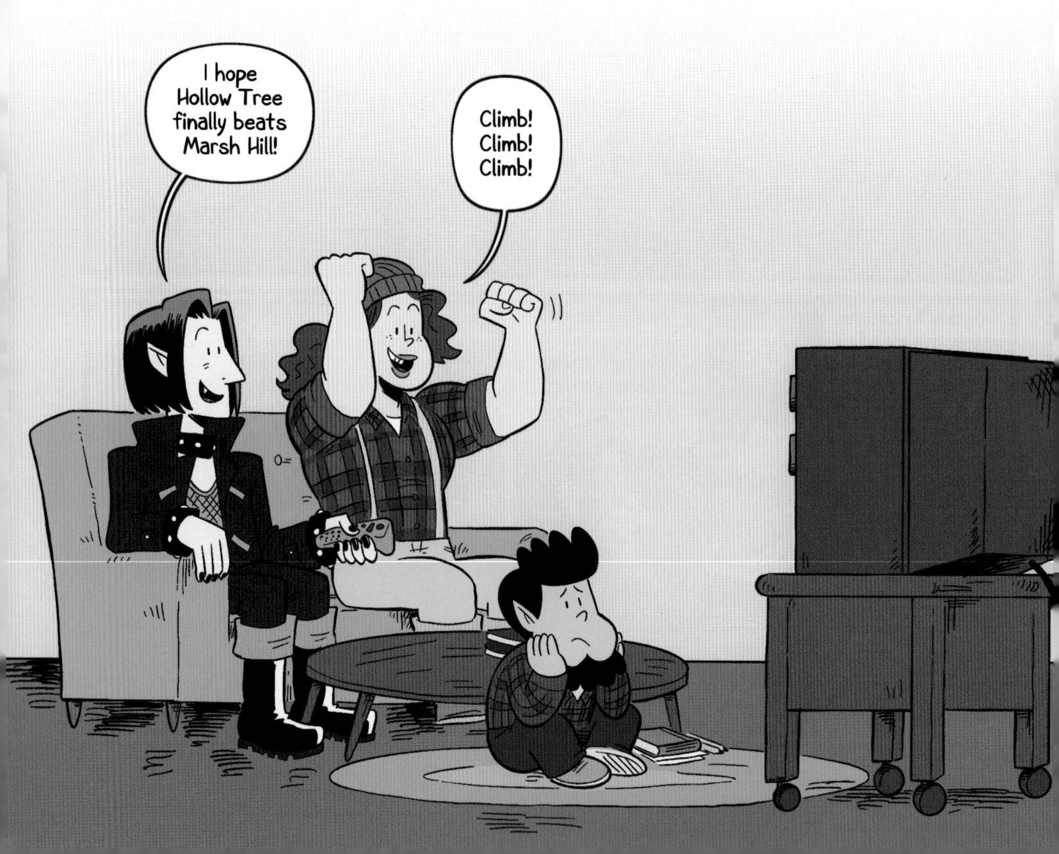
I hope Hollow Tree finally beats Marsh Hill!
Climb! Climb! Climb!

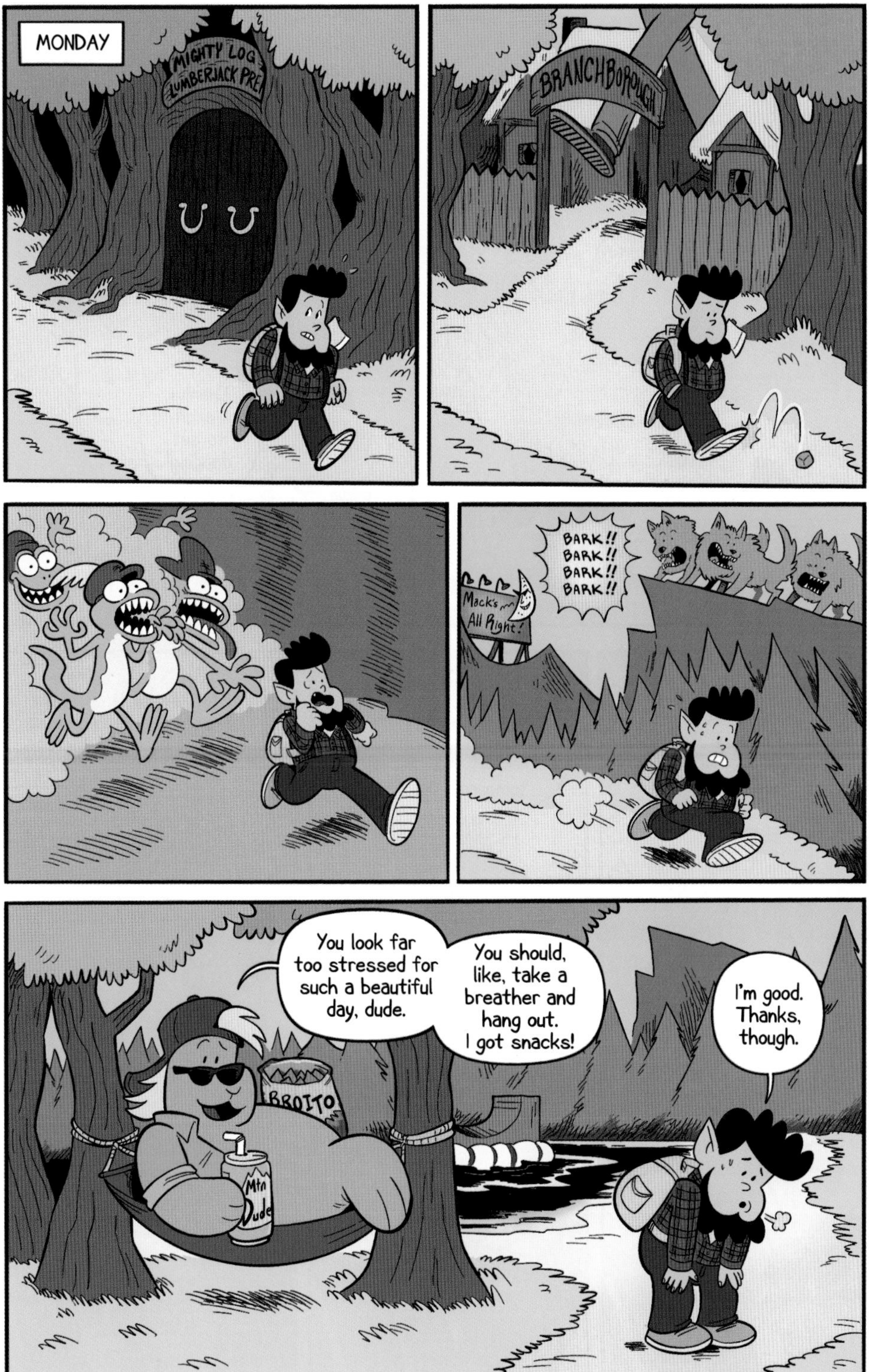
MONDAY
MIGHTY LOG
BRANCHBOROUGH
BARK!! BARK!! BARK!! BARK!!
Mack's All Right!
You look far too stressed for such a beautiful day, dude.
You should, like, take a breather and hang out. I got snacks!
BROITO
Mtn Dude
I'm good. Thanks, though.

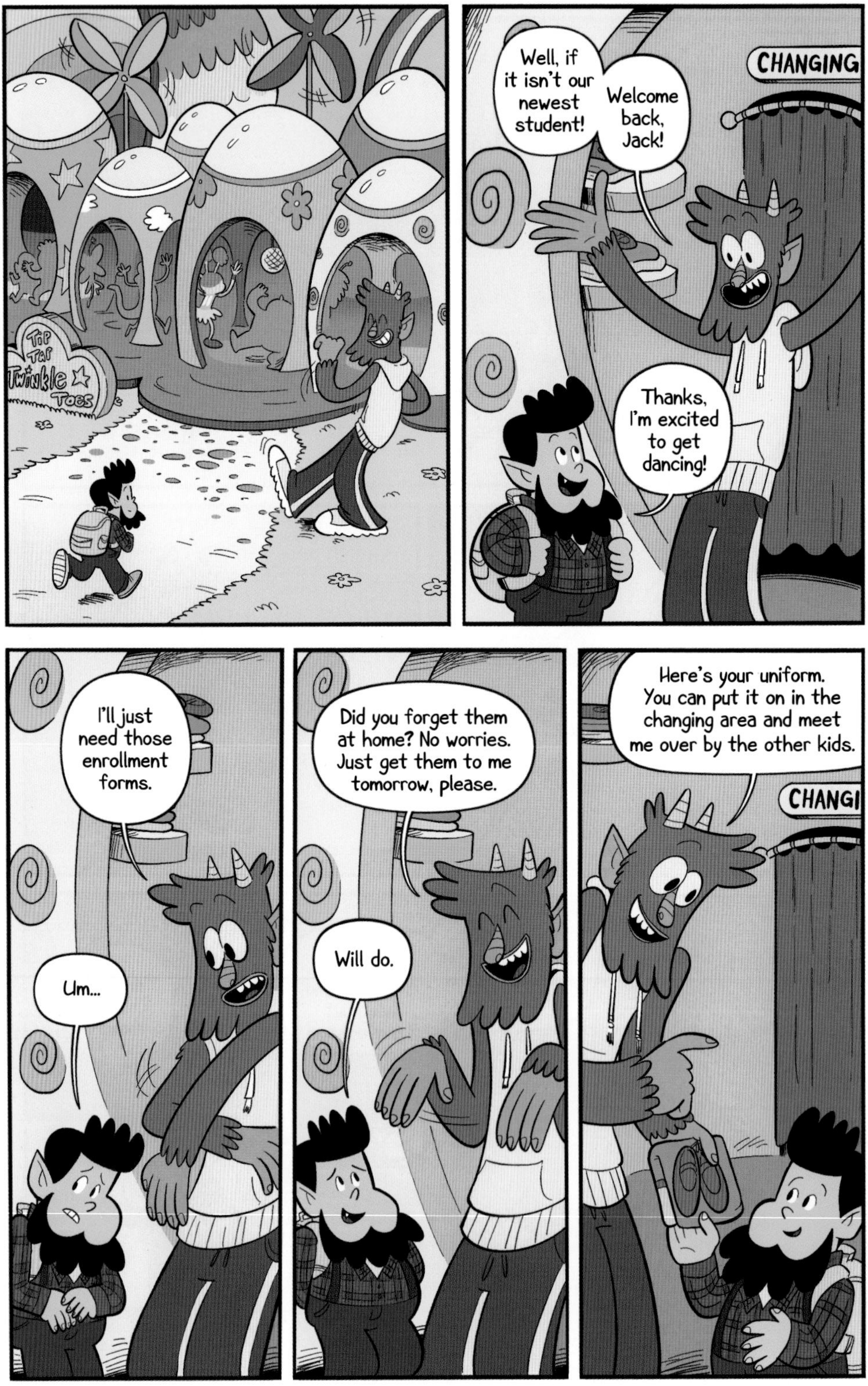
Tip Tap Twinkle Toes
Well, if it isn't our newest student!
Welcome back, Jack!
CHANGING
Thanks, I'm excited to get dancing!
I'll just need those enrollment forms.
Um...
Did you forget them at home? No worries. Just get them to me tomorrow, please.
Will do.
Here's your uniform. You can put it on in the changing area and meet me over by the other kids.
CHANGI

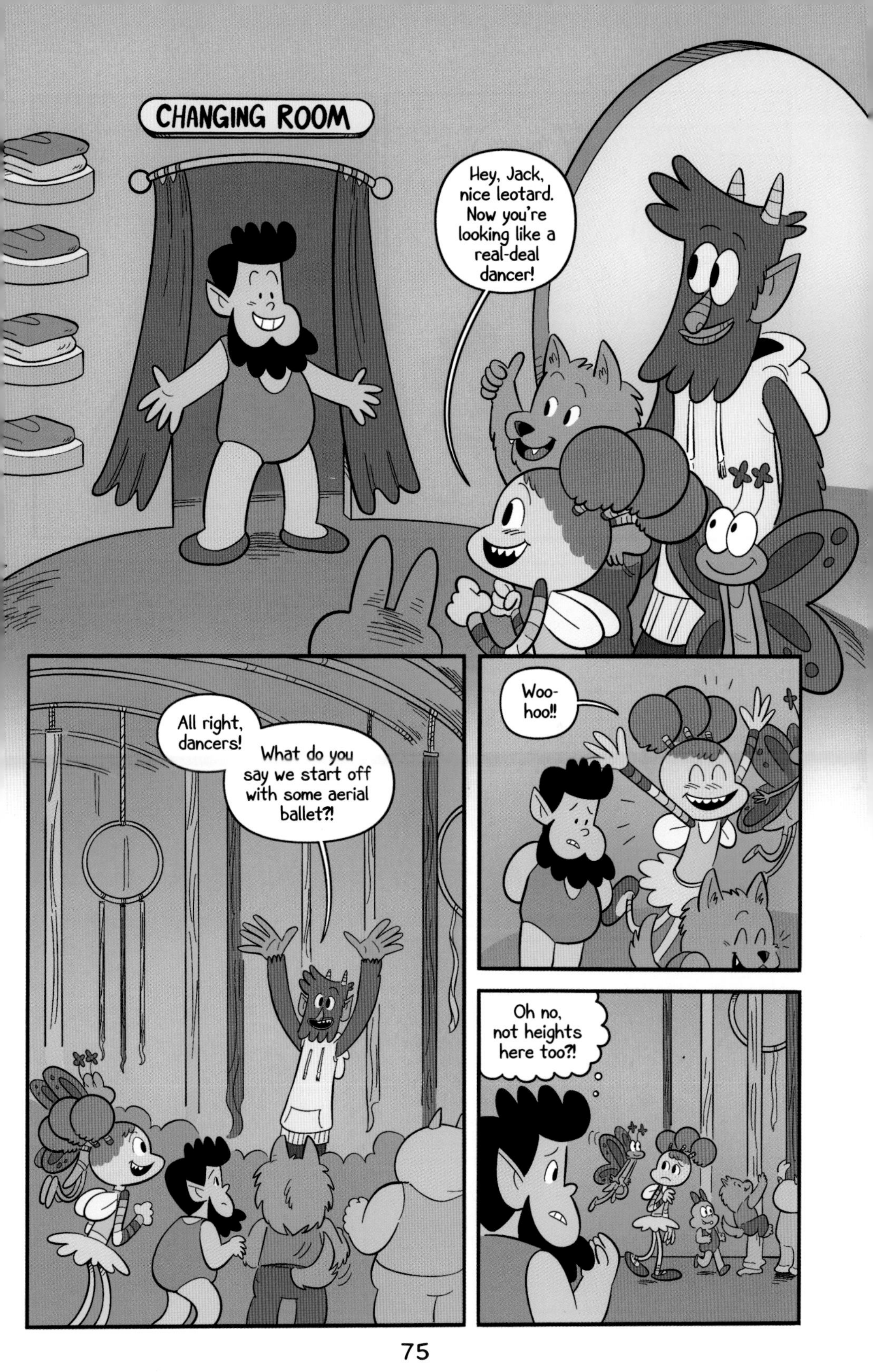
CHANGING ROOM
Hey, Jack, nice leotard. Now you're looking like a real-deal dancer!
All right, dancers!
What do you say we start off with some aerial ballet?!
Woo-hoo!!
Oh no, not heights here too?!

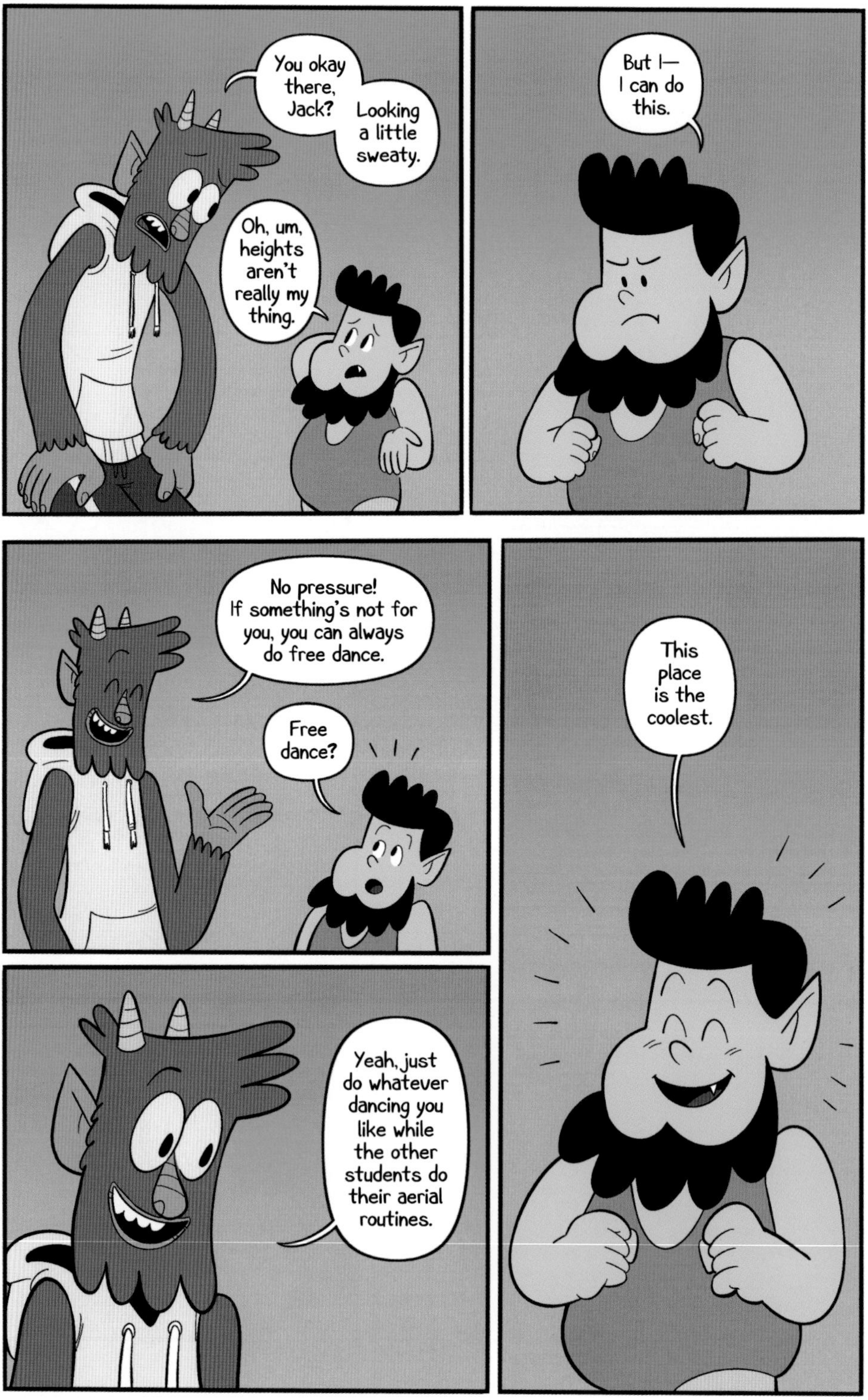
You okay there, Jack?
Looking a little sweaty.
Oh, um, heights aren't really my thing.
But I— I can do this.
No pressure! If something's not for you, you can always do free dance.
Free dance?
Yeah, just do whatever dancing you like while the other students do their aerial routines.
This place is the coolest.

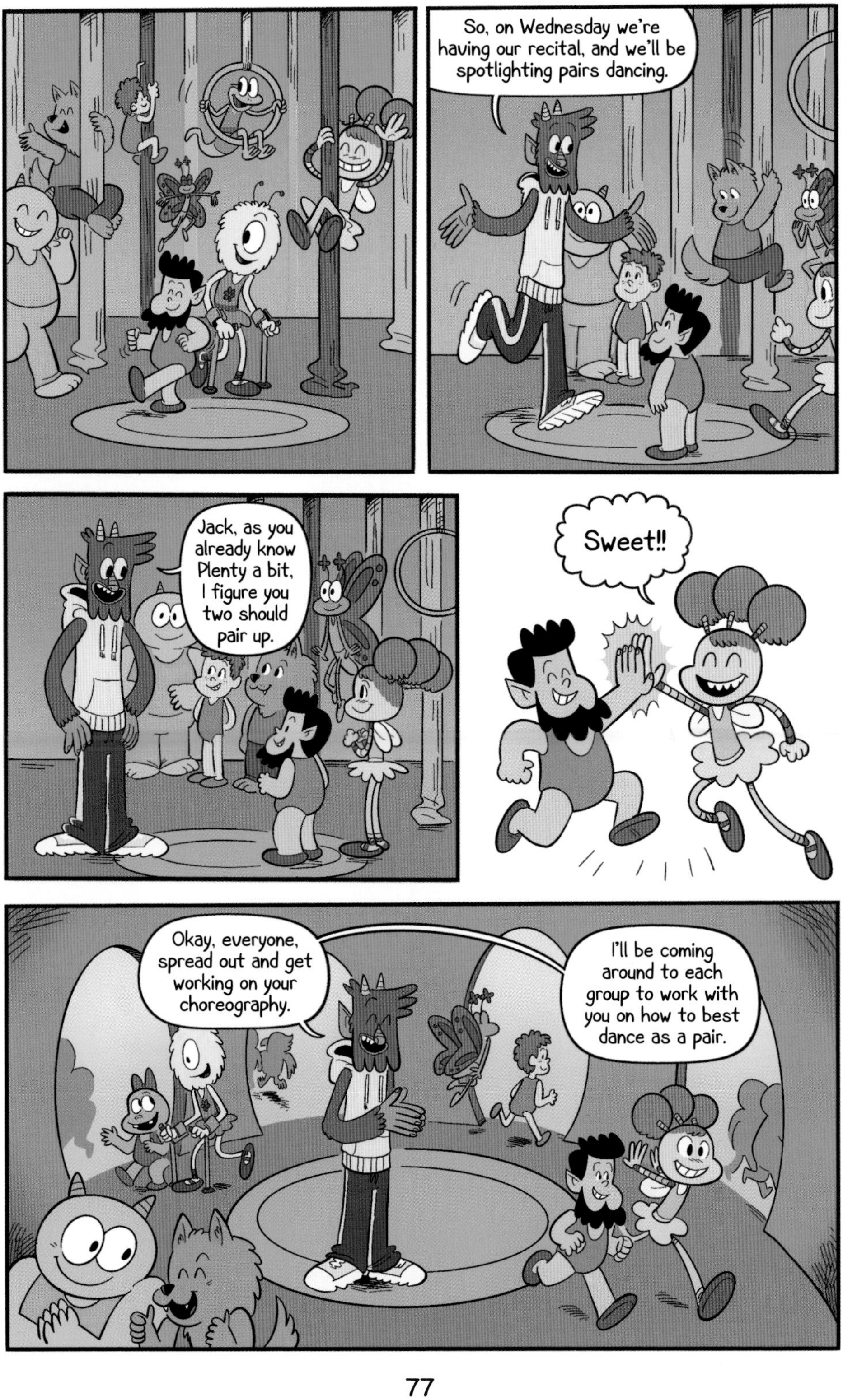
So, on Wednesday we're having our recital, and we'll be spotlighting pairs dancing.
Jack, as you already know Plenty a bit, I figure you two should pair up.
Sweet!!
Okay, everyone, spread out and get working on your choreography.
I'll be coming around to each group to work with you on how to best dance as a pair.

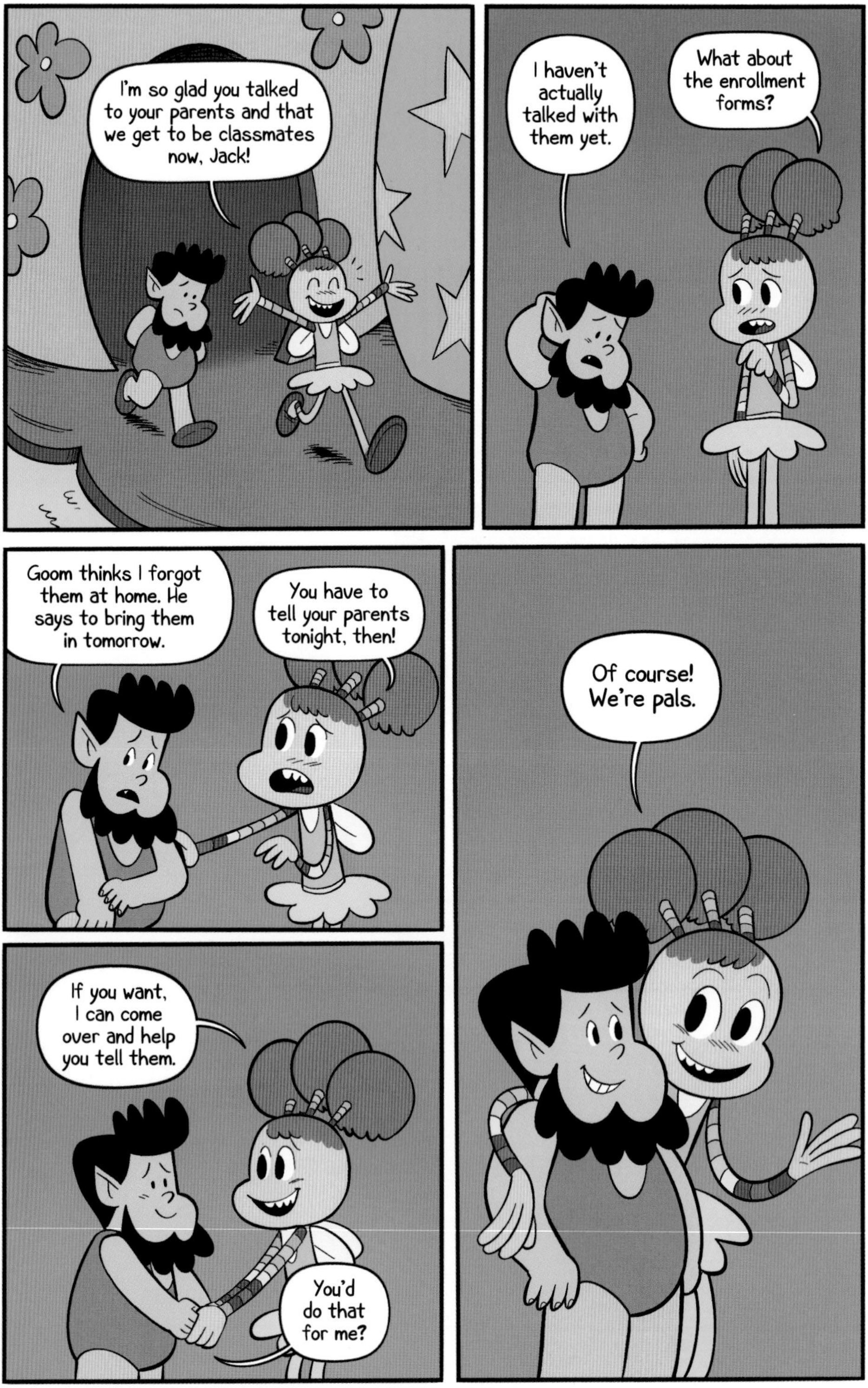
I'm so glad you talked to your parents and that we get to be classmates now, Jack!
I haven't actually talked with them yet.
What about the enrollment forms?
Goom thinks I forgot them at home. He says to bring them in tomorrow.
You have to tell your parents tonight, then!
If you want, I can come over and help you tell them.
You'd do that for me?
Of course! We're pals.

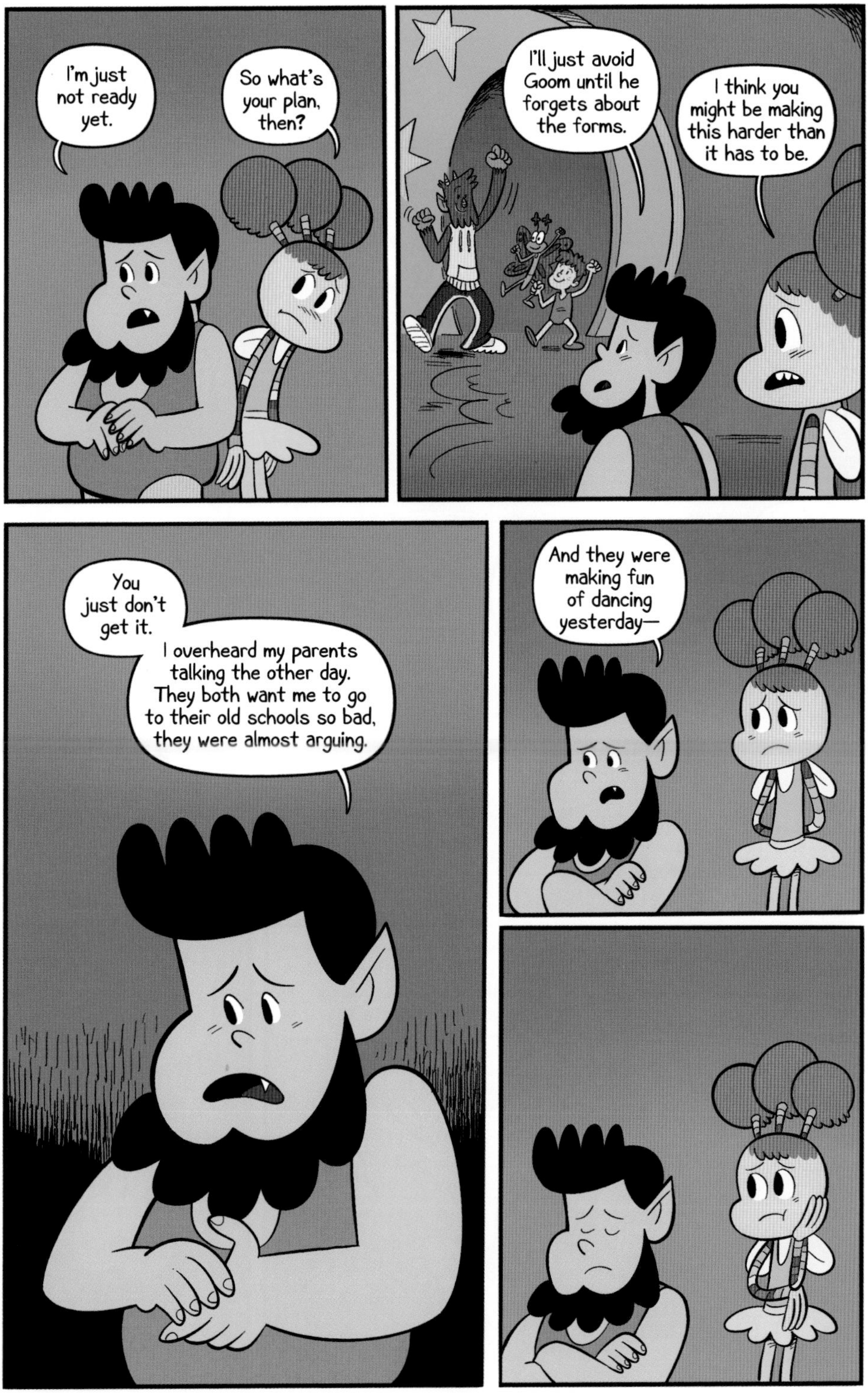
I'm just not ready yet.
So what's your plan, then?
I'll just avoid Goom until he forgets about the forms.
I think you might be making this harder than it has to be.
You just don't get it.
I overheard my parents talking the other day. They both want me to go to their old schools so bad, they were almost arguing.
And they were making fun of dancing yesterday—

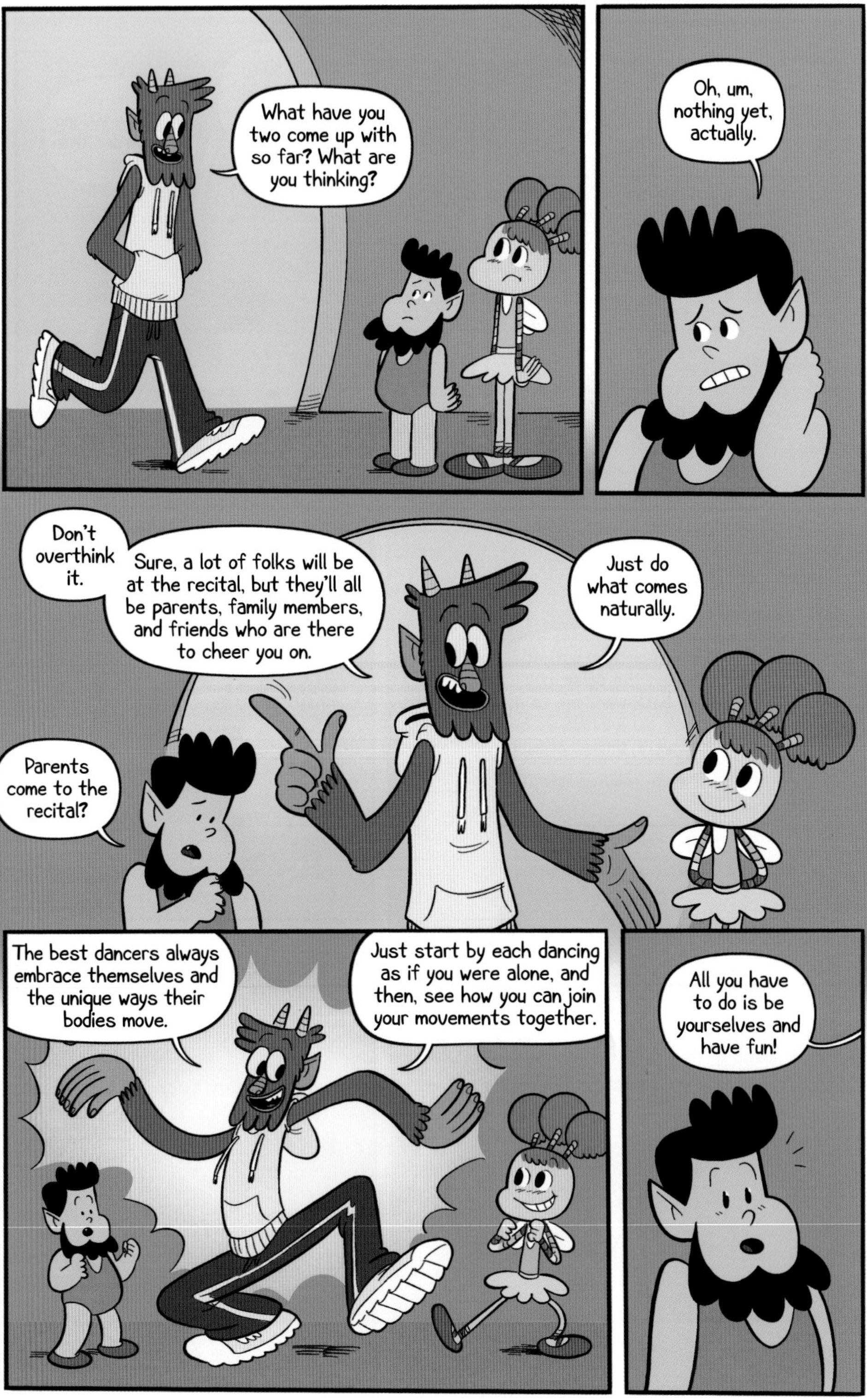
What have you two come up with so far? What are you thinking?
Oh, um, nothing yet, actually.
Don't overthink it.
Sure, a lot of folks will be at the recital, but they'll all be parents, family members, and friends who are there to cheer you on.
Just do what comes naturally.
Parents come to the recital?
The best dancers always embrace themselves and the unique ways their bodies move.
Just start by each dancing as if you were alone, and then, see how you can join your movements together.
All you have to do is be yourselves and have fun!

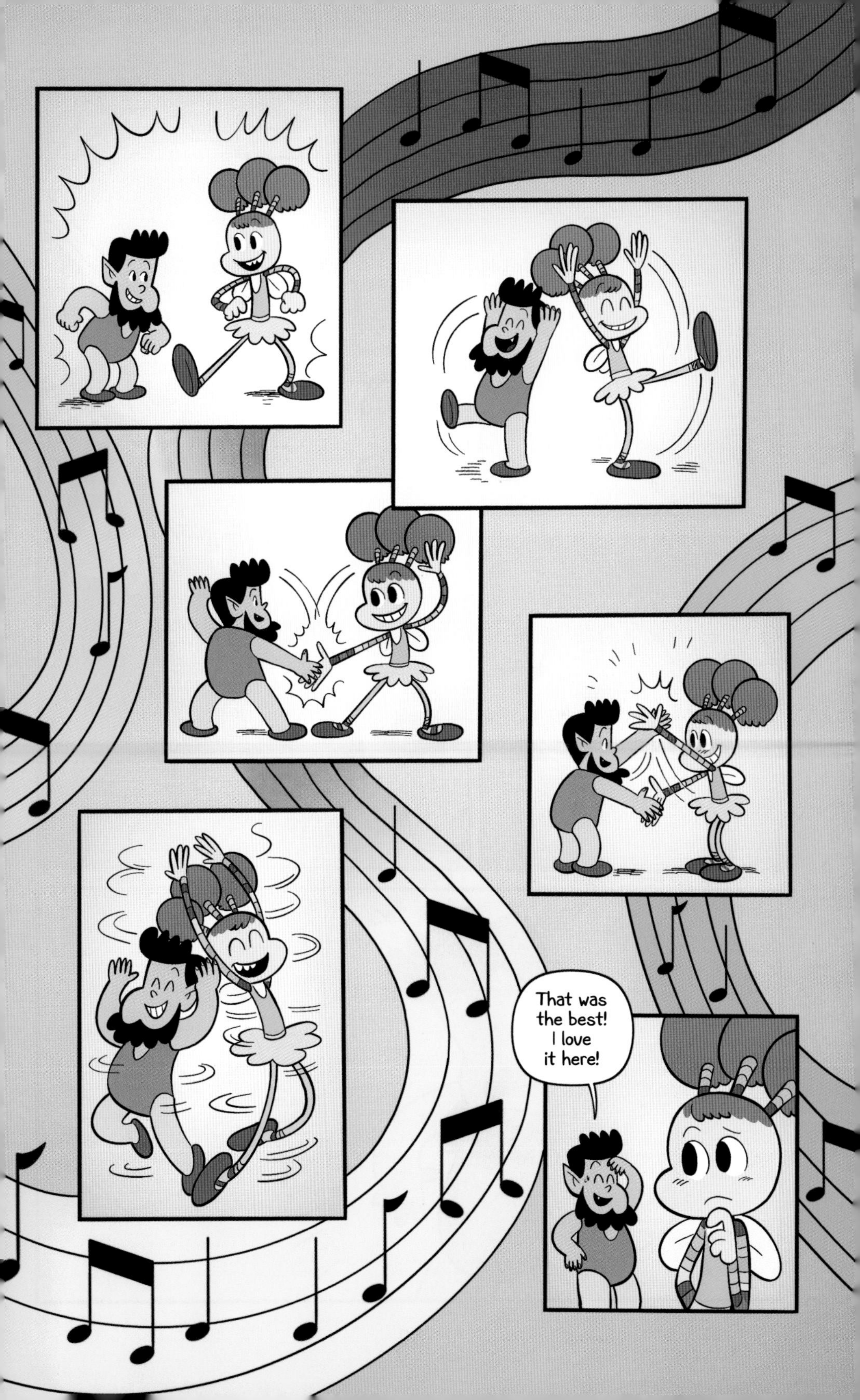
That was the best! I love it here!

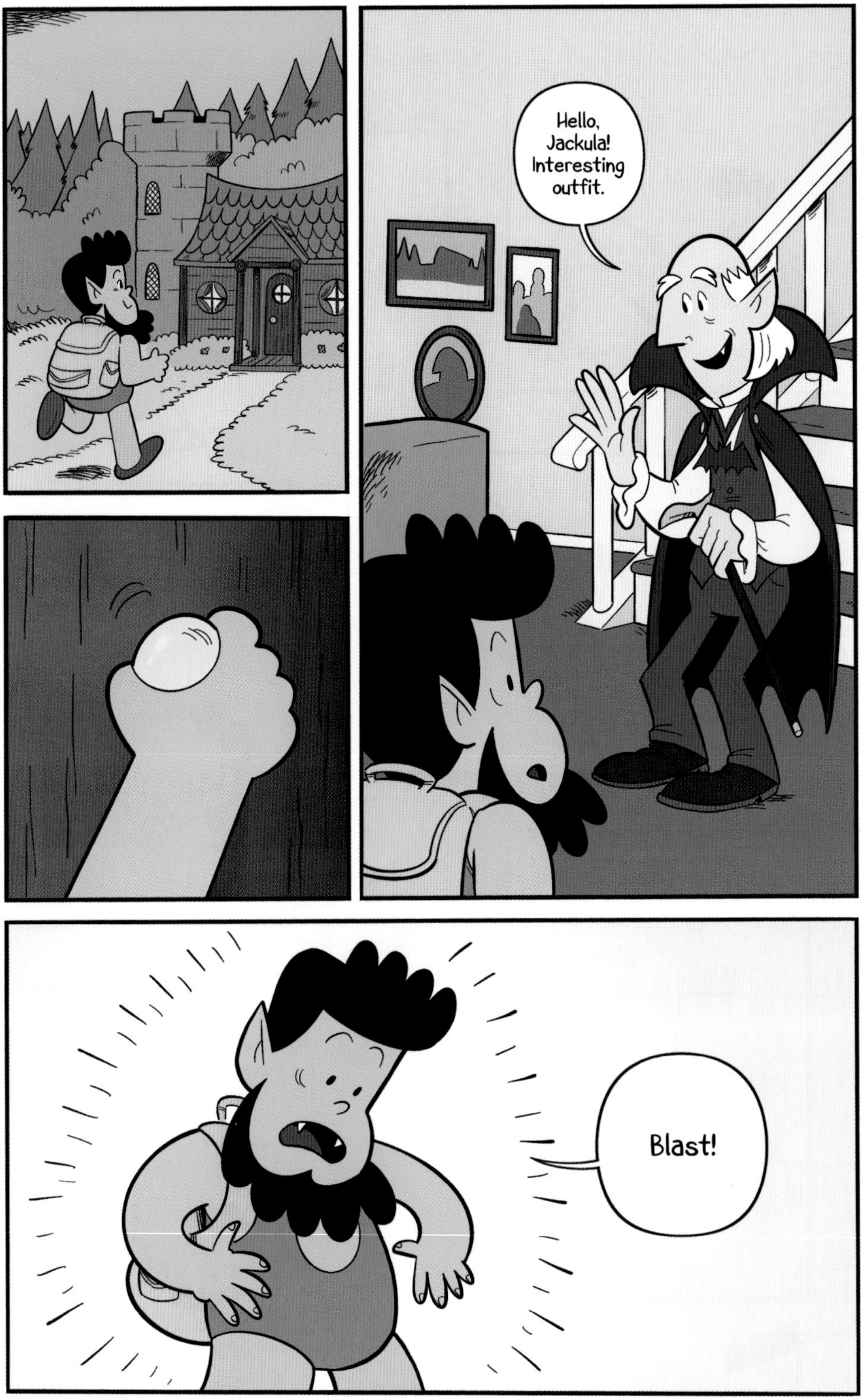
Hello, Jackula! Interesting outfit.
Blast!

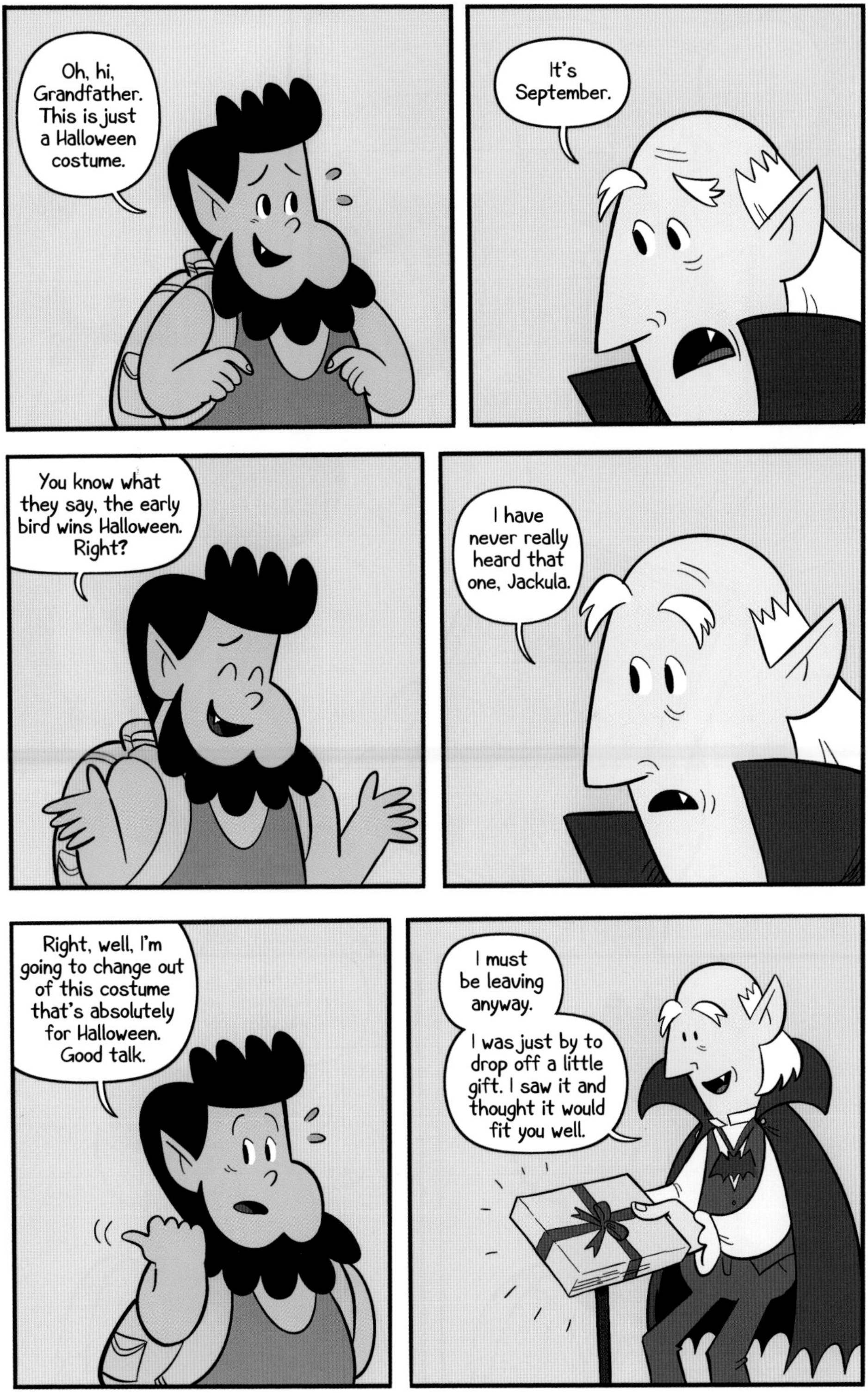
Oh, hi, Grandfather. This is just a Halloween costume.
It's September.
You know what they say, the early bird wins Halloween. Right?
I have never really heard that one, Jackula.
Right, well, I'm going to change out of this costume that's absolutely for Halloween. Good talk.
I must be leaving anyway.
I was just by to drop off a little gift. I saw it and thought it would fit you well.

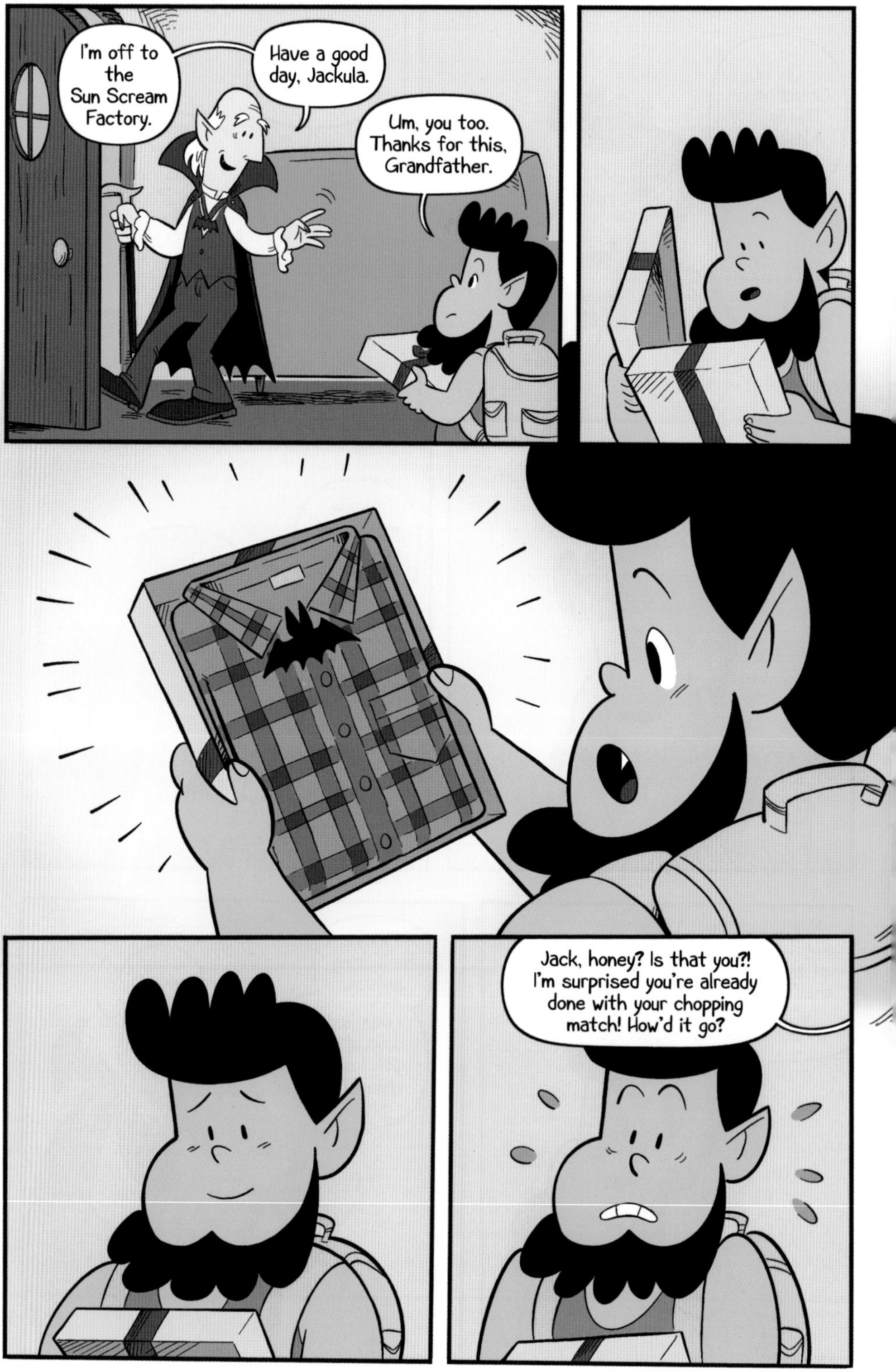
I'm off to the Sun Scream Factory.
Have a good day, Jackula.
Um, you too. Thanks for this, Grandfather.
Jack, honey? Is that you?! I'm surprised you're already done with your chopping match! How'd it go?

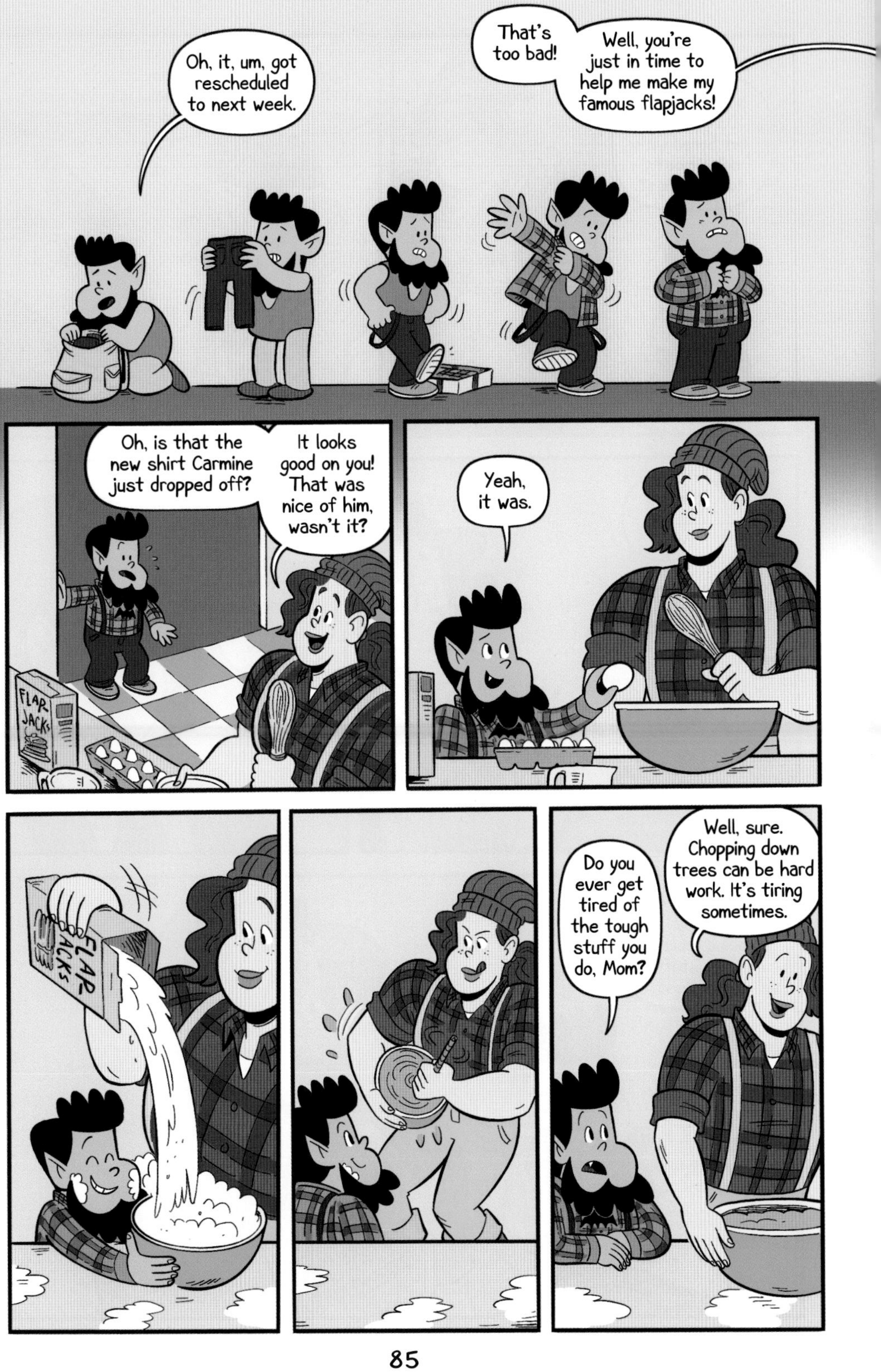
Oh, it, um, got rescheduled to next week.
That's too bad!
Well, you're just in time to help me make my famous flapjacks!
Oh, is that the new shirt Carmine just dropped off?
It looks good on you! That was nice of him, wasn't it?
Yeah, it was.
FLAP-JACKS
FLAP-JACKS
Do you ever get tired of the tough stuff you do, Mom?
Well, sure. Chopping down trees can be hard work. It's tiring sometimes.

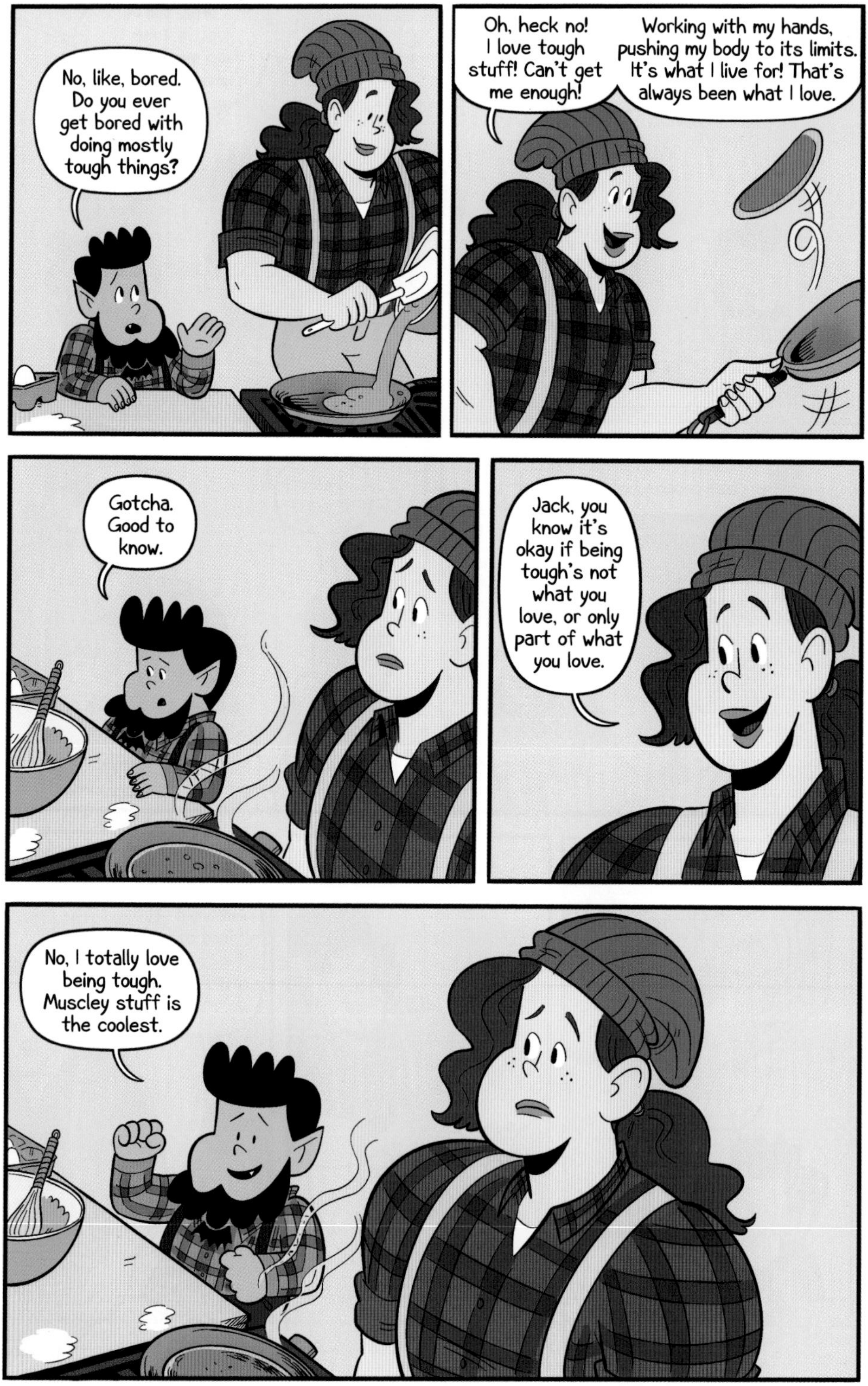
No, like, bored. Do you ever get bored with doing mostly tough things?
Oh, heck no! I love tough stuff! Can't get me enough!
Working with my hands, pushing my body to its limits. It's what I live for! That's always been what I love.
Gotcha. Good to know.
Jack, you know it's okay if being tough's not what you love, or only part of what you love.
No, I totally love being tough. Muscley stuff is the coolest.

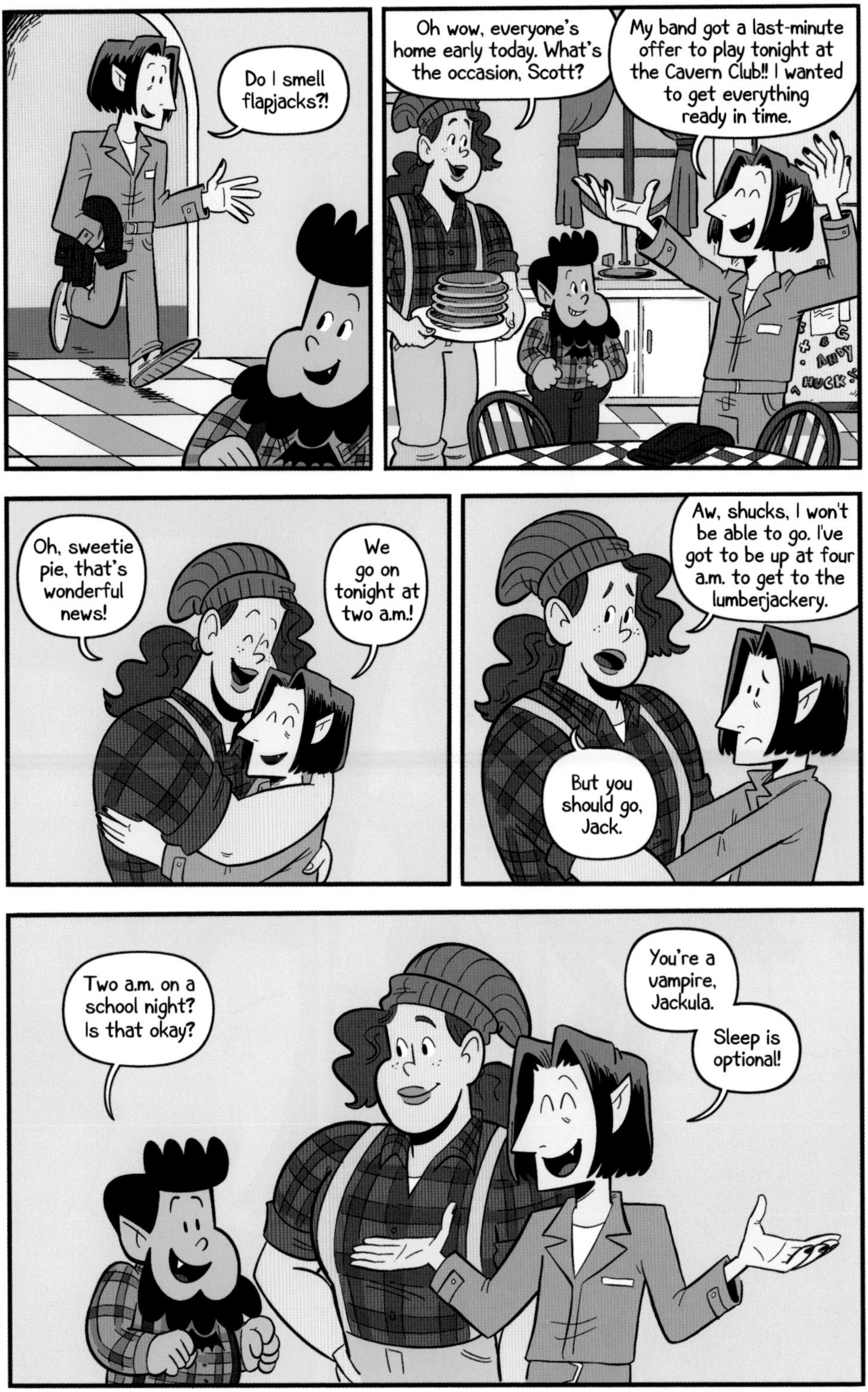
Do I smell flapjacks?!
Oh wow, everyone's home early today. What's the occasion, Scott?
My band got a last-minute offer to play tonight at the Cavern Club!! I wanted to get everything ready in time.
Oh, sweetie pie, that's wonderful news!
We go on tonight at two a.m.!
Aw, shucks, I won't be able to go. I've got to be up at four a.m. to get to the lumberjackery.
But you should go, Jack.
Two a.m. on a school night? Is that okay?
You're a vampire, Jackula.
Sleep is optional!

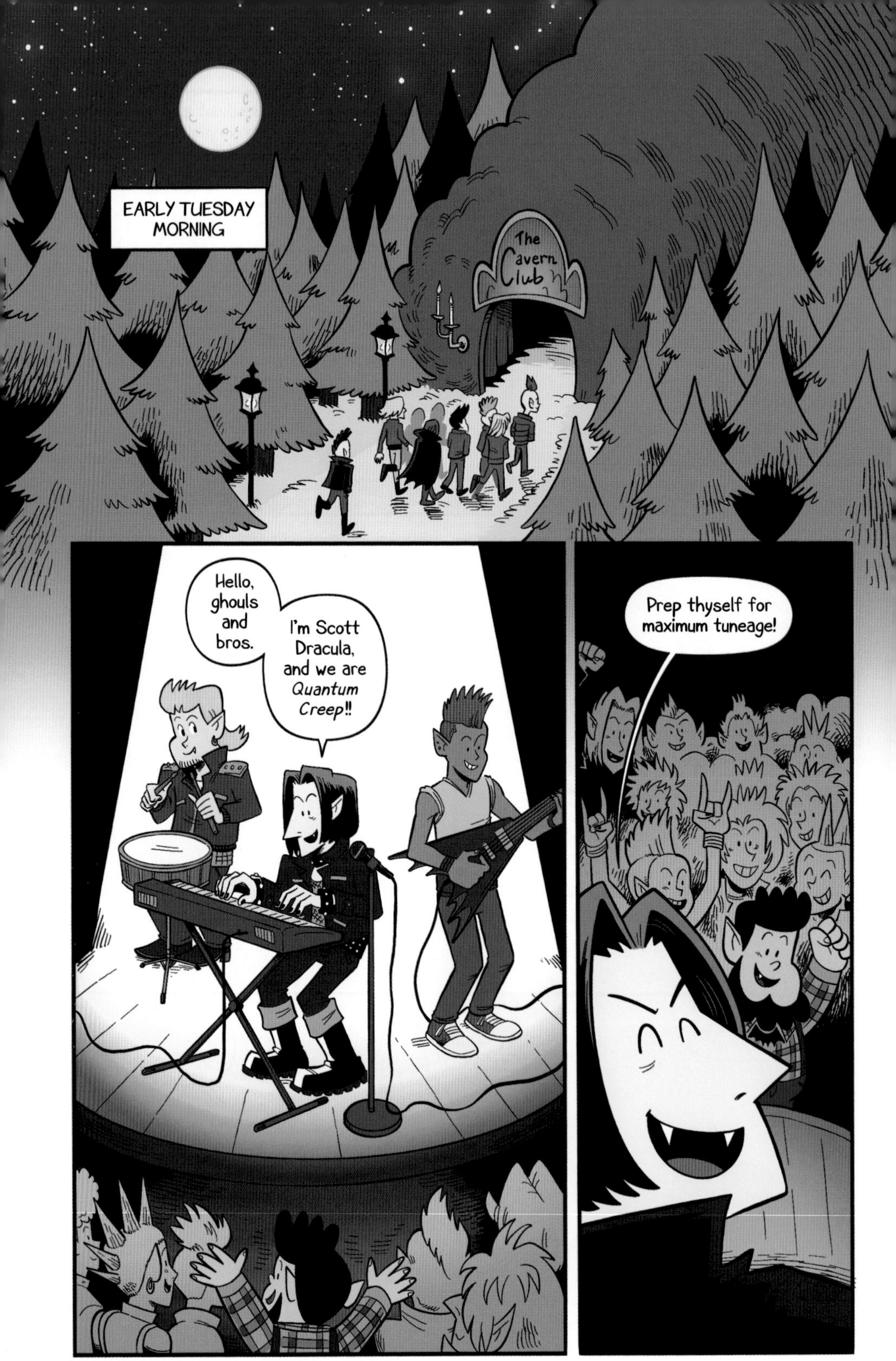

EARLY TUESDAY MORNING
The Cavern Club
Hello, ghouls and bros.
I'm Scott Dracula, and we are *Quantum Creep*!!
Prep thyself for maximum tuneage!

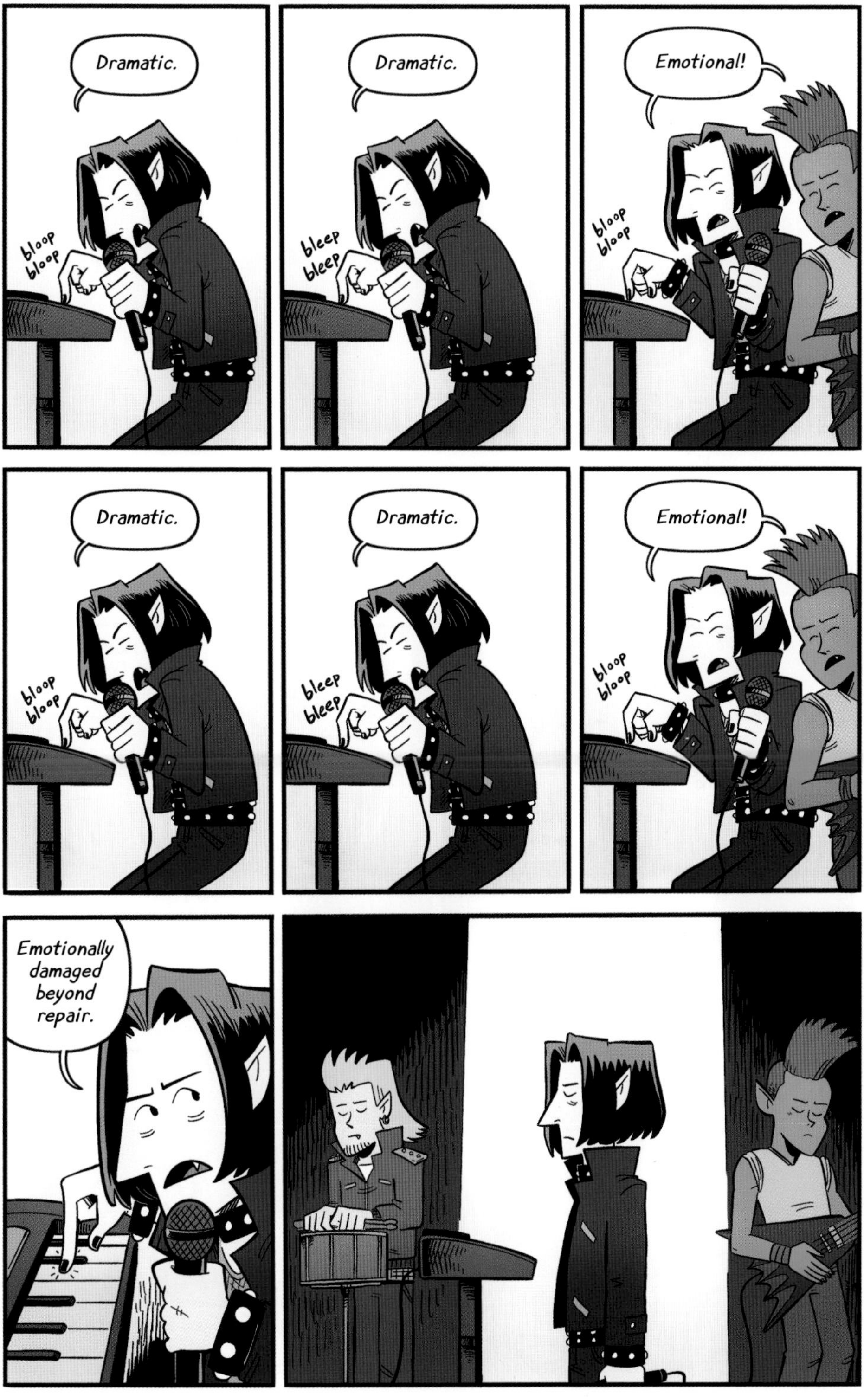
Dramatic.
bloop bloop
Dramatic.
bleep bleep
Emotional!
bloop bloop
Dramatic.
bloop bloop
Dramatic.
bleep bleep
Emotional!
bloop bloop
Emotionally damaged beyond repair.

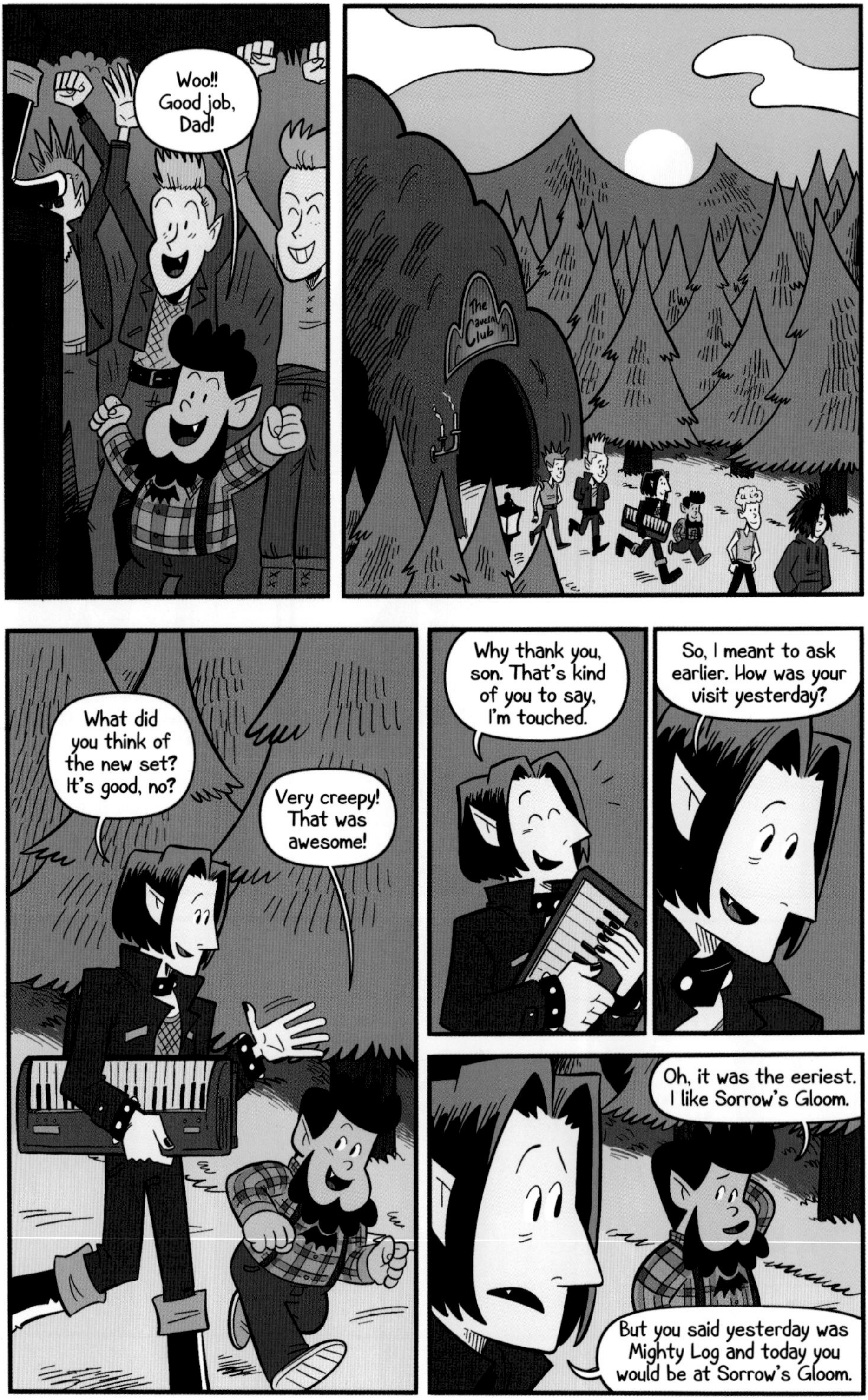
Woo!! Good job, Dad!
What did you think of the new set? It's good, no?
Very creepy! That was awesome!
Why thank you, son. That's kind of you to say, I'm touched.
So, I meant to ask earlier. How was your visit yesterday?
Oh, it was the eeriest. I like Sorrow's Gloom.
But you said yesterday was Mighty Log and today you would be at Sorrow's Gloom.

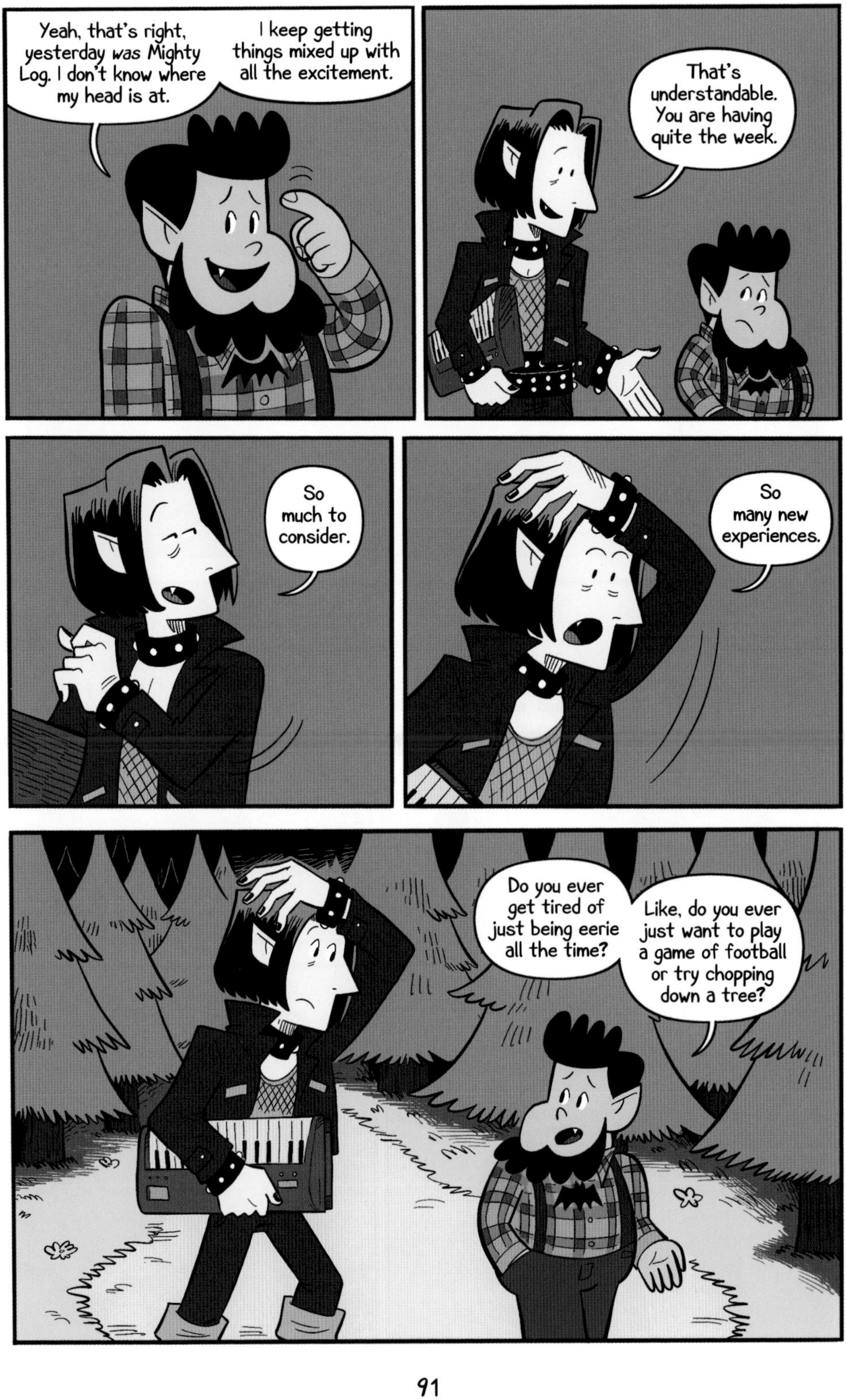
Yeah, that's right, yesterday *was* Mighty Log. I don't know where my head is at.
I keep getting things mixed up with all the excitement.
That's understandable. You are having quite the week.
So much to consider.
So many new experiences.
Do you ever get tired of just being eerie all the time?
Like, do you ever just want to play a game of football or try chopping down a tree?

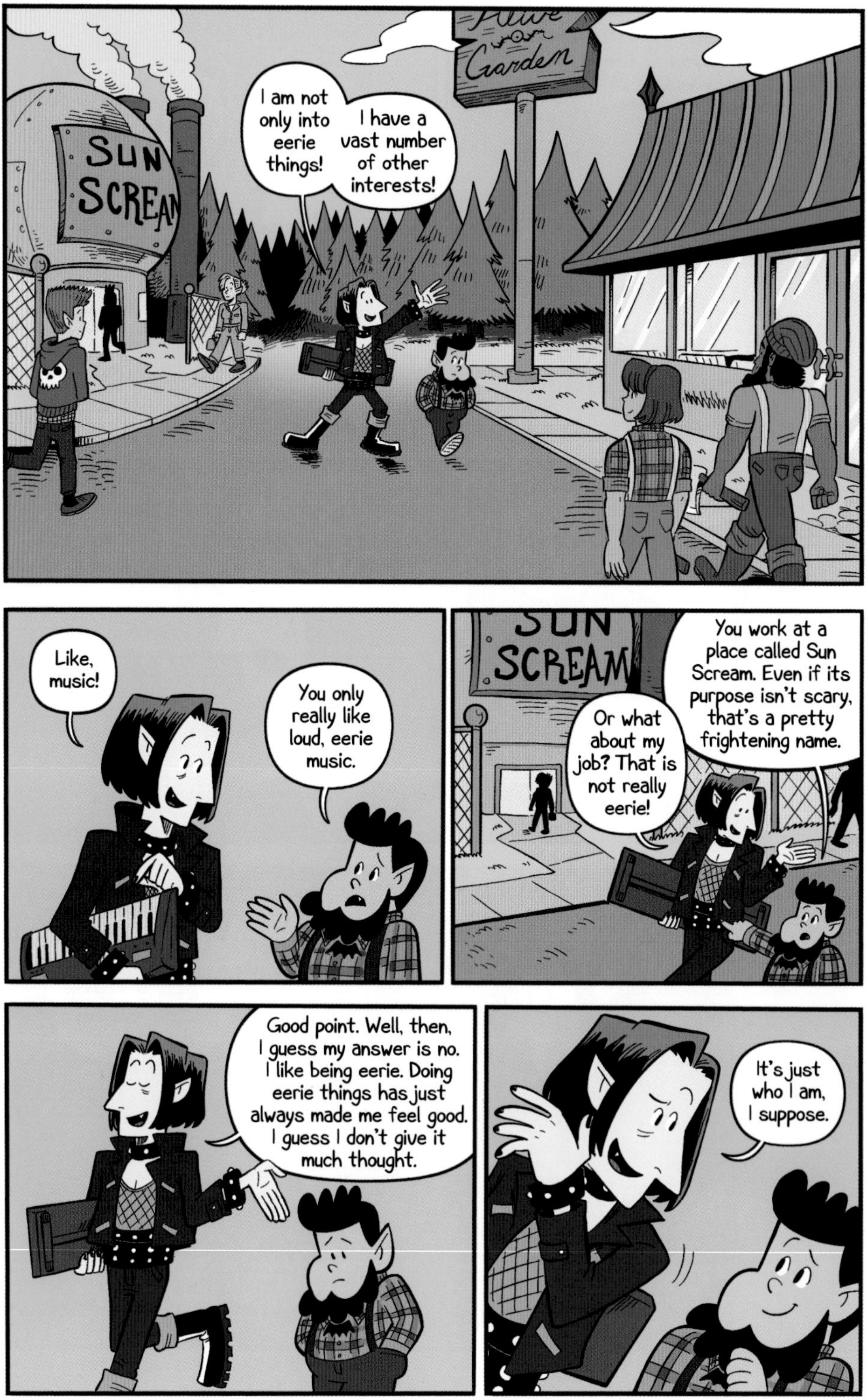
Garden
SUN SCREAM
I am not only into eerie things!
I have a vast number of other interests!
Like, music!
You only really like loud, eerie music.
SUN SCREAM
Or what about my job? That is not really eerie!
You work at a place called Sun Scream. Even if its purpose isn't scary, that's a pretty frightening name.
Good point. Well, then, I guess my answer is no. I like being eerie. Doing eerie things has just always made me feel good. I guess I don't give it much thought.
It's just who I am, I suppose.

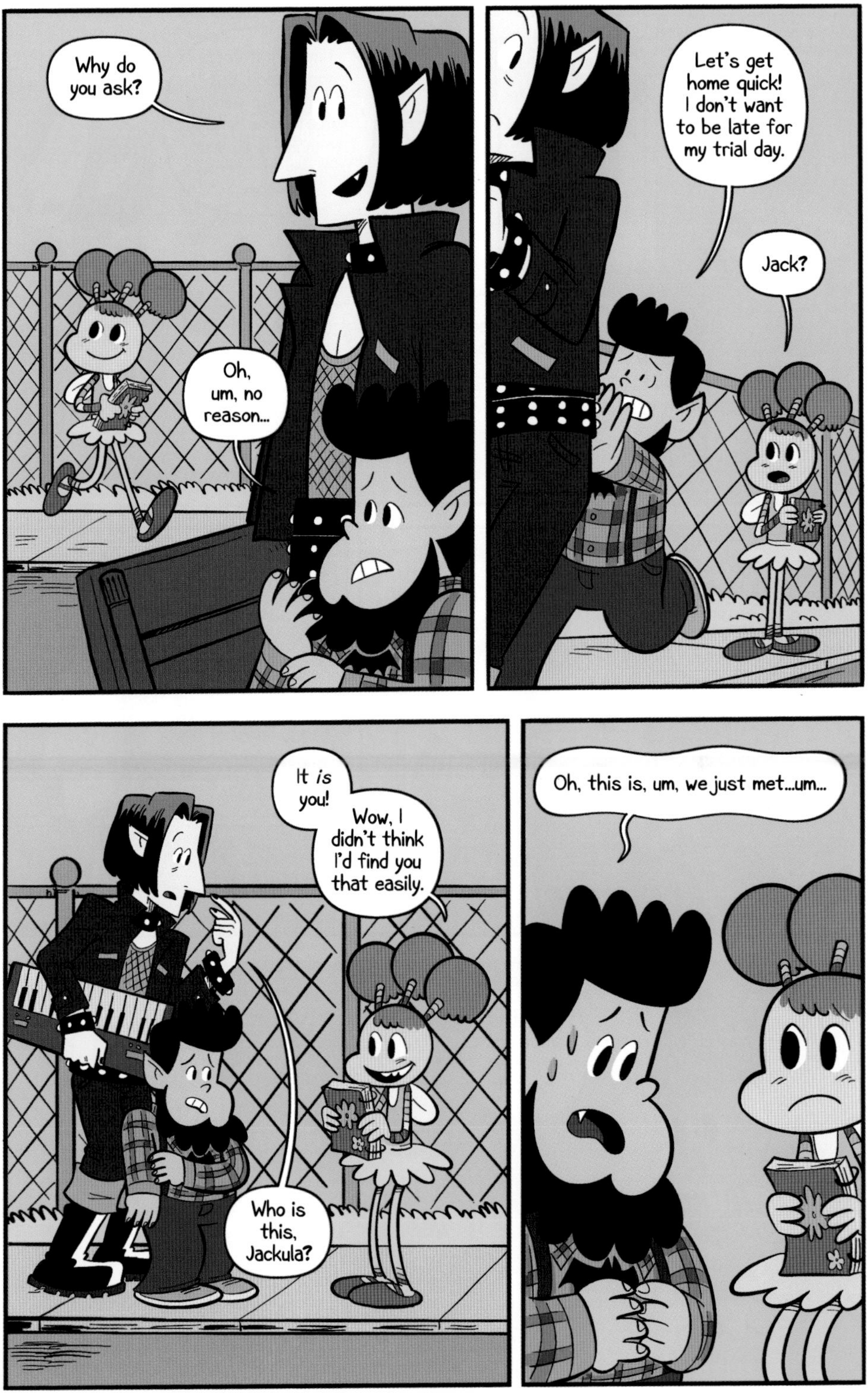
Why do you ask?
Oh, um, no reason...
Let's get home quick! I don't want to be late for my trial day.
Jack?
It *is* you!
Wow, I didn't think I'd find you that easily.
Who is this, Jackula?
Oh, this is, um, we just met...um...

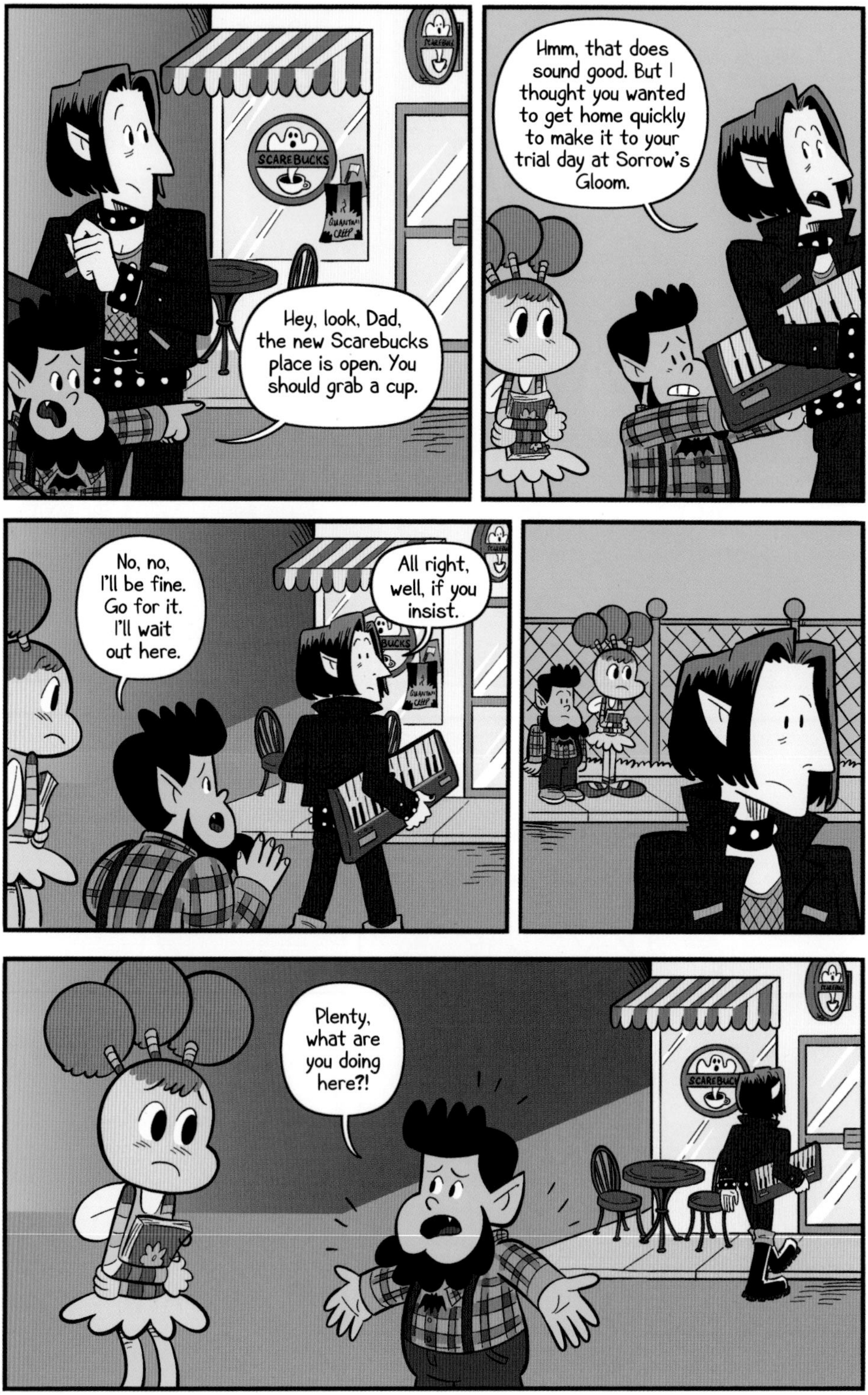
SCAREBUCKS
QUANTUM CREEP
Hey, look, Dad, the new Scarebucks place is open. You should grab a cup.
Hmm, that does sound good. But I thought you wanted to get home quickly to make it to your trial day at Sorrow's Gloom.
No, no, I'll be fine. Go for it. I'll wait out here.
All right, well, if you insist.
Plenty, what are you doing here?!

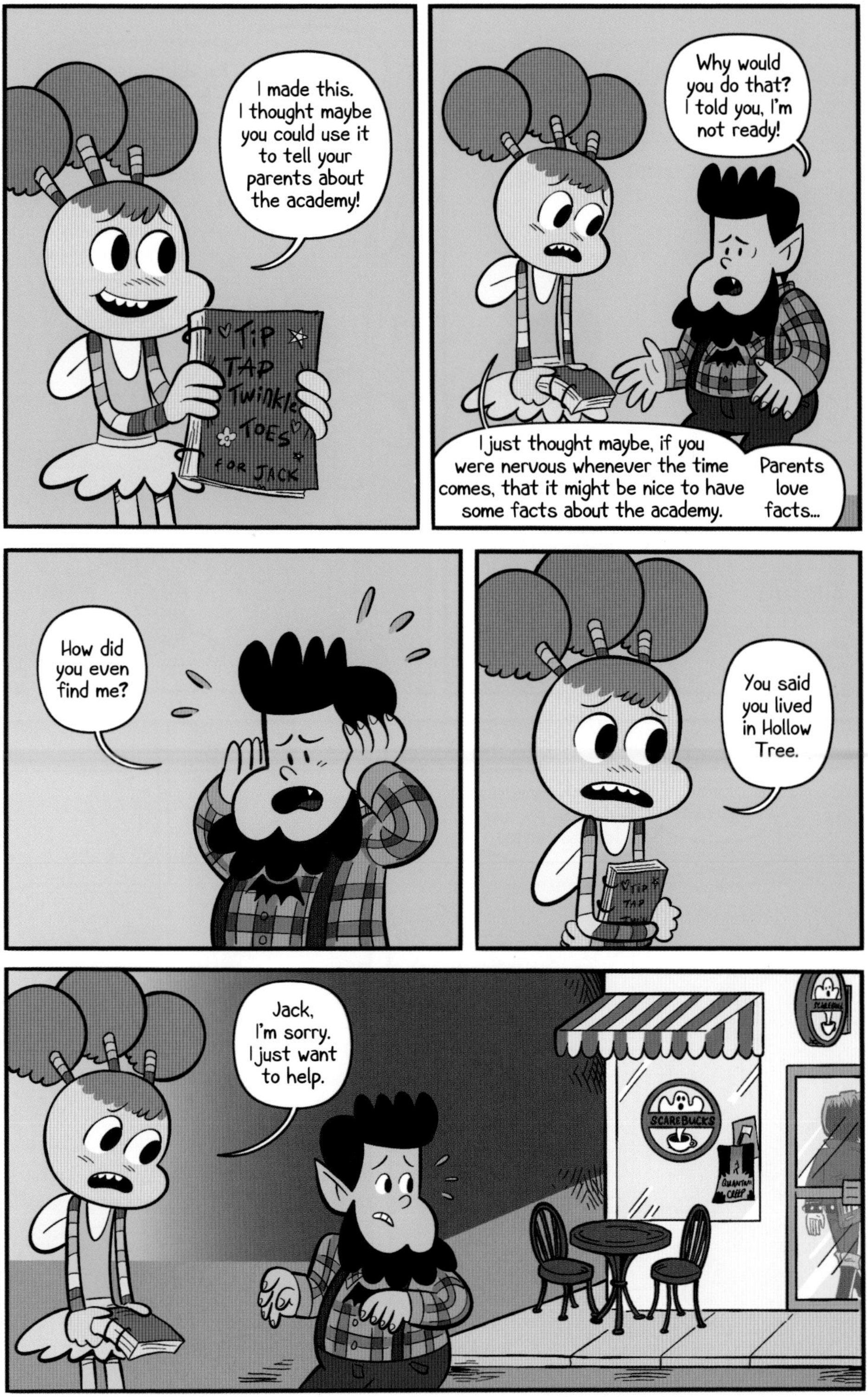
I made this. I thought maybe you could use it to tell your parents about the academy!
TIP TAP Twinkle TOES FOR JACK
Why would you do that? I told you, I'm not ready!
I just thought maybe, if you were nervous whenever the time comes, that it might be nice to have some facts about the academy.
Parents love facts...
How did you even find me?
You said you lived in Hollow Tree.
Jack, I'm sorry. I just want to help.
SCAREBUCKS

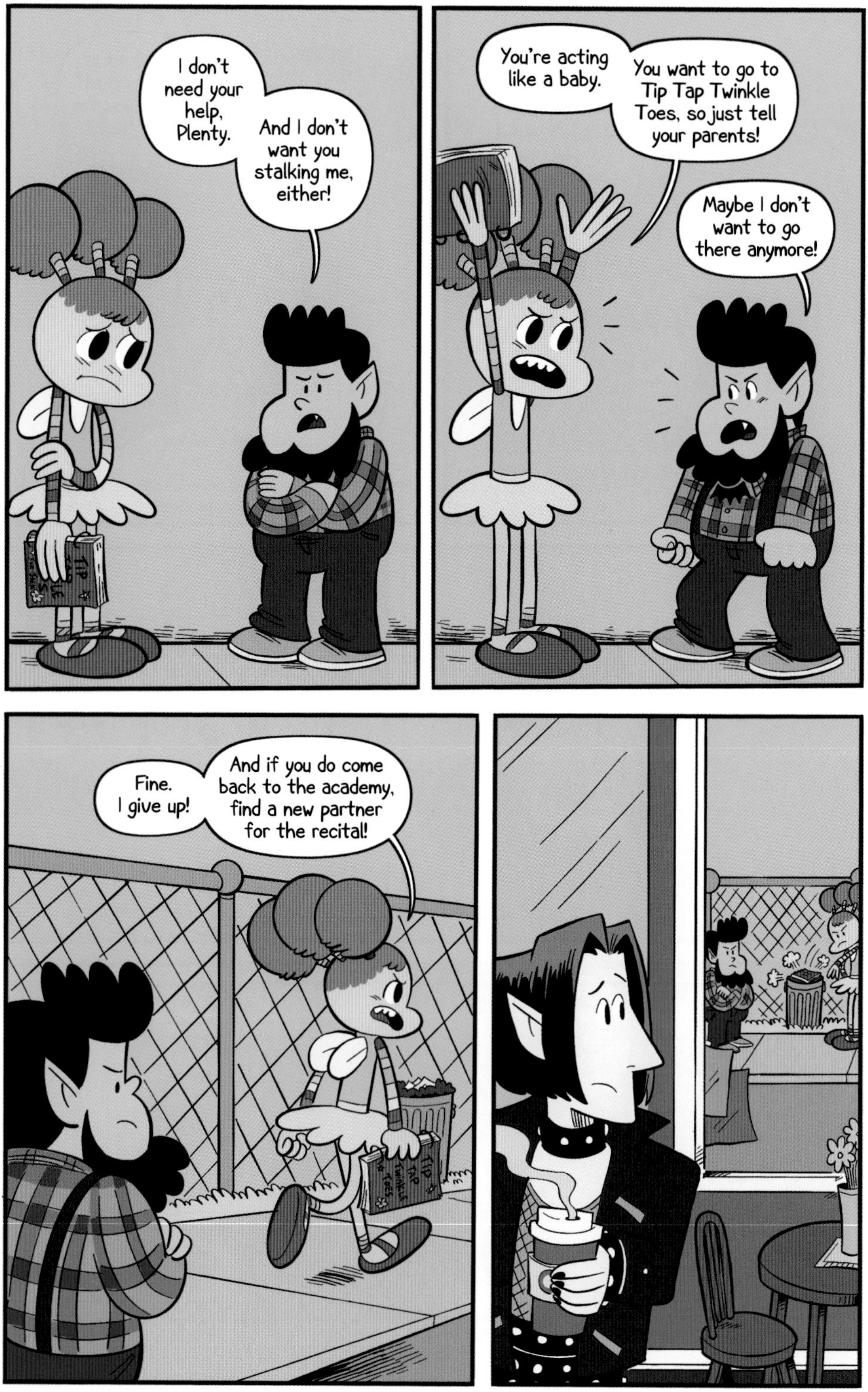
I don't need your help, Plenty.
And I don't want you stalking me, either!
You're acting like a baby.
You want to go to Tip Tap Twinkle Toes, so just tell your parents!
Maybe I don't want to go there anymore!
Fine. I give up!
And if you do come back to the academy, find a new partner for the recital!
TIP TAP TWINKLE TOES

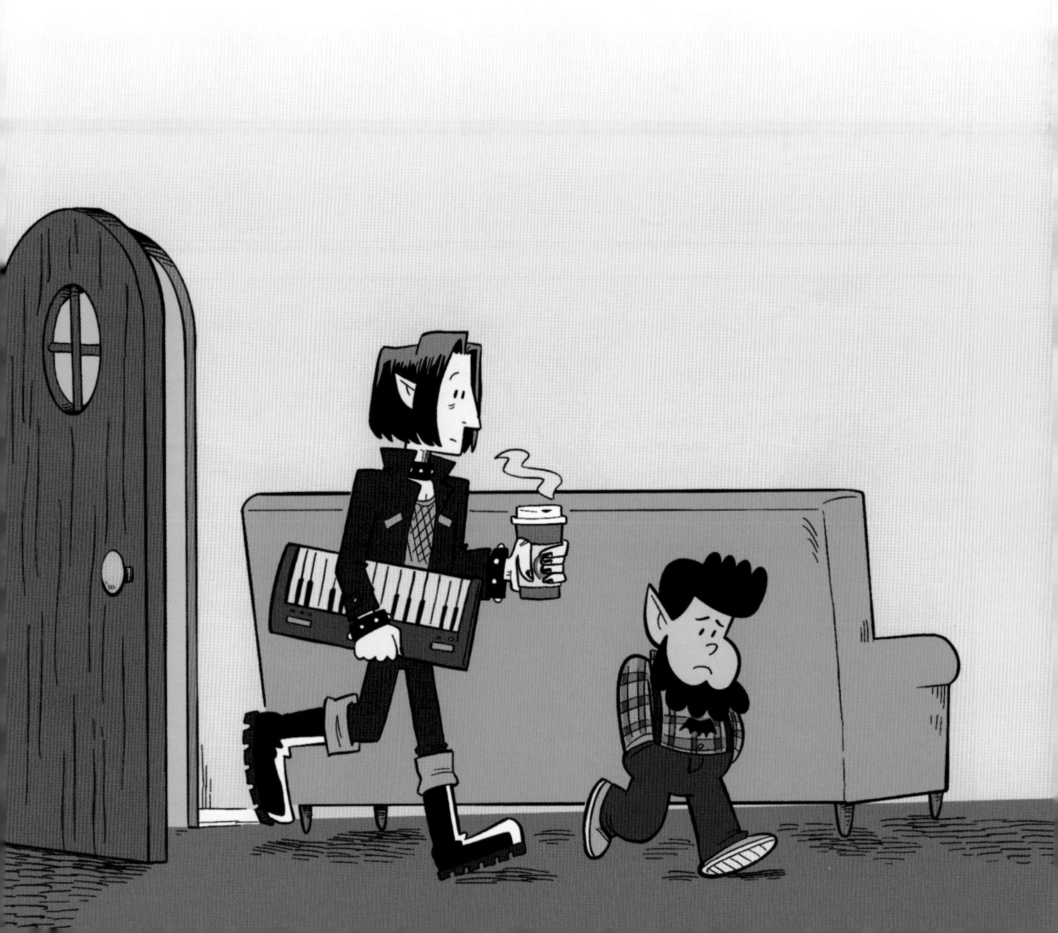

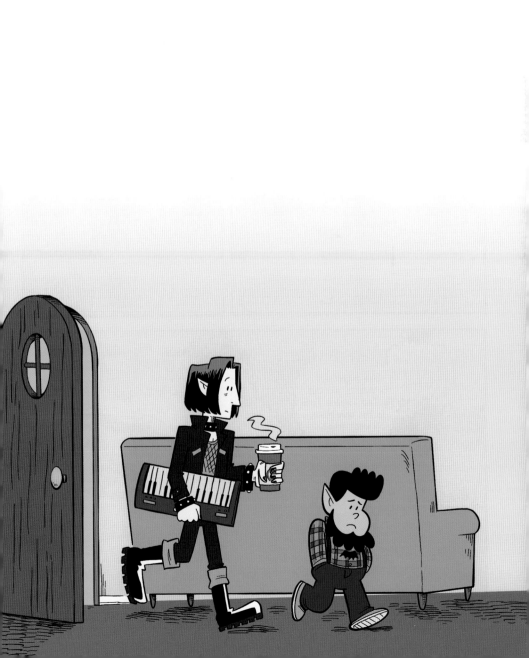

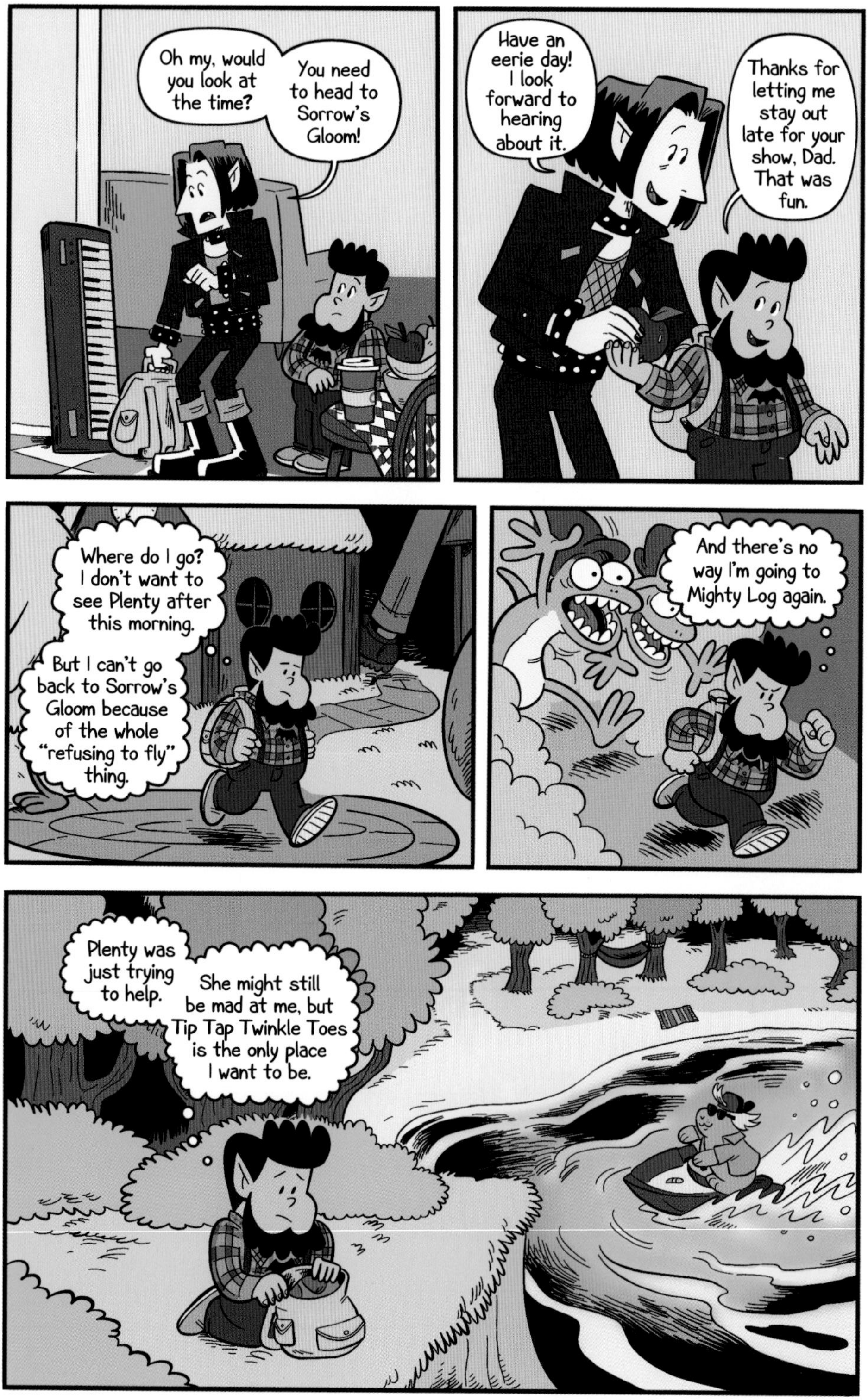
Oh my, would you look at the time?
You need to head to Sorrow's Gloom!
Have an eerie day! I look forward to hearing about it.
Thanks for letting me stay out late for your show, Dad. That was fun.
Where do I go? I don't want to see Plenty after this morning.
But I can't go back to Sorrow's Gloom because of the whole "refusing to fly" thing.
And there's no way I'm going to Mighty Log again.
Plenty was just trying to help.
She might still be mad at me, but Tip Tap Twinkle Toes is the only place I want to be.

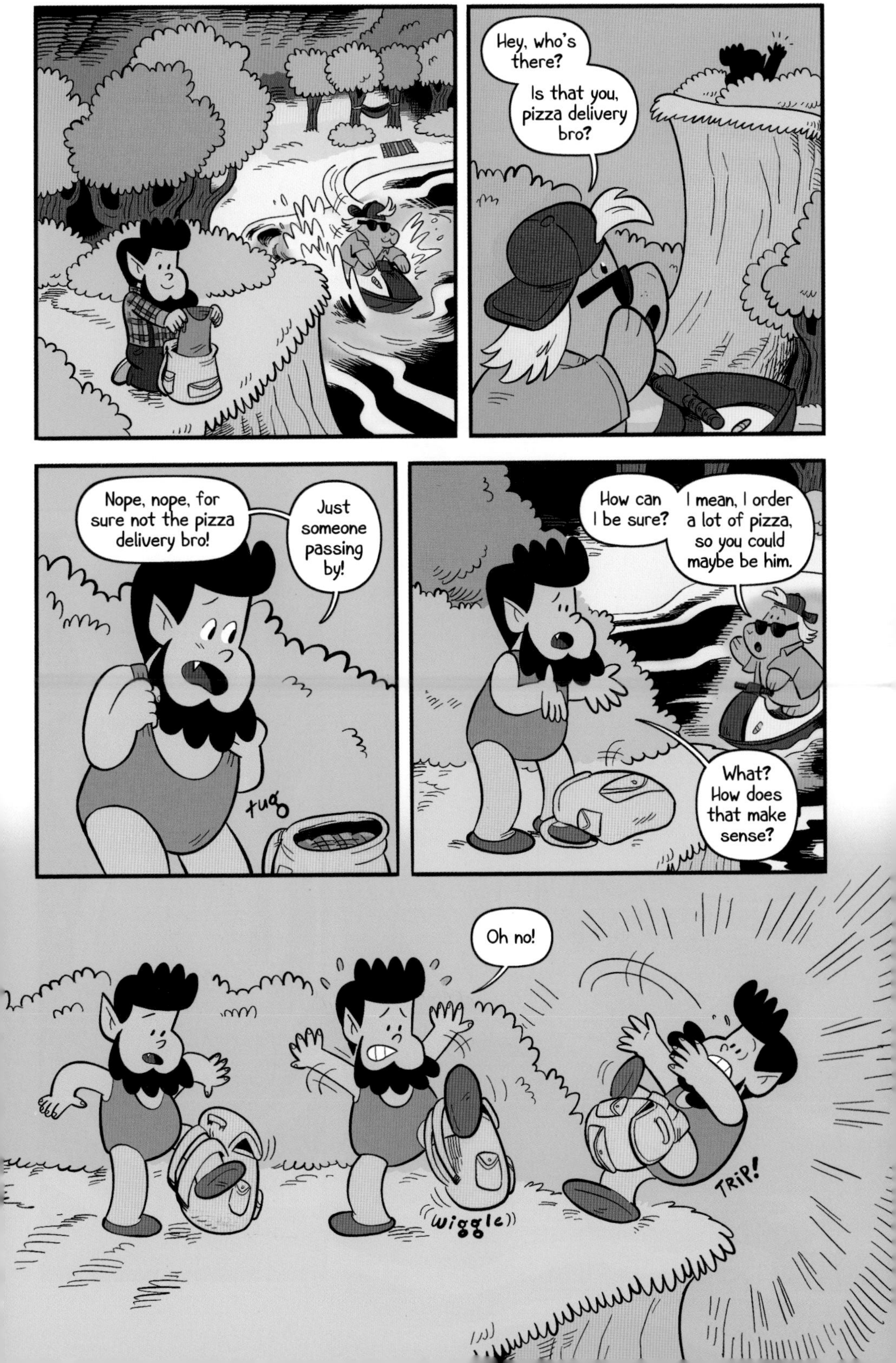
Hey, who's there?
Is that you, pizza delivery bro?
Nope, nope, for sure not the pizza delivery bro!
Just someone passing by!
tug
How can I be sure?
I mean, I order a lot of pizza, so you could maybe be him.
What? How does that make sense?
Oh no!
wiggle
TRIP!

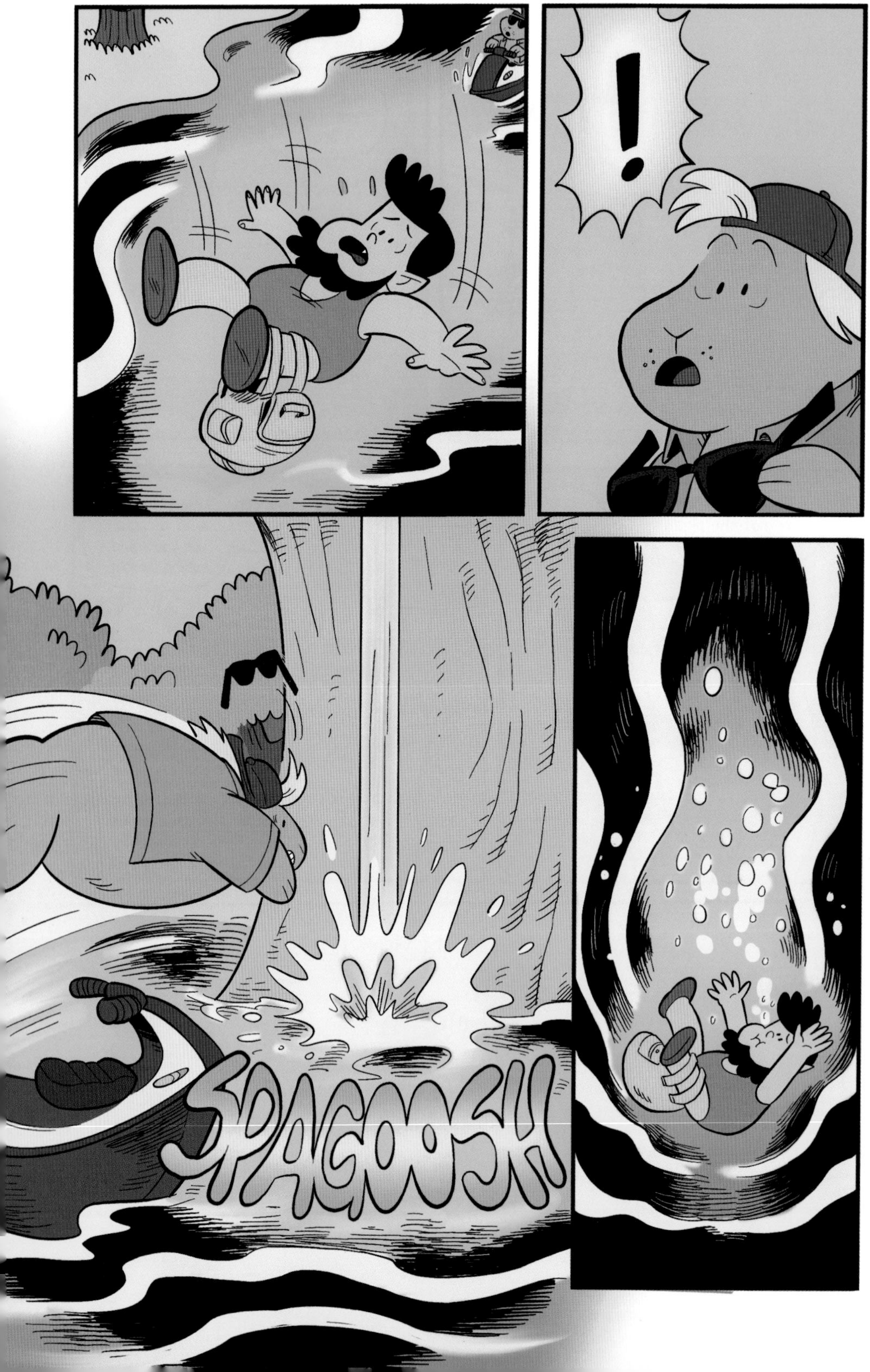
!
SPAGOOSH

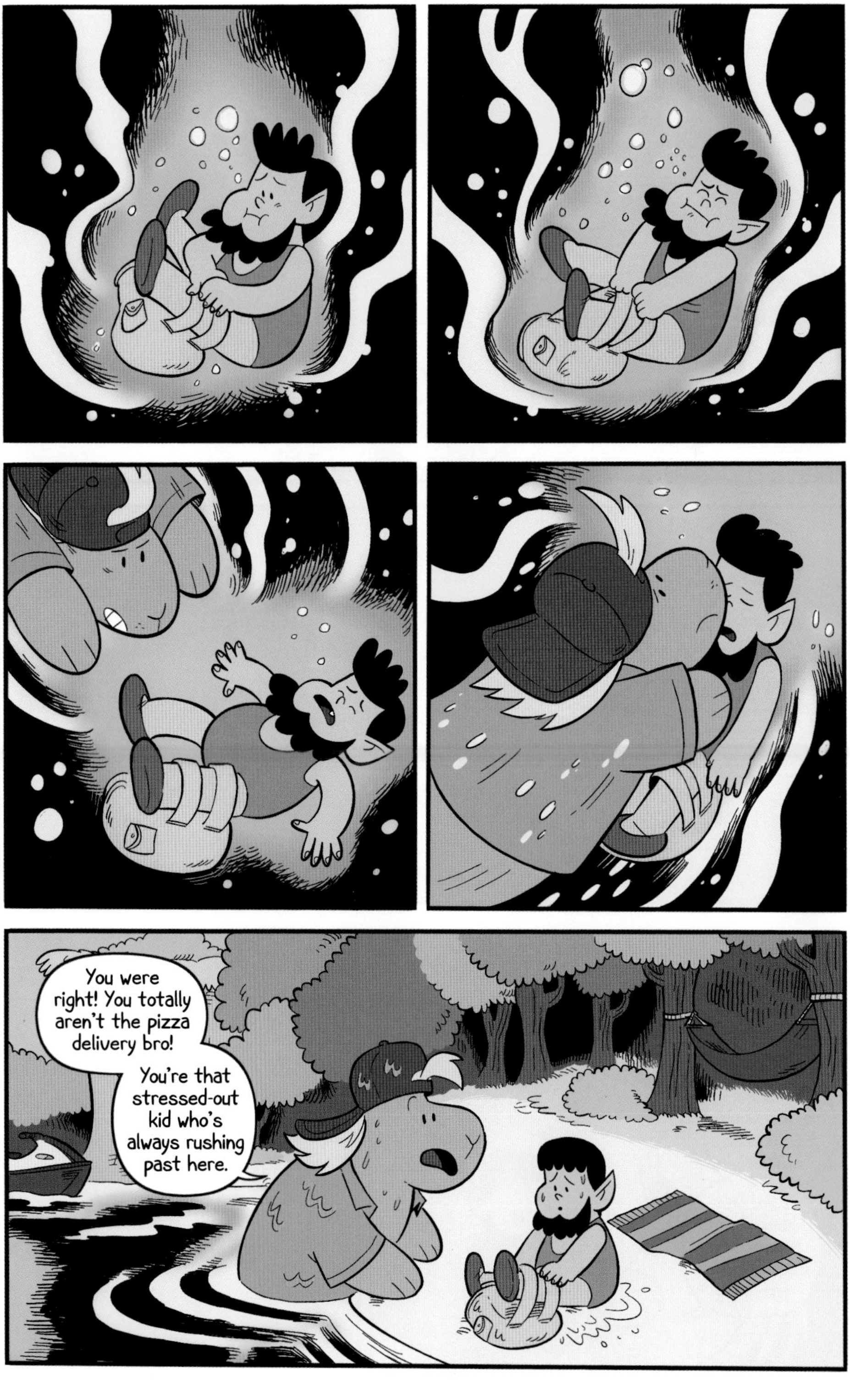
You were right! You totally aren't the pizza delivery bro!
You're that stressed-out kid who's always rushing past here.

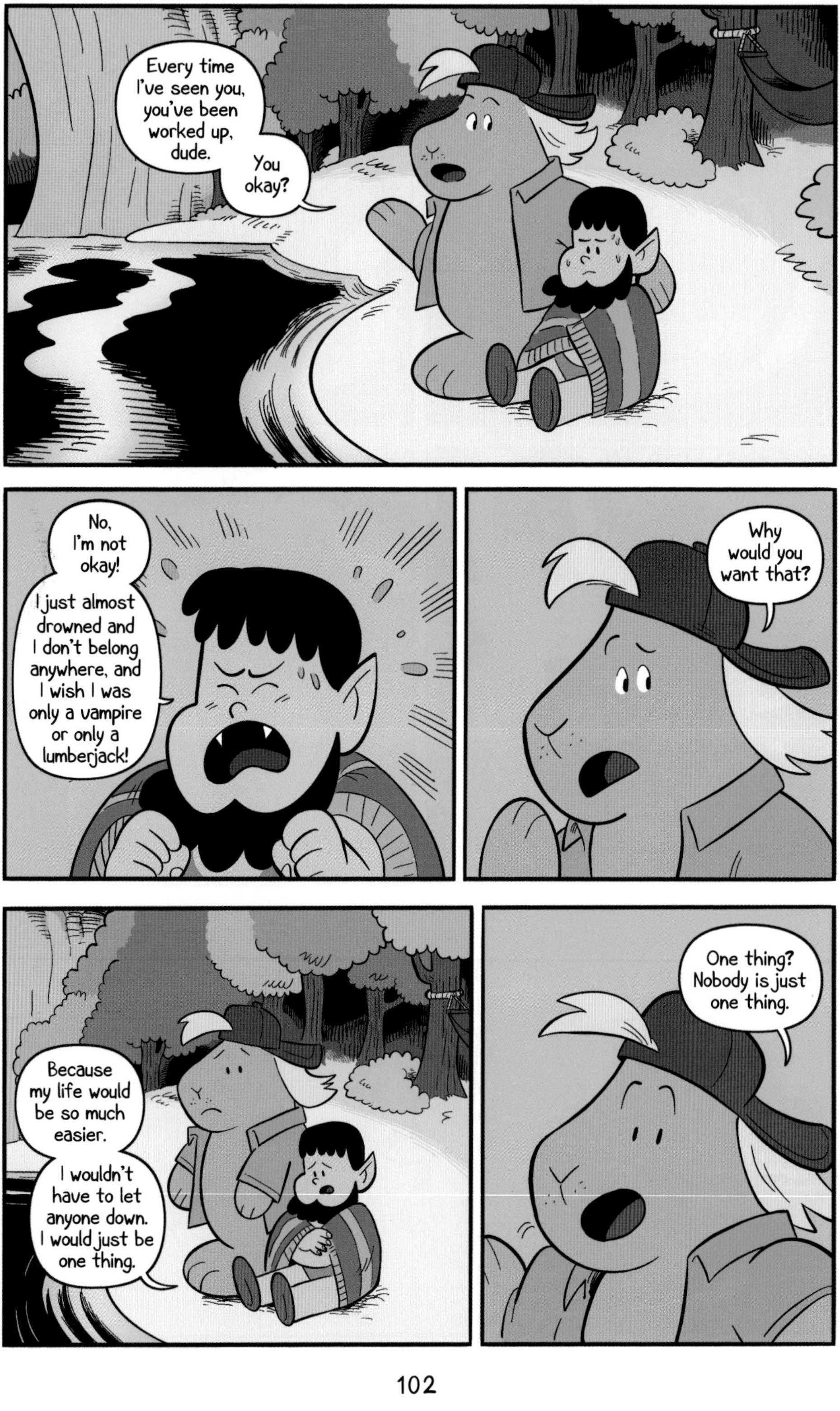
Every time I've seen you, you've been worked up, dude.
You okay?
No, I'm not okay!
I just almost drowned and I don't belong anywhere, and I wish I was only a vampire or only a lumberjack!
Why would you want that?
Because my life would be so much easier.
I wouldn't have to let anyone down. I would just be one thing.
One thing? Nobody is just one thing.

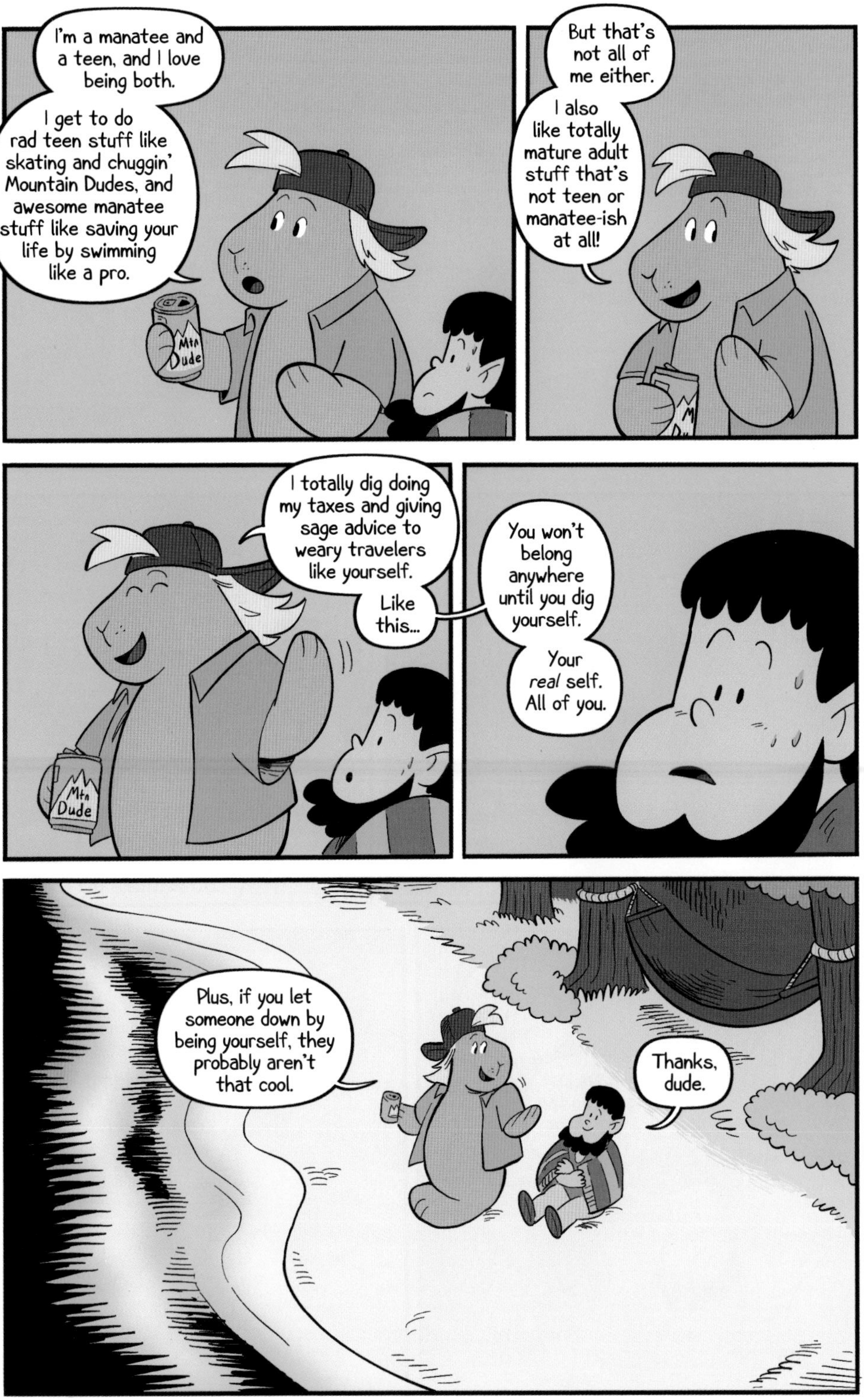
I'm a manatee and a teen, and I love being both.
I get to do rad teen stuff like skating and chuggin' Mountain Dudes, and awesome manatee stuff like saving your life by swimming like a pro.
Mtn Dude
But that's not all of me either.
I also like totally mature adult stuff that's not teen or manatee-ish at all!
I totally dig doing my taxes and giving sage advice to weary travelers like yourself.
Like this...
Mtn Dude
You won't belong anywhere until you dig yourself.
Your *real* self. All of you.
Plus, if you let someone down by being yourself, they probably aren't that cool.
Thanks, dude.

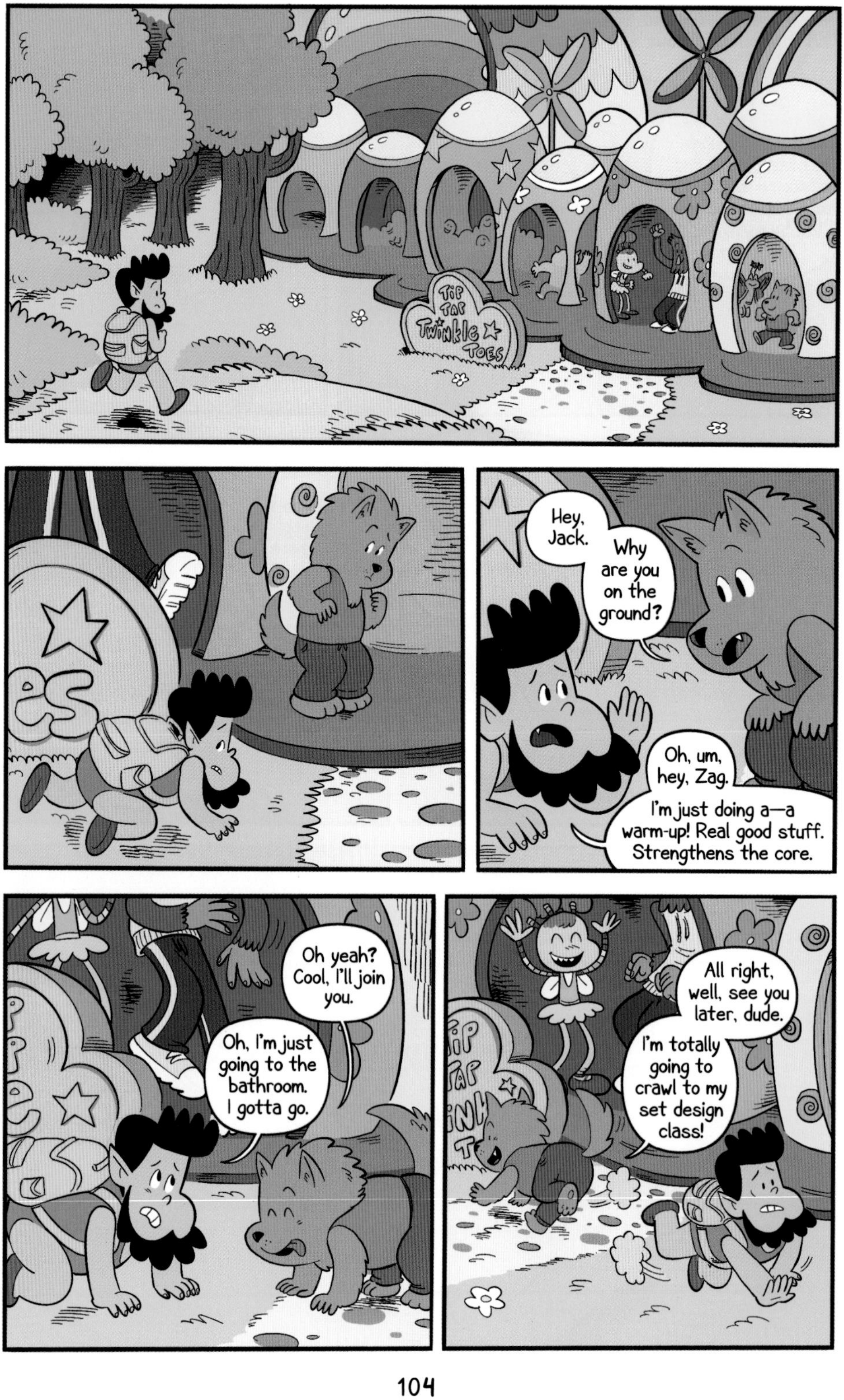
TIP TAP TWINKLE TOES
Hey, Jack.
Why are you on the ground?
Oh, um, hey, Zag.
I'm just doing a—a warm-up! Real good stuff. Strengthens the core.
Oh yeah? Cool, I'll join you.
Oh, I'm just going to the bathroom. I gotta go.
All right, well, see you later, dude.
I'm totally going to crawl to my set design class!

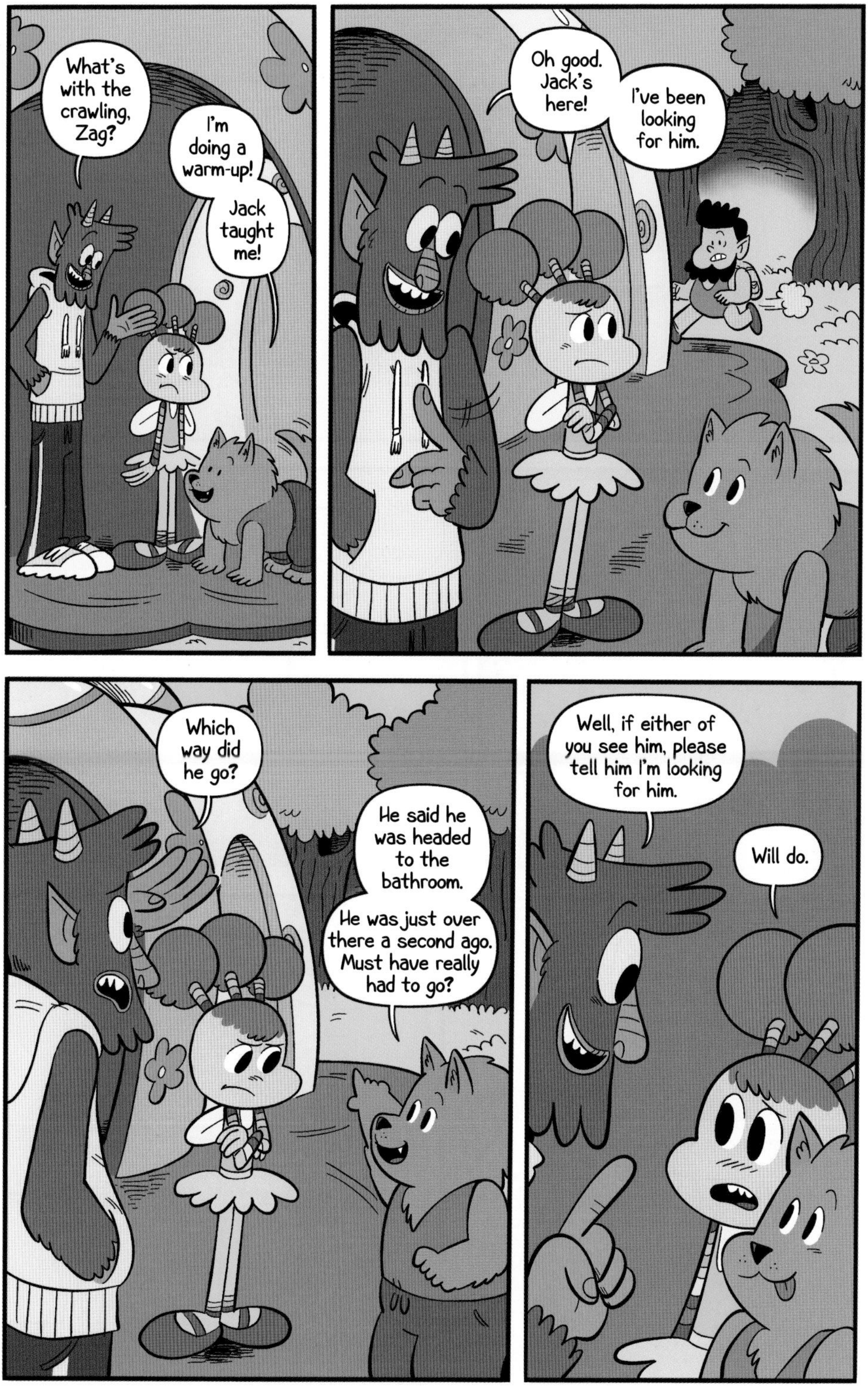
What's with the crawling, Zag?
I'm doing a warm-up!
Jack taught me!
Oh good. Jack's here!
I've been looking for him.
Which way did he go?
He said he was headed to the bathroom.
He was just over there a second ago. Must have really had to go?
Well, if either of you see him, please tell him I'm looking for him.
Will do.

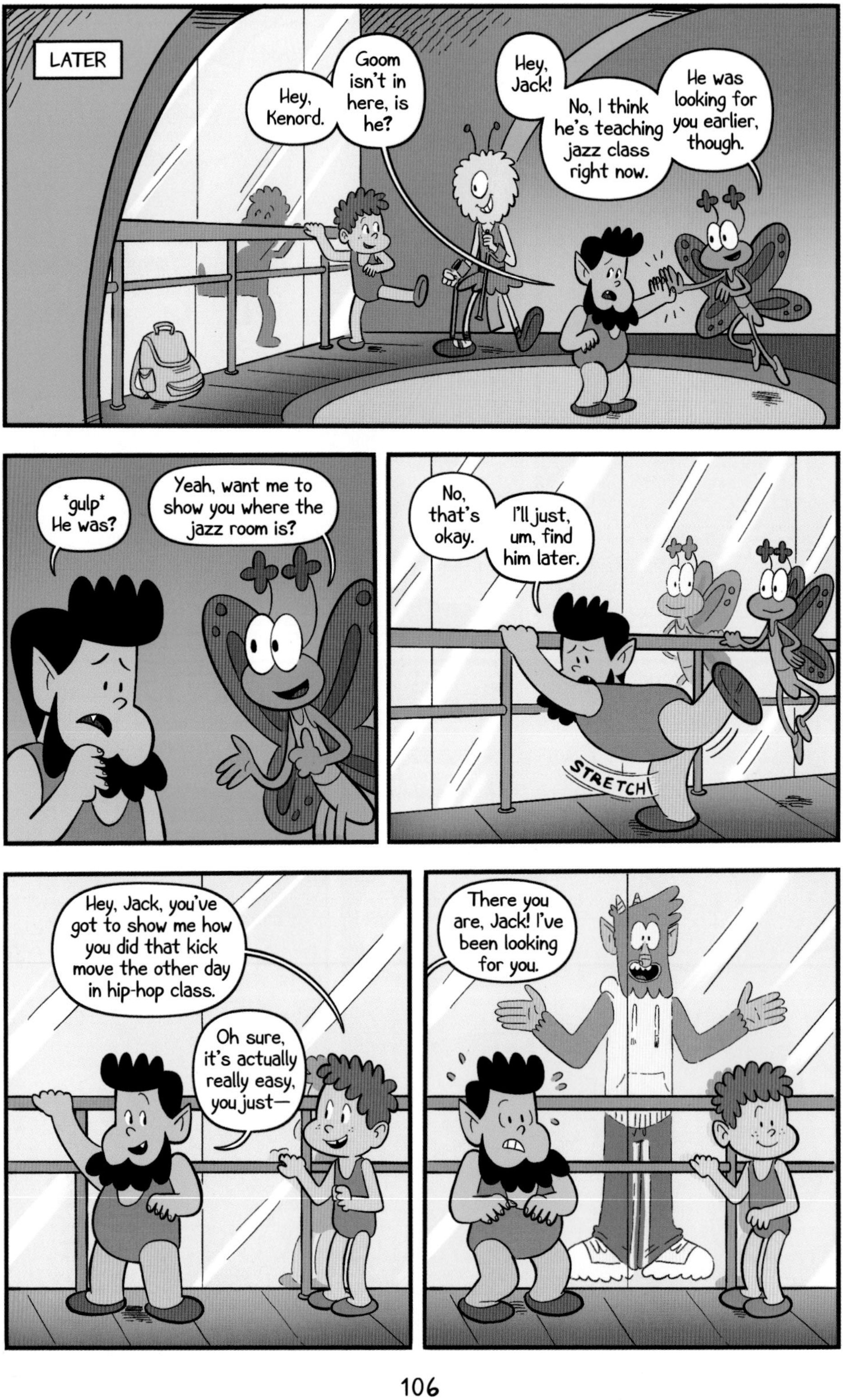
LATER
Hey, Kenord.
Goom isn't in here, is he?
Hey, Jack!
No, I think he's teaching jazz class right now.
He was looking for you earlier, though.
gulp He was?
Yeah, want me to show you where the jazz room is?
No, that's okay.
I'll just, um, find him later.
STRETCH
Hey, Jack, you've got to show me how you did that kick move the other day in hip-hop class.
Oh sure, it's actually really easy, you just—
There you are, Jack! I've been looking for you.

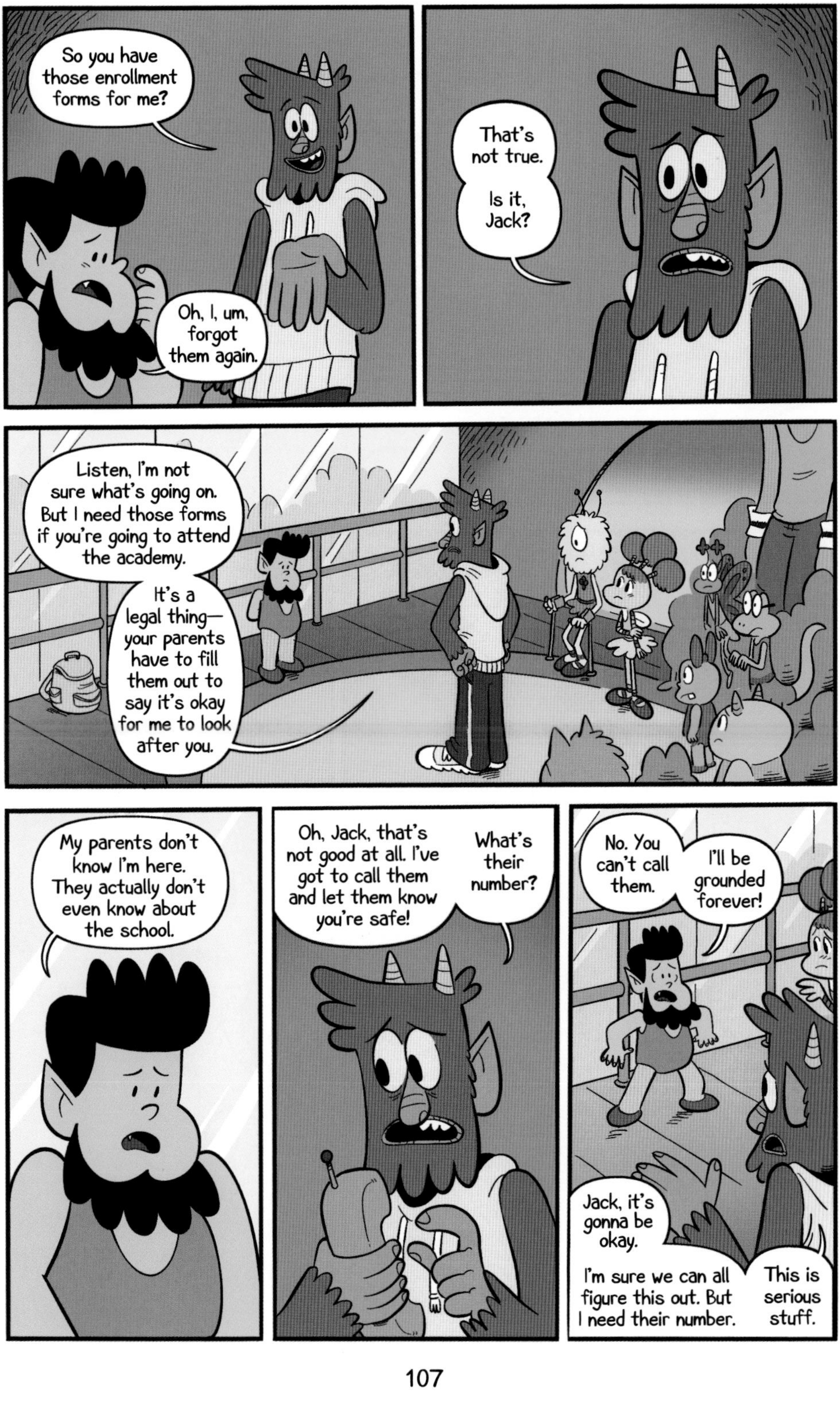

So you have those enrollment forms for me?
Oh, I, um, forgot them again.
That's not true.
Is it, Jack?
Listen, I'm not sure what's going on. But I need those forms if you're going to attend the academy.
It's a legal thing— your parents have to fill them out to say it's okay for me to look after you.
My parents don't know I'm here. They actually don't even know about the school.
Oh, Jack, that's not good at all. I've got to call them and let them know you're safe!
What's their number?
No. You can't call them.
I'll be grounded forever!
Jack, it's gonna be okay.
I'm sure we can all figure this out. But I need their number.
This is serious stuff.

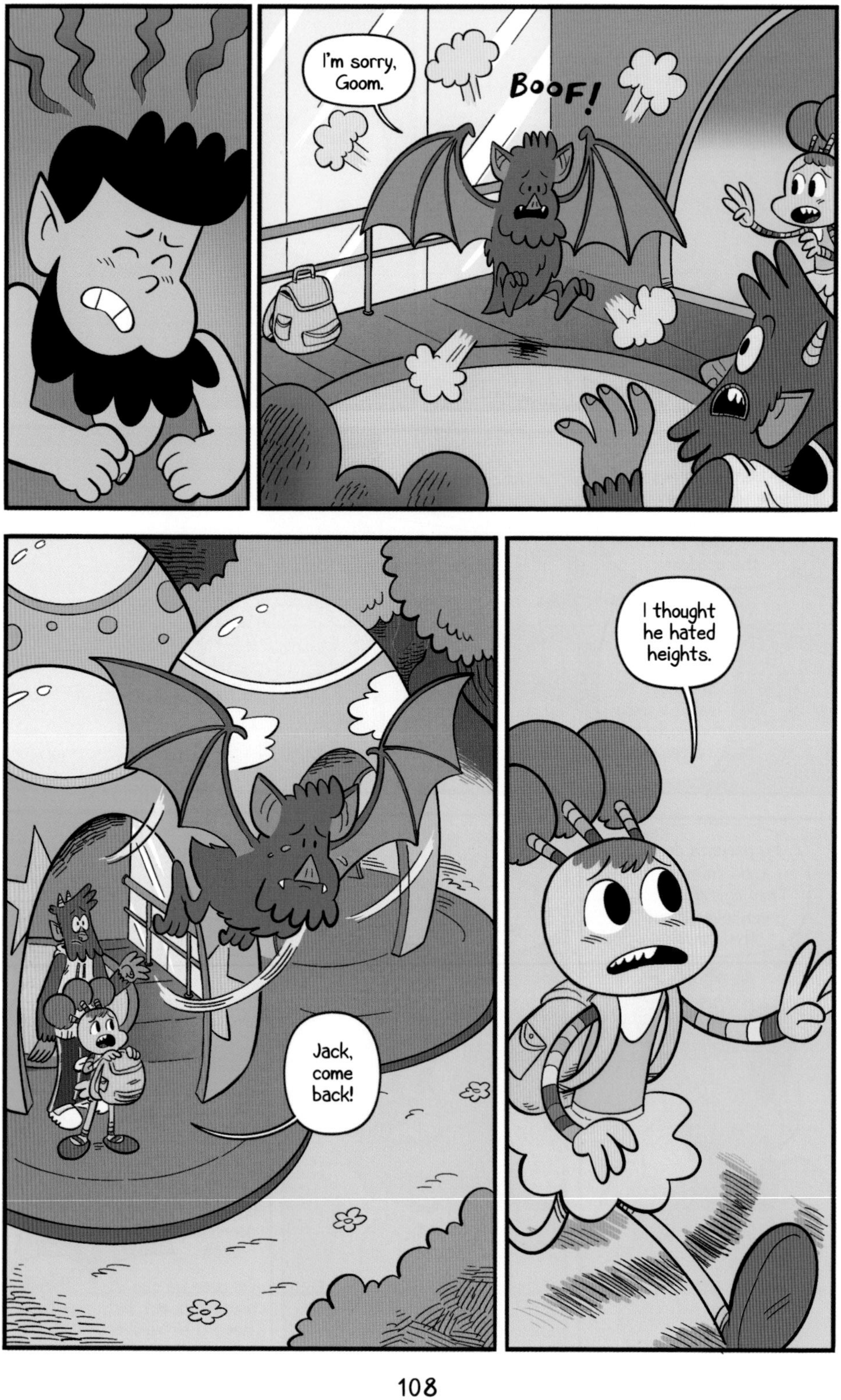
I'm sorry, Goom.
BOOF!
Jack, come back!
I thought he hated heights.

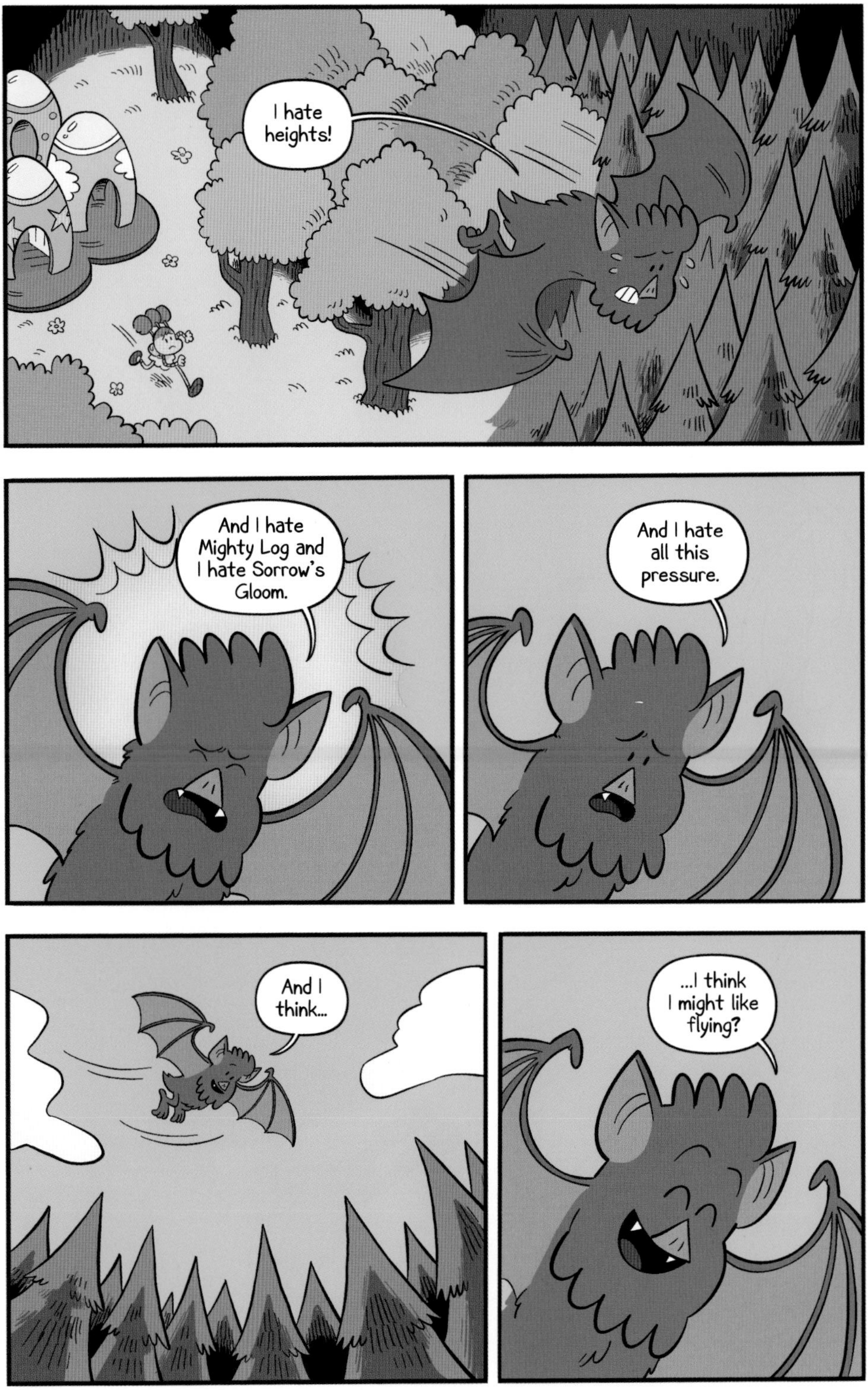
I hate heights!
And I hate Mighty Log and I hate Sorrow's Gloom.
And I hate all this pressure.
And I think...
...I think I might like flying?

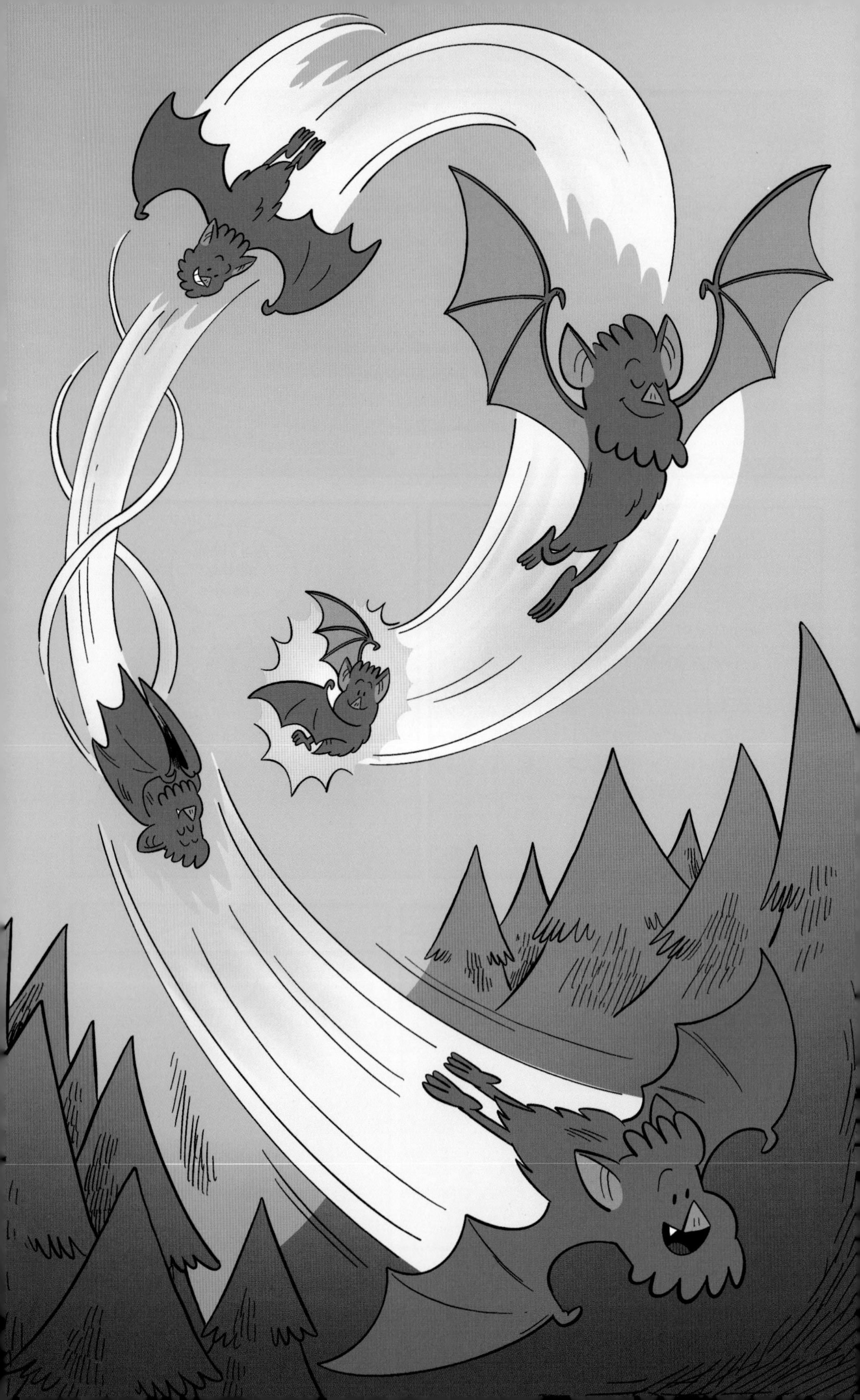

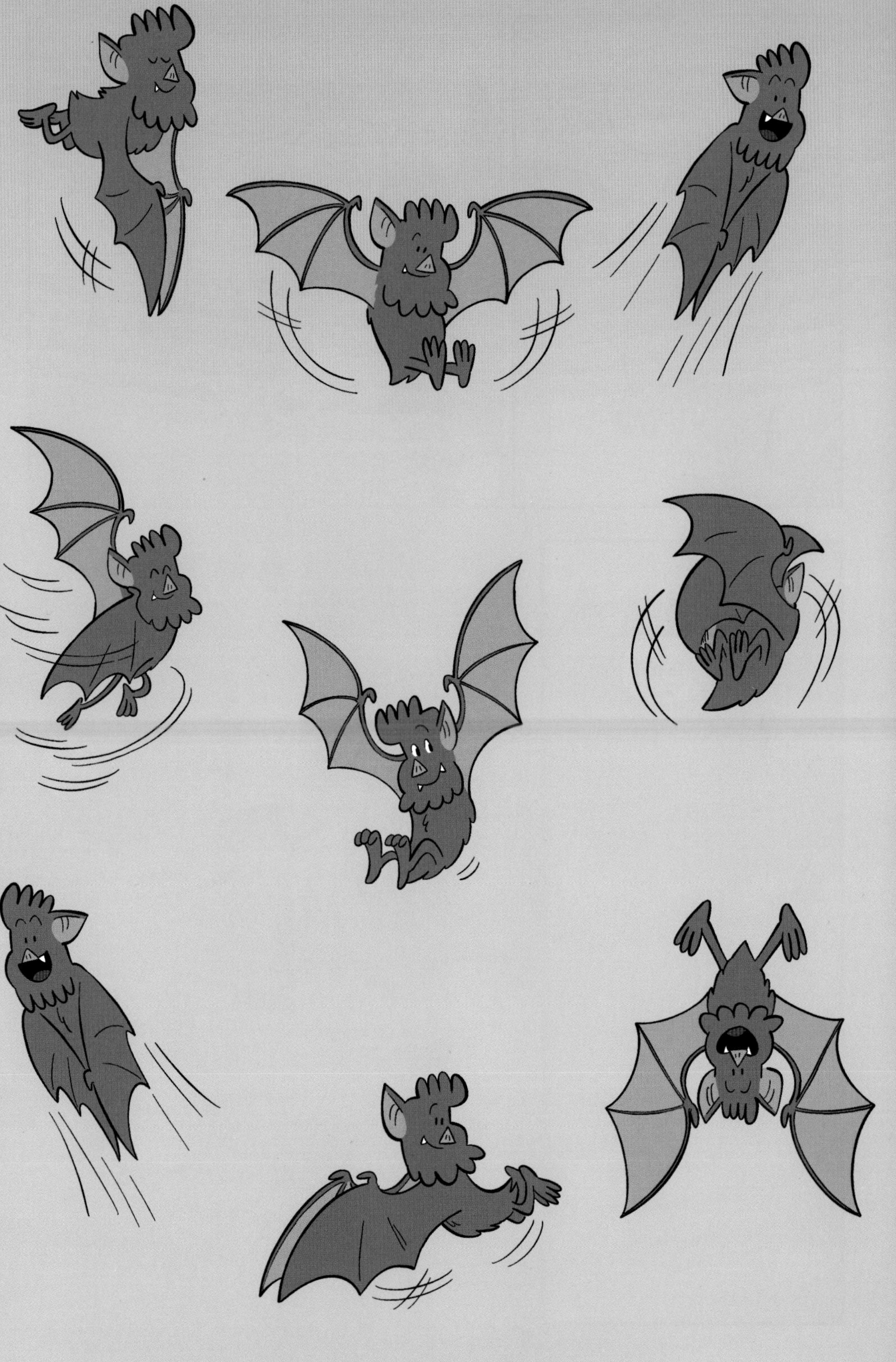

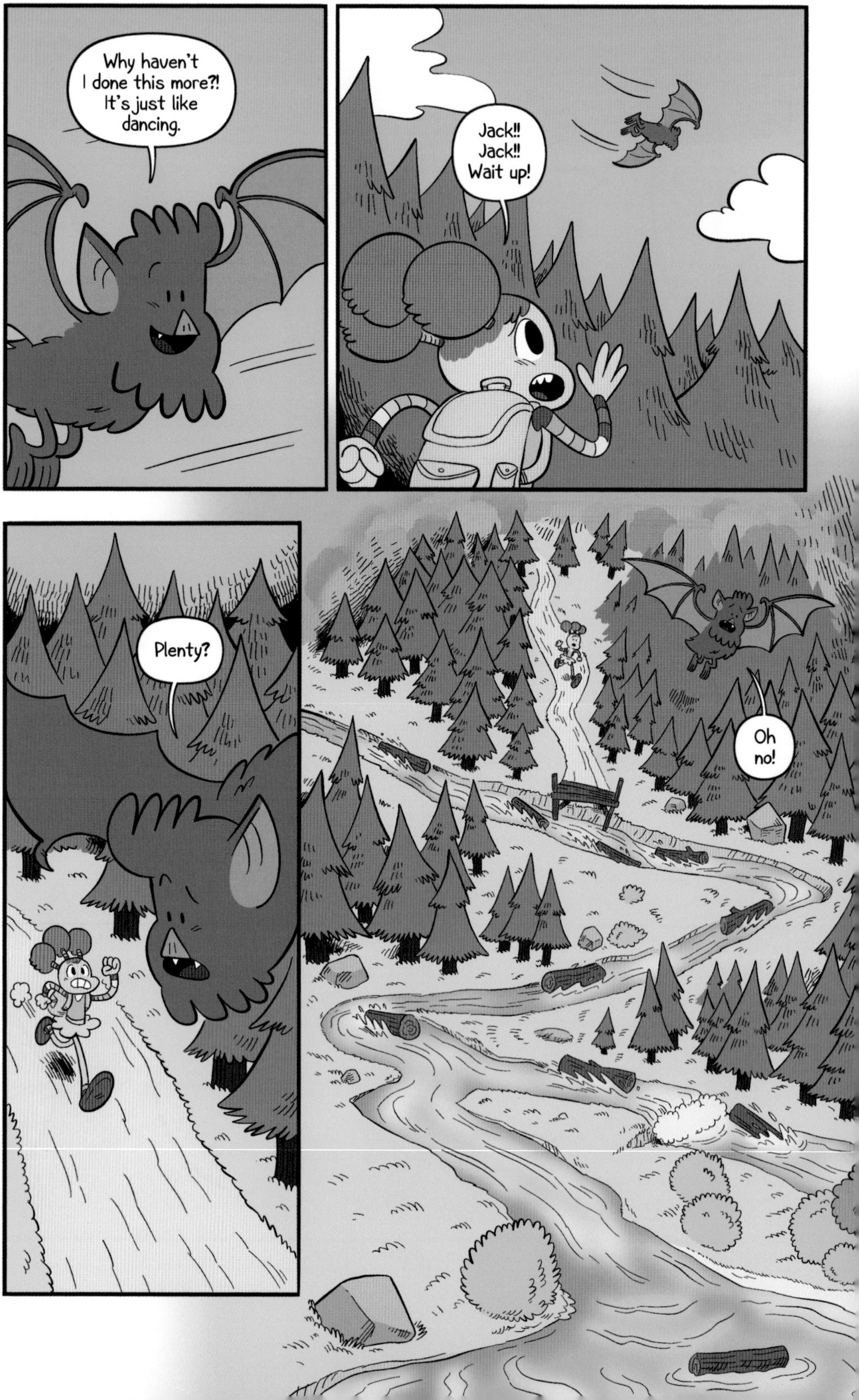
Why haven't I done this more?! It's just like dancing.
Jack!! Jack!! Wait up!
Plenty?
Oh no!

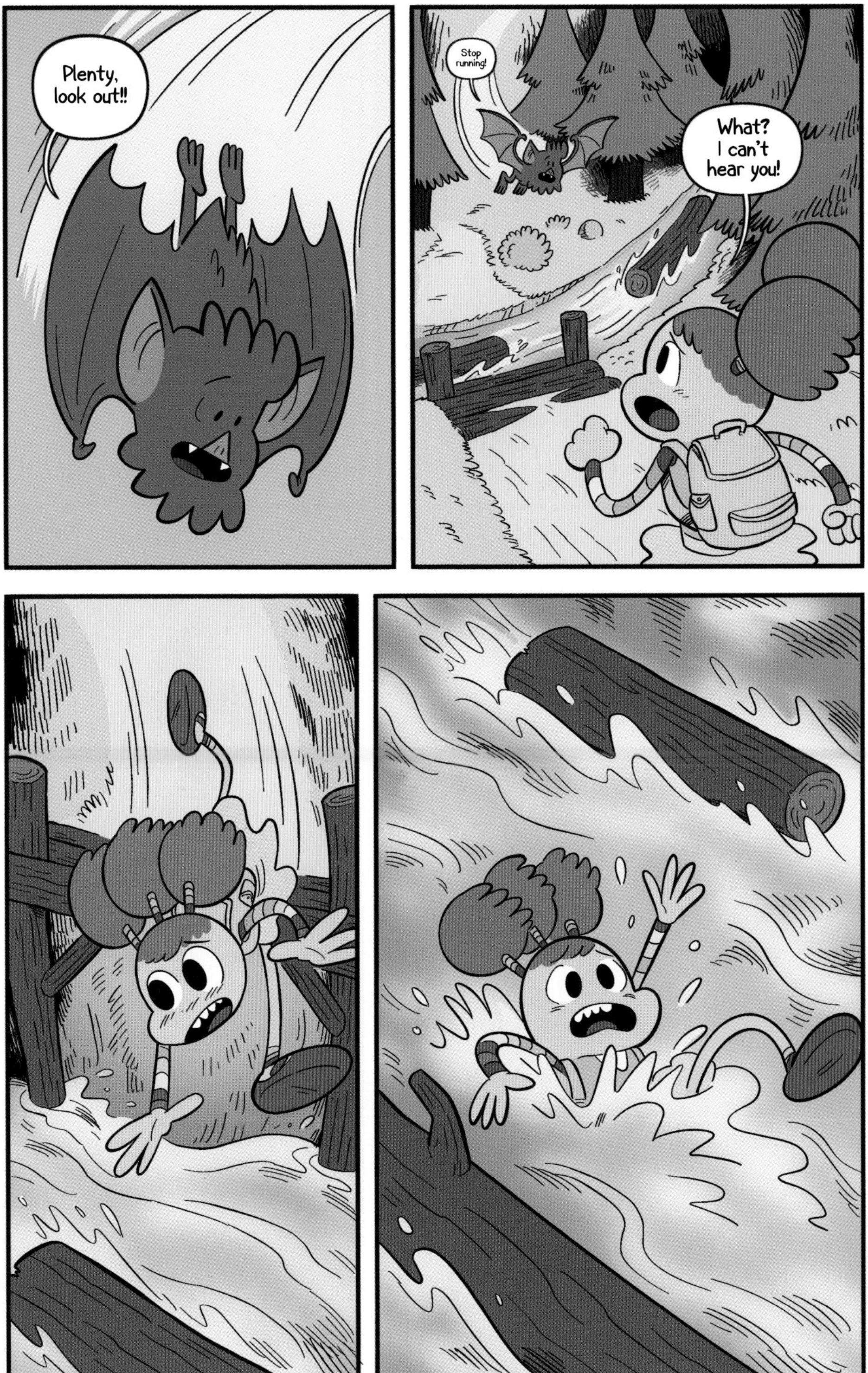
Plenty, look out!!
Stop running!
What? I can't hear you!

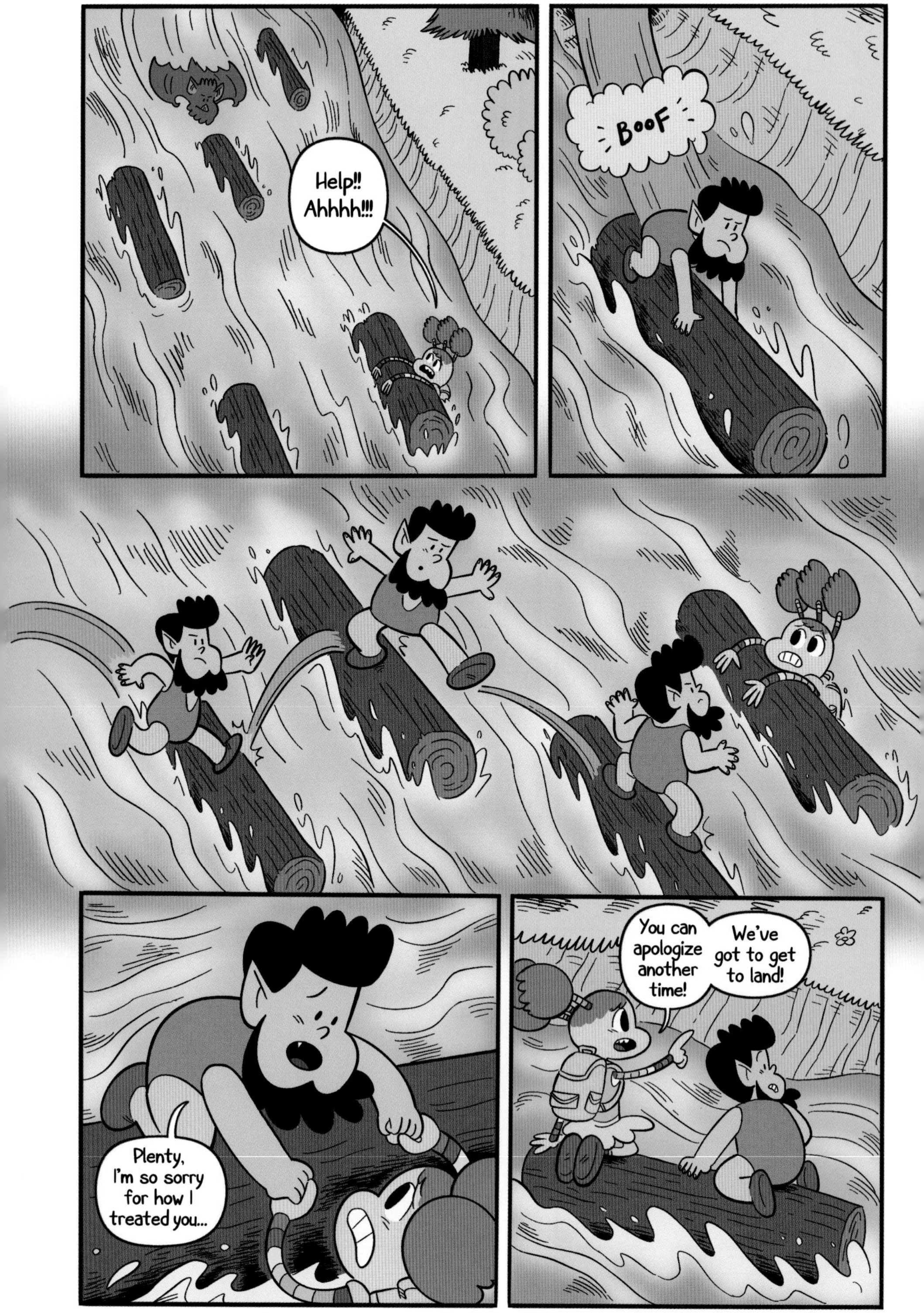
Help!! Ahhhh!!!
BOOF
Plenty, I'm so sorry for how I treated you...
You can apologize another time!
We've got to get to land!

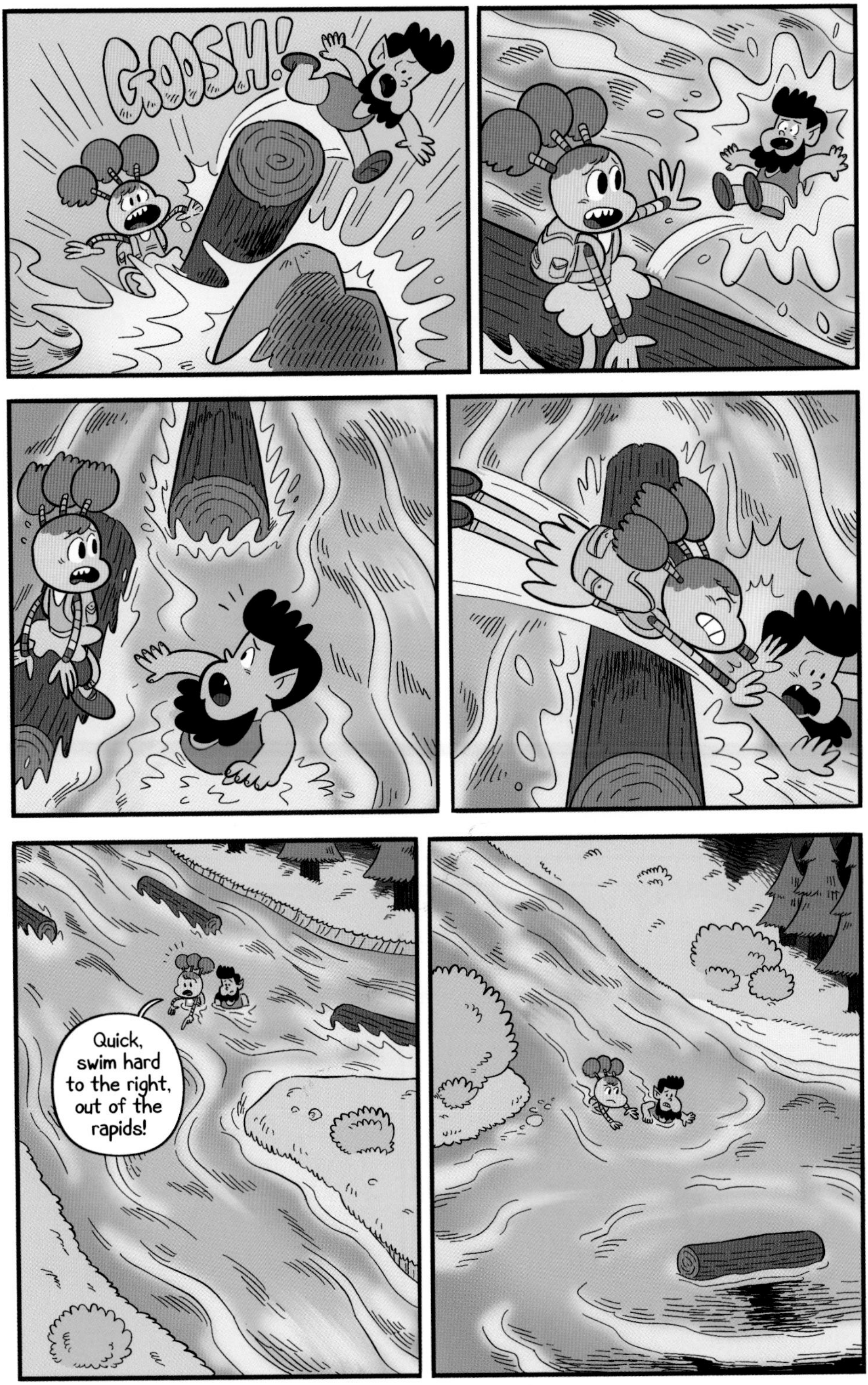
GOOSH!
Quick, swim hard to the right, out of the rapids!

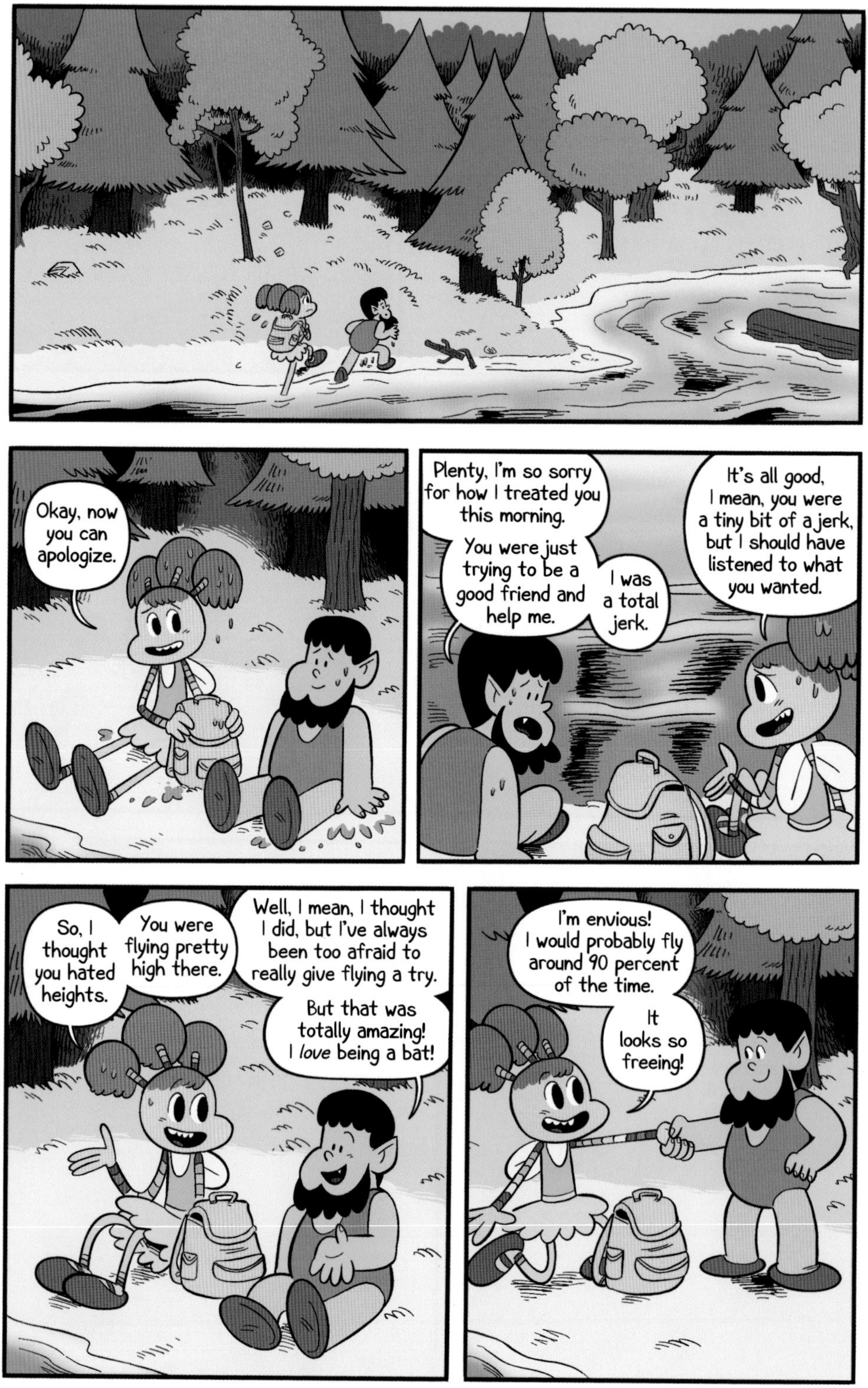

Okay, now you can apologize.
Plenty, I'm so sorry for how I treated you this morning.
You were just trying to be a good friend and help me.
I was a total jerk.
It's all good, I mean, you were a tiny bit of a jerk, but I should have listened to what you wanted.
So, I thought you hated heights.
You were flying pretty high there.
Well, I mean, I thought I did, but I've always been too afraid to really give flying a try.
But that was totally amazing! I *love* being a bat!
I'm envious! I would probably fly around 90 percent of the time.
It looks so freeing!

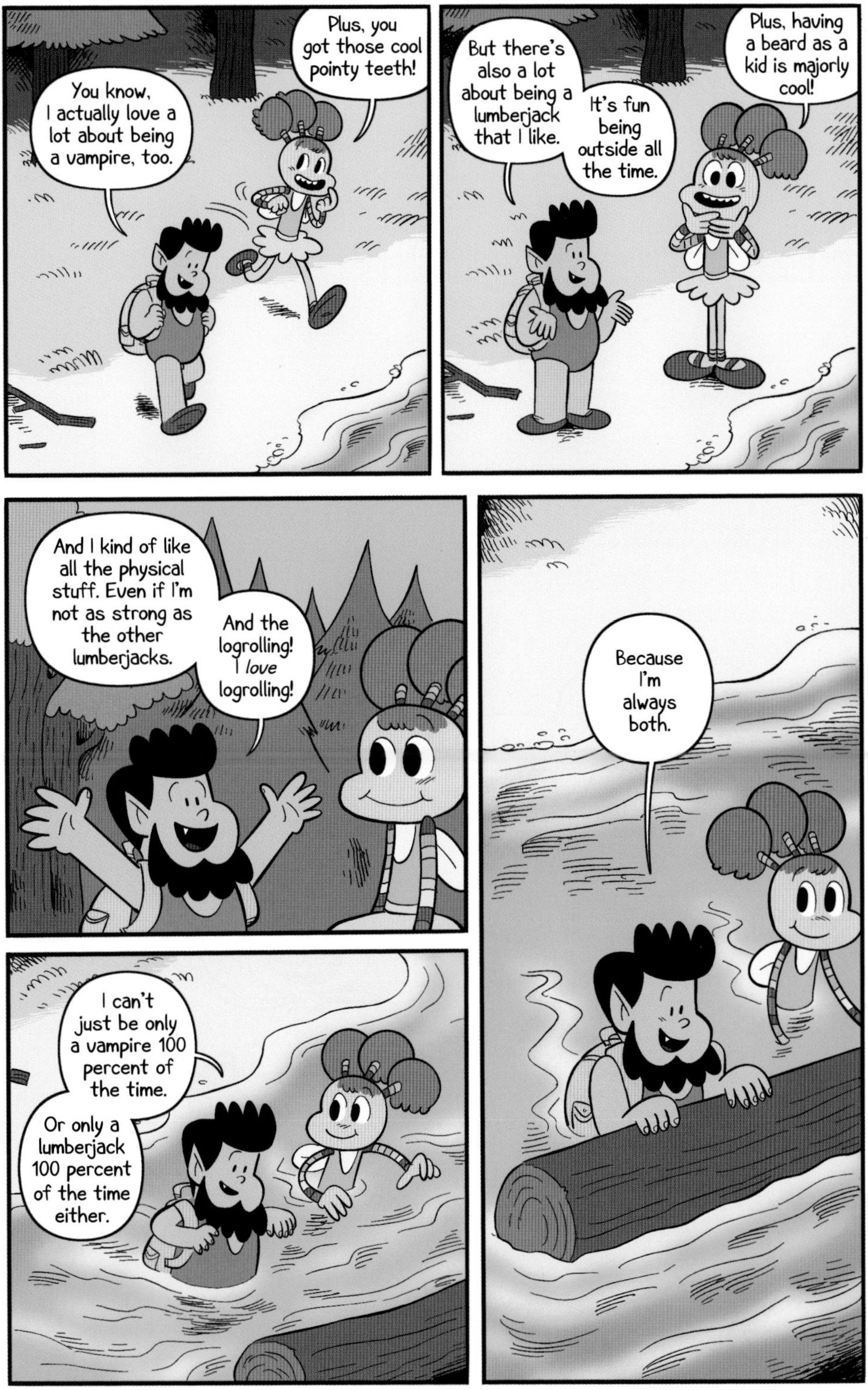

You know, I actually love a lot about being a vampire, too.
Plus, you got those cool pointy teeth!
But there's also a lot about being a lumberjack that I like.
It's fun being outside all the time.
Plus, having a beard as a kid is majorly cool!
And I kind of like all the physical stuff. Even if I'm not as strong as the other lumberjacks.
And the logrolling! I *love* logrolling!
I can't just be only a vampire 100 percent of the time.
Or only a lumberjack 100 percent of the time either.
Because I'm always both.

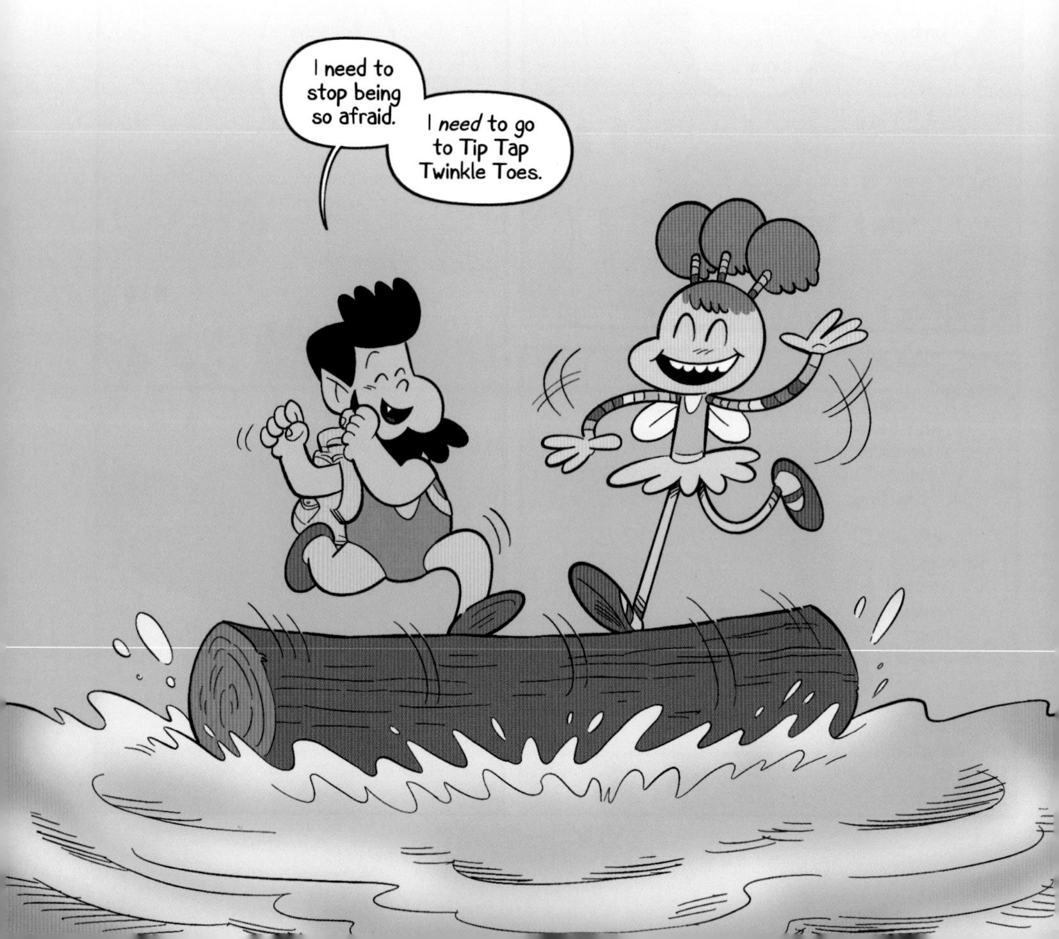
I need to stop being so afraid.
I *need* to go to Tip Tap Twinkle Toes.

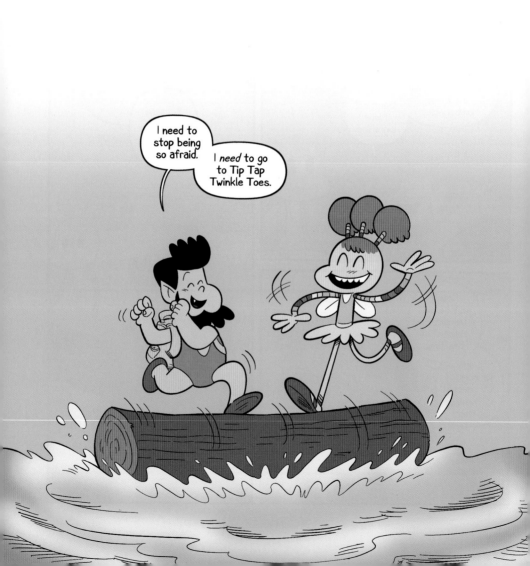

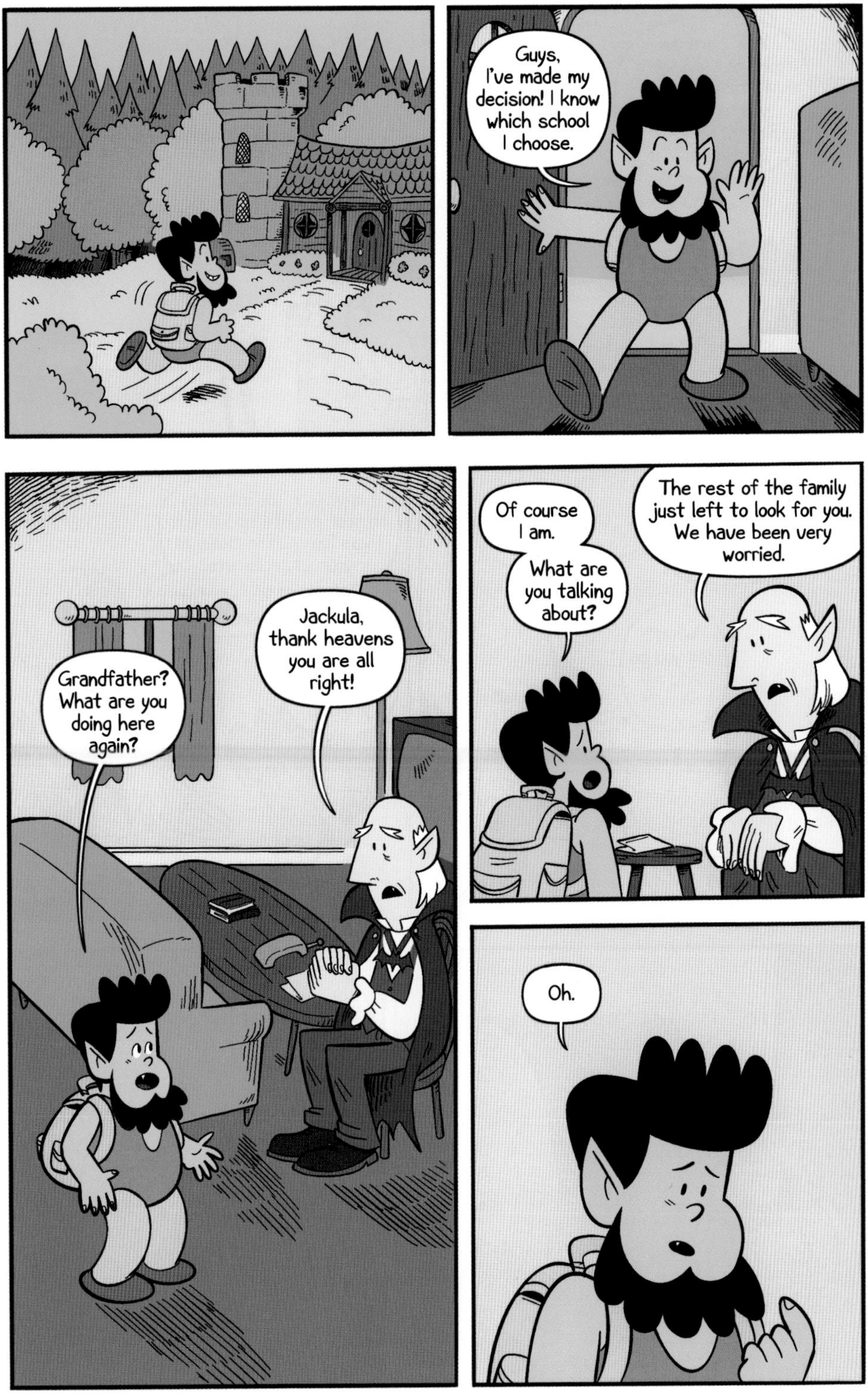
Guys, I've made my decision! I know which school I choose.
Grandfather? What are you doing here again?
Jackula, thank heavens you are all right!
Of course I am.
What are you talking about?
The rest of the family just left to look for you. We have been very worried.
Oh.

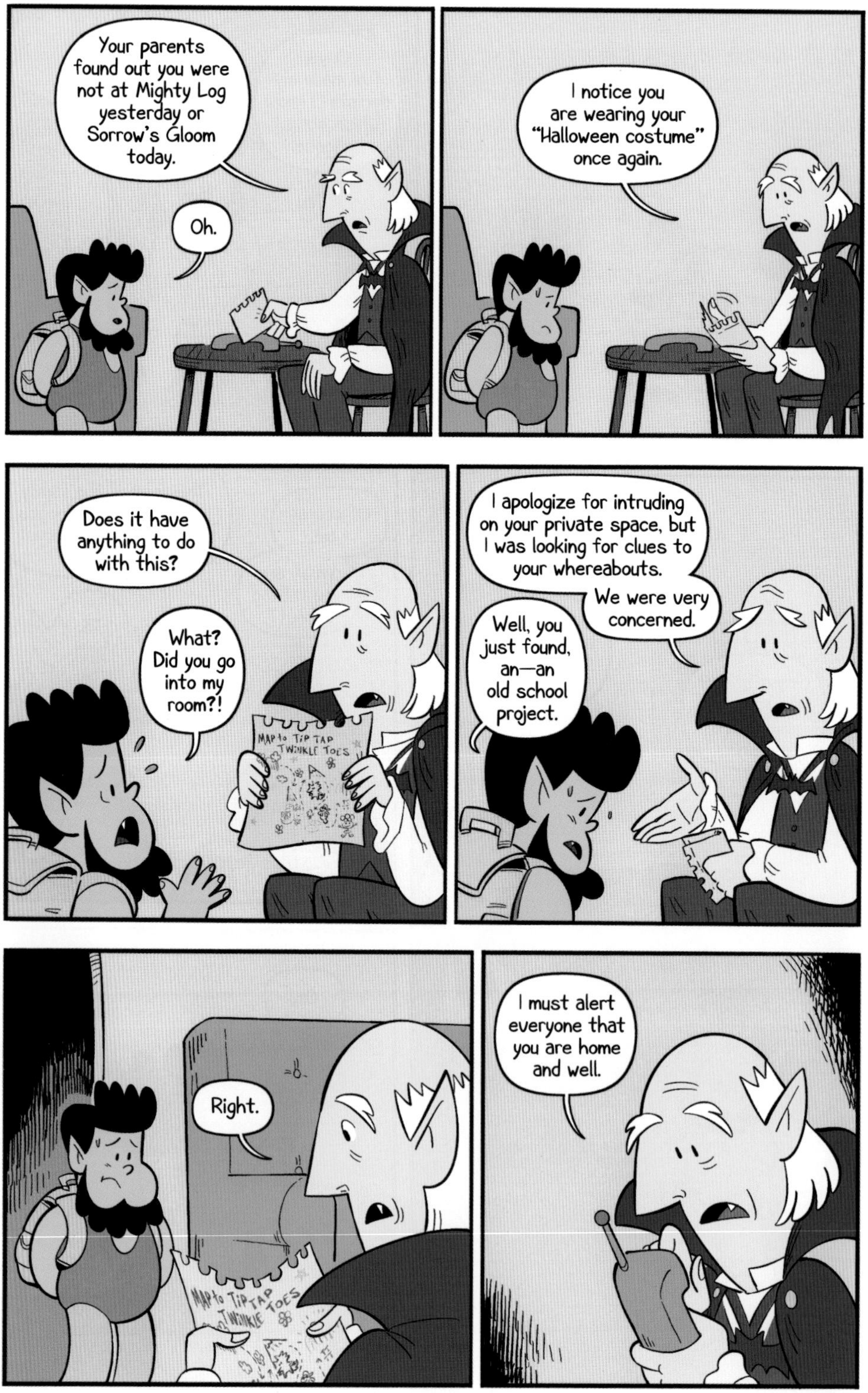
Your parents found out you were not at Mighty Log yesterday or Sorrow's Gloom today.
Oh.
I notice you are wearing your "Halloween costume" once again.
Does it have anything to do with this?
What? Did you go into my room?!
MAP to TIP TAP TWINKLE TOES
I apologize for intruding on your private space, but I was looking for clues to your whereabouts.
We were very concerned.
Well, you just found, an—an old school project.
Right.
MAP to TIP TAP TWINKLE TOES
I must alert everyone that you are home and well.

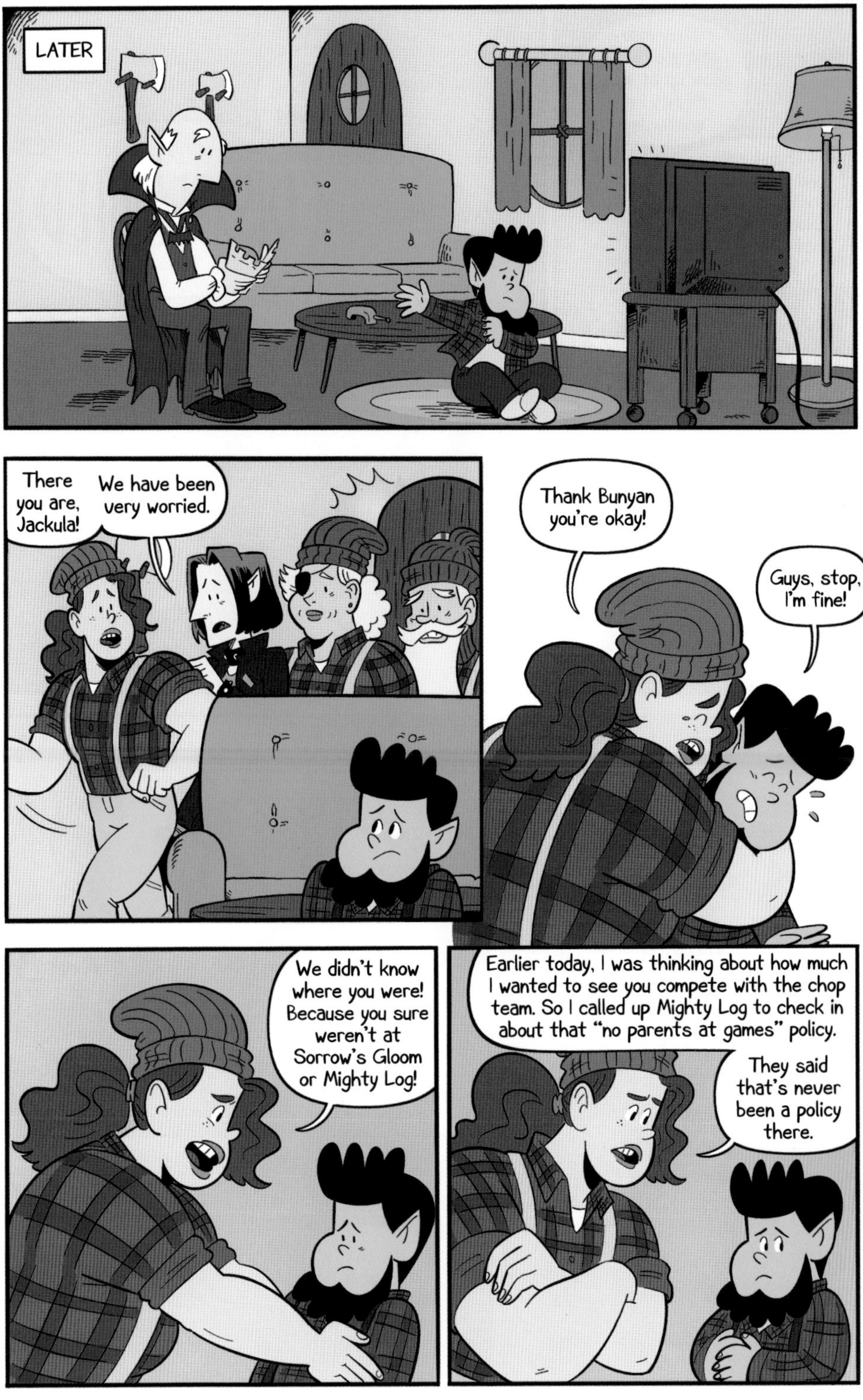
LATER
There you are, Jackula!
We have been very worried.
Thank Bunyan you're okay!
Guys, stop, I'm fine!
We didn't know where you were! Because you sure weren't at Sorrow's Gloom or Mighty Log!
Earlier today, I was thinking about how much I wanted to see you compete with the chop team. So I called up Mighty Log to check in about that "no parents at games" policy.
They said that's never been a policy there.

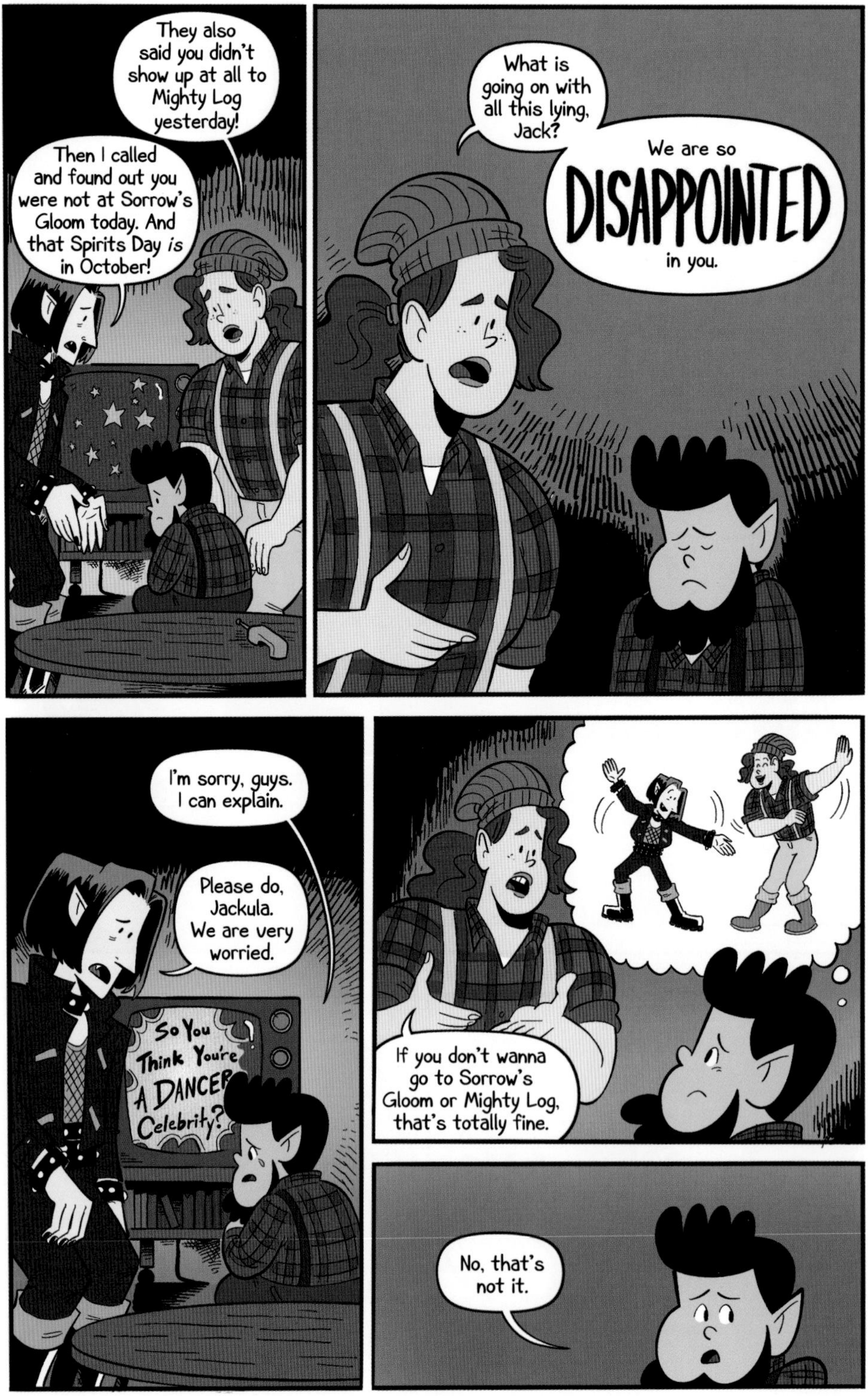
Then I called and found out you were not at Sorrow's Gloom today. And that Spirits Day *is* in October!
They also said you didn't show up at all to Mighty Log yesterday!
What is going on with all this lying, Jack?
We are so DISAPPOINTED in you.
I'm sorry, guys. I can explain.
Please do, Jackula. We are very worried.
So You Think You're A DANCER Celebrity?
If you don't wanna go to Sorrow's Gloom or Mighty Log, that's totally fine.
No, that's not it.

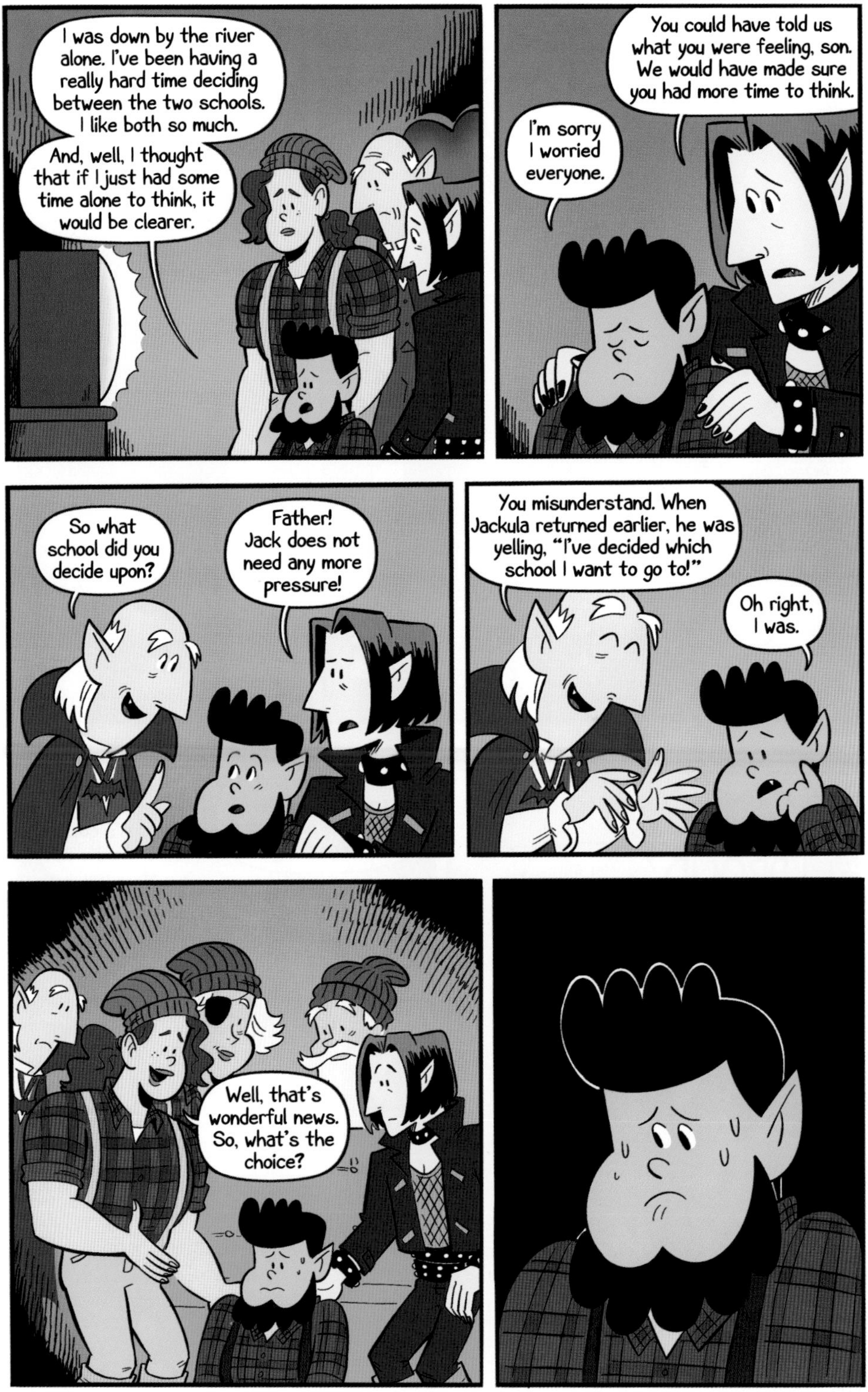
I was down by the river alone. I've been having a really hard time deciding between the two schools. I like both so much.
And, well, I thought that if I just had some time alone to think, it would be clearer.
You could have told us what you were feeling, son. We would have made sure you had more time to think.
I'm sorry I worried everyone.
So what school did you decide upon?
Father! Jack does not need any more pressure!
You misunderstand. When Jackula returned earlier, he was yelling, "I've decided which school I want to go to!"
Oh right, I was.
Well, that's wonderful news. So, what's the choice?

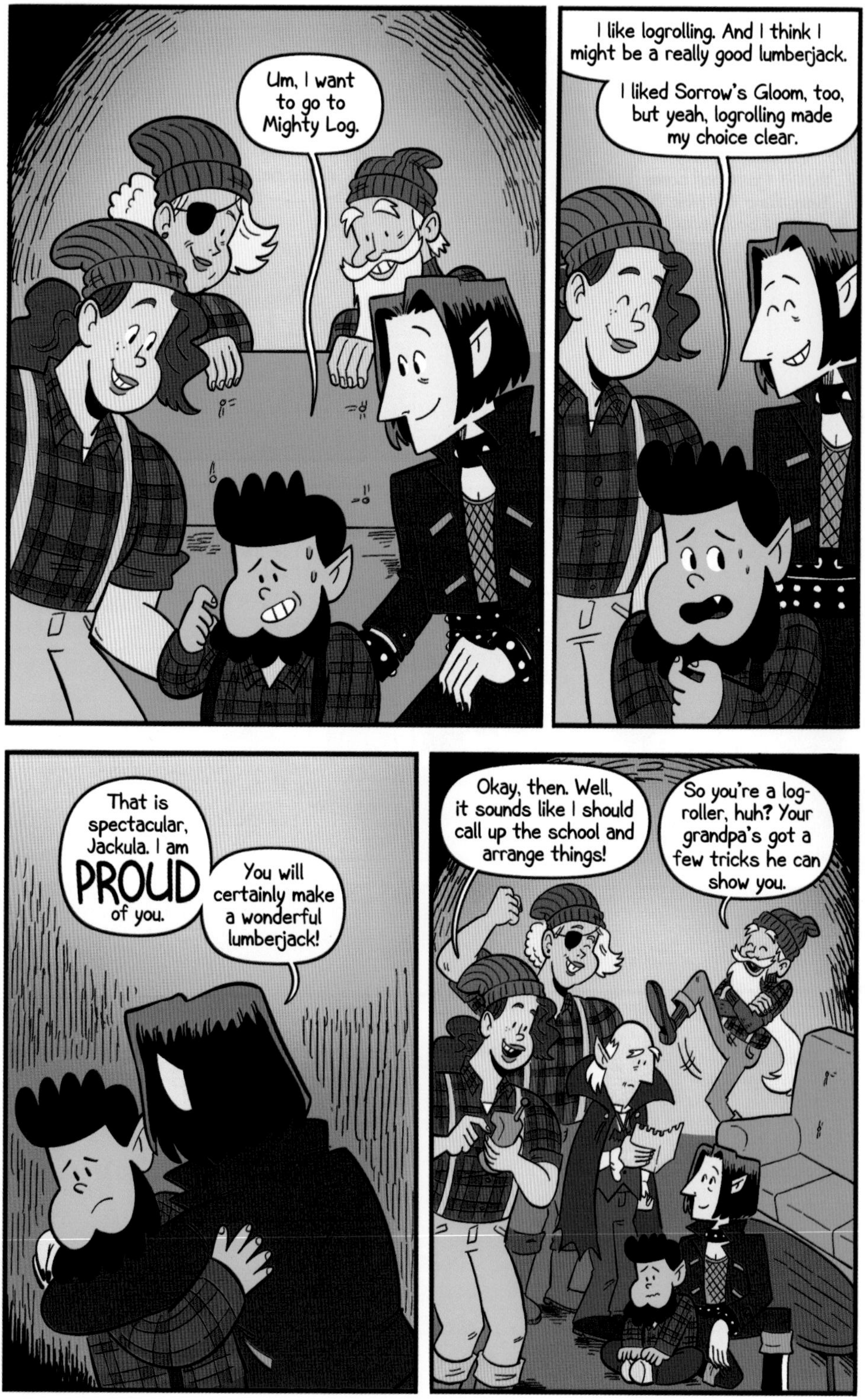
Um, I want to go to Mighty Log.
I like logrolling. And I think I might be a really good lumberjack.
I liked Sorrow's Gloom, too, but yeah, logrolling made my choice clear.
That is spectacular, Jackula. I am PROUD of you.
You will certainly make a wonderful lumberjack!
Okay, then. Well, it sounds like I should call up the school and arrange things!
So you're a log-roller, huh? Your grandpa's got a few tricks he can show you.

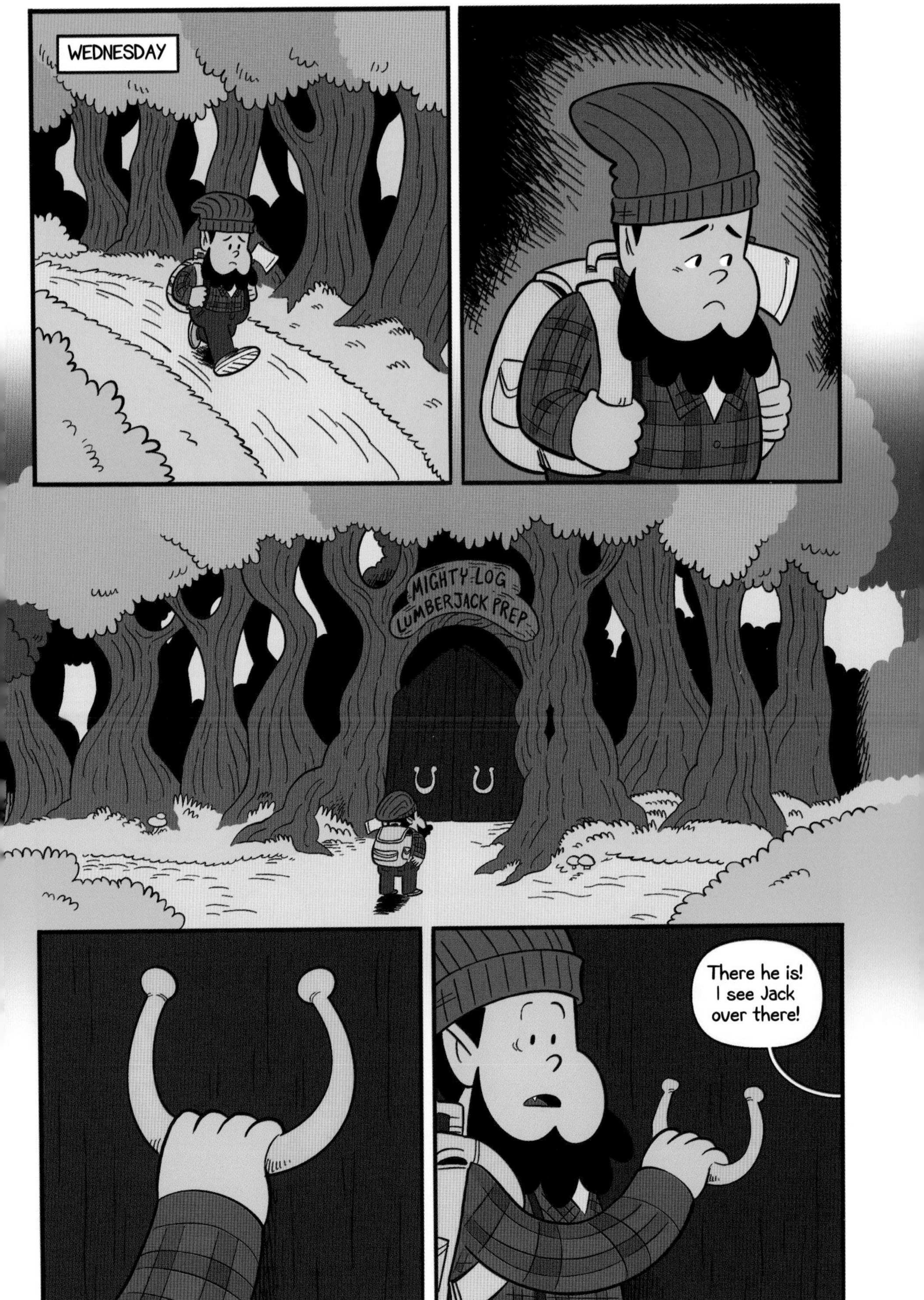
WEDNESDAY
MIGHTY LOG
LUMBERJACK PREP
There he is!
I see Jack
over there!

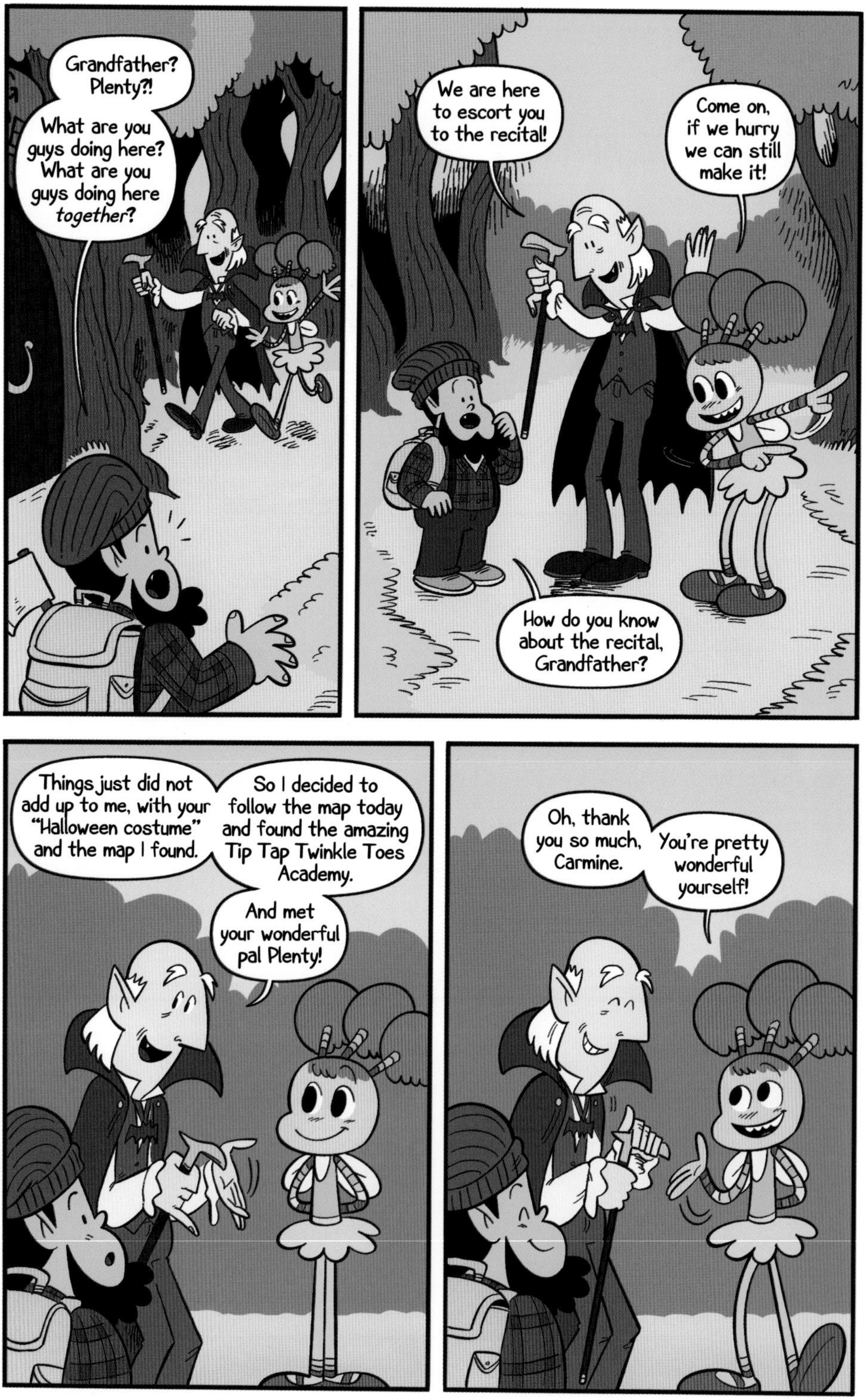
Grandfather? Plenty?!
What are you guys doing here? What are you guys doing here *together*?
We are here to escort you to the recital!
Come on, if we hurry we can still make it!
How do you know about the recital, Grandfather?
Things just did not add up to me, with your "Halloween costume" and the map I found.
So I decided to follow the map today and found the amazing Tip Tap Twinkle Toes Academy.
And met your wonderful pal Plenty!
Oh, thank you so much, Carmine.
You're pretty wonderful yourself!

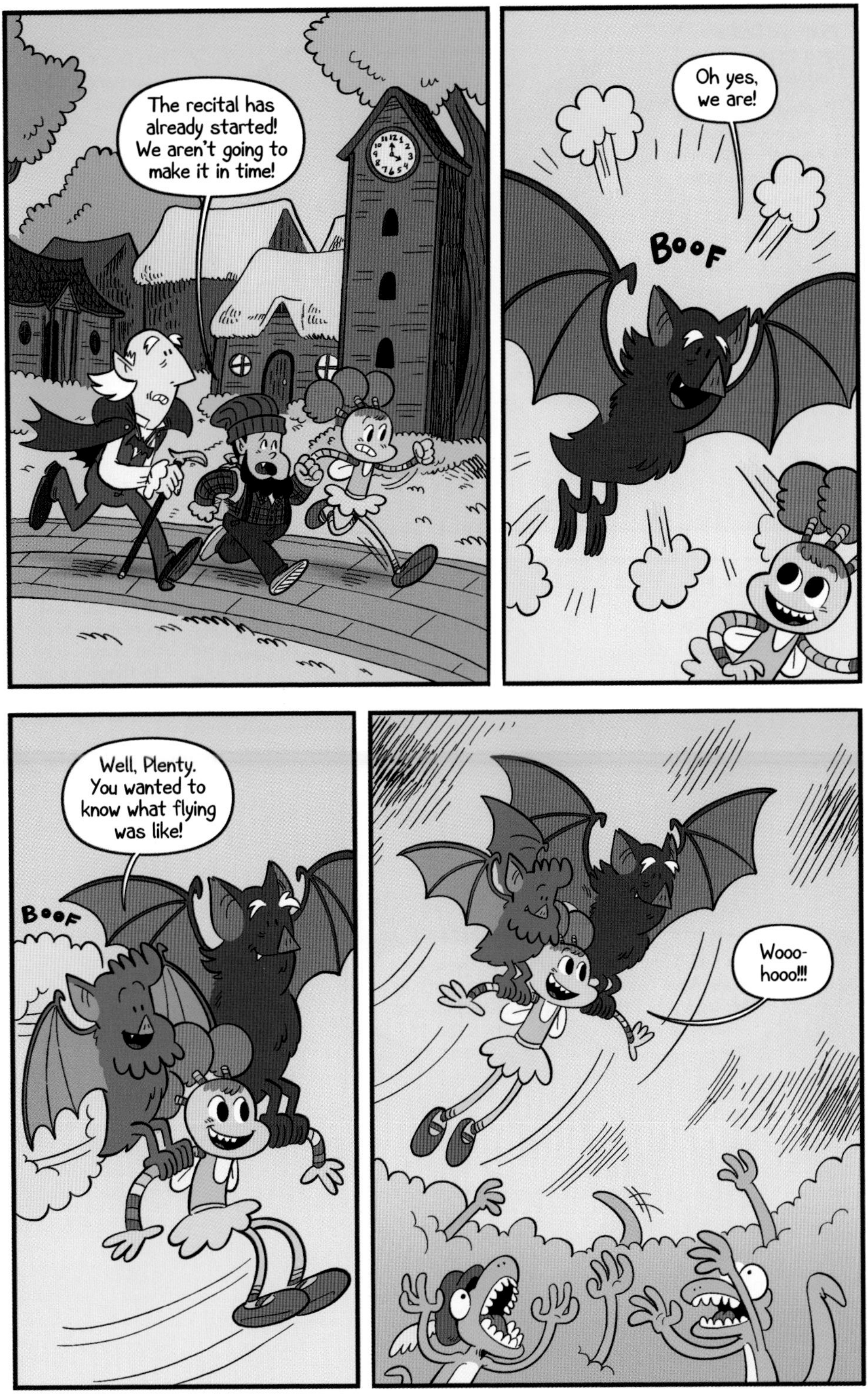
The recital has already started! We aren't going to make it in time!
Oh yes, we are!
BOOF
Well, Plenty. You wanted to know what flying was like!
BOOF
Wooo-hooo!!!

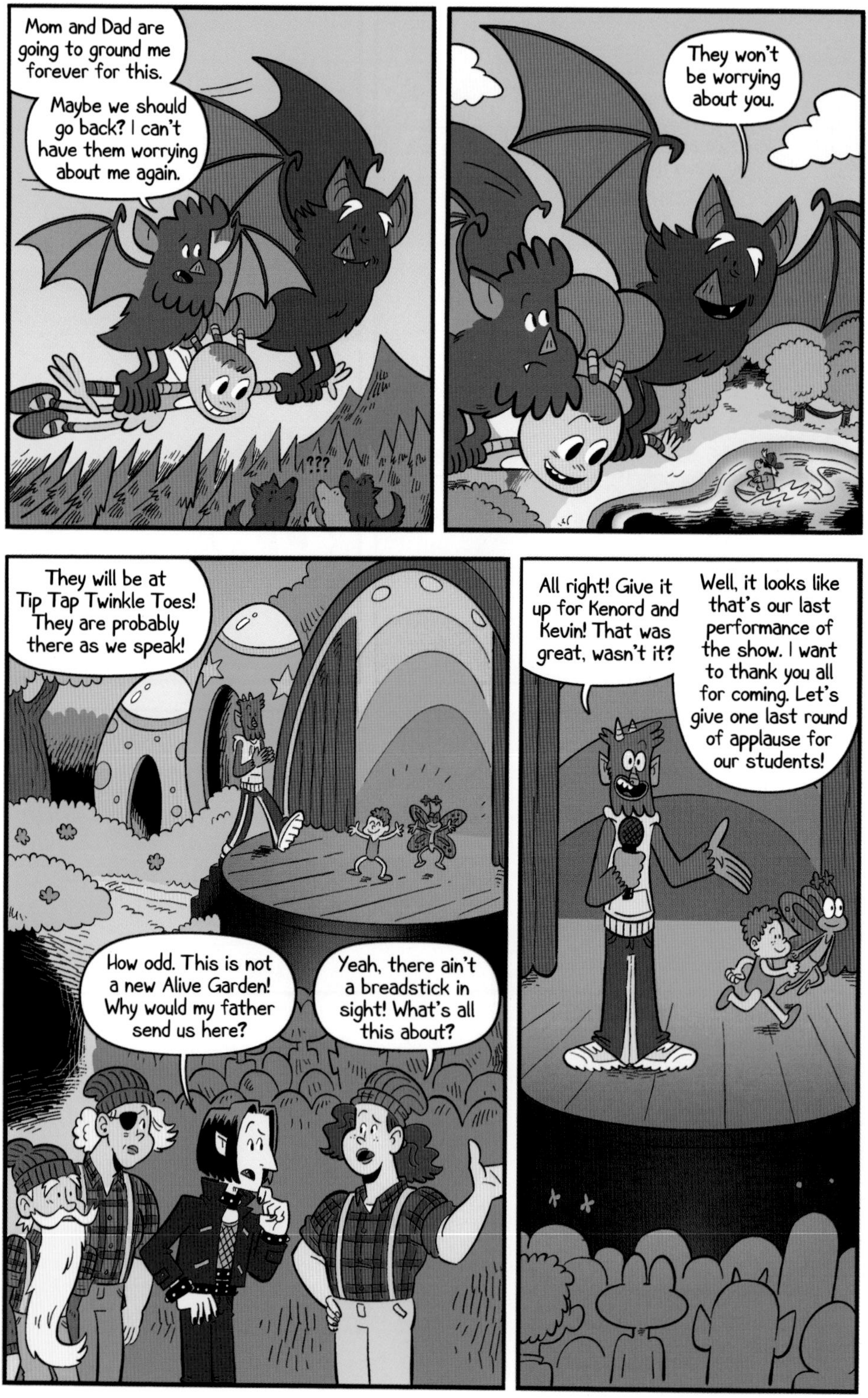
Mom and Dad are going to ground me forever for this.
Maybe we should go back? I can't have them worrying about me again.
???
They won't be worrying about you.
They will be at Tip Tap Twinkle Toes! They are probably there as we speak!
How odd. This is not a new Alive Garden! Why would my father send us here?
Yeah, there ain't a breadstick in sight! What's all this about?
All right! Give it up for Kenord and Kevin! That was great, wasn't it?
Well, it looks like that's our last performance of the show. I want to thank you all for coming. Let's give one last round of applause for our students!

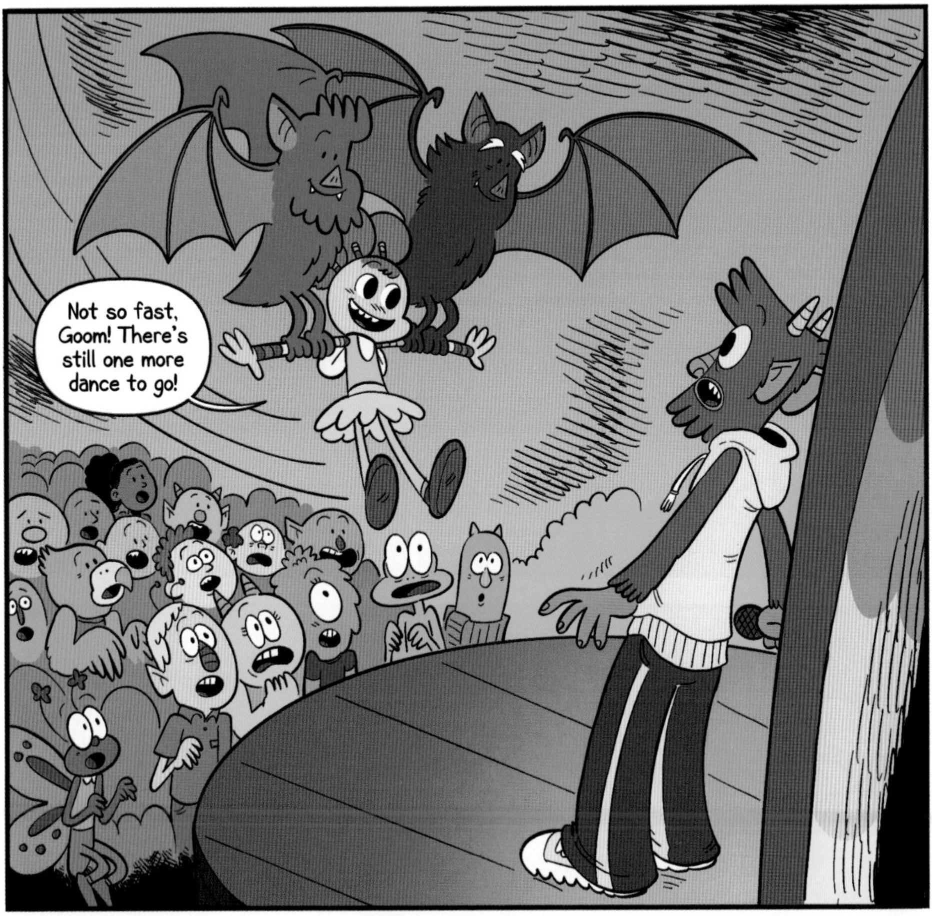
Not so fast, Goom! There's still one more dance to go!

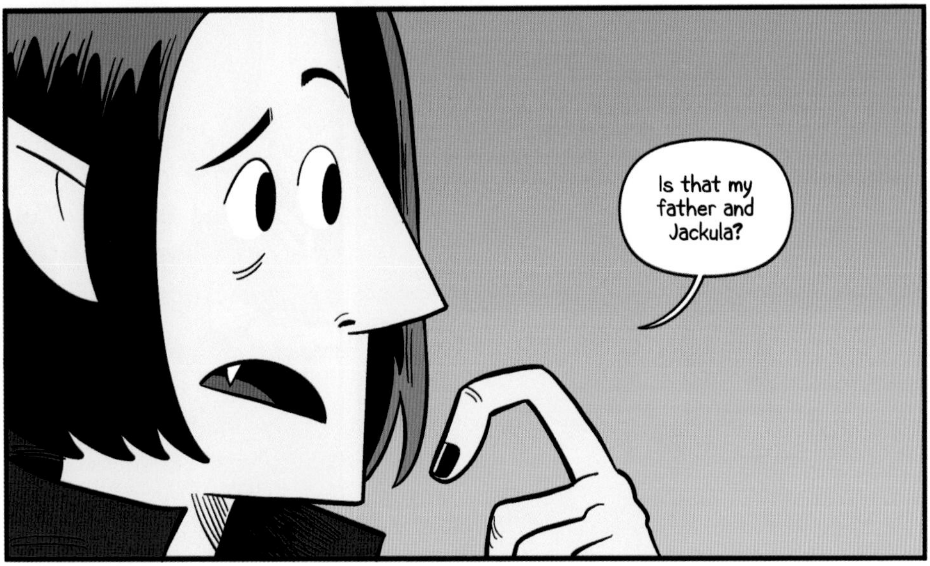
Is that my father and Jackula?

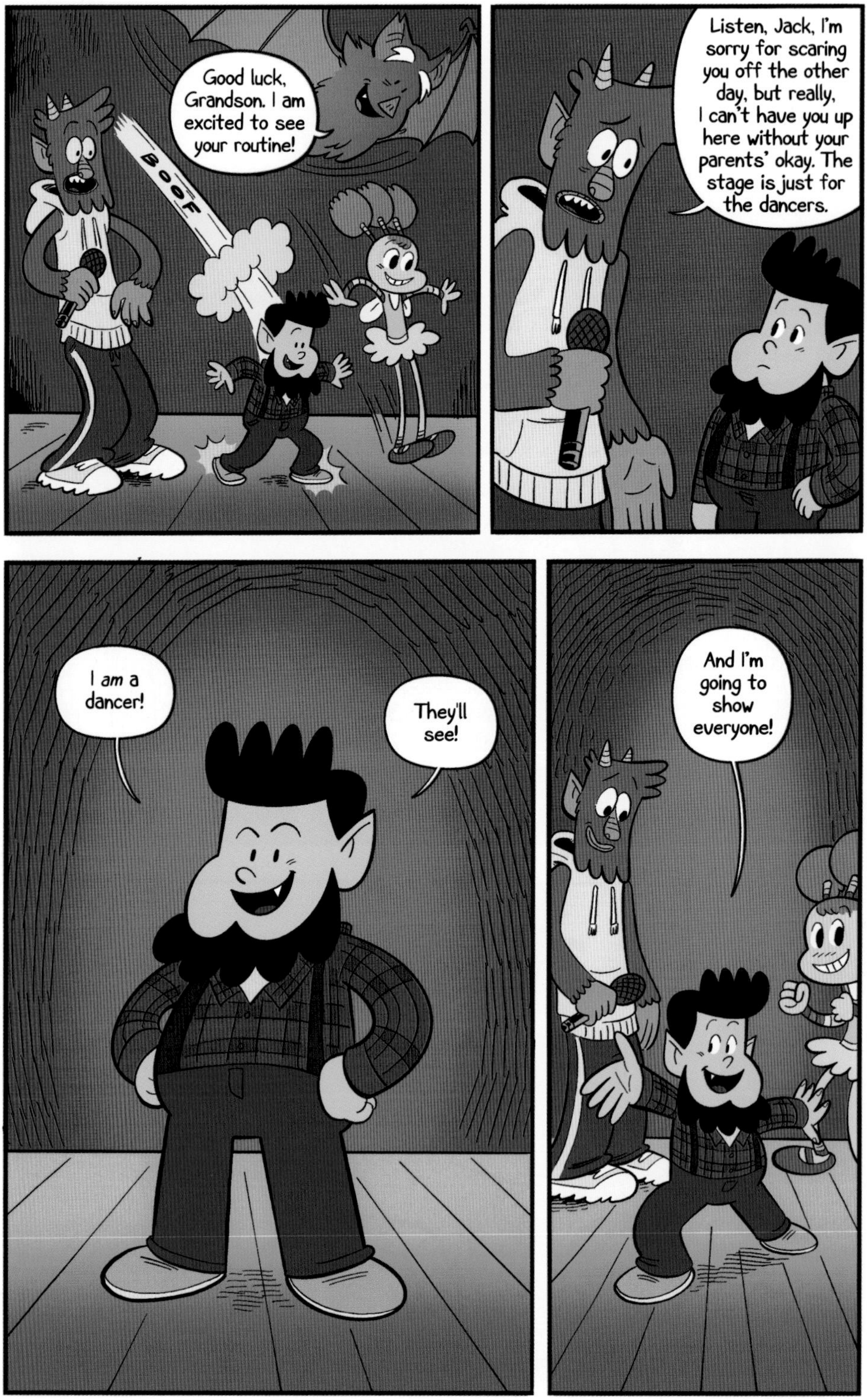
Good luck, Grandson. I am excited to see your routine!
BOOF
Listen, Jack, I'm sorry for scaring you off the other day, but really, I can't have you up here without your parents' okay. The stage is just for the dancers.
I *am* a dancer!
They'll see!
And I'm going to show everyone!

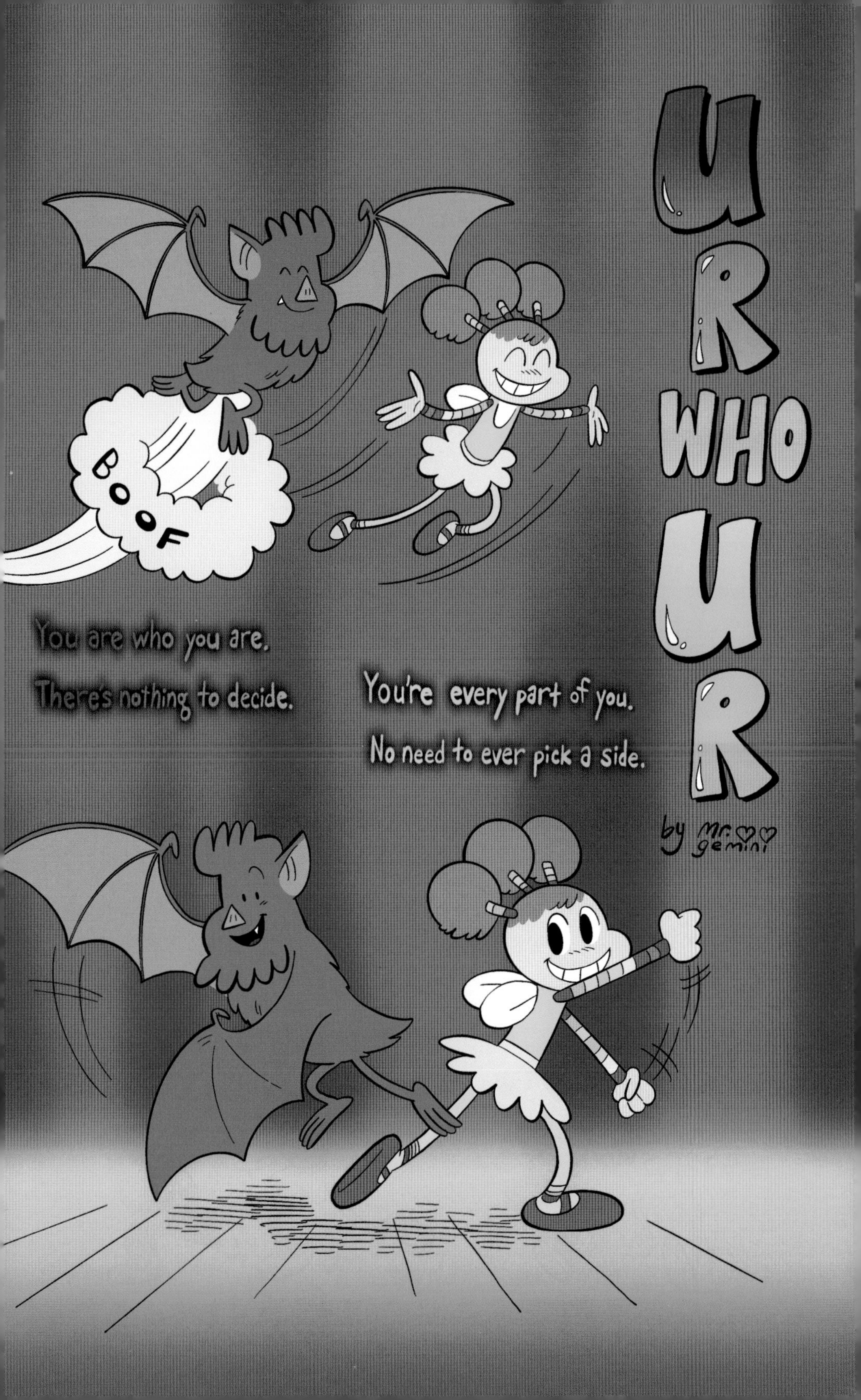

U R WHO U R
by Mr. gemini
BOOF
You are who you are.
There's nothing to decide.
You're every part of you.
No need to ever pick a side.

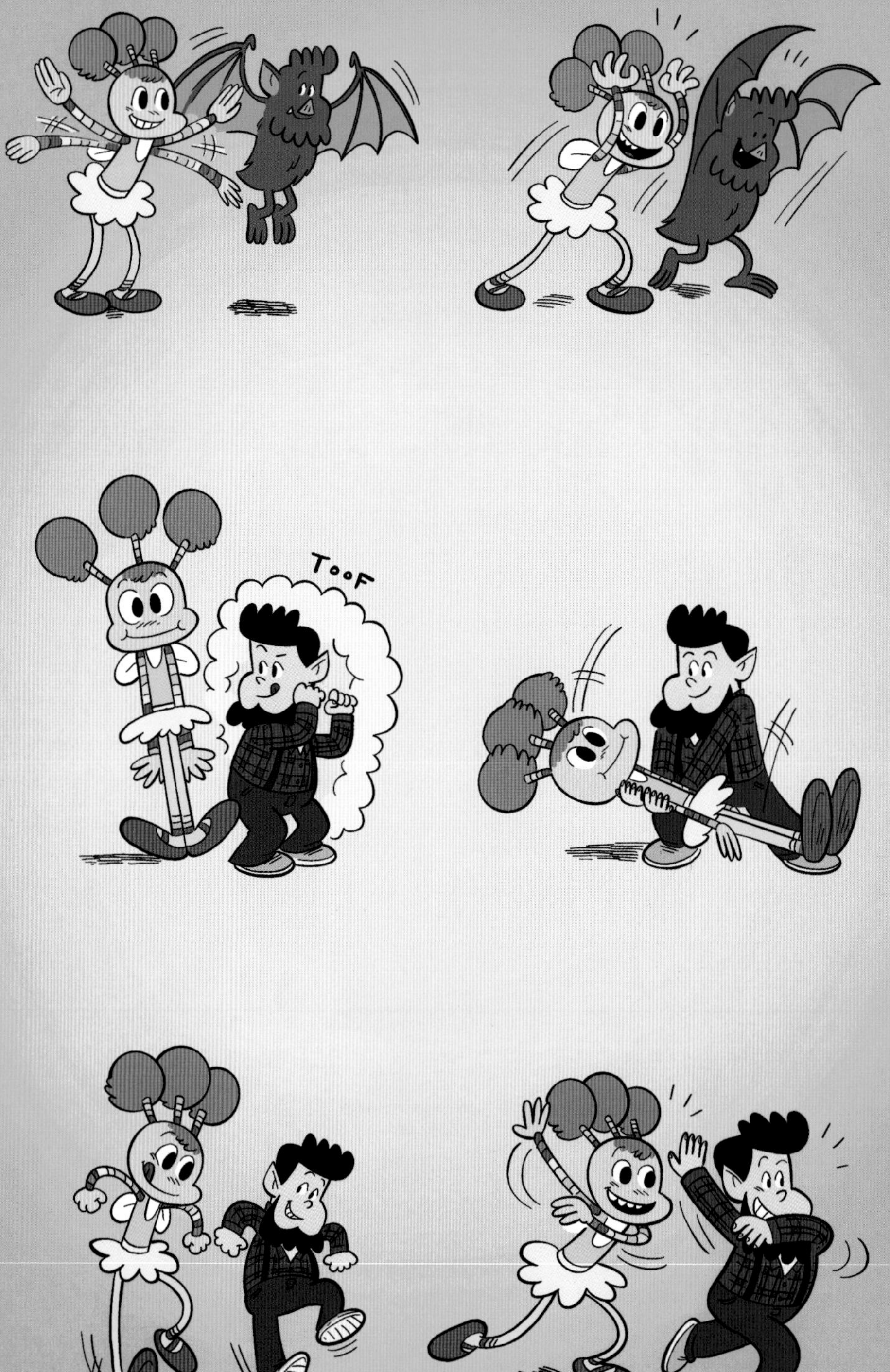
TOOF

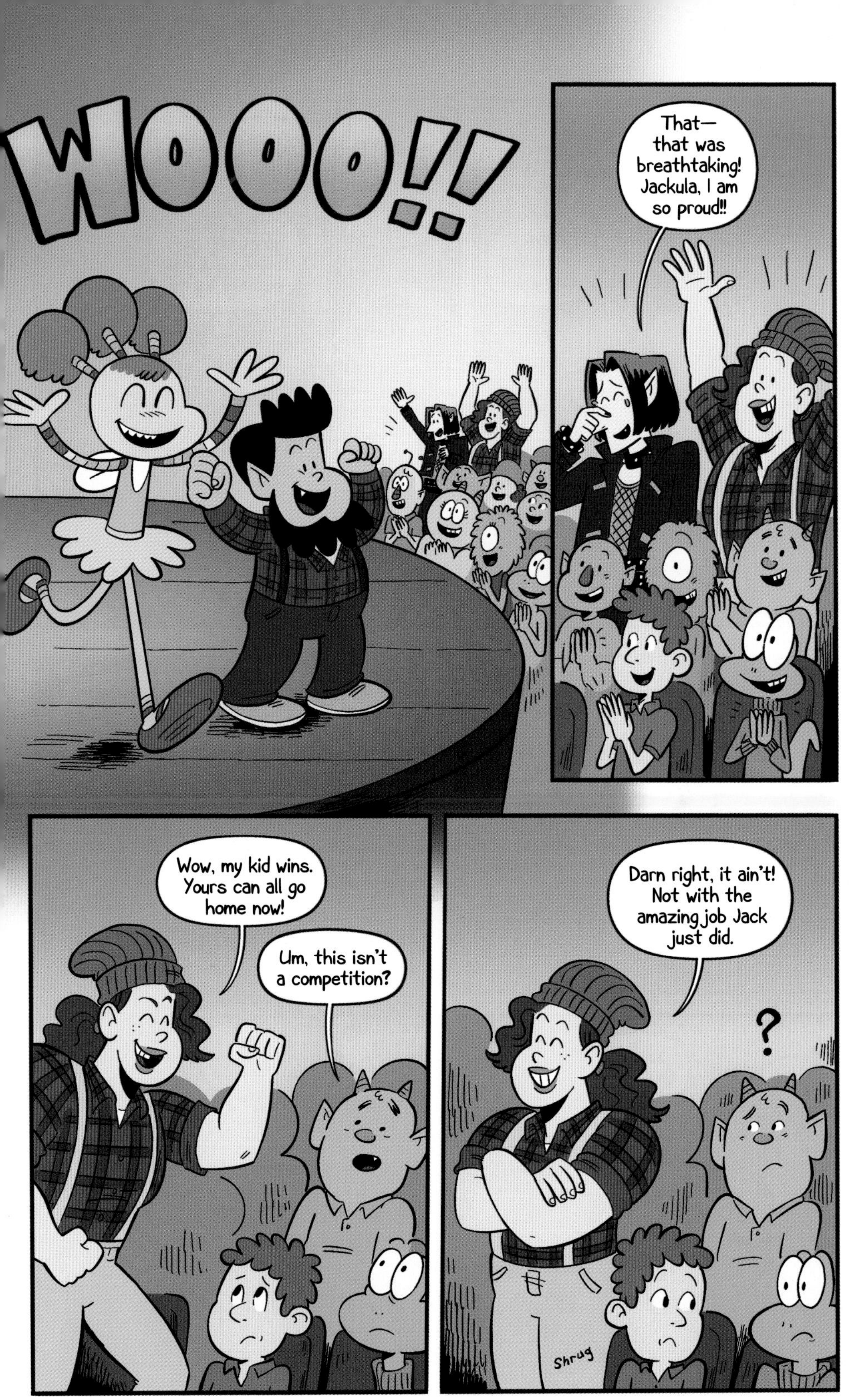
WOOO!!
That—that was breathtaking! Jackula, I am so proud!!
Wow, my kid wins. Yours can all go home now!
Um, this isn't a competition?
Darn right, it ain't! Not with the amazing job Jack just did.
?
Shrug

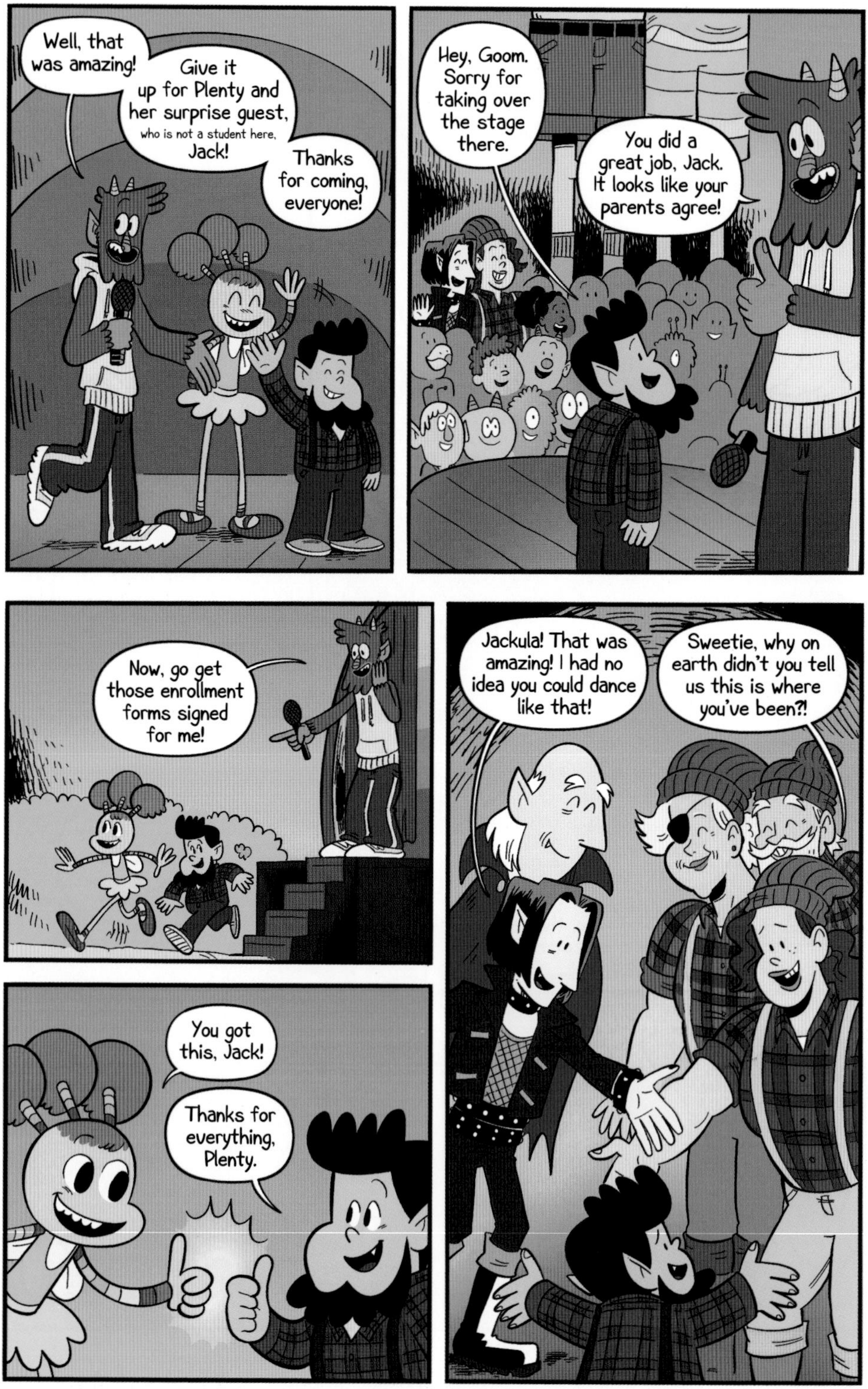
Well, that was amazing!
Give it up for Plenty and her surprise guest, who is not a student here, Jack!
Thanks for coming, everyone!
Hey, Goom. Sorry for taking over the stage there.
You did a great job, Jack. It looks like your parents agree!
Now, go get those enrollment forms signed for me!
You got this, Jack!
Thanks for everything, Plenty.
Jackula! That was amazing! I had no idea you could dance like that!
Sweetie, why on earth didn't you tell us this is where you've been?!

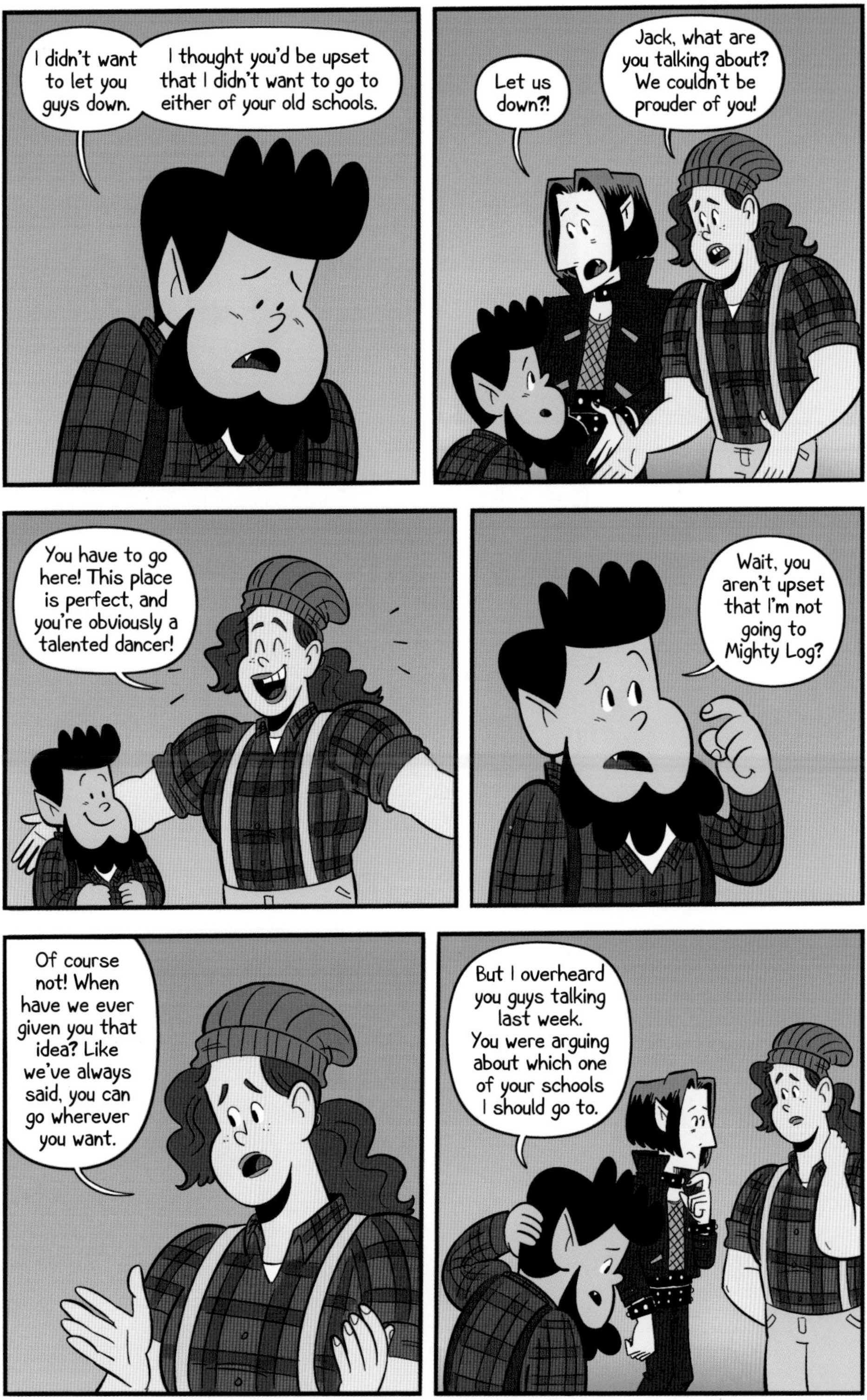

I didn't want to let you guys down.
I thought you'd be upset that I didn't want to go to either of your old schools.
Let us down?!
Jack, what are you talking about? We couldn't be prouder of you!
You have to go here! This place is perfect, and you're obviously a talented dancer!
Wait, you aren't upset that I'm not going to Mighty Log?
Of course not! When have we ever given you that idea? Like we've always said, you can go wherever you want.
But I overheard you guys talking last week. You were arguing about which one of your schools I should go to.

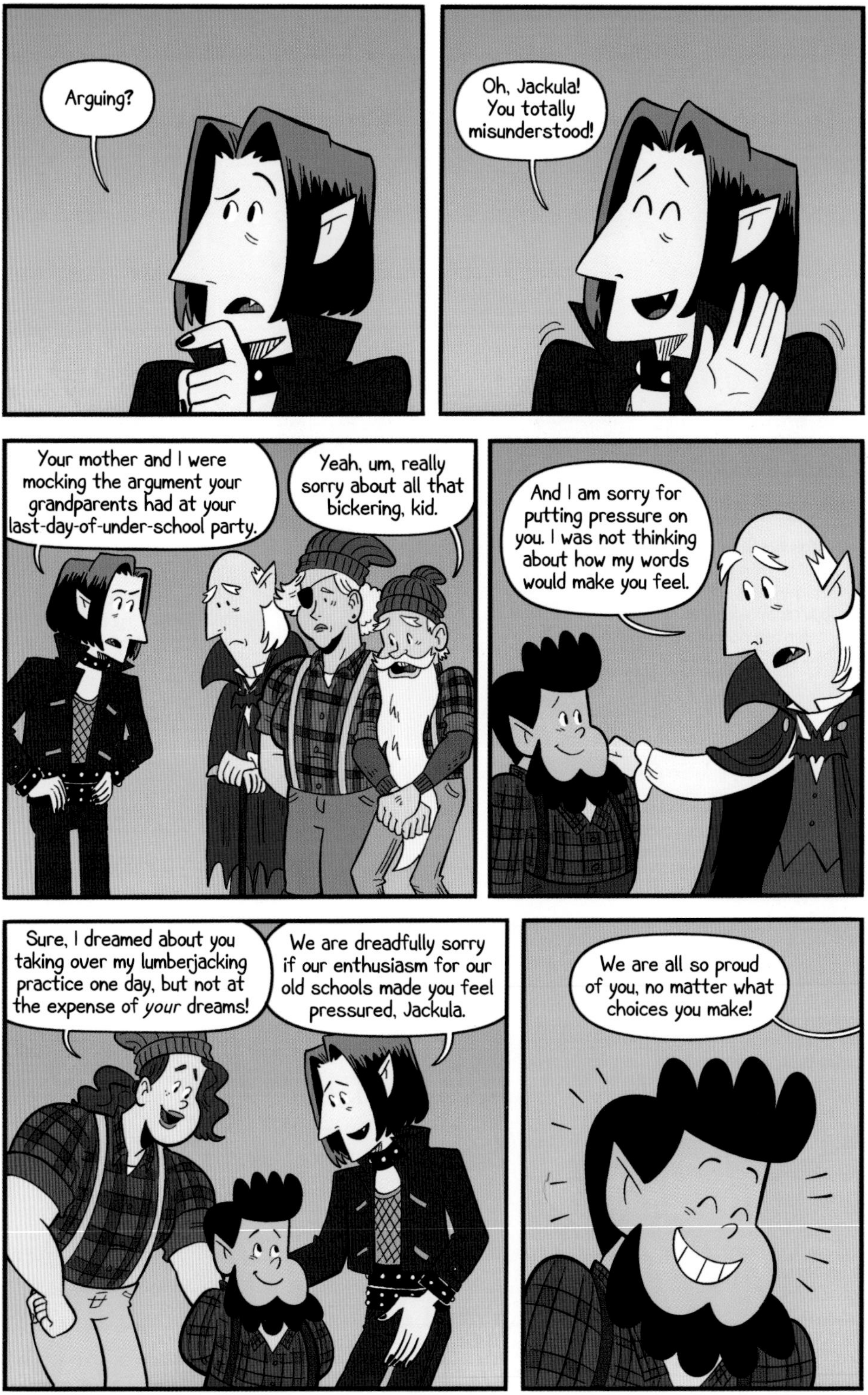
Arguing?
Oh, Jackula! You totally misunderstood!
Your mother and I were mocking the argument your grandparents had at your last-day-of-under-school party.
Yeah, um, really sorry about all that bickering, kid.
And I am sorry for putting pressure on you. I was not thinking about how my words would make you feel.
Sure, I dreamed about you taking over my lumberjacking practice one day, but not at the expense of *your* dreams!
We are dreadfully sorry if our enthusiasm for our old schools made you feel pressured, Jackula.
We are all so proud of you, no matter what choices you make!

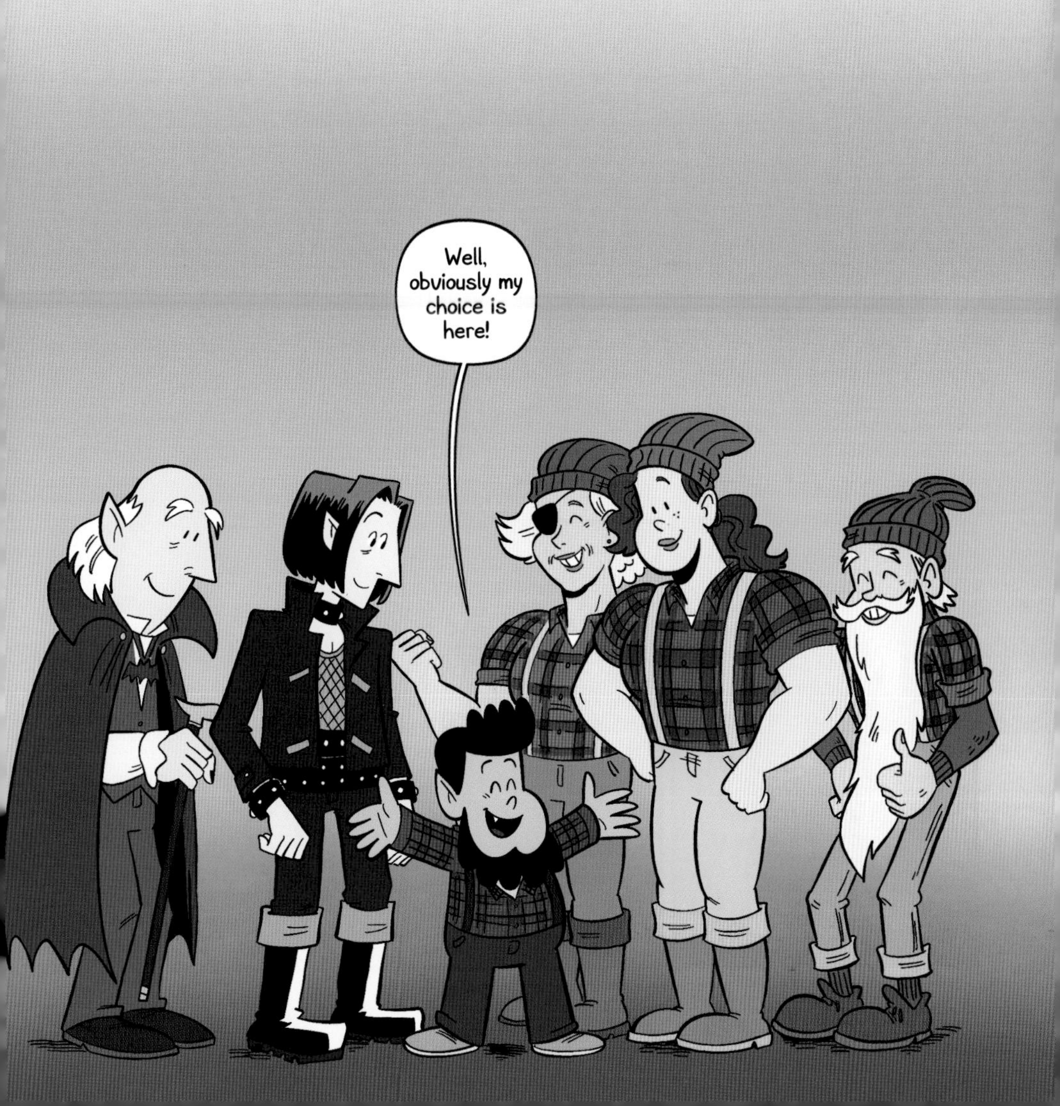
Well, obviously my choice is here!

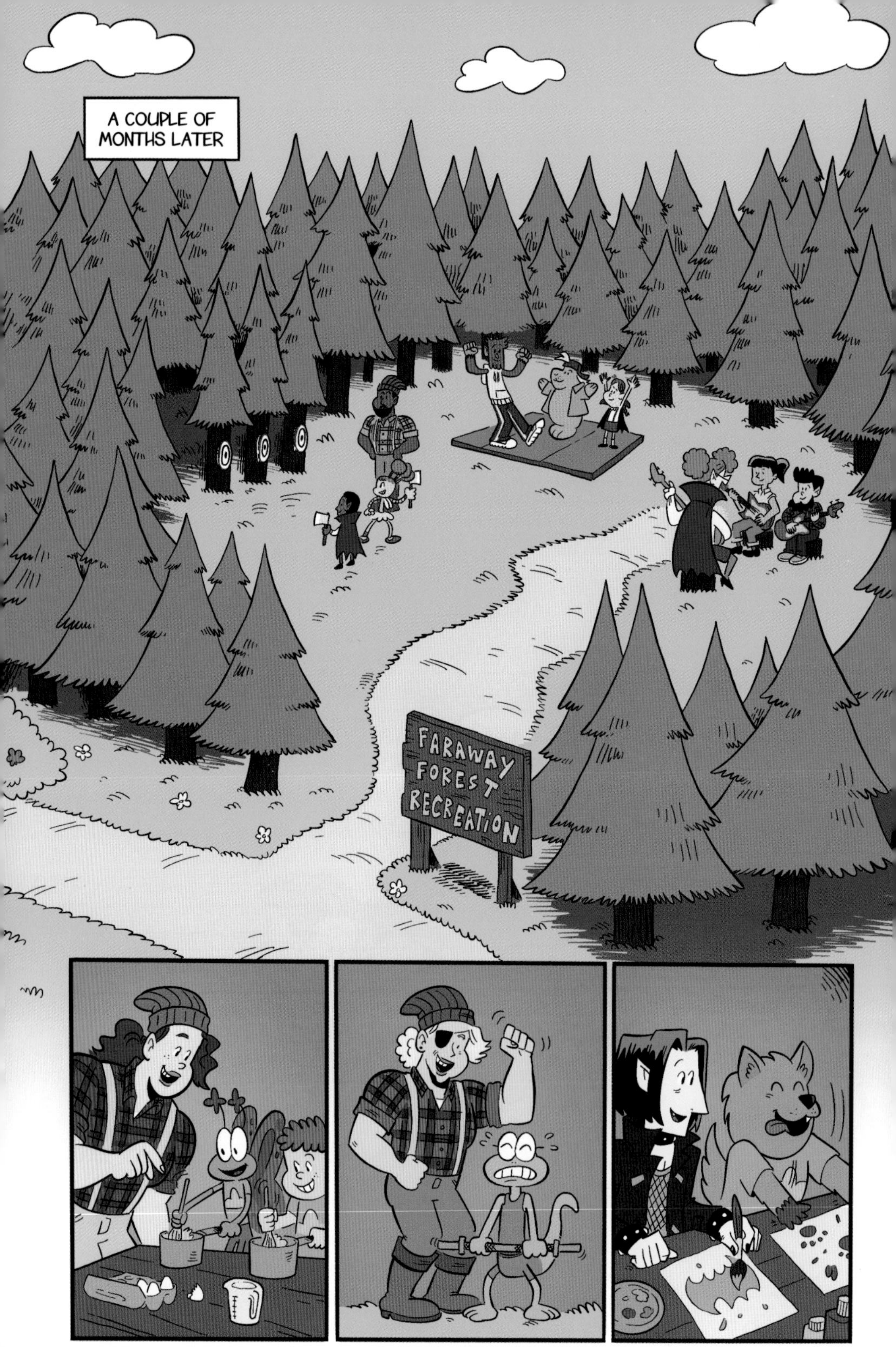
A COUPLE OF MONTHS LATER
FARAWAY FOREST RECREATION

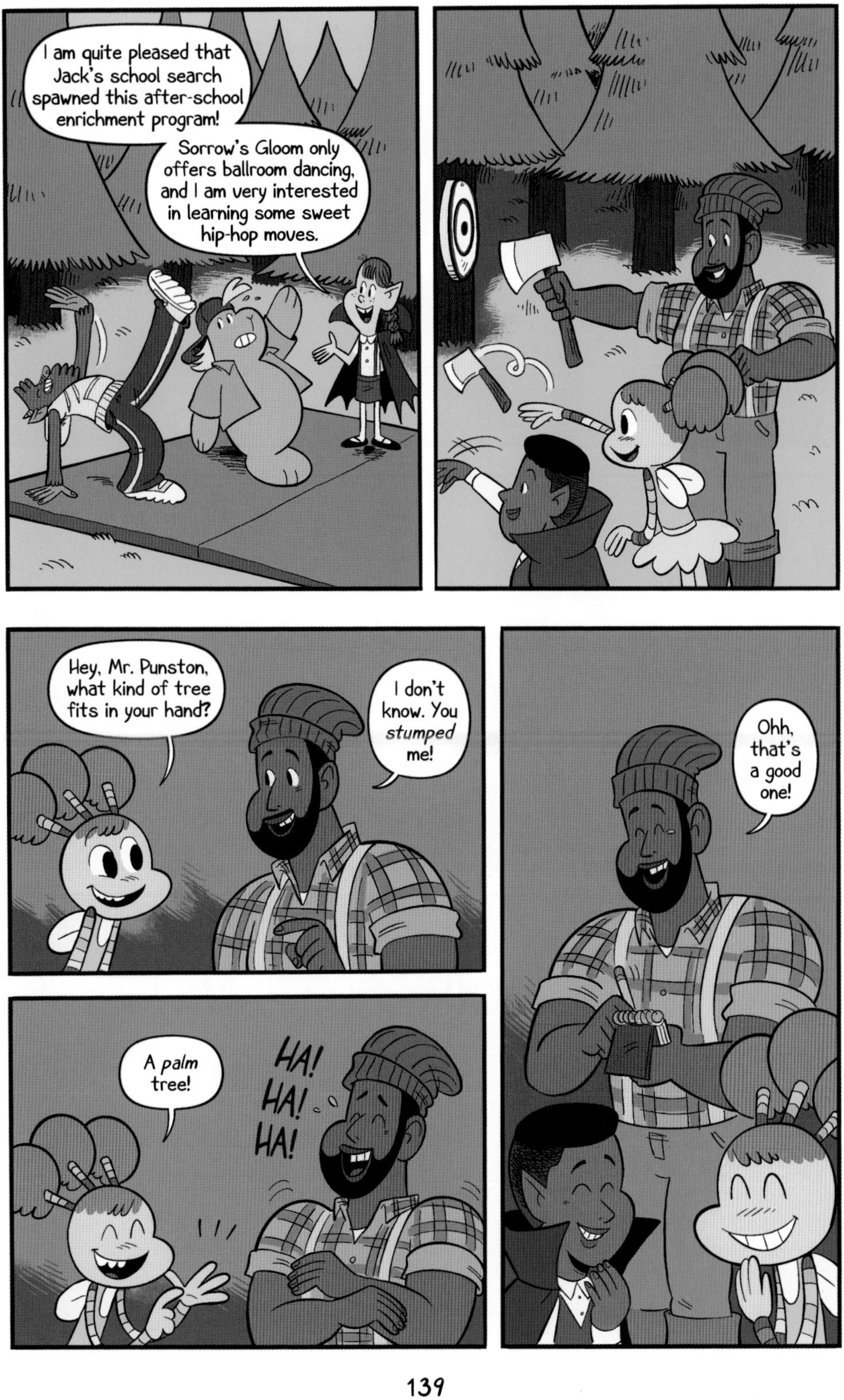
I am quite pleased that Jack's school search spawned this after-school enrichment program!
Sorrow's Gloom only offers ballroom dancing, and I am very interested in learning some sweet hip-hop moves.
Hey, Mr. Punston, what kind of tree fits in your hand?
I don't know. You *stumped* me!
A *palm* tree!
HA! HA! HA!
Ohh, that's a good one!

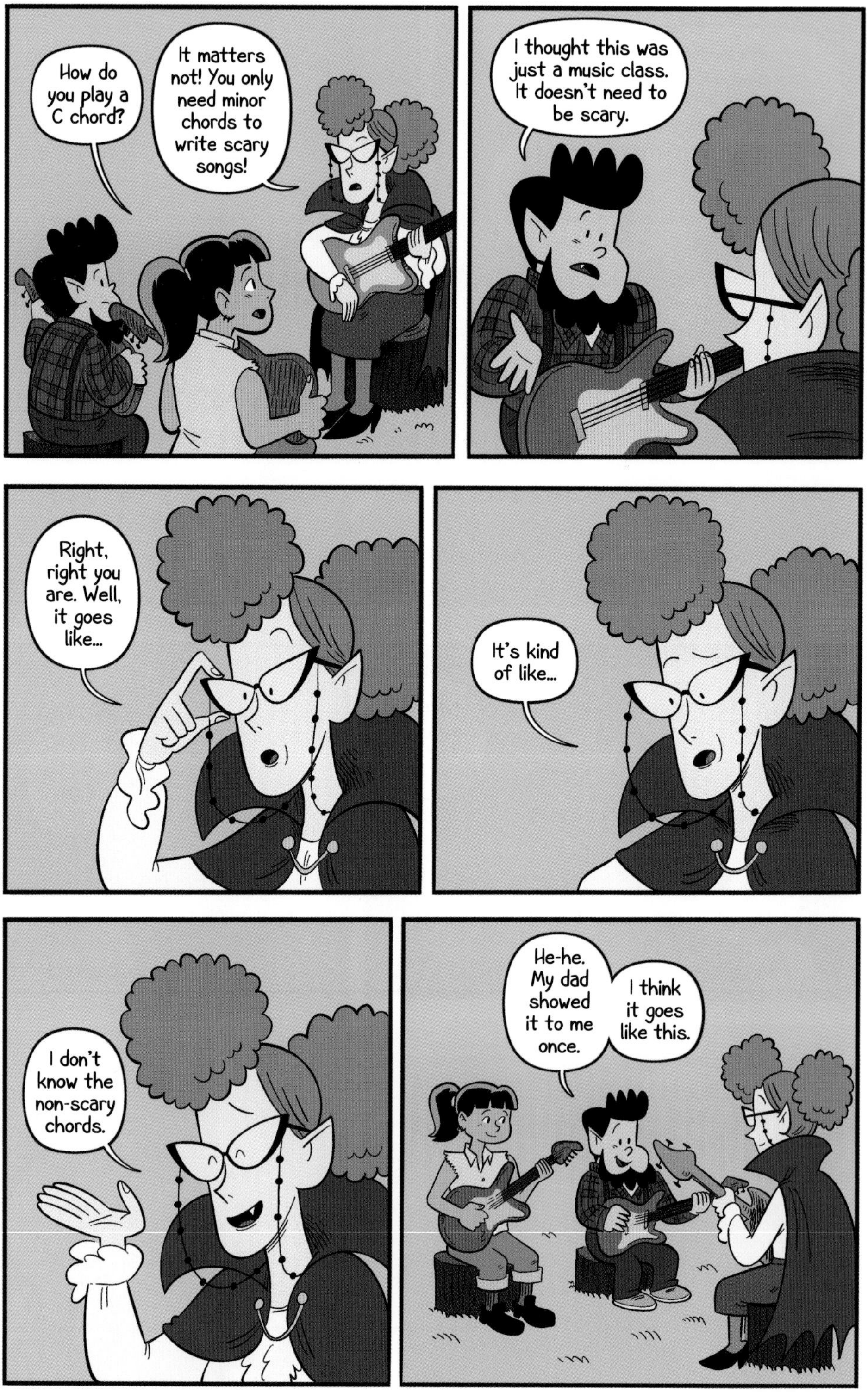
How do you play a C chord?
It matters not! You only need minor chords to write scary songs!
I thought this was just a music class. It doesn't need to be scary.
Right, right you are. Well, it goes like...
It's kind of like...
I don't know the non-scary chords.
He-he. My dad showed it to me once.
I think it goes like this.

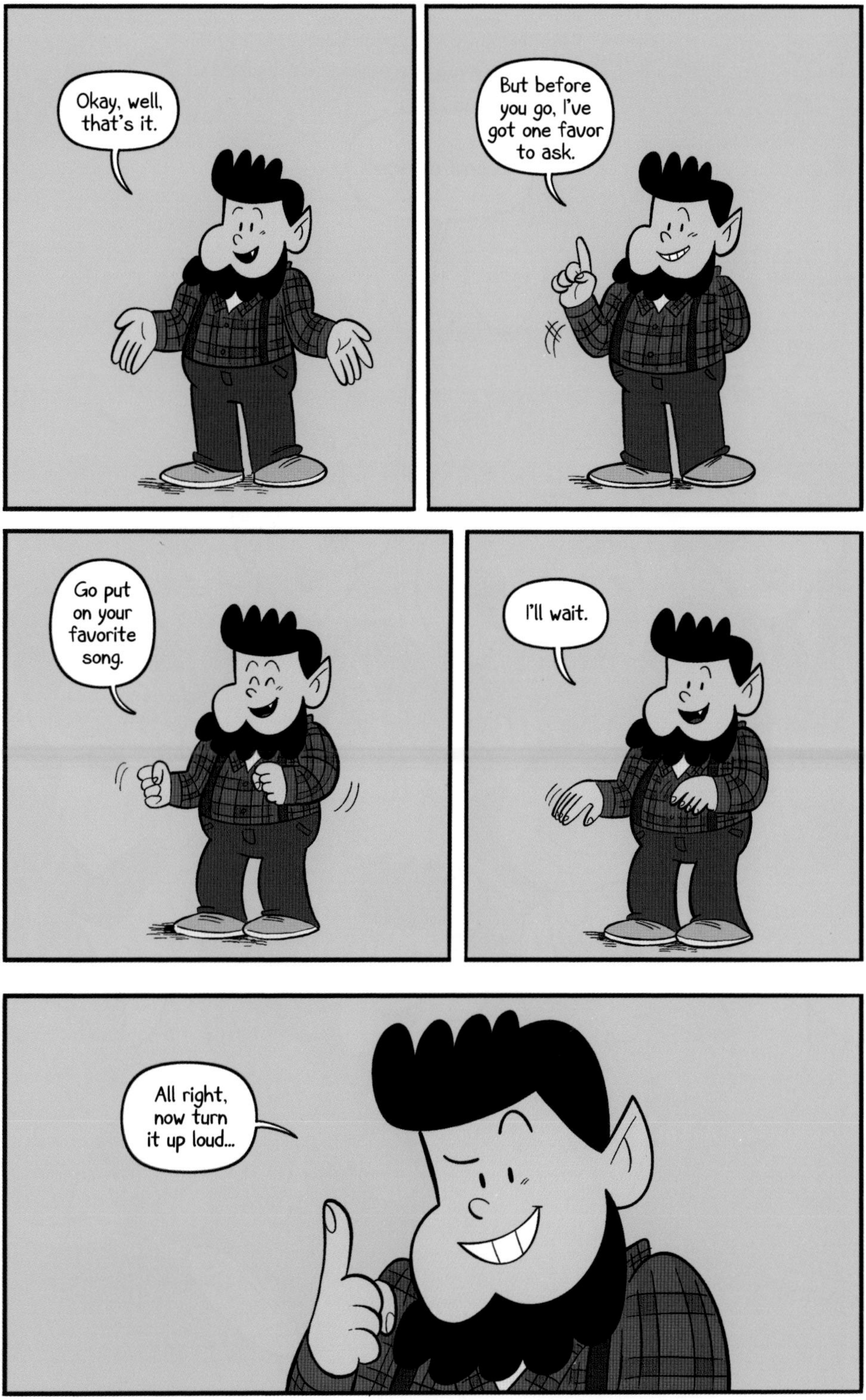
Okay, well, that's it.
But before you go, I've got one favor to ask.
Go put on your favorite song.
I'll wait.
All right, now turn it up loud...

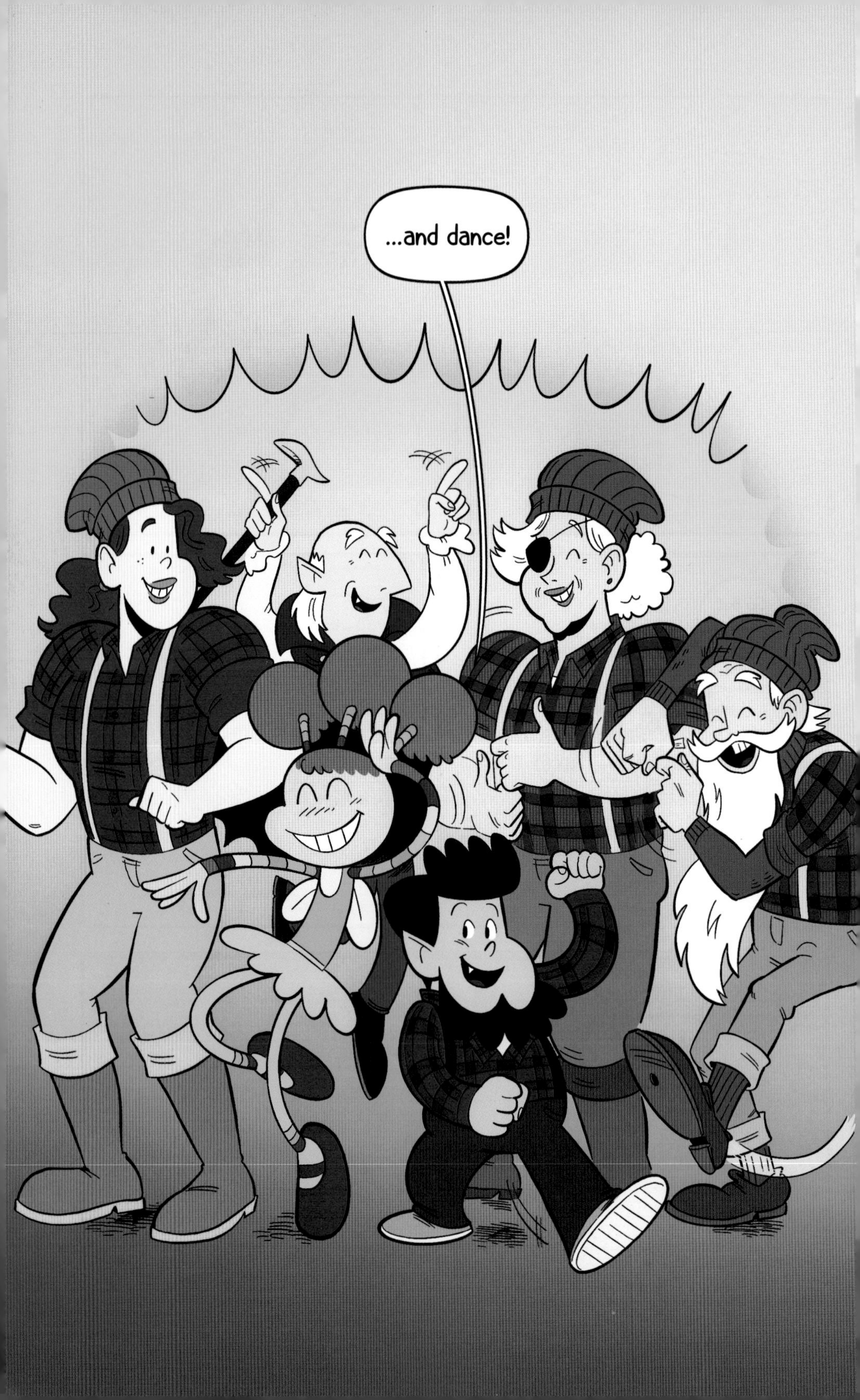
...and dance!

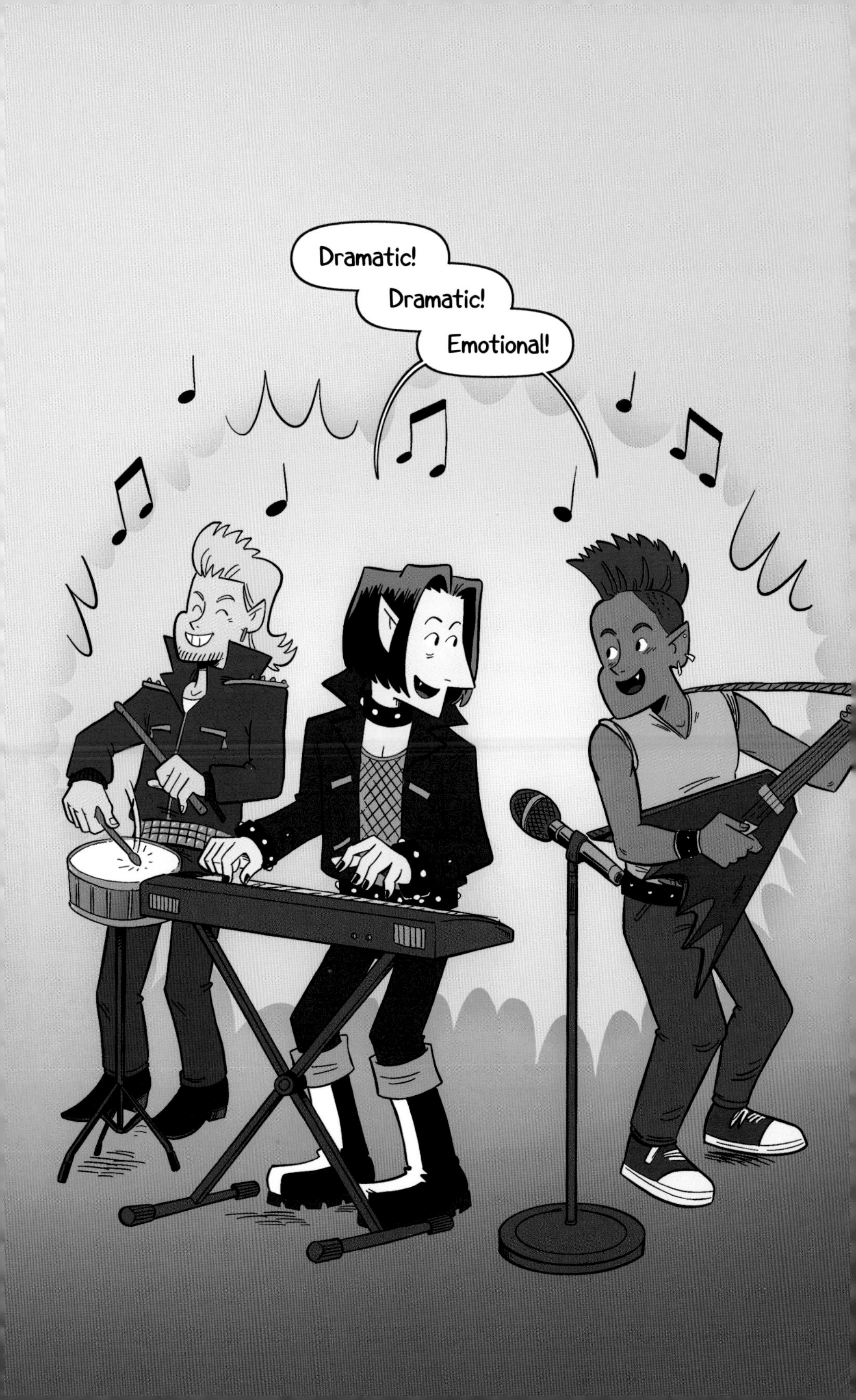
Dramatic!
Dramatic!
Emotional!